The Sea Eagles

Books by John Jennings

THE SEA EAGLES

*A story of the American Navy
during the Revolution; of the
men who fought and the ships
they sailed and the women who
stood behind them.*

JOHN JENNINGS

GARDEN CITY, N. Y.

Doubleday & Company, Inc.

1950

TO THE MEN AND WOMEN OF THE
UNITED STATES NAVY, AND OF
THE NAVAL RESERVE, WITH WHOM
I TOOK A VERY MINOR PART IN
A MUCH MORE RECENT STRUGGLE
FOR HUMAN LIBERTY, THIS BOOK
IS MOST AFFECTIONATELY
DEDICATED

Yet, freedom, yet thy banner, torn,
   but flying,
Streams like the thunder-storm *against*
   the wind;
Thy trumpet voice, though broken
   now and dying,
The loudest still the tempest
   leaves behind;
Thy tree hath lost its blossoms,
   and the rind,
Chopp'd by the axe, looks rough,
   and little worth,
But the sap lasts,—and still
   the seed we find
Sown deep, even in the bosom
   of the North;
So shall a better spring
   less bitter fruits bring forth.

LORD BYRON—*Childe Harold's Pilgrimage*
   Canto iv, Stanza xcviii

In Explanation
and Acknowledgment

HERE is a novel whose purpose—to be honest—is primarily to entertain. It is true that it deals, too, with matters of history and the nation's story. But it tells also of other things that are timeless. And for this it must be allowed a certain latitude in the telling.

I have invented in these pages—to be sure. I have omitted some small details of the record which have seemed to me to have little or no bearing on the tale. Some who are familiar with the actual chronology may be startled to find Joshua Barney in Dublin in 1774 instead of 1772. Others may frown to find omitted any mention of the young sea dog's little escapade with the mysterious Austrian beauty aboard the Ostend packet and in the Low Countries, following his escape from Mill Prison. An account of these adventures, exciting as they may have been, is not essential to this narrative. They have nothing to do with our story. We have left them out.

Yet even those who may object to these slight alterations will admit that they do not change the course of history. No deviation from the truth has been made in the account of any important event. Where the fictitious characters who have been drawn here are plunged into actual occurrences, they do not alter by their presence the direction of the stream. They do not take Destiny by the hand and guide it. They go along as actual characters in situations which truly happened; the details of the event and the behavior and reactions of the individuals involved have been reported as accurately and fully and with as much care as the records will permit. Where such records have been lacking in complete details, I have attempted to supply them from my own imagination, as it has seemed to me, from a careful study of the end results, that they must have come about.

The records of the American Navy and Merchant Marine during the course of the American Revolution are woefully scant. This fact is especially apparent to anyone who has attempted to run down minor details of fact. The story, however, in its general outlines is there, and while a full bibliography in a novel is neither feasible nor desirable, mention of a few authorities is appropriate for the sake of those who may wish to explore the subject further. Gardner W. Allen's *A Naval History of the American Revolution* deals mainly with operations. C. O. Paullin's *Navy of the American Revolution* concentrates similarly on administrative matters, though both, necessarily, pass over many details. E. S. Maclay's *History of the United States Navy* and his *History of American Privateers* also deal with the general background. Greater details of the lives of the redoubtable Joshua Barney, of Lambert Wickes and John Barry, and of the lot of American naval prisoners of war during the Revolution will be found in *Sailor of Fortune,* by Hulbert Footner, *Joshua Barney, Forgotten Hero of the Blue Water,* by Ralph D. Paine, *Lambert Wickes, Sea Raider and Diplomat,* and *Gallant John Barry,* by William Bell Clark, *Revolutionary Incidents of Suffolk and Kings Counties,* by Henry Onderdonk, Jr., and *American Prisoners of the Revolution,* by Danske Dandridge. This is by no means an exhaustive list of the works consulted in the preparation of this story, but the reader who is interested in delving further into details will find in them a good deal of information. He will also find in them complete and exhaustive bibliographies and notes, which he may be sure I, too, have followed. I take this opportunity to thank the authors of these books, both living and dead, for the help they have so inadvertently given me.

It is not possible for an author, in these days, when space is at such a premium, to give thanks by name to every person who has given him a helping hand, or to explain all that was in his mind when he wrote. In the main his work must stand for itself, and those to whom he is grateful must accept his blanket acknowledgment and know in their hearts that he meant each and every one of them.

A few, however, in this case, have given such particular assistance that they must be mentioned. First, the idea that a lusty sea yarn could be woven about the fabulous adventures of Joshua Barney—only about a third of whose incredible career is covered here—was first suggested in 1943 by Lieutenant L. H. Hurlbert, USNR, of Buffalo, New York, when he and the author were both stationed at the naval air station at Quonset Point, Rhode Island. During the interval between that time and this the research was done and the plot worked out. When the time for writing the story came, Howard Rowe, librarian of the Santa Barbara Public Library, and his staff were more than co-operative. They did everything in their power to run down material and make it available to me. When the task of editing and cutting and working over the original manuscript had to be done, Colonel and Mrs. Melvin Sims, of Pasadena, and Mrs. Phyllis Waller, of Santa Barbara, gave me invaluable and generous assistance. Not least among those who advised me and helped me reshape the first draft and put it into its final form were my agent, Harold Matson, and my editor, Lee Barker, both of New York.

But one person who helped me in the preparation of this book, above all others, deserves thanks and gratitude and praise for all she has done. Her help and her patience have actually amounted to collaboration. I speak of my wife, Virginia Jennings, who has researched and read and criticized and suggested, corrected and revised with me. To her, and to these others, and to all the rest I have not mentioned, I give my sincere and heartfelt thanks.

JOHN JENNINGS

Santa Barbara,
California. 1949.

Contents

I
THE REDEMPTIONER

II
YANKEE MEN-OF-WAR

III
PRIZES AND PITFALLS

I

The Redemptioner

1. *Dublin*

THE CITY glistened, drab and wet, in the late November twilight. The gray stones, the dun cobbles, the dismal smoke that hung from the chimney pots were as listless as the eyes that the passers-by turned to watch the Lord Lieutenant's carriage sweep past. The rain that sifted gently from the lowering sky was like the tears of countless thousands of Irishmen and -women falling endlessly upon the land.

Under the lions of Essex Bridge, where Capel Street gathered itself for the leap across the Liffey, Kenny Boyle took his stand and waited. Under the skirt of his coat he held a cobble, picked from a pile a little way up the quay. When the Viceroy's carriage flashed in view he fetched it out and took careful aim. He would have let it fly, too, but for the stranger who caught at his wrist.

"Leave go o' me!" cried Kenny urgently.

"I will not!" retorted the stranger grimly.

They fell to wrestling for possession of the rock; and if he had not been so weak with belly-pinching hunger, Kenny was sure he could have broken free. As it was, while they struggled the carriage whipped by, and then there was no more chance. Seeing it so, Kenny dropped the cobble and lashed out at the stranger. But the other ducked and came back easily with a crack to Kenny's nose that fetched the claret and stretched him on his back. It was just luck that none of the Watch noticed.

Kenny got his fists under him in the muck and was coming back for more. But the stranger met him with his feet braced and one fist cocked and his left hand outstretched with his own handkerchief offered.

"Here!" he was saying in a slurred voice. "I didn't mean that, but you asked for it. Here! Use this!"

Until then Kenny had not had a close look at the other lad. Now he stopped to examine him, hostilely, to be sure, but nonetheless curiously. The stranger was wearing a blue coat and buckled shoes, and his black hair was caught in a neat queue under an enormous three-cornered hat. He was a little shorter than Kenny, perhaps, but straight and strong. His eyes were uncommonly dark, and his mouth was small and sensitive, even a touch sensuous, you might say, but by no means soft.

"What for would ye be doin' that?" Kenny demanded.

"Are you mad?" replied the stranger. "Why would you fling a rock at the poor old man?"

"Because I hate every bloody Sassenach that puts foot to Irish sod!" Kenny growled. "If that's aught t' ye."

"It is not!" the other told him, still in that odd slurring tone. "But I tell you 'twas a fool thing you were about to do. Man! I doubt you'd even have hit him, and all you'd have had for it would be a foot of cold steel in your belly——" He paused, and his dark eyes raked Kenny. "At that, I'd guess it's more than you've put into yourself in quite a while!"

"Who are ye?" Kenny demanded. "Ye don't think like an Irishman. Nor have ye th' sheepnose bleat o' a Sassenach!"

"You do me honor!" The stranger laughed. "I've no more love for them than yourself. Barney's the name—Joshua Barney, of Baltimore, in Maryland."

Kenny's Irish truculence gave way abruptly to curiosity. America had been much in his mind of late. Trouble was brewing there, so they said; and wherever there was arguing with the English there would be opportunity for an Irishman. If ever a man needed to look at the face of fortune, it was himself then.

"A Yankee!" he exclaimed. That would explain his accent.

"Your servant!" Joshua Barney made a sardonic leg. "But you've the advantage of me now. Perhaps you'll wipe your face and do me the honor?"

"Kevin Boyle!" the Irishman muttered gracelessly. He scrubbed at the blood on his lips and chin and belatedly bethought himself of his manners. "Kenny I am for short. I come from Tralee, in County Kerry, an' 'tis but a few days I've been in Dublin."

"Then we've that in common," the American told him. He studied Kenny's gray eyes and sandy-red hair and thin figure thoughtfully. "I only arrived from Liverpool myself today. 'Tis a pleasure to make the acquaintance of a lad of spirit. Will you accept my fist on it, and let us forget our differences?"

Kenny scowled but accepted. Barney grinned.

"I tell you—will you sup with me?"

"I thank ye!" Kenny stiffened.

"Come on, man!" cried Joshua. "Just to look at you leaves me half famished. As for paying your footing, you'll have the chance. I've to find passage home for myself and my brother-in-law. Perhaps you can help me."

"I've told ye I'm but new here meself——" began Kenny.

"Aye! But 'tis that much longer than myself," Joshua interrupted. "Besides, I've no mind to eat alone. 'Tis devilish lonesome! Come! I'll leave it to you to name the place."

Kenny scowled. He was no beggar, but it was true that his pockets were as empty as his stomach, and he had been forced since his arrival to keep body and soul together with scraps flung from the kitchen and an occasional crust of bread and a bowl of thin soup doled out at the gates of the hospitals. If this Yankee insisted, he reflected, why should he refuse?

"I know naught o't, but I've heard th' Black Monk bespoke," he said half apologetically. "'Tis run be a felly named Cunningham an' his doxy—Great Kate. 'Twill be rough, I daresay, but th' food, 'tis said, is fair enough. But perhaps ye'll not be wantin' a place so low?"

Barney chuckled.

"'Twill be no worse than a hundred others I've seen! Let's go!"

They found the Black Monk at the bottom of a blind alley off Cole's Quay, not far from the Liffey. In the dusk they might have missed it had they not been looking for it, for the old sign had rotted away, and all that remained to show that the tottering old house was an inn was the iron bracket, from which the board had hung, jutting stark and bare from the wall.

"This must be it," Kenny said dubiously, his hand on the latch. Joshua grinned in the creeping dark.

"Lead the way! What's an adventure worth that leaves no doubt?"

They pushed open the door and found themselves in a long, low-ceilinged room, half lighted by a few guttering candles, hazy with the smoke of strong tobacco, and rank with the stink of unwashed bodies, stale beer, and pot-stilled whisky. A number of long tables ranged down the center, and at one end a hot fire of sea-coal chunks glowed redly in the maw of the grate. Along each side were several murky booths, from the depths of which came snatches of wanton laughter. At their entrance the hum of conversation died, and they could feel the eyes of the patrons swing and study them suspiciously. Kenny hesitated, but Joshua stepped confidently in front of him and looked about.

At one of the tables a tremendous woman stood up and swept toward them; a big, blowzy slut with breasts that wobbled obscenely under the loose, stayless lacings of her grease-spattered bodice. This must be Great Kate herself, Kenny thought as she planted herself solidly before them, barring the way, her arms akimbo and her muddy blue eyes surlily challenging. Kenny's rags seemed to reassure her, but obviously she was suspicious of Joshua.

"Ye seek somethin'?" she demanded.

Joshua appeared in no way cowed.

"We're no bailiffs, if that's what you fear, madam," he retorted. "Set yourself at ease. All we want is a warm place to sit, a dram or two, and a bit to eat."

Her air of hostility vanished before his assurance and gave way to dissolute servility.

"Well, now! If that's all we can be servin' yer honors—will yiz be plazed t' folly me?"

She led them across to a dingy, grubby booth near the grate. As they took their places she leaned upon the table, bending down confidentially, revealing her pendulous bosoms without shame.

"Will there be no other little thing?" She leered at Joshua. "We've foine beds above, an' lusty wenches t' fill 'em."

"Thank you, no!" Kenny noticed approvingly that his companion seemed neither shocked nor distressed. Rather, he was faintly mocking. "At the moment we've naught on our minds but our bellies. Will you serve us grog, and then send food—the best you have? My friend is hungry."

She gave Joshua an almost contemptuous glare and turned.

"I'll see to't!" she snorted, then raised her voice in strident summons. "Moira! Moira? Divil take th' biter!"

At the table, behind her, Joshua lifted one quizzical eyebrow at his companion. Kenny flushed.

"I told ye I knew naught o't! How would I——"

"You're no Dubliner—that's evident!" Joshua smiled. "How does it happen I find you here like this?"

A hot retort sprang to Kenny's tongue, but he bit it back in time. Joshua had no reason to pry, he reminded himself. The question was prompted by no more than friendly curiosity.

"'Tis not long to tell!" he growled. "Me father died not long since, an' 'twas clear some o' us had t' get out an' fend for ourselves."

Joshua nodded understanding.

"He—he was a free trader, me father. Maybe ye'd call him a smuggler?" Kenny's look was challenging, but he found no criticism in Joshua's look. Vaguely, indeed, he sensed a certain sympathy, and the need to rid himself of some of the bitterness that was in him welled up and overflowed. "He'd a lugger we used t' run to France an' Spain——"

"You're a sailor, then?" Joshua looked interested.

"As much that as anythin', I'll allow." Kenny shrugged. "He raised me t' th' sea. I know th' Bay o' Biscay as well as th' palm o' me hand. An' if there's a port ye want to reach between Finisterre an' Ushant, I can put ye into it blindfolded. If I'd not been down o' a sickness when he was taken I'd been with him then, an' likely not here now!"

"What happened?" Joshua prodded him.

"Happened?" Kenny spoke savagely. "They hung him! What else? Th' damned preventive men caught him back o' th' Seven Hogs, under Magharee Island, an' they raised th' gallows tree at his own very door for his family t' be seein'! D'ye wonder I've hate for th' bloody Sassenachs in me heart?"

"I do not!" said Joshua emphatically. "But what did you hope to accomplish with one small rock?"

"What else would I be doin' meself?" Kenny was defiant.

"Little enough—alone," Joshua replied grimly. "But has it struck you that if all who had reason combined——"

"Boh!" cried Kenny. "That's treason, they'll tell ye, an' hang ye for that too! I tell ye, Irishmen have been fightin'——"

"I don't speak only of the Irish," Joshua broke in. "Look you! I've naught against the English personally, as you have. But as a nation I resent much of their way. America—my country—is big. There's space enough in more than one of our provinces for all the Isles together. Yet they treat us as if we existed for their good alone! Are we to be taxed to support the Crown and a Parliament that's no use to us —that has no thought for our problems? No, man! I tell you, there's destiny across the ocean, and there are those of us who think it our own——"

"Ho, what are ye plottin' now, th' two av ye?" The voice that broke in upon them was fresh and taunting, but musical. Joshua straightened almost guiltily and glanced up. The girl who slid the tray of food and drink upon the table between them was laughing and pretty. Her eyes were green and tantalizing, and the reflection of the candles' light was coppery in her hair. Under her bodice her breasts

seemed plump and firm, ripe for the plucking. Joshua covered his
confusion with boldness. He laughed and caught her about the waist,
dragging her half across the table to plant a kiss on her mouth.

"Why, here's a pretty bite!" he cried. "Give me your lips, sweet-
heart! I swear, if there were a way it could be done I'd take you with
me to America!"

"Ah, be off wid yer blarney, now!" She laughed. "Why, sure 'twas
Kate herself said ye had naught on yer moinds but food an' drink!
An' God love us, yer friend looks like he needed thim!"

She twisted away with a quick, laughing peck at his cheek, and
green eyes met Kenny's for an instant with a flash of sympathy.

"If there's aught more ye need, call for Moira!" she told them, and
then, with another quick look at Kenny, she was gone.

Joshua laughed as he watched her go.

"There's a tempting morsel!" he cried. "But here's food—and drink!
Here's health to you and me, and to our friends, and bad luck to our
enemies! Let's be at it!"

He lifted his mug of poteen, and Kenny followed his example.
After that they tackled the smoking hot stew in silent, honest concentration, for Kenny was starved, and if Joshua was not so hungry,
at least it was suppertime and he had food on his mind. Only when
they had mopped up the last of the rich brown gravy did Kenny
speak.

"Ye said 'twas passage t' th' Colonies ye were seekin'," he said. "But
'tis a fact I've not been long enough in Dublin to learn aught o' th'
ships here. If I could be helpin' ye——"

"You can!" Joshua interrupted him. "Two heads are better than
one. You can help me find one out. I'll be glad enough to pay a commission for the service. 'Tis honest work."

Neither of them noticed the big man who loomed beside the table
until he spoke unctuously, interrupting them.

"Excuse me, gintlemin! I could not help overhearin'. Is it a ship ye
want?"

They looked up at him, startled. He was an enormous man with a
vast head of unkempt brown hair and small pale eyes like blue
agates. His chin was covered with a growth of reddish stubble, and
his old brown velvet coat was dirty, untidy. Joshua glanced across
the table, but Kenny shrugged denial and shook his head slightly.
The man offered what was evidently intended as an ingratiating
smile.

"Th' name's Cunningham," he said. "Me an' Kate run th' place. I might put ye in th' way o' what ye seek."

"You know of a ship?" Joshua asked.

"I do," Cunningham assured him. "Have ye seen th' *Dolphin* be any chanc't? She's th' big vessel laying in th' Liffey a bit down from the Batchelor's Walk."

"Off the Abbey Dock?" Joshua asked.

"Th' very one!" Cunningham beamed.

"I saw her as we came in past her in the packet," Joshua said. "She looks stout and well rigged."

"Aye! An' ye'll see she's well found, too, ye may lay to that!" Cunningham went on earnestly: "She sails for Philadelphia within th' week, an' it happens Cap'n O'Shea himself sits across th' room now. If ye say th' word I'll be askin' him t' step this way."

"Why not?" Joshua nodded.

Cunningham hesitated.

"There'll be a small commission, ye understand?" he said. "But even so I might be able t' save ye considerable over th' regular cost."

"I'll give you ten per cent—if I ship in her," Joshua told him curtly, and the man was gone. While they waited his return Kenny studied Joshua.

"D'ye trust him?" he demanded.

"No further than I can see him." Joshua grinned. "But what's to lose? I don't have to take it if I don't want it, and if there's a passage in it, why, then my search is done. At least I know the ship."

He was still speaking when Cunningham returned, picking his way through the murky haze, followed by a stocky, black-browed man who glowered at them curiously, unsmilingly, and a little mistrustingly. But there seemed little doubt that Seumas O'Shea was what he claimed to be, for at Cunningham's suggestion he silently produced his papers to prove it and laid them before Joshua. The American gave them a cursory glance and then nodded toward the vacant seats across the table. They sat down, and it was Cunningham who bawled to Moira to fetch poteen for himself and the "gintlemin." She seemed almost nervous when she served them, Kenny noticed; nor did she smile or linger. Her green eyes caught his for the flicker of an instant before she was gone, but he could not read anything in them but a sort of fright. He guessed that she was afraid of the big man, and he hardly blamed her for that. He would be, too, if he worked in the place. But O'Shea and Joshua were speaking.

"Cunn'ham says ye seek passage to America." The captain stated it flatly.

" 'Tis a fact I need two." Joshua nodded. "One for myself and one for my brother-in-law."

O'Shea glanced questioningly at Kenny.

"Mr. Boyle is just a friend," Joshua told him. "No, Captain Drysdale and I fetched the brig *Lydia* from Baltimore to Liverpool, where she was sold under us. He sent me on ahead to find passage. I look for him to arrive by packet day after tomorrow."

"A seaman?" O'Shea looked mildly interested.

"One of the best!" Joshua assured him. "You've room for us?"

"I can give ye cabins aft." O'Shea nodded slowly.

"And found?"

"Th' same as meself an' th' rest o' th' officers," O'Shea replied. " 'Tis plain fare but ample. If ye want fancies ye'll have t' provide 'em yerselves."

"That's fair enough." Joshua nodded. "And the cost?"

"I don't like t' be bargainin', Mr. Barney"—O'Shea's eyes narrowed slightly—"so I'll name me bottom price at th' start. Ye can take it or leave it—twenty quid!"

Joshua's expression did not flicker, although he knew the sum to be less than half the amount usually asked for accommodation in the Philadelphia packets. William Drysdale, notoriously close with a penny, had given him forty-five guineas for each of them and orders to bargain. If he could get both for that price, counting in the commission, it would be a feather in his cap indeed. Cunningham, misinterpreting his silence, apparently thought that an explanation was needed.

"Cap'n O'Shea owns his own vessel," he said, "an' takes but a few passengers aft. Th' profit is all to his own pocket. 'Tis why he can be affordin' t' do it so cheap."

Joshua nodded. From his own experience he knew it was not an unusual arrangement, especially in a cargo vessel. What a few chance passengers might pay was clear profit, and certainly there had been nothing about the ship as they had passed her in the river to make him think there was aught wrong with her.

"Very well!" he said. " 'Tis done—and here's my hand on it!"

2. The "Black Monk"

KENNY watched Joshua count out the money, while Captain O'Shea wrote out billets of receipt, with feelings of mingled pleasure and regret. He had begun to have a liking for this dark American, and while he was pleased that Joshua had seemed to find so easily what he sought, he was also sorry that it should be so soon. At the same time he was conscious of a prickle of jealousy. It was all so easy, he thought, if you had the money to pay for it. He was abruptly conscious of Cunningham's eyes upon him, studying him covertly, and he flushed.

"What about yerself?" Cunningham demanded in a low voice. The others were busy. They did not hear the exchange. "Why don't ye go too? Ye'd like to—eh?"

"What'd I be givin' for passage price?" Kenny tried to pass it off with a laugh. "Th' linin' o' me pocket?"

"That might be taken care o'!" said Cunningham casually.

Kenny stared at him, but O'Shea and Joshua had finished by now. Joshua put the tickets in his pocket and stood up.

"Well, gentlemen!" he said. "I thank you! Captain Drysdale and I will come aboard as soon as he arrives. In the meantime, if you'll excuse me, I'll be off to my own quarters, for I've some sleep to catch up on!"

"Ye'll have one for th' road?" Cunningham invited.

"If you don't mind!" Joshua shook his head. "I've had my share for the evening."

Kenny started to rise too. But Cunningham stopped him.

"There's no need for ye to go too, is there?" he demanded. "Wait a bit. I want a word with ye."

Kenny hesitated and glanced at Joshua. The American smiled.

"Stay if you like—I can find my way."

He counted out the commission he had promised and handed it to Kenny, cutting short his protests with a laugh.

"Nonsense! Didn't you fetch me here and put me in the way of it? 'Tis only fair. If you need aught of me, I'll be at the Duke of Leinster till sailing. Good night, gentlemen."

He nodded and was gone before Kenny could rise and follow.

Perhaps it was to divert the Irishman and blanket any unease he may have felt that Cunningham raised his voice.

"Moira! Three more o' th' same! Look alive!"

When she brought the order Kenny glanced at her, but she seemed almost to avoid his eye. Cunningham lifted his mug, watching him sardonically.

"So!" he exclaimed. "Well, then! Here's t' a safe v'yage an' a merry one fer th' *Dolphin!*"

Whether the man had noticed his interest in the girl or not, Kenny could not tell. But of one thing he was sure. Half starved as he had been, he was in no condition to undertake a bout of heavy drinking. Already he could feel the fumes of the stout pot-stilled whisky spreading through his thin frame. It was warming, delicious, almost a drowsy sensation. But it was also a warning one.

At the same time he could scarcely refuse Cunningham's toast if he wanted to find out what the big man had meant. No more could he decline the round that O'Shea insisted upon buying. And once that had been downed he had no choice but to take his turn and call for still another for the three of them. Kenny began to feel that if he did not soon swing the talk around to where he wanted it, it would be too late. Under that spur he took the bull by both horns.

"What was it ye were sayin'?" he demanded. "Ye hinted a passage could be arranged."

Cunningham turned his pale eyes upon him.

"Ye said ye'd no money on ye?" he growled.

"Only what ye saw Mr. Barney pay over to me."

"How much was that?"

"Two quid!" Actually there was something more, but Kenny saw no reason to admit it.

Cunningham and the captain exchanged glances.

" 'Tis only eight pound in th' steerage," O'Shea said.

Cunningham nodded.

" 'Tis enough for an earnest," he replied, and swung toward Kenny again. "Th' cap'n an' meself, we've been through enough hard times t' know what 'tis like! We've a soft spot for them with a will but not th' way! We've made it our business t' give a helpin' hand here an' there."

"Aye?" Kenny looked from one to the other suspiciously. "What kind o' a helpin' hand?"

Cunningham chuckled. He seemed to take no offense.

"I tabbed ye for a smart lad!" he cried. "'Tis clear ye're not one t' leap out o' th' box till ye've seen if th' bailiff's about. Our offer's simple. Pay me yer two quid for a binder. Then give me yer note o' hand for twelve more at ten per cent, an' we'll give ye passage t' America an' th' chance t' be payin' it back."

Kenny studied him unsteadily. Obviously Cunningham and the captain would share the profits. But there must be more to it than that. He was conscious of the fact, but in his fuddled state he could not put his finger on the catch.

"I don't see——" he began.

"Why, love ye, lad!" Cunningham boomed almost too jovially. "O' course there's somethin' in it fer us. But 'tis only what's fair! I take th' two quid an' sell yer note t' O'Shea fer six more—an' that's me own profit. He'll carry ye t' Philadelphia. There ye'll be payin' him or th' agents he names th' twelve pu'n' an' interest, such as th' note's drawed t' then—an' that'll be his!"

"I'll have time t' be payin' it?" Kenny scowled.

"As much as ye like!" Cunningham laughed. "O' course th' note'll draw interest, but 'tis not much. God's upright man! That shouldn't be hard. A bright, honest lad like yerself'll have no trouble findin' work in America. Ye'll earn th' sum in no time! Come! What d'ye say?"

He reached in his pocket and brought out a sheaf of papers and slapped them on the table between them.

"Sign these!" he said. "An' then 'tis done!"

Kenny scowled at the dog-eared documents, but they were only a blur of legal mumbo-jumbo to him at that point. The thing *seemed* reasonable. He lifted his eyes to O'Shea, and the dark man nodded. Kenny looked back at Cunningham.

"How d'ye know I'll not be skippin'?"

"I've no fear," Cunningham assured him. "'Tis easy t' see ye're honest. But even if we made a mistake an' picked a wrong 'un, there'll be bailiffs in th' Colonies. Th' note'll be on record, an' I doubt ye want t' end yer days in a debtors' jail!"

"Ye c'n be sure o' that!" Kenny growled.

"Then what's t' be waitin' for?" Cunningham demanded.

He held out a pencil and shoved the grimy paper along the table. He kept his hand unobtrusively over the top of the sheet, but Kenny never noticed.

"Sign there—an' there," Cunningham said. "One copy for me an' one fer th' cap'n."

"Do I get none fer meself?" Kenny protested.

"What need?" Cunningham looked pained. "O'Shea'll give ye his copy marked 'Paid' when ye fetch him the money."

Kenny could see nothing wrong with that. He signed.

"There now!" cried the big man, snatching up the sheets quickly. "'Tis done! Seumas—yer copy! What d'ye say, Boyle? D' we sluice our gob on't?"

"Eh?" Kenny blinked and tried to shake some of the buzz from his ears. "D'ye think I should?"

"Certain!" Cunningham retorted. "'Tis not every day a man gets passage t' America. God's squeaker! There's times when I wish I could be goin' meself!"

The drinks were before them before Kenny could protest.

"Happy voyage!" was the toast again, and when it was downed Kenny was so sleepy he could scarcely keep his eyes open.

"Ye said ye'd two quid," Cunningham reminded him, not nearly so jovial now that the papers were signed.

"Ooo-ah! S' I did!" Kenny yawned.

He fumbled in his pocket, counting out the money by the feel of the sovereigns. He clung with fuddled stubbornness to his determination not to reveal that he had anything more. Cunningham watched him sharply and grinned as he pocketed the coins.

"There now!" He leered without humor. "That's all o't. There's naught more t' be done save go aboard when 'tis time t' sail. Mind ye're there then, or I'll have th' beadles onto ye!"

Kenny only half heard him. His head felt as if it were spinning round and round, and he was so sleepy with the drink they had urged on him that he could scarce stay awake. Indeed, at that point, he wondered vaguely why he should. The thought, having once crept into his mind, took quick root.

"'N tha' case, might's well stay ri' here!" he said owlishly, then put his head down upon his folded arms before him on the table and went instantly to sleep.

"Took ye at yer word, looks like, Will'm." O'Shea grinned.

Cunningham's reply was unprintable. O'Shea rose.

"Leave him be!" he grunted. "He ain't doin' no harm, an' he might as well sleep it off here as anywhere. What'd ye give him, anyway? It hit him like a white squall."

"I have me own ways!" Cunningham growled.

"Aye! Takin' ways!" O'Shea snorted at his own joke. "Well, I got t' shove off. Send 'im along before sailin'. I c'n always make use o' 'em!"

He winked, and Cunningham rose and strolled with him to the door, paying no further heed to the lad sleeping on the table. When O'Shea was gone he remembered a matter in the kitchen that needed his attention.

How long he slept so, Kenny never knew. It was still dark, and the room seemed even smokier, dimmer, though the candles hardly seemed much shorter, when he was roused by someone persistently shaking his shoulder.

"Hist!" whispered a girl's voice. "Wake up, darlin'! Wake up, duck! Wake up, now, will yez?"

He opened his eyes and found the green-eyed serving wench bending over him.

"Wha—— Where'm I?" he grunted sleepily, and closed his eyes once again. The whole top of his head felt as if it were being stripped off. He groaned.

"Ah, come now," the girl whispered again, almost frantically. "Come along, poor lamb! Sure ye must o' been fair starved fer sleep fer even his filthy potions to be hittin' ye so. Come on!"

She tugged at his sleeve, and he pulled away irritably.

"I wan' stay here!"

"Ye can't stay here, duckie," she wheedled. "There's no tellin' th' things he'll be doin' t' ye if he comes back an' finds ye. Come along, now. I'll give ye me own bed t' sleep in, for 'tis that ye need. But ye must be quick about it an' folly me before he catches ye. I swear, th' devil's got eyes in th' back av his head!"

Before her insistence Kenny dragged himself erect and stumbled after her. She led him by a circuitous route around the edges of the room, where they were least likely to be noticed, and finally caught up a guttering candle from one of the booths and thrust him quickly through a door that he had not previously noticed at the side of the room opposite to that on which he had been sitting.

Beyond the door they found a narrow, dingy hallway, at one end of which there was a rickety flight of stairs leading up into the gloom of the house above. At the other end was a stout oak door that he guessed vaguely must lead to the alley outside. He was about to speak, but she motioned him to silence and led the way up the creaking stairway. In the upper hall the blackness seemed even more opaque, oppressive, more threatening; and the feeble rays of the candle, as they passed along, struggled to reveal fitfully a row of closed doors from behind which came rhythmic creaks and wanton titters, ribald whisperings, tremulous half sighs, and once or twice the sharp sound of ecstatically caught breath.

If the girl was embarrassed she gave no sign of it. She led him to the very end of the hall, where she thrust open a door and ushered him into a little cubbyhole of a room furnished only with a rickety bed, a cracked chamber pot, a tottering commode, a basin, and a pitcher of icy water.

"'Tis yours?" he asked, gazing about him. He was thoroughly awake now, and his head felt as if it held all the devils of hell hammering to get out.

"Me very own, duck! An' yours fer as long as ye need it!" she assured him, then evidently as an afterthought: "What's yer name, darlin'?"

"Kenny," he told her. "Kenny Boyle. What for did ye bring me here?"

"Could anny woman's heart resist ye, an' ye so handsome an' so helpless an' needin' a place t' lay yer head so bad?" she demanded. "Ah, Kenny boy, 'tis sleep ye need now. Creep into th' bed yonder an' rest, but be leavin' th' latchstring out, an' as soon as I can be leavin' belowstairs I'll come creepin' up t' ye t' lie beside av ye an' hold ye close in me arms an' give ye love an' comfort."

Kenny was no prude. But he was proud. He wanted to do his own choosing. He tried to tell her so; started to shake his head, and winced.

"Ah, ye poor lamb!" she cried out. "What've they done t' ye?"

"It must have been th' drink," he admitted ruefully.

"Ye didn't sign anythin', did ye?" She looked at him tensely, as if she had just thought of the possibility.

"Only me note," he told her, "fer a passage t' America."

"Only yer note?" she cried ferociously. "Ah, th' damned scaw banker! Ah, Kenny, d'ye not know what 'tis he's made ye do? Ye've signed yer indenture! Ye've given yerself t' be redeemed at auction when ye come t' th' Colonies! They'll sell ye there fer a term o' slavery! Ah, th' dirty, thievin' scoundrel——"

"No!" Kenny was white with the shock of it. He'd heard of redemptioners but never thought to be one. "No! He'd not?"

"Would he not?" Moira demanded furiously. "Would he not now? I tell ye, 'tis one av his dirty ways av makin'——"

Behind Kenny the door burst open. Moira broke off with a little gasp. Kenny whirled to see Cunningham framed in the doorway, with Great Kate leering evilly over his shoulder.

"So, ye gallows bait! So, I find ye sneakin' off with one o' me wenches t' cheat me when me back's turned!" the man roared. "Kate saw ye slip out an' sent for me, an' a good thing she did, too, for I heard her tell ye! Aye! Now ye know th' way o't! What're ye goin' t' do about it?"

He glowered at Kenny and came a step into the room.

"Fer a fact," he snarled, "I'll be givin' ye somethin' else t' chew on! Somethin' ye can be tellin' that fine friend o' yers, Barney, when ye give 'im a squint at th' twist I'll be puttin' in yer gig! He'll find it out fer himself in time, but ye may as well be tellin' him. He's not got th' bargain he thinks in th' *Dolphin*. Let him get his foot aboard, him an' his fine brother-in-law, an' he'll find th' cabins he's got're a lot closer th' bilges than they are astern!"

He swung furiously on Moira.

"As for ye, ye thripenny upright!" he snarled. "I've th' right medicine for ye! Here, Kate! While I tend t' him, take 'er below an' trice 'er up in th' buttery where th' neighborhood won't be roused be 'er yowls. Make 'er fast t' th' gratin's an' get th' clothes off her back! I want t' be seein' her skin curl!"

He reached for the cringing girl.

"Leave her alone!" yelled Kenny.

"Hoity-toity!" Cunningham leered. "Who says?"

Kenny flung himself savagely upon the man. He heard Moira scream and Great Kate bawl some filth, though what she said he could not tell, for he was fighting with everything that was in him. Once—twice—three times he drove his fists into the great slab face. But Cunningham did not seem to feel the blows. Much as a man would brush at an irritating fly, he lifted one huge balled fist and struck. Kenny was lifted from the floor and flung across the room by the force of the blow. Light burst like a fiery fountain before his eyes. He caromed off the bedstead and slammed against the wall and then dropped. Desperately he made an effort to scramble back across the great gulf of silence that seemed suddenly to have gaped between himself and the rest of the room. He got one fist under him, and then one knee, and was reaching for the bedframe for further support, by which to drag himself erect, when Cunningham's boot crashed against the side of his jaw.

Again the lights flashed, and as if at a distance he heard the man's savage snarl.

"There! Leave that keep ye quiet till I get t' ye, ye little devil!" Then came the clap of darkness, and he knew no more.

3. Moira

KENNY came back to himself with the wet fingers of the fog trailing across his face and with the stench of offal rising in the grim dawn all around him. His head seemed ready to burst, and for a moment he wondered if there was a whole bone left in his body. He could not remember at first what had happened. Then slowly it came back to him. He sat up gingerly, prodding himself tenderly here and there. His jaw was swollen and sore, and he guessed both eyes were black. His ribs were tender. But evidently nothing was actually broken.

He glanced about him and was able to recognize the place in which he lay. He was in a narrow cul-de-sac some distance from the Black Monk. No doubt Cunningham had dumped him there in the dark to divert suspicion from the house itself. It was not unusual, Kenny reflected, to find dead bodies in the city with cracked heads or broken necks or knife wounds in their backs or throats. Almost any of the warrens and runs of Dublin was like to produce its quota, and no one ever thought anything about it.

He put his hand in his pocket to see if he had been robbed as well of the few bits of silver he had had left of what Joshua had given him. To his surprise the money was still there. Cunningham must really have thought him dead and been thoroughly frightened to have neglected to search him! Or could it be that he was frightened for another reason? The recollection of Moira and of the man's fury at her kindness nagged at Kenny like a sore tooth. He was worried about her and what might have happened. And there was something else that troubled him, though at first he could not put the finger of his memory upon it. Then it came to him suddenly—the jeering reference to Joshua Barney and the passage he had taken; the hint that the Yankee had not bought the accommodation he thought he had. Of course Cunningham was enraged when he had said it. He would never have let such a thing slip if he were not. Still, Kenny felt that he owed Joshua an account of it. The American assuredly had the right to know and to take such steps as he thought best to counteract the innkeeper's evil design.

It was yet early in the morning, which was as well, for it gave Kenny a chance to clean up before showing himself at the Duke of Leinster; to wash some of the muck and offal from his clothing and to bathe his aching face in icy water. Yet when Joshua saw him he gaped.

"Kenny!" he cried. "What the devil happened to you?"

Ruefully Kenny explained, leaving out no detail, so far as he could remember it, of all that had happened after Joshua had left.

"I seem t' have fetched ye naught but trouble," he mumbled. "At least I thought ye should be knowing what 'twas he said about th' *Dolphin* an' th' passage ye've taken."

"We'll see about that!" replied Joshua grimly, and then smiled a little at the Irishman. "At least I am grateful to you for being so honest with me. You could have let it go entirely, you know, and I'd be none the wiser."

"What d'ye take me for?" growled Kenny.

Joshua laughed and clapped him on the back. Kenny winced.

"Not for a blackguard, in any case!" the American cried. "Come! Let's be laying the tale before the port commissioner. He'll have an answer for it, I'll warrant!"

They found the port commissioner in a little cubby of an office in the customhouse, a gray, blocky man as grim and dour as the buildings themselves. He listened sourly to Kenny's story and snorted impatiently when it was done.

"An' what d'ye expect me t' do?" he demanded. "Can I be runnin' wi' hankersops t' dry th' eyes o' every fool that's let himself be tricked into signin' an indenture? What——"

"Be damn'd t' ye, ye gray-jawed gundyguts!" Kenny cried hotly. "I ask ye naught fer meself! I know what 'tis that I've done, an' I've me own way o' dealin' with that. But Mr. Barney, here, has paid his good money fer a first-class passage, an' 'tis fer yerself t' be seein' he's not cheated o' that!"

Joshua started to protest, but Kenny waved him to silence.

"Have done!" he growled, and glowered at the commissioner. "Are ye goin' out with him, or must we be carryin' it higher an' callin' on th' magistrate fer a warrant?"

The gray man sighed and reached for his hat.

"We might's well go an' see what we can do with O'Shea. Hawkins! Have th' cutter manned an' readied, an' give us a pair o' armed guards."

"That's more like it!" Kenny nodded. "Now ye've me story. It'll be better I don't go with ye. 'Twill only be rilin' t' O'Shea if he sees me, an' I've no mind t' be settin' foot in th' *Dolphin* till I must!"

Joshua and the commissioner found the *Dolphin* lying, just as O'Shea had described her, off the Abbey Dock in the lower stream. As they swarmed over the side Joshua was aware of a rank stench about her that was faintly reminiscent of a prison, and as he swung his leg over the rail he saw that she was patched and battered, not nearly so well found, apparently, as she had seemed when he saw her from the deck of the packet.

"Used t' carry transported prisoners." The grizzled commissioner grinned as he saw Joshua's look of doubt. "Now O'Shea specializes in redemptioners. She ain't a nice ship. D'ye still want to sail in her?"

"Captain Drysdale will be more interested in the penny saved than the quality of the accommodations." Joshua nodded.

Captain O'Shea met them, black-browed and a little apprehensive, as they dropped to the deck. The sight of Joshua startled him, but the presence of the port commissioner and the two armed customs men was more alarming.

"Gentlemen?" he growled warily.

The commissioner came straight to the point.

"We've been talkin' with a lad named Boyle," he said.

"Boyle!" O'Shea looked startled.

"Aye!" retorted the commissioner dryly. "He'd serious things t' report, Cap'n!"

"As f'r instance?" O'Shea was wary, suspicious.

"As for instance that he was told be one Cunnin'ham that ye'd no intention o' givin' Mr. Barney, here, th' accommodations he paid for but meant to put him an' his brother-in-law in th' steerage with yer redemptioners."

Captain O'Shea looked relieved. He laughed.

"Why, gentlemen," he cried, "I don't know what Mr. Cunningham has said, but sure ye cannot be holdin' me t'account fer't! 'Pon me word, I'd no such notion! If ye're a mind t'it, Mr. Barney, I'll be pleasured t' show ye th' cabins aft I've put aside for ye an' give ye me writin' in th' presence o' th' commissioner that they're yer own."

He could not resist a glance at the two armed guards who stood stiffly to one side. Joshua nodded.

"I'll take you on that, Captain!" he growled.

Kenny was waiting for them at the customhouse. The commissioner gave him a venomous glare.

"Damned wild-goose chase!" he blustered. "Nothin' t'it! I've a mind t' lodge a complaint o' ye."

"'Tis my own notion OShea was frightened by the show of force." Joshua shook his head. "At any rate, we've the assurance now. If you like, I'll vouch for Mr. Boyle."

"I swear t'ye, 'twas th' truth I told ye!" Kenny cried.

"Hmmph!" growled the commissioner. "Well, ye've no more need o' me. I'll give ye good day."

When they were back on the rain-swept street Joshua glanced sidewise at his ragged companion.

"I believe you, Kenny," he said, "and thanks! But what about yourself?"

"I'll see ye aboard," Kenny replied shortly.

"Aboard?" Joshua was surprised. "Man, you've no need to go! You were tricked——"

"Tricked!" Kenny shrugged. "Aye, so I was. But I've given me word, an' I'll not be goin' back on't. If I would, I've set me fist t' paper an' signed me name. Cunnin'ham's right. If I don't show aboard, I'll be snatched fer debt, an' what's best, d'ye think—t'be sent as a redemptioner, or transported as a prisoner? 'Tis six o' one an half a dozen o' t'other!"

The American chuckled.

"You're a stout lad, Kenny!" he exclaimed. "And an honest one! You can be sure of one friend in the cabin, at least. Why don't you find yourself some decent quarters and get some rest? You need it."

In her room at the Black Monk, Moira O'Connell opened her eyes reluctantly and ran cautious hands over her body under the rough covers. Her back was fiery, and she all but cried out at the touch of the blanket upon it. Inside and out she felt bruised and battered, and when she recalled the things that Cunningham had done to her in the buttery before she lost consciousness she buried her face in the pillow in shame and half wished that she were dead.

At the same time, however, being the woman she was, she was

already beginning to put such thoughts behind her and consider what she might do to strike back. What she had seen Cunningham do to Kenny had made her even more furious, and her mind reached automatically to the point at which he and Kate seemed most vulnerable. In addition to their other activities, she was well enough aware, they were receivers of stolen goods. Where they might conceal their loot she did not know, but it seemed to her that here was her one best point of attack. It did not occur to her that they might make use of her own room as a hiding place.

To judge from the way the light came in at the window, it must be close to noon. It would be the quietest time about the house. If she could slip out for a moment unseen, she could report her suspicions to the authorities and be back before anyone realized she had been gone. Quietly she rose and dressed and then slipped down the stairs and out the alley door. Once outside, she turned her steps swiftly in the direction of the magistrate's court.

When he left Joshua, Kenny set about finding a place to lodge, as his friend suggested. In Little Ship Street, far enough removed from the Black Monk to be out of harm's way, he felt, he found the place he sought. A shabby little house with a large room on the ground-floor front. The widow who kept the place evidently was accustomed to students and beggars, for she asked no questions but merely asked her two shillings a day in advance.

He supped at a stall in High Street, which was as much as he could afford, and when he left in the gathering dusk, his feet turned toward Cole's Quay almost automatically, for whether or not he admitted it to himself, he was concerned for Moira. He had no intention of entering, for the last person he wanted to see was Cunningham. But he did have some notion that he might find opportunity to speak with her.

He found the alley and had not much more than taken his stand at the dark side, in a doorway opposite, before a dozen men with lanterns and staves came swinging into the way. They'd be bailiffs, he was sure, from the look of them, lighting the way fleetingly with their candles, yet making no sound.

God save them, he thought. They'd all be taken and carried off to the New City Gaol; and he was glad then that he had come by, for he felt he might be of some real help to her. They did not see him, half hidden in the shadow, but swung past without realizing he was there. In a flicker he made up his mind and mingled with them. Apparently they did not notice in the gloom, and the next instant they were thrusting in a rush through the door into the familiar room, smoky and evil-smelling, and the folk at the long tables were turning about and lumbering to their feet.

"Ho, Jerry! Mike!" cried out their leader. "Take watch here be th' door, an' leave none in 'r out!"

He whirled and leveled a long finger at the blowzy Kate.

"Yon's th' cock bawd!" he cried. "Seize on 'er, Rafferty! Where th' devil's Cunnin'em?"

At the back of the room a door banged, and as it closed Kenny caught a glimpse of the innkeeper bolting through.

"After 'im, Patrick! Shawn!" cried the chief bailiff. "Upstairs, th' rest av ye! Lively now!"

He disappeared through the hall door, and the room settled into a sullen silence, broken only by Kate's foul cursing. Kenny slipped around toward the side and, to his relief, came upon Moira hiding in a booth.

"Kenny!" she whispered, startled.

"Moira!" he hissed at her. "Keep out o' sight. I see 'em comin' in an' I thought ye might be needin' me."

He felt for her hand as he squeezed in front of her, and he had no more than hidden her when the two men who had been sent in pursuit of Cunningham came pelting back.

"He give us th' slip!" they yelped. "Where's Tom?"

"Th' dirty scapegallows rat!" shrieked Kate.

"Upstairs!" said one of the men at the front entrance.

But the two bailiffs were no more than halfway to the hall door when the man, Tom, burst in with his fists full of rings and baubles and his face crimson.

"Where's th' wench that gave th' information?" he bawled.

"Aaaah!" Kate's snoring exclamation held both relief and realization. "So! Moira's room? Eh! Th' hizzy! I could be tellin' yez did ye ask——"

"Shut yer face, ye Munster heifer!" retorted the man. "Ye've enough in yer own room t'explain later! An' how did ye know where they were? Where is she?"

Behind Kenny, Moira gasped.

" 'Twas planted there!"

Kenny covered her exclamation.

"Look in th' back!" he croaked from the depths of the booth.

Tom did not pause to see who had spoken. He dived through the kitchen door, with the two others at his heels. Kenny reached over and snatched up a heavy mug from the table and lobbed it across the room, toward the far side. As it smashed against the far wall, the place flew into an uproar.

"Hist, now!" He caught Moira's hand. "Folly me!"

He slipped out of the booth, with the girl behind him, and was through the door in a twinkling and into the hall. Overhead they could hear the heavy running steps of the other bailiffs, attracted by the noise of the brawl below.

"Quick now!" He snatched at her arm and drew her to the end of the hall and pushed open the door. Feet were just beginning to appear on the stairs when they stepped out into the alley and the door closed behind them. In the darkness outside they turned and ran, out into Cole's Quay and then up toward the city. Not till they slackened their pace was Moira able to say, panting beside him:

"Kenny! Kenny darlin'—ye've got t' believe me! I didn't——"

"Save yer breath!" he told her roughly.

They said no more then until they reached the house in Little Ship Street. Cautiously Kenny glanced inside. Then, reassured, he turned and beckoned Moira in. She followed him, slipping quietly into the darkened room. Only when they were inside and the door closed behind them did she turn to him again.

"Kenny darlin', will ye be believin' me—please!" she whispered. "I didn't steal it. 'Twas hid there on purpose."

Gently he drew her to him.

"I believe ye, Moira. I believe ye, lass," he said.

4. The "Dolphin"

KENNY woke suddenly, to find the day come and Moira beside him, studying him through sober and affectionately troubled eyes, the color of clear green seas over the kelp-covered rocks. For a moment he was surprised, then he remembered and smiled.

"Was it well ye slept?"

" 'Tis true, Kenny!" She sighed contentedly and snuggled against him. " 'Twas blessed peace!"

"Ye'll need not be goin' back there."

The way he touched her cheek gently as he said it showed how kindly it was meant. But when he had said it the full implication of the words touched them, and they sobered and were quiet.

"I must be goin'," she said, finally, flatly. "'Tis naught but trouble I'll be bringin' yerself here."

"No!" he protested. "We'll think of something."

"They'll be seekin' after me," she reminded him.

"There must be some way," he replied.

She shook her head hopelessly.

"Hold on a bit now!" he cried. "What about th' American?"

"He'd never!" she objected. "Would such as him——"

"Hist!" he retorted. "He'd never be tellin'. 'Tis th' very thing t' catch his fancy, an' sure 'tis a chance. Wait here now while I'll be goin' an' seein' him."

She seemed doubtful still, and it did not occur to him that her reluctance might be the remnants of an almost forgotten modesty.

Joshua Barney was at breakfast when he found him. The American glanced at Kenny's face and smiled slightly.

"Don't tell me you're in more trouble!" He grinned.

"Well-l-l——" Kenny hesitated. "'Tis not trouble exactly."

Joshua flung himself back in his chair.

"You do seem to get yourself involved," he remarked.

Kenny flushed and told him what had happened. Joshua waved him to a seat and poured him a cup of coffee.

"And what would you like me to do?" he demanded finally.

"Well—we thought——" Kenny stumbled. "That is—I——"

Joshua scowled into his cup.

"You want me to help the wench, is that it?"

"Since you put it so——" Kenny nodded.

Joshua frowned.

"Why should I?" he demanded. "She's naught to me, and I've got to draw the line somewhere!"

"If 'tis meself——" Kenny flushed and half rose.

"Oh, sit down," Joshua told him. "Don't be so touchy. 'Tis just that you must see it. After all, when my brother-in-law comes I'll have to account to him. He advanced the money."

Kenny looked mollified and a little hopeless.

"Aye!" he agreed. "But all th' same, I was hopin' ye'd feel a little responsible——"

"Responsible—I?" Joshua stared at him.

"For sure!" Kenny nodded. "Was it not yerself stopped me from throwin' th' rock?"

"What's that got to do with it?"

"D'ye not folly me?" Kenny cried. "But for ye I'd never have gone t' the Black Monk. An' if I'd not done that, I'll ask ye, how could I be snatchin' her from under th' noses o' th' bailiffs? An' there's t' say naught o' th' fact that if we'd not gone we'd not have found ye a vessel t' be carryin' yer brother-in-law an' yerself t' America at half cost!"

Joshua laid back his head and roared.

"Kenny! Kenny!" He chuckled. "Damned if you don't make it all sound reasonable! All right, then. Since you say that's the way of it, wait a bit while I get my hat and coat and we'll go and see what can be done."

They went back together to the house in Little Ship Street, where Kenny was pleased to find Moira up and dressed and the room all straightened out as neat as a pin. There was no chair, and the girl bounded up from the bed on which she had been sitting, blushing as rosily as any bride. Joshua smiled.

"Good day to you, Moira."

"An' good day t' yerself, sir." She curtsied awkwardly and gave him a shy look from beneath her long lashes, studying him. He flushed a little, and Kenny scratched at his neck uncomfortably.

"Kenny tells me you've a problem," Joshua said.

A wisp of a smile touched her lips.

"There's th' plain truth av it, yer honor——"

"Joshua!" he interrupted her.

"Joshua!" She smiled at him openly then. "We were hopin' yerself might be thinkin' av a way out."

Joshua chuckled.

" 'Tis plain Dublin's no place for you," he replied. "And since you must leave it, there's one obvious way."

"Obvious, is it?" Kenny broke in a little irritably. "Sure we've not seen it!"

"There's th' God's truth," Moira added. "What is it?"

"The *Dolphin*, of course," Joshua replied to them both.

"The *Dolphin*?" Clearly they had not thought of the ship.

"Of course!" Joshua retorted a little impatiently. "Captain O'Shea had no hesitation in accepting Kenny's indenture. I doubt he'd balk at taking your own, Moira."

Kenny caught his tongue in his teeth to bite back the reply that came to it. Joshua was right at one point, at least. There was a way out, if a disagreeable one. Moira was less reticent.

"Are ye a damned scaw banker, too, then?" she cried.

"I don't understand!" Joshua was stiff, no less quick to temper than herself. Obviously she was offering him no compliment.

"Moira! Moira!" Kenny put in quickly. "There's no way t' be lookin' at it. Mr. Barney—Joshua's here t' be helpin' us. 'Tis but a suggestion he's offered." He turned quickly to the American. "Don't ye be mindin' her. 'Tis sensitive she is. 'Tis so they call a man—like Cunningham—that makes a livin' persuadin' innocent folk t' trade their indentures in return for a passage."

"Is that it?" Joshua looked insulted. He clapped on his hat and turned to the door. "Well, then, if that's what you think, I can do no good here!"

"No! Wait, Joshua!" Kenny cried.

Hearing the desperation in his voice, Joshua turned back with his hand on the latch, and both of them stared at the girl. She lifted her head defiantly and returned their gaze.

"Hark to me, Joshua—and ye too, Kenny," she said. "I've been too long in th' world not t' be knowin' men an' th' ways o' them. Ye should be knowin' 'em too! Now, d'ye be tellin' me yer own selves—what'd be th' result was I t' be takin' yer advice an' sellin' me indenture t' Cap'n O'Shea—or anyone?"

She paused and scowled bleakly.

"Moira——" Kenny tried to interrupt.

"Hush, Kenny Boyle!" she cried. "Ye know well, th' both o' ye, what'd happen. D'ye think I've a mind t' be set on th' block an' sold t' some lecherous old scrimshanks fer th' thankless task o' gracin' his bed an' board? No, I thank ye! A wench I may be, an' a thorough good-natured one at that! But even laced mutton may be proud av its smell, sorrow be me sops! I'd romp with none but av me own choosin'——"

She stopped abruptly, angry at them and angry at herself for having said what she had. Joshua looked embarrassed and then broke into a laugh. It was an instant before Kenny, too, broke into a grin, but his hurt showed in his eyes.

"D'you know," said Joshua, "there's truth in that!"

Kenny nodded miserably. "There's one other way."

"What's that?" Joshua looked at him curiously.

" 'Twas a savin' be more than half ye made when ye took passage in the *Dolphin*," Kenny hinted.

Joshua glanced quickly at the girl.

"That's true," he admitted. "But you don't know William Drysdale. 'Twould pleasure him a good deal, to say nothing of making up for a lot of discomfort, if I could show him a profit on the deal."

"Ye could still be showin' him a profit"—Kenny blew on the fire when he saw the kettle warm—"if ye were to use a bit o' yer savin' t' buy a passage for her. An' who'd be th' wiser?"

Joshua nodded thoughtfully, his reluctance evident in his scowl. Then abruptly he saw the eagerness in their eyes.

"Damn me!' he cried. "I shouldn't be thinking of it. But you make me hound if I do and hound if I don't. All right, if that's the way of it! I'll do it!"

They cried out in unison, "God love ye!"

Moira ran to him and threw her arms about him, while Kenny grasped at his hand with tears of gratitude in his eyes.

"Oh, come now!" cried Joshua, embarrassed. " 'Tis not so much as all that. Stay close here, both of you, until I get back. But, mind! Not a word of this to my brother-in-law. He'd have my hide off my back if he knew of it."

He was back within an hour and a half with Moira's ticket in his wallet and a supply of food in a basket.

"Ye have it?" cried Kenny, bounding up excitedly. "God love ye, Joshua! After ye'd left I began t' be fearful lest O'Shea refuse ye——"

Joshua grinned at him and Moira.

"He was not happy, I tell you," he replied, "when I named our passenger for a young lady—— No fear, Moira! I was careful not to tell him who you were. But I think he was afraid to refuse me aught since I'd been aboard last with the commissioner. I think the show of force set him back on his heels. Here!"

He gave them the receipts and put the basket of food down on the table.

"I learned about Cunningham too," he went on, not giving them a chance to speak. "The tale of the raid is about town now. Kate was taken to New City Gaol, and so were a number of others. Cunningham got away—Lord knows where! They're still on the watch for you, Moira, so you'd best stay hidden here till sailing time. You'll not need to go out, for I've fetched enough in the basket to feed you both."

"Bless ye, Joshua!" the girl cried, and he colored violently when she kissed him impulsively.

"Avast, now!" he exclaimed. "I'll look in on you if I can, but if I should not have the chance, here's what to do."

He gave them specific instructions then as to boarding the *Dolphin* and promised to be on the lookout for them on board.

The time that followed before their departure was not long—less than forty-eight hours, in fact—but it seemed to both Kenny and Moira an interval of blessed peace and escape, a moment of rest from the cares of their all too grim world. Joshua looked in on them once, but he did not stay, for he saw that they were content enough merely to be alone together.

William Drysdale, Joshua's brother-in-law, came in from Liverpool, stepping from the packet to the soggy Dublin quay exactly at the time he had said he would—scarcely a matter for surprise to the younger man, for Captain Drysdale never did anything but on a precise schedule. He was tall, thin, almost emaciated, with a sallow skin, wispy hair, and a rheumy eye. He was close to middle age, and his nose seemed to wear a perpetual dismal droop at the end, while his mouth was wide and thin and petulant, with bloodless lips permanently pursed and turned down at the corners. He was as unlike his younger relative as it was possible for a human being to be, and Joshua had never seen him smile, nor ever expected to. Drysdale's greeting to his brother-in-law, who served also as his first mate, was curt and sour.

"Ye got th' passages?"

"Aye!" Joshua had learned to be taciturn with him.

"Hmmmph!" Drysdale sniffed. That anyone else could carry out orders exactly as given never ceased to surprise him, though it never occurred to him to offer a word of approval. "How much did it cost ye beyond what I gave ye?"

"As a matter of fact"—Joshua permitted himself a curl of the lips—"'twas at a saving of thirty guineas. The *Dolphin's* not much of a vessel, but I'd say she was seaworthy. She sails with tomorrow morning's tide."

"Well, now!" Drysdale exclaimed, almost merrily for him. "Thirty guineas, ye say? Hmmmph! She *can't* be much. I never heard o' her!"

"Well, you'll have your chance to become acquainted." Joshua grinned openly at him then.

They went on board the *Dolphin* as soon as they had dined, and even Joshua was as glad that they had waited that long, for on the eve of sailing the stench he had noticed about the vessel before was even more overpowering. As soon as his feet touched the deck Drysdale sniffed and bellowed.

"What th' devil is this that ye've got us aboard?" he demanded. "I swear, by God an' by Jesus, 'tis a damned felons' transport 'r a redemption ship!"

"Aye! She carries redemptioners, but what of that?" Joshua pretended not to notice the stink.

"What o't? What o't, he asks! Damn my eyes!" roared Drysdale. "D'ye not smell it? I'll warrant ye will when once we've put t' sea an' th' hatches're battened down on 'em! A damned blackbirder is what she is for aught o' difference there is, save that her cargo is white! What th' devil d'ye mean gettin' me passage aboard?"

"You told me to save pennies, and I followed your orders." Joshua was not cowed by his bluster. "I took the cheapest I could find!"

"Ye find somethin' wrong with me ship, gentlemen?" They whirled at the sound of the voice behind them, to find Captain O'Shea staring at them hostilely. Joshua nodded distantly and presented his brother-in-law. Drysdale did not offer to shake hands.

"Ye'll not be likin' it, Captain?" O'Shea growled. "D'ye want yer money back?"

This was the crucial moment, Joshua was aware. O'Shea would be only too happy to refund their money and be rid of them. If he did so it was likely his brother-in-law would learn of the ticket he had bought for Moira. But he counted upon Drysdale's penuriousness. He held his breath. His brother-in-law scowled, hesitated, then gave way to his nature.

"We'll sail with ye, but I'll not pretend t' deem yer vessel better'n a floatin' pigsty!"

Joshua grinned inwardly and drew a breath of relief.

The weary afternoon dragged itself away. Hour after dingy hour plodded out of the future and dropped off into the past, beyond recalling. As the time for their departure approached, the steerage passengers began to come out to the ship, in driblets first, and then by the boatload; a few alone, but most of them under the watchful eye of the scaw bankers with whom O'Shea had done his business. Twice the captain found opportunity to drag Joshua aside and question him furtively about Kenny.

"He's not come yet."

"He'll be along," was as much as Joshua would tell him.

"By God! If ye're coverin' him!" O'Shea growled.

"Don't fear, Captain," Joshua retorted. "He'll be here when 'tis time to sail!"

As the redemptioners came out they were herded together and driven below the forward hatches, like so many sheep, into the steerage, near the already stinking bilges. The ship had not had a thorough scrubbing since she had entered the trade, Joshua judged, and her bilges must be full of offal, to judge from the stench. What was worse, as the people came out to her and were crammed below, more than two hundred of them crowded into a space that allowed them no more than ten square feet for each, the air about them grew more and more unbearable. Joshua could not help wondering if his brother-in-law was not right, after all. Their own quarters were aft, in the Great Cabin, in tiny individual cubbyholes opening off the main saloon—less cramped, perhaps, but yet gloomy. He scarcely looked forward to the voyage.

At the house on Little Ship Street, Kenny and Moira watched the hours slip by with mingled emotions. In a sense they were excited at the prospect of being on their way to America, and they saw the hour of departure approach with apprehension and reluctance, for it meant a separation of their two worlds. As dusk drew near Moira went to him and gathered his head in her arms.

"Don't ye be worryin', Kenny darlin'," she crooned. "Sure 'tis not everything we'd be wantin', but 'tis a step in th' way, an' th' rest'll be workin' themselves out. Ye'll see! There were some said I'd th' power o' second sight, an' I see love an' luck for ye."

He gathered her in his arms.

"Then 'twill be well for yerself, too, Moira," he told her, "for ye're a sweet lass, an' I—I love ye!"

Perhaps that troubled her more than anything he had said.

When the darkness filled the streets with the creeping fingers of the fog, they gathered their few scant belongings and went down to the quays. There they found a waterman to set them aboard the *Dolphin*. As they came over the side of the ship Kenny wrinkled his nose but said nothing. A quartermaster met them on deck.

"Yer names?" he demanded sourly.

"Boyle——" Kenny began.

"Forrad, in th' steerage, both o' ye!" the man growled.

"What're ye sayin'?" Kenny flared.

A figure loomed out of the dark at the quartermaster's elbow, and Kenny broke off, relieved at the sight of Joshua.

"Mistress Connor stays aft," Joshua barked at the man, and Kenny noticed that he had deliberately revised Moira's name. "I'll show her to her cabin. You look to Mr. Boyle's comfort, and see that you're civil about it, unless you've stomach for a taste of the rope's end!"

"Aye, aye, sor!" The man touched his forelock. Apparently he understood the voice of authority, whatever clothes the speaker might wear.

"We'll see you later." Joshua nodded briefly to Kenny and then took Moira's elbow and turned her quickly toward the after companion, whispering in her ear as he led her. "Smartly, now. Into your own cabin, and don't show yourself on deck till we're well at sea."

He showed her below and let her into her tiny cubby opposite his own. She thanked him with her green eyes as she stepped ahead of him and gave him a quick touch of her fingers. Then she was gone inside. He waited until he heard the key turn in the lock and, sure at last that she was safe, turned and crossed to his own cabin and tumbled into his berth. What they would do next was a thing they could decide among them once they were under way. And there would be plenty of time for that in the slow crossing that lay ahead of them. In the meantime his greatest worry was his own conscience. He did not like much the trick he had played on his brother-in-law. Still, he was too tired to lie long awake in contemplation of it. He started to turn the thing over in his mind. But then, as his thoughts reached for it, as he lay in the darkness, it slipped away from him and was gone. Before he was aware of it, he slept.

5. The Voyage

HE WOKE to the gentle kick and pitch of the ship and the heel of her as she took the wind on her larboard quarter, and knew they were well out of the river. When he came on deck it was to find them running free, with the wind whistling a shrill dirge in the rigging and the vessel lurching along drunkenly as the great green rollers hissed under them, lifted them, and then dropped them again stern first. Off to westward, against the lowering horizon, the black mountains of Wicklow loomed dark and threatening. There were not many of the ship's people yet abovedeck; only a few sailors moving about, battening down hatches, stowing gear against the coming voyage. Joshua went below to break his fast and found the majority of the ship's officers and his fellow cabin passengers already before him.

They hardly seemed an impressive lot. Captain O'Shea, black-browed and surly, sat at one end of the long table, glaring sourly down its length at William Drysdale, who, when he returned the look at all, did so with equal distaste. The vessel's third mate, Manus MacNamara, was a wizened little man in an immense watch coat who shivered as he nursed his steaming mug of rum and tea. Joshua guessed that he had just come off duty, and the table conversation confirmed his guess. Owen Griffith, the second mate, a sharp-faced Welshman, had the deck, it seemed. Felix Kelly, the first mate, was huge, red-faced, and hearty. Fingal O'Meara, sailing master, was aged, worn, and weary, a gray-faced man who had probably come up from before the mast, while Nicholas Giveney, the purser, and Gilbert Clough, the surgeon, were plainly flashy sports, this morning somewhat the worse for wear.

The other passengers, it seemed to Joshua, were quite as ill-assorted. Henry Thompson and Stephen Mowbray were Americans, traders from someplace in New Jersey; the former long and lean and unhappy-seeming, the latter short and squat and round, and always with an affable, almost servile grin. Of the two, Joshua preferred Thompson, for, sour as he was, he was an outspoken patriot, while Mowbray seemed all too ready to run with the hare and ride with the hounds with never a "no" for anyone. The three other gentlemen, Brian Cavanaugh, Eustace Long, and Gideon Galt, were all petty traders from London; men of a type to patronize such a ship as a matter of habit rather than as anything out of the ordinary. Apart from Moira, there were no women in the cabin, and Moira did not put in her appearance that day. Joshua gathered that she was sea-sick, for when he knocked at her door later in the morning, she groaned out to him to go away and let her die.

As for the rest of the passengers—the redemptioners crammed in the steerage forward and below—their lot was certainly unenviable. True, Joshua did not go down into the holds for a close look at them, but he could not help seeing the squalor and misery, the crowded filth of their quarters, as he passed to and from the heads, in the eyes of the ship, nor help being conscious of the fetid stench of them rising like a rushing blast from the open companionways. And even if he had not been made so aware of it, Kenny would have told him. He found the Irish lad, soon after breakfast on that first day, leaning gloomily on the fo'c'sle rail, staring across the leaden waters toward the haze-blued hills of his homeland.

"'Tis yerself?" Kenny growled as he came up, no more than slipping his glance sidewise, then staring out again toward shore. "How is it aft? More comfortable, I daresay, than we have it forrad."

"I daresay." Joshua shrugged. "But hardly the best, you can be sure of that."

"How's she?" Kenny asked.

"Uncomfortable. I take it she's no sailor."

"'Twill be th' first time she's set foot aboard ship," Kenny said soberly, "poor lass. At least she's a place t' herself—not like th' poor devils below."

"'Tis so bad as that?" Joshua demanded.

"Bad, d'ye say?" Kenny cried. "I tell ye, man, ye've no notion o't! We're packed like shot in a locker; men, women, an' childern, layin' foot t' foot, with scarce a place t' be layin' our heads. Th' swill they fetch us fer food is not so good as we feed t' th' pigs at home, an' already half o' 'em are sick an' losin' their guts across th' felly next to 'em! When it comes real weather they'll be battenin' us down under hatches, like as not, and then there'll be nor light nor air! They'll be dyin' like flies then, mark me words!"

"Aye!" Joshua swore hopelessly. "I'd a notion 'twas somewhat like that. I wish there was something I could do. But I see naught! At least it can't last forever."

Kenny spat into the hissing sea and glanced sidewise at the American.

"No?" he said. "Perhaps ye're right. But still, 'twill be forever for some. I've a curiosity about yerself. I know me own need, an' th' girl's aft. But 'tis none o' yer own. Why did ye hold out yer hand t' us? That I can't be tellin'!"

Joshua smiled at him wryly.

"I'm damned if I can tell you myself," he replied. "Maybe 'twas because I liked the look of you both and have a sympathy for the way you feel. Perhaps 'tis because I've a notion that we'll soon have need of men like yourself in America. Why else would I advance what's not my own?"

"There's twice ye've spoke o' that," Kenny growled, ignoring the question. "Are ye so sure, then, 'twill come?"

"As sure as I stand here!" Joshua told him emphatically. "I may be an Englishman, by the way it is now. But I'm an American first, and I tell you 'tis so! The time is near for us to hit out for ourselves— to declare our own independence! And when it comes you'll not find me far behind——"

Kenny glanced at him almost cynically.

"Ah, it must be nice t' be independent enough in yer means," he said, "t' be thinkin' such things! Fer meself an' th' girl, I'll be glad enough t' be buyin' meself free an' makin' me own way——"

"Oh, that'll come, never you fear!" Joshua laughed.

The steward's gong clanged at the after companion, summoning him to the midday meal.

"I must be going," he said.

"Look out for her," Kenny admonished him.

"I'll take good care of her," Joshua promised, smiling.

"Not too good, mind!" Kenny replied.

They both chuckled at the remark, yet there was more in the words than either could then see. In her tiny cabin, at the moment Moira was beyond caring what might be in the future, or even with being greatly concerned whether she lived or died. She was hearty and healthy, however, and she recovered her equilibrium more rapidly even than she admitted to Joshua, who took it upon himself to see that she had, by tray, such sorry food as the vessel offered. By the time Dublin lay twenty-four hours behind them she was nibbling at the viscous mess, and long before the end of their first week at sea she had grown accustomed to the motion of the ship and was as ready to come on deck as she would ever be. Yet she continued to keep herself hidden from the rest of the passengers, pretending illness, for her own very good reasons. She wanted to think things out, and she could find strength enough in her own heart to insist that her thoughts be not disturbed by any influences outside.

Her heart had sung its own sweet song as she came aboard with Kenny; and her first impulse, as soon as she had laid aside her nausea and felt able to lift herself from her berth, was to run to him and find comfort in his arms. It was a fact that she felt drawn to the handsome young Irishman in a way that she had never felt drawn to any man since she had left home—and she had known many. Moreover, he had been good and kind to her and he had helped her.

Yet as she thought of that she realized that, perhaps for those very reasons, there was a different course that she must follow.

She was no fool. There was real worth in this boy who had come so unlooked for into her life. Despite his Irishism, despite the moods and shadows that swept across him with the speed of light and made him so quick to shift from tenderness to anger, from merriment to despond, she could recognize the qualities that shone through like a bit of white skin glimpsed through a ragged tear in an old pair of breeches. He had loyalty, above all. Where he gave his hand he would not be quick to withdraw it. He had courage that would keep him fighting against odds, as she had seen him struggle back against the brute Cunningham until consciousness itself left him. He had a tenderness and a gentleness that did not impair the strength of his convictions.

In the gloom of her cabin she worked this out for herself. What, she demanded of her own heart, had such as she to offer him? He deserved a better chance than he would have with her. He should be free to find a woman who would give him love and happiness, a home and children; a woman who would support him in his ventures and comfort him when he was down; who would guide him toward the promise of his future and never let any shadow of a questionable yesterday fall across the path. But for the love and the comfort, could she offer him any of these?

It took longer than that for her to reach her decision. But she came to it in the end because of the very honesty of her own heart. And when she did make up her mind, she knew, too, that for his own sake he must be turned away. Knowing him as she did by now, she was aware it would not be easy. It would be a bitterness for him, and for a time it might shake his faith in womenfolk. But he was young yet, and a healthy male animal. He would get over that when the proper girl came his way. For herself she was too straightforward in her thinking not to realize the pain of it. Yet for him it must be done, and, having made up her mind so, she thrust that thought aside and set to mapping her plans.

Her first thought, having come to it, was for Joshua as the instrument most ready to her hand. She liked the dark Yankee well enough to feel a small tingle of titillation at the thought of a game with him. Nor would he, she had some reason to believe, be altogether averse to it if he were encouraged. In the days they had been at sea it had amused her to pretend carelessness, to let the blanket slip from her chin as she raised up and took the tray from his hands, leaving her exposed to the hips. Then she would fumble and flush prettily, as she had learned to do in her trade, and it somehow pleased her to see the gleam that came into his eye; nor was she unaware of the tensity with which he held himself in.

It may have been that essential honesty of the man that decided her against the plan, though, more, it was because the complete wanton would be more effective to her scheme. There was no question in her mind that Kenny would be jealous of Joshua. But he could quarrel with one man. He could hardly feel the same toward many. The resentment he might direct toward Joshua if she were to single him out would—indeed, it could only—be turned upon her if she flaunted her favors promiscuously for all. That course would turn him from her most effectively, and at the same time it would not alienate Joshua from him—and she had particular reason for wanting them to remain friends.

Since she had made her decision and laid her plans she lost no time putting them into effect. She borrowed needle and thread from Joshua, who, sailor-wise, carried a kit always in his baggage; and she begged from him an old mulberry suit, a lace stock, and some linen shirts that he had no use for. With these she busied her fingers deftly, and on the fifteenth day after their sailing she appeared one noon at dinner in the dress she had made, laughing and flirting and as gay as if she had just stepped aboard. Even Joshua was astonished at what she had accomplished with her few makeshift pieces. As for the rest of the cabin, both passengers and ship's people, they made it clear that they thought her ravishing, and she lost no time taking advantage of that.

Joshua was astonished and pleased, even intensely admiring at first. But it was not long before all that gave way to bewilderment, and from that he passed to rank disgust and even outrage. For Moira left no doubt as to her calling or her intention of practicing it while she was aboard. Captain O'Shea clearly thought it a great joke on Joshua, whom he obviously judged to have brought the wench aboard for his own purposes. He would have taken her into his own cabin, for his own exclusive use, but Moira was too astute for that; she set up her shop in her cabin and accepted all comers freely and brazenly. But the worst of all, it seemed to Joshua, was that she absolutely refused to be bothered with Kenny.

"Ah!" she cried flippantly once, when he ventured to tax her with it. "Sure, we're all aboard now. 'Tis every wan fer his own self! What d'ye think now he c'ld be offerin' th' likes av me?"

"He could offer his heart," he told her seriously, "and the love of an honest man—both of which he's already done, it seems to me, to say nothing of what he's done for you. There'd be no need for you to live like this if you'd see that."

"Go on with yez!" she cried, and tossed her red curls while her lips laughed, if her green eyes were grave and shadowed. "Who'd be havin' th' like av that when there's both fun an' profit t' be had aft here?"

He gave her a scowl of repugnance and turned on his heel.

"What about yerself, Joshua?" she called after him. "Will ye not be comin' t' see me?"

He did not answer.

After that he tried to avoid her, and it seemed to him that the climax came when, responding to the call of nature one night, he stepped out toward the heads from his own cabin at the very instant Will Drysdale emerged from hers, most obviously adjusting his nightshirt. No word passed between them, but the older man scowled furiously, flushed to the roots of his hair, and scurried to his own cubby. The next night, when the stars were out and the seas quiet and Joshua was alone on deck, Moira came to him and fell into step beside him.

"Joshua," she said.

"Leave be!" he told her gruffly. "Why aren't you below with your friends?"

"You're angry with me." She pouted.

"That's hardly the word!" he retorted.

"Ah, Joshua," she said softly. "Don't be feelin' so. 'Tis th' only trade I know."

"Is it necessary—here?" he growled.

"It is!" she told him stoutly. "I've me own reasons, an' I'll not be botherin' yerself!"

He ignored that. She put her hand in her bosom and drew out a little sack of coins.

"Here! 'Tis th' price av me passage. Pay back yer brother-in-law!"

"Do you think I'd touch that?" He recoiled.

"Sure, an' why not?" She laughed. "I've but made him take it out av th' one pocket and put it in t'other!"

Even Joshua was forced to smile grimly. Reluctantly he accepted the sack.

"If it had been my own," he said, "I'd not take it."

"If it had been yer own," she retorted, "I'd not be askin' ye to!"

That very night he turned over the money to Drysdale with a certain relish he could not repress, and explained. His brother-in-law did not see the humor of it.

"So ye used th' money I advanced to buy passage for a slut?" he cried. "Igod, mister! Yer folks'll hear o' this!"

"Suit yourself." Joshua shrugged. "But in that case you'll leave me no choice but to tell how 'twas repaid!"

"Ye damned rebel!" Drysdale called after him, but there was no further question upon that point.

But the problem was not so simple as that. In a world as small as the *Dolphin's* it would have been difficult to conceal the activities of the one woman passenger in the cabin even if she had tried, and Moira had no wish to keep it hidden. The word of the nightly revels aft spread forward into the steerage, and Kenny was not alone affected by it. To be sure he heard it, at first incredulously, and then with fury, and finally with a burning bitterness toward her. He had been fond of the girl. He had been ready to overlook what had gone before. That had been forced by circumstances, he felt, and he had been willing to put it behind them and hold out his arms to her. But there was no excuse for this now. And what was worse, he was inclined to hold Joshua accountable. A certain reserve first, and then open hostility grew in him, and he began to feel almost an active dislike for the dark American. They never spoke in those brooding days.

In the meantime the *Dolphin* plodded her bumbling way westward. Fastnet Rock fell behind, and the storms of the December Atlantic buffeted them. They had a few mild days until they passed to northward of the Bermudas and crossed the Gulf Stream, but the slops they were served remained the same, and there were days at a time when they were caged below hatches and no one aboard seemed to care whether they lived or died. Indeed, six of their number gave up the struggle and were buried at sea, though none of the afterguard seemed concerned unless it was Joshua Barney and his brother-in-law, Will Drysdale, who said the brief prayers over the canvas-encased bodies. Captain O'Shea, evidently, was too much engrossed with his wench and his bottle; and the nightly bacchanal in the cabin was a source of bitter comment forward.

They had battled winds and seas two thirds of the way across, it seemed, and it was almost February by the time they crossed the Great Current. There the furies of winter swooped down upon them, and they pitched and rolled and bucked under bare poles, while the captain and his cronies drank and made merry aft with never a thought, apparently, for the men and women and children under hatches, stifling in the cargo space forward. They could not hear Drysdale growl:

"Be damned t' ye, Captain O'Shea! If ye don't put away yer woman an' yer bottle, begod, an' get on t' Philadelphia, I'll have t' take command myself! We can't be hangin' forever in mid-ocean!"

Nor could they hear O'Shea's growled retort:

"Try it!"

All they knew was that they were abandoned to die in this waste of water, and none cared what became of them.

Kenny sat, grim and dour, in the foul stench of the steerage, and in the smoky light of the single whale-oil lantern stared into his mess kit at the viscid mess of slops that had been lowered to them in a bucket in the name of food. Somewhere amid the shadows forward a child was whimpering. The endless sound of it angered him; not against the child, but against those who could allow such things. A voice spoke at his elbow.

"I've four av 'em like that an' a wife t' boot! They'll never live t' see Philadelphy at this rate. Three days now, since we left th' Great Current behind, we've not made a foot westin'!"

"Aye, I know." Kenny glanced up to see a blue-jawed Belfast-man, Walsh, beside him. "But what's t' be done?"

"There are them"—Walsh's black eyes flashed—"will folly us if we take th' lead. Me an' ye're th' only sailormen o' th' lot!"

"'Tis mutiny ye suggest!" Kenny told him.

"Is it t' be mutiny, then, or death?" the Belfastman retorted. "An' they sittin' aft in th' cabin enj'yin' th' fat?"

Forward the child wailed again. Kenny thrust his mess kit aside and rose.

"Then what're we waitin' for?" he demanded.

Supper, such as it was, was on the table, and it seemed to Joshua that the night was more than usually raucous. Captain O'Shea was early drunk, and Moira had more than was good for her, though she never seemed to take so much that it interfered with her sense of profit. All but MacNamara, who had the deck, were there, waiting for the mess steward to clear away the remnants of the first course.

and those with a mind to it were making the most of the bibulous interval when the hubbub rose on the deck forward and Mac-Namara's voice came down the scuttle, high-pitched and frightened.

"Cap'n! Cap'n O'Shea! Come quick! Th' steerage passengers're up an' comin'!"

For a drunken man, Captain O'Shea moved swiftly. He lurched to his feet and dived into his own cabin. He must have kept the piece ready for just such an emergency, for he was out again in an instant with a pistol in his fist. Almost before the rest of them could move he was streaking up the ladder. Then Griffith and Kelly were at his heels, and close behind them were Drysdale and Joshua. The scene that met their eyes as they burst out on deck was tense, startling. The waist was crowded with grim, half-starved men moving aft determinedly. Joshua recognized Kenny at their head, but before he could cry out O'Shea wheeled to the rail and leveled his pistol.

"Stand where y'are!" he hiccupped.

Some of the redemptioners wavered, but Kenny still came forward.

"Halt!" roared O'Shea, and it was clear he was becoming panicky. "Stop 'r be Jasus I'll shoot!"

"Shoot 'n' be damned!" Joshua heard Kenny growl.

O'Shea's finger was whitening against the trigger as Joshua dived forward. His shoulder struck against the man's gun arm and tossed it up, just as the piece went off harmlessly into the air. At the same instant, almost as if they had planned it so, so closely was it timed, William Drysdale moved in behind the captain with a belaying pin. Joshua saw O'Shea's head jerk with the force of the blow, and the sound of it was a dull "thuck" in the whine of the wind. Captain O'Shea dropped like a felled ox, and Drysdale stepped astraddle of his body. So abrupt was it, so surprising, so unexpected, that no one moved. Even Kenny stopped and stood rooted to the deck.

"I've been threatenin' t' take command o' this vessel if need came!" Drysdale's voice came clear above the wind. "Now 'tis done—ye lads'll have me to deal with!"

He tapped the rail before him with the belaying pin.

"D'ye know what 'tis like forrad?" Kenny demanded.

"I've a notion," Drysdale retorted dryly. "I'll do my best fer ye."

"What d'ye call yer best?" Kenny was still belligerent. His eye met Joshua's truculently but showed no sign of recognition.

"I can't be responsible for th' quality o' th' stores that were fetched aboard this floatin' hogsty in Dublin!" Drysdale's sharp eye did not miss the glance that passed between the Irishman and his brother-in-law. "But since I command now I'll tell ye 'twill be share an' share alike from now on. Steerage passengers'll have th' same as those in th' cabin. Seamen in th' fo'c'sle'll change places with th' women an' children in th' hold—see t' that, Mr. Griffith!"

"Aye, aye, sir!" The habit of obedience was strong in the second mate.

Drysdale stepped aside and prodded the inert O'Shea with his toe. "You, Mr. Kelly! Get this below and iron him to his berth. I'll return his vessel to him when we reach Philadelphia. Mr. Mac-Namara, get th' men aloft an' shake out royals an' t'gallants. Fetch her about on th' larboard tack an' reach sou'westward! D'ye want t' be forever sittin' in this millpond?"

"Aye, aye, sir!" replied both Kelly and MacNamara together. Whatever else Drysdale might be, he was a competent seaman, and both officers and crew accepted his easy assumption of command as an almost natural thing. In the waist a growl of approval went up from the assembled redemptioners, and the crowd began to break up and drift back toward their quarters.

"One other thing!" Drysdale bawled. The steerage people halted and faced about, half hostilely. "We'll get on t' Philadelphia as fast as we can," Drysdale went on. "In th' meantime, though, you"—he pointed to Kenny—"an' yerself, Joshua, ye'll pick guards—an equal number from th' steerage, th' crew, an' from th' folk aft! 'Twill be for them t' keep th' peace aboard—an' I'll hold th' pair o' ye t' account for it. D'ye understand?"

With that, having fixed the responsibility for the whole mess where he felt it properly belonged, his sour eye took on an even more sardonic gleam, and he turned on his heel and dropped down the companionway.

"See to't!" he rapped back over his shoulder as he went.

Things went better after that. Kenny could scarcely say he was happier, for his bondage continued, and that could not be blinked. Moreover, his new duties brought him in contact necessarily with Joshua. To be sure, Joshua had done everything he could ask to help him, but he was sore and hurt at Moira's conduct, and he had no way of knowing that Joshua had no part in her encouragement until the latter spoke. To Kenny, and indeed to all the steerage, all of the afterguard were tarred with the same stick. Their blackness was only a matter of degree.

Fortunately Joshua took matters in his own hands when they met to draw lots for the distribution of watches. Kenny was stiff and distant. Joshua was hot-tempered.

"Hark to me, sulky man!" he flared out. "I've a notion what you're thinking, and I'll tell you now 'tis not so. I'm sorry things have fallen out as they have aft. But I'll tell you I've had no part in it—not so much as a shilling's worth!"

That settled that question, at least, yet the air remained strained between them. They cast their lots and apportioned their own and their men's time, Joshua himself drawing the midwatch, from twelve to four. After that they parted formally, coolly polite.

Things went more rapidly then, which pleased Joshua as well as Kenny, for they were both fed to the teeth with the business and looked forward to being shut of it. With a restoration of order and a sound commander to push her, the *Dolphin* made reasonable time, and for once the winds seemed to shift in their favor. They came in sight of the black, low-lying shore toward the end of the month. And Joshua, on watch, felt a tingle of excitement as he leaned upon the rail and identified the familiar landmarks at the mouth of the Delaware through the thin, bitter-bright, winter moonlight. This was America—his land! He was not aware of the girl beside him until she spoke.

"So 'tis home again ye are now, Joshua."

He looked around at her and moved a little aside. When he did not speak she went on a little wistfully.

"I know ye've little regard fer me, Joshua," she said, "an' I'll not be blamin' ye. But there's a thing or two I'd be askin' av ye."

"Favors?" His voice was cynical.

"Not fer meself!" she retorted bitterly. "I'll make me own way in a hard world. How much would ye be sayin' a man's bond'd bring on th' block in Philadelphy?"

"Kenny?" He glanced at her sharply.

"Kenny!" she retorted defiantly.

"He'd not have you!" he told her cruelly.

"'Tis not what I'm askin' ye," she reminded him.

"He's half starved and skinny." He calculated swiftly. "He'd hardly be called a good risk. Say—twenty pounds."

She put her hand to her bosom once more and drew out a small bag of coins, yet warm from their resting place between her breasts.

"You've had a profitable voyage!" He was caustic.

"That's as ye look at it." She counted out a handful of gold pieces and held it out toward him. "Here! There's thirty-five guineas t' be sure av it——"

"You want me to bid him in? Is that what you're asking?" He drew back, putting his hands behind him.

"Please, Joshua——" she began.

"D'you think he'd want it?" he demanded roughly. "D'you think it would please him to know that his price was a handful of dirty gold—made the way that was?"

He saw her eyes glisten wet in the moonlight and, in spite of himself, felt shame for the way he had spoken.

"Ye've a right t' yer thoughts," she said harshly, "an' I'd not be arguin' with ye. But will ye be sayin' that's anny dirtier than anny other money that'd be buyin' him? 'Tis fer himself an' his freedom I ask ye to do it. He's a right to that. He need never be knowin' where 'tis from."

"What is it you're trying to tell me?" he demanded a little more softly.

She turned and stared down at the black water, trying to put her thoughts into words.

" 'Tis but just this," she said finally in a voice so low that he had to bend close to hear. "Ye're a good man, Joshua. An' so will he be. Whatever I am meself, so much can I be seein'. I've trust fer yerself. But I've a different feelin' fer him. Never before in me life did I love a man like this! But I'm tellin' ye now—an' I want ye should promise it to me that ye'll never be breathin' a whisper av it to annyone, least av all to himself—I love him, Joshua!"

"Why, then——" Joshua began, half exasperated.

"I know what ye'll be sayin'," she interrupted him. "Ye'll say all I'd need to be doin' was leave things as they were an' he'd be havin' me. But 'tis not so simple as that. Ye've seen what it is that I am. An' ye know yerself th' good lad he is. There's no power on earth or in heaven above can be makin' me over! Without me he can go far. With me—I'd just be a drag on him. Ye know it."

He stared at her with a new feeling of respect.

"And it's for that you want me to take the money?" he demanded. "Is it for that you've been doing—all this?"

"What else?" The question was simple, and there was no mistaking the bitterness in her voice. Yet there was pride in it too. Joshua bowed low before her and laid humble fingers upon her arm.

"Moira O'Connell!" he said. "I owe you an apology. I'm proud to have known you, and no man will ever say aught against you in my hearing without having me to reckon with!"

She laughed with a little catch in her throat.

"Go along with yer blarney!" she cried, and held out the coins in her hand again. "Here! Will ye be takin' 'em now an' be doin' as I ask av ye?"

He accepted the money and dropped it into his pocket with an air of embarrassment.

"If I had it myself," he told her, "I'd say keep it and carry the cost myself. But I'll not get my wages until I am back in Baltimore, and in the meantime I'm dependent on my brother-in-law. But I'll see 'tis repaid to you someday!"

They leaned shoulder to shoulder on the rail after that, and he pointed out to her the landmarks of the Delaware that loomed in the light of the moon: Cape Henlopen to the south, Cape May a little more clearly seen to northward upon their starboard bow, and the white rips of the Overfalls in between. But all the while he was thinking.

"How will I know where to send the money when I get it?" he asked.

"Sure, now!" She laughed. "Our paths'll be crossin' again someday. Ye can be givin' it to me then."

"How can you be sure of that?"

She sobered a little with a quick, Irish change of temper.

"'Twas not fer naught they were callin' me Moira Mohr O'Connell in Limerick before I left!" she retorted. "'Black Mary'll' be the English av it. 'Tis as I told Kenny, there's times when th' power av second sight is in me, an' this'll be wan av them!"

"Go on!" he gibed. "What else do you see?"

She closed her eyes.

"Not all I'll be tellin'!" she replied, darkly serious. "Some good an' some bad—some that'll be very bad fer all av us! But fer yerself, Joshua, I see it comin' out as ye'd wish. I see ye in command av yer own ship—a man-av-war, she'll be, an' yerself fine an' proud in a fine blue coat with red facin's an' a gold epaulet on yer shoulder!"

"You and your second sight!" Joshua slapped at the rail before him and scoffed, laughing. "That shows what you know of it. The British wear blue and white, and the French have white and gold! But who ever heard of blue and red? I'll challenge you to name such a navy! Go ahead! Name it!"

But she did not laugh as she stared back at him.

"Ye'll see!" was all she said.

6. Articles of Indenture

KENNY BOYLE leaned upon the rail in the crowded waist of the *Dolphin* and stared moodily at the slate-gray sky and the jumbled chimney pots and roofs of Philadelphia, half covered with sooty snow, and at the bleak warehouses and the icy, muddy morass of Water Street. For almost a week they had lain moored alongside the wharf while Seumas O'Shea arranged his auction, and in all that time Kenny had seen no more of America than this.

So much was, perhaps, natural in the circumstances, and it did not account entirely for his sense of loneliness and abandonment. As soon as the vessel had tied up to the shore Captain Drysdale had returned the command of her to Captain O'Shea, whereupon all of the cabin passengers immediately fled ashore, never even so much as stopping to say good-by. Joshua and his brother-in-law were among the first to go, and for all his dull resentment Kenny could understand a little why the American might not seek him out. After all, he had done his part. But that Moira should slip off without so much as a fare-ye-well seemed to him the crowning touch. He kept reminding himself that he should have expected little else; that doubtless she was shamed to face him after her behavior during the voyage. Nevertheless, he could not still the little shrill voice of bitterness that nagged at his thoughts. It was only another proof of the faithlessness of woman—so the little demons kept reminding him; and in his black Irish fit Kenny was ready to believe it.

But the long wait and its black hours of brooding seemed past now, and despite his dread of the future Kenny was at least relieved that this much was over and done. They had been turned out on deck early and herded in a knot in the waist. Ashore a few little knots of people began to converge upon one of the nearby warehouses. While the redemptioners waited in chill idleness on deck a ragged handbill was passed from hand to hand among them. When it came to him Kenny looked at it curiously:

! ! ! VENDUE ! ! !   **! ! ! VENDUE ! ! !**

JUST ARRIVED FROM DUBLIN BY THE SHIP
DOLPHIN
A CHOICE SELECTION OF MEN AND WOMEN
REDEMPTIONERS

200 will be Sold at VENDUE, at Meachum's Warehouse, at half past TEN, in the MORNING, March 2nd, 1775, at TERMS ranging from THREE to FOURTEEN years. Among them will be Found a Number of Excellent COBBLERS, TANNERS, SMITHS, CARPENTERS, STILLERS, WOODWORKERS and SERVANTS, as well as a Selection of COMELY and CAPABLE Housemaids! There are also a few SAILORS and FIELD HANDS & sum that is suteable for CLARKS, SCHULEMASTERS, TUTORS, &c, &c. Offered for SALE for the Acct of Seumas O'Shea, Capt. Ship DOLPHIN.

"That's today!" said Walsh, who had been reading over his shoulder.

"Aye—like so many sticks o' furniture," retorted Kenny.

"An' what were ye expectin'?" Walsh shrugged. "At least we'll be shut o' this devil's ark!"

When the time came they were herded down the gangway by guards, picked from the crew, and crowded as rapidly as possible across the wharf and into the long warehouse. Inside a crowd of buyers milled, smelling vaguely of sweat and mildew and human spittle. Kenny noticed that a good many of them were chewing tobacco and were not particular where they spat.

At one end of the long, drafty building there was a raised platform with a rough table upon it of boards laid across a pair of sawhorses. The redemptioners were crowded in a body to one side of the platform, and Kenny saw Captain O'Shea standing near the table, evidently discussing the forthcoming sale with a black-haired, blue-jowled, beetle-browed man, who later proved to be the vendue master. Kenny felt O'Shea's eye rake sourly across him, dark and vengeful, and he was glad at least that after today he would be out of his reach.

The sale itself was a simple enough procedure. The redemptioners were called up in alphabetical order and made to stand upon the table, where they were turned this way and that for all to see, while prospective buyers were allowed to come up and examine them; to poke and prod and pry, to examine their teeth and feel their ribs and flanks and legs, while the gods of the galleries—who were there only for the amusement of it—offered jeering and insulting remarks. When they had been duly displayed, the vendue master took the stand with his hammer and the auction began. Since his name began with a "B," Kenny was called up early. O'Shea leered at him without humor as he scrambled up on the table.

"Naow, then!" called the vendue master. "Here's a stout lad, an' young, too! He's——"

"Scrawny as an alley cat!" jeered a voice at the back.

Kenny gritted his teeth.

"He might look a mite peaked," the vendue master admitted, "but that's th' passage. He'll fill out with good feedin', an' he's strong an' wiry fer his size!"

"Fifteen guineas!" said a familiar voice from one side of the room, near the back.

O'Shea slewed around and stared furiously in the direction of the voice, and heads turned and craned for a sight of the fool who would open the bidding so high without even troubling to make an examination. Kenny looked, too, although he hardly needed to do so, and stiffened as he recognized Joshua. The American nodded toward him reassuringly, but Kenny did not return the gesture. The vendue master grunted in surprise but quickly recovered.

"Seven years this'n has signed up fer!" he called. "An' by trade he's a sailor. Do I hear sixteen guineas?"

"I said fifteen!" Joshua corrected him flatly.

"I beg yer pardon, young sir! FIFteen—do I hear sixteen? FIFteen, do I hear SIXteen? Gentlemen! Don't tell me ye're goin' t' let this good smart sailor lad go for such a song!"

No one answered. With the rest, Kenny was sure at first of Joshua's foolhardiness in offering such a sum to begin with. But now it seemed that there was a method in his bid. By setting it high to begin with, Joshua had evidently frightened off other bidders who might otherwise have been tempted to pyramid their offers.

"FIFTEEN!" cried the vendue master plaintively. "Won't someone say sixteen? Fifteen I have! Who will give sixteen? Have I no bidders? No? Well, then! Going once! . . . Going twice! . . . AND going three times andsoldtoth'young gent-in-th'-blue-coat! Off th' table, boy! Pay yer money to th' beadle, sir, an' take yer man!"

Kenny scrambled down, his ears burning, while Joshua came forward. For the first time Kenny noticed Captain Drysdale at his heels, glowering even more than usual. He and O'Shea exchanged sour looks but did not speak to one another. As they approached the beadle's table Kenny caught the last of the captain's growled aside to Joshua:

"—satisfied with your bargain. Ye needn't look t' me t' pay it!"

"Don't fear for your money, Will!" Joshua retorted.

In silence Kenny watched Joshua pay over the sum and accept his bond of indenture in return. There was something almost grim about it, it seemed to him. Then Joshua took his elbow and nodded toward the door. He walked in silence, a little bitter and ashamed that Joshua should so have taken advantage of what he knew. He would much prefer to have been bought by a complete stranger—if buying had to be. In the slush and mud outside Joshua turned to his brother-in-law.

"All right, Will," he said. "Thanks for coming. We'll have business to attend now. Why don't you go along to the inn? We'll meet you there later."

Drysdale turned on his heel without comment and disappeared, taking his sour gloom with him. Joshua grinned at Kenny.

"Come on!" he commanded. "We'll want to do something about those rags."

Kenny did not trust himself to reply. He walked at Joshua's elbow in silence up along Water Street, thence left up the muddy bluff bank and into the broader, airier expanse of Market Street, where even in his gloom Kenny was surprised to see the place so much more a city than it had appeared from the decks of the *Dolphin* below. Joshua presently led him to a dark-looking building with leaded windows. As they entered Kenny was surprised to find himself in a well-appointed shop. At their entrance a little man with a tape measure about his neck bustled out of the back and approached them.

"Yah, gentlemens!" He smiled. "What is it I can be doing for you?"

"My friend needs outfitting," Joshua told him.

Kenny found his tongue.

"I'll be askin' no man's charity!" he growled.

"'Tis not charity," Joshua retorted. "You forget, I've your indenture in my pocket. The law requires me to clothe and feed and house you."

Kenny flushed sullenly but could find no reply, and the shopkeeper set to work to lay out the goods Joshua requested. The thing took longer than they expected, but when it was done Kenny stood equipped in new shoes and stockings, new breeches and a coat that was plain but serviceable, a hat and a plain caped overcoat. Even his underclothing was new, and he was conscious of a twinge of guilt at his own sullenness. Yet he was unable to help himself. He could not forget that Joshua owned him, body and soul, for seven years, and his pride found this hard to bear. When they stepped outside the short winter's day was already growing dark. Joshua led the way a short distance up Market Street, and as they went he ventured a remark.

"I've seen naught of Moira since we came ashore," he said. "Have you?"

"No!" Kenny spat disgustedly into the gutter. "That I have not. Nor'll I be wantin' t' lay eyes on th' slut!"

Joshua reddened and seemed about to reply, then evidently changed the words even as they left his lips.

"You're a surly beggar, Boyle!" he said, not weighing the words too carefully. "You could be misjudging the girl."

"Could I now?" jeered Kenny. "Don't ye be tellin' me! They're all th' same!"

Joshua only looked as if he felt it not worth while to argue.

Inside the Black Horse Inn the lights were bright and cheerful and a fire blazed upon the hearth. But Joshua did not pause below. Instead he led Kenny upstairs to a set of rooms, where the walls were warm and mellow and a smaller grate glowed. As they entered William Drysdale glanced up sourly. Joshua nodded at him and then looked at Kenny with pride.

"Looks different, eh?"

Drysdale grunted.

"Now ye've got him, what d'ye propose t' do with him?"

"With your permission, we'll dine first," Joshua retorted.

Kenny retreated to a place in the corner, holding himself glumly silent while the supper was ordered. Nor would he be drawn into conversation while the beefsteak and kidney pie was being served and they ate. When they were done Drysdale flung his napkin on the table.

"Now then!" he growled. "Will ye tell me what it is ye're plannin'?"

Joshua reached in his pocket and drew out a handful of papers.

Kenny recognized his own indenture. The American held it out to him.

"'Tis yours," he said simply. "Take it and good luck!"

Kenny stared first at the papers and then at Joshua's face, and his own skin darkened.

"'Tis not so simple," he said. "No, thank ye!"

Joshua blinked at him in surprise.

"I gave me bond fair an' in faith," Kenny explained. "'Twas yerself that bought it."

"It was," Joshua agreed.

"Well, then," said Kenny, "I'll be servin' out me time, either till 'tis run or I've earned th' money t' be buyin' it back. It may be th' law ye must be clothin' an' feedin' an' shelterin' me, but I doubt there's aught in it that says ye must be givin' a man back his pledged word—an' that I'll not accept. No! Fer better or fer worse, Mr. Barney, ye've bought me, an' I'll not be walkin' free until I've earned th' right to't. Now ye may give thought t' that!"

Joshua sat back in his seat and stared at him, openmouthed.

"I'm damned!" he exclaimed. "At least you've guts if not judgment!"

The sound that Drysdale made in his throat might almost have been a chuckle.

"Caught yerself a tartar, eh?" he grumbled.

7. *Home Port*

THEIR JOURNEY to Baltimore was scarcely comfortable. It was cold and muddy, and it rained continuously. The heavy stage wagon slithered and slogged and jolted over the rutted road, and mired or was in danger of oversetting a dozen times a day. Baltimore itself proved a smaller, hillier, muddier replica of Philadelphia, with steep quagmired streets and a harbor to take a sailor's eye. They stepped down stiffly at the Fountain Inn and walked the last mile or so, picking their way amid the bottomless puddles. Near the top of Federal Hill they came to a big rambling house of red brick. It was not the largest or most pretentious of the town's houses. But it was the grandest place Kenny had ever set foot inside.

They did not wait for an answer to their knock but went directly in. Kenny found himself in a large square hall with a gracefully curving stair rising at the back. At either side doors opened, on the left into the dining room, on the right to a large drawing room. It was there that the short, rather buxom, middle-aged woman appeared at the sound of the street door's closing thump. From the fleeting look of pleasure in her eyes, from her high coloring and the shape of her face, Kenny knew her even before Joshua spoke.

"Mother!"

"Joshua, my son!" she cried, and held out her arms. Over his shoulder she caught sight of Drysdale. "And Will, too! Oh, but 'tis good to see you both! We've looked for you this month past."

" 'Twas a weary passage," Drysdale growled. He would have said more, but at that moment she noticed Kenny.

"And this?" she suggested.

Joshua recalled himself abruptly and whirled.

"This is Kenny—Kevin Boyle, my friend, from Dublin."

"Welcome, Kenny!" Mary Barney smiled and held out her hand. "Any friend of Joshua's is a friend to all of us here."

"Me deepest thanks t' ye, ma'am." Kenny felt stiff and awkward, but he managed a creditable leg.

Drysdale glanced toward the drawing room, from which the sound of voices could be heard.

"Ye've a party?" he asked. "Who's here?"

Kenny caught the swift darkening of Mary Barney's eyes and was uncomfortably aware that all was not well. As the stranger in the house he was perhaps quicker to notice what in the excitement of their home-coming the others missed.

" 'Tis no party, Will," she said quickly. "Naught but a family gathering. Come in—all of you."

She took Joshua by the arm and swept with him into the drawing room. As they passed through the doorway Kenny was at once both dazzled and curious. Half a dozen candles in tall silver sticks brightened the gathering dusk. The furnishings were tasteful and comfortably simple, though the high-backed wing chairs and the twin settees flanking the huge fireplace seemed to him opulent indeed. The bright log fire on the hearth he had already learned to accept as an almost inevitable part of life in this country.

But he had no time for more than a glance about the room. A murmur of welcome rose at Joshua's appearance, though he thought he detected a note of restraint in it. In the next instant he himself was being presented.

Alice, Joshua's eldest sister and Captain Drysdale's wife, stood by the near couch, tall and thin and nearly as ascetic-seeming as her husband. Across from her a pretty, brightly vivacious but obviously empty-headed blonde was introduced to him as the next eldest sister —Caroline, or Callie; Mrs. Ben Wales, to give her her married name. William was the oldest brother. He was a merchant from Norfolk, big and bluff and hearty. Arthur, next after him, was thin and slightly bald, reticent, retiring. Robin, the youngest, was a bright black-eyed child of eight or nine.

Near the fireplace stood two young men about Kenny's own age. Edric Wales, Caroline's brother-in-law, was short, slim, wiry, but barrel-chested and cocky. He was sleekly handsome and obviously aware of it. Kenny was instantly repelled, irritated, by his expression of positive superiority, and he took an immediate dislike to the man. Nor did Wales seem to think more highly of him. Neither offered his hand, and both merely acknowledged the introduction with a cool bow. Sam Smith, at the other side of the fireplace, was just a heavy-set, round-faced, rather good-natured young man. But it remains a fact that Kenny scarcely heard his name pronounced, for his glance had already gone beyond him to the dark girl standing near his elbow. She could not have been more than sixteen or seventeen, but there was no question of her breath-catching loveliness. She was smiling a little, her dark eyes bright, her lips parted slightly, revealing twin rows of small, flashing white teeth, while her black hair shone in the candlelight with the sheen of a feather dropped from a black cock's wing in the woods on the slopes of the Slieve Mish or the hollows of Macgillicuddy's Reeks.

"And this is my youngest daughter, Barbary," Mrs. Barney was saying.

Kenny fetched himself up sharply, aware that he was staring.

"Mistress Barbary," he said gravely. "Sure 'tis honored I am t' be makin' yer acquaintance. I hope ye'll be forgivin' me if I sh'ld be a bit mixed at first. 'Tis so many that ye are——"

Barbary's smile seemed to him to deepen with amusement at his brogue, and his Irish temper flared, raw and sensitive, no doubt because of the recent rasping of his own self-esteem.

"Is it wrong, then, th' way I speak?" he demanded.

Joshua cut in quickly:

"Where's Father?"

There was a sharp, sudden hush; a stiffening, as if they had all been dreading the question and were now bracing themselves for the answer. Perhaps because of his own raw hurt Kenny was sensitive to it. He took a step toward Joshua. At the same time Mary Barney let slip her courage and looked stricken.

"He—he's gone, Joshua!" she whispered. "Dead! 'Twas an accident. He was shot, hunting ducks in the marshes with Robin. We buried him yesterday."

For an instant there was no sound in the room. Because he himself had so recently known the numbing weight of just such news Kenny was the first to recover his wits. He put an arm about Joshua's shoulders. Barbary was watching, frowning a little, as if she were puzzled, but he was hardly aware of that. He turned to Mary Barney.

"Perhaps, ma'am," he suggested gently, "if he could be havin' a minute or two to himself now——"

"Of course." The older woman nodded swift understanding.

The room to which she led them was at the end of the hall on the next floor; a warm room with a comfortable personality. Tall windows looked south and east, and the furnishings were such as might be expected in a man's room: a pair of tall poster beds, a desk, a chest of drawers and a simple commode, and an easy chair.

" 'Tis his own room," she told Kenny as she showed them in. "We're so crowded now, I know you'll not mind sharing it."

"O' course not!" He had spent his life in a cottage not much larger than that room, but he did not tell her that.

"He needs a friend," she told him. "You'll stay with him?"

"As ye wish, ma'am," he replied.

"We'll be having dinner in an hour," she said. "I can send up a tray if you think——"

"Thank ye, ma'am." Kenny shook his head gently. "That'll not be needful. We'll be down."

She drew the door closed, and Kenny could hear her steps moving softly away. He turned toward his companion. Joshua flung himself down upon one of the beds and buried his face in the pillows. For a moment Kenny gazed at him compassionately. Then quietly he went around to sit on the other bed.

It was a long time, it seemed to him, before either of them spoke. Then Joshua lifted his head and stared at him out of hard-hurt yet still dry eyes. Kenny nodded slightly.

" 'Tis hard for ye," he said. "I know. 'Tis not so long since I knew it meself."

"You—told me." Joshua's dark eyes eased just a shade in their tortured look. "I understand better—now."

"Whist!" There was appreciation as well as sympathy in Kenny's voice. "Th' hurt'll be an old one t' me now. Maybe I can be offerin' ye a bit o' comradeship t' help ye over a sorry time."

"You'd help me?" Joshua was surprised.

"Why not?" Kenny shrugged. "Was it not yerself held yer hand out t' me? There was a thing I had t' be thinkin' out fer me own self, th' time me father died an' I went up on th' hills above th' curlin' sea an' lay down on me belly an' poured out me own tears on th' green sod. 'Twas this: I'd a mother meself, an' brothers an' sisters, like yer own. When I'd got a bit over th' wild grief in me I took thought o' them, an' it come t' me then that there wasn't a one o' them that wasn't just as hurt an' sore an' grievin' as meself. Then I was thinkin' that 'twas fer me t' be puttin' a bold face on it fer their sakes. 'Twas not fer me t' be always remindin' them o' their wounds. 'Twas better t' be givin' 'em some sort o' cheer an' a stout heart. That'd be th' way me own father'd be wantin' it, an' I'll warrant 'twould be th' same with yours."

Joshua sat up.

"By God, Kenny!" he cried. "You're right! You make me shamed for the way I showed it."

"No need for that," Kenny told him. " 'Twas a sudden gust out o' a clear sky, an' ye'd not be th' truehearted lad I think ye if it did not strike ye all aback! But now ye've th' way o't ye know what's t' be done. 'Twill be near suppertime. Shall we be goin' below an' let them be seein' ye've got a good hold o't?"

Joshua grimaced ruefully.

"Aye!" he said. "But one thing first. I've already offered your indentures once. I wish——"

Kenny stood up and shook his head.

"Thanks t' ye," he said, "but I've told ye th' feelin' I have about that. Leave me be earnin' 'em. 'Tis as much as I can be askin' t' repay ye for what ye've done fer me."

"If you feel so"—Joshua looked at him intently—"I can't insist on it. But here's my hand, at least! I hope you'll think of me rather as a friend than as the holder of your bond."

Kenny was pleased when they went down to join the others, for it seemed to him that the group brightened perceptibly at their reappearance. Edric Wales and Sam Smith had left, he was glad to discover, and he found himself at the long table between Robin and Caroline and directly opposite Joshua and Barbary—an arrangement that was also a cause for a certain satisfaction, for he had to admit, even to himself, that he felt a nagging curiosity about the dark girl, and from where he sat he could study her unobtrusively.

But the evening was one of swift changes and nuances; of events and questions. They were scarcely settled before Robin wanted to know all about the voyage. Joshua turned him off casually enough, and Drysdale was too busy with his trenchering to be bothered with answers. But Caroline kept the subject alive.

"Did you come in the same ship with Joshua, Mr. Boyle?" she asked.

"Th' very same, ma'am," he assured her. "But——"

Perhaps it was as well that he got no further, for he might have said more than he intended. But at that very moment an immense Negress entered from the kitchen, carrying a smoking bowl of oyster stew. Kenny's jaw dropped and he stared at her until she had set it down upon the table and withdrawn from the room. The others gaped at him.

"What's the matter, Mr. Boyle?" Barbary asked.

"Will ye be forgivin' me rudeness?" Kenny cried. "Never before did I lay eyes on an Indian!"

A shout of laughter rocked the table.

"That's no Injun!" Robin spoke scornfully. "Cassie's a black nigra from Africa."

"Is it th' truth ye say?" Kenny grinned at him. "Well, now, 'tis six o' one, half dozen o' t'other, for I never clapped eyes on one o' them either. We've none o' th' dark folk in Ireland."

"Oh, we've lots of them here," Robin assured him. "They're slaves mostly."

"Are there no other kind?" Kenny felt he was floundering. This might be dangerous ground.

"Why, yes." Barbary misunderstood him. He had meant to ask if none of these were free, but she thought he was making a distinction of color. "There are both black and white. Transported criminals and indentured servants are really little better, though we've never had a white slave in this house. Daddy wouldn't——"

"Strength t' him!" Kenny's sensitive temper flared again. He glowered at her belligerently. "D'ye approve yerself o' a system that'd take a man's liberty from him?"

She was surprised at his outburst and a little piqued. Her own temper showed in her heightened color.

"As a matter of fact, Mr. Boyle," she retorted, "I never thought much about it. But I don't think——"

"Perhaps 'twould pay ye t' give it some thought!"

Joshua broke in hastily, diverting the trend of the talk.

"As an Irishman," he said, "Kenny's a bit sensitive in the matter of personal liberty. I daresay he'll be as interested in developments here in the Colonies as the rest of us. What of it, Bill? Arthur? What's happened since we were gone?"

"Not so much that you could say a fight's begun"—Will Barney grinned—"but enough to show the way the wind lies. A congress of the Colonies met in Philadelphia in September, after you sailed. The Boston men have not let things lie, but stated their grievances at Suffolk County in October. And Importation Agreements have been applied, and our merchants have agreed not to deal with Britain. 'Tis said they're close to blows in New England."

"Damned rebels!" Captain Drysdale growled sourly.

"Is it rebellion," cried Joshua, "for men to stand for their own rights?"

"'Tis rebellion to deny th' power o' Parliament an' th' authority o' th' Crown!" Drysdale retorted.

"Will's right," Callie put in. "The least we can do is let the King's ministers decide what's best."

"I suppose that's what Ben Wales says!" Barbary put in.

It was clear that she was still resentful, but she gave way to her brother, whom she clearly idolized. The fact served Joshua's purpose of drawing the discussion away from Kenny, but it also showed that even among them opinion was not altogether unanimous. Obviously Will Drysdale was a crown partisan. But evidently Alice, his wife, did not altogether agree. From the talk it was equally apparent that Ben Wales, Callie's husband, was a Tory, and that his views were merely echoed by her. Arthur did not commit himself, but Kenny gathered that he was as yet neutral. On the other hand, Will Barney was an ardent patriot, only surpassed in his political convictions by Joshua himself. Barbary, who seemed to be devoted to them both, was equally militant. Mrs. Barney appeared to lean moderately to the Whigs, while Robin, outspoken as any child, was as fiery a patriot as Joshua.

Kenny, listening, wondered where he would stand in the issues.

Certainly he had no love for the British. At the same time, would a man cut his own throat to spite his stomach? For the time being, at least, he was satisfied to listen and to snatch an occasional glance at Barbary across the table. She was certainly pretty enough. But what a temper! Each time he looked at her he was conscious of a prickle of antagonism—a feeling far beyond any he should have felt as a result of their brief clash. Toward the end of supper Drysdale interrupted to inject a more practical note.

"I don't want t' argue," he growled nasally. "I jedge William's estate's been settled?"

"Oh, Drysdale, hush!" his wife cried. "Yes, the will's been read. I'll tell you all about it later."

"Then we've got no call t' go into that." He gave her an icy glare and went on: "But there's somethin' else. What's t' do next, hey?"

"I don't see——" Mary Barney began grimly.

"Wait a minute! Wait a minute, now!" he grumbled. "I only want ye t' know what I aim t' do, an' ye can chart yer own courses accordin'. Before I left here last year John Smith offered me command o' th' *Sydney*, tradin' t' th' Mediterranean. She'll be sailin' in a couple o' weeks. I weren't sure I'd take her till I got here. Now I reckon I will. Joshua—if ye're a mind t'it I'll make ye th' same offer as before —first mate's berth?"

Joshua scowled, then nodded.

"Better count me in, Will."

Across the table Kenny caught Joshua's eye. The American's nod was barely perceptible. When they rose from the table Kenny waylaid the captain.

"What d'ye want?" Drysdale had never been friendly.

"Ye were speakin' o' a ship." Kenny stood his ground. "Would ye have a berth aboard for another hand?"

Drysdale glowered at him. No reasons of friendship swayed him, but Joshua held Kenny's indenture. There was a good chance he could obtain the Irishman's services at a rate considerably below the usual.

"I'll give ye twelve shillin' a month before th' mast."

Kenny stiffened angrily. He knew that to be half the amount usual. But still there was the indenture. This way, at least, he would be earning back something.

"I'll take ye!" was all he said.

Joshua was furious when he learned what had been offered. But

Kenny persuaded him that it was best to let matters stand. Long after they had gone to bed and Kenny could hear Joshua's rhythmic breathing, indicating that he slept, the Irishman lay awake, staring at the gray outline of the window, turning the day's events over in his own mind.

He kept coming back to the question—what was he to do? He felt confused by the overwhelming rush of things. What was he, he asked himself, but a beggar? A ragged, nondescript, shoddy nobody; a poor Irish pauper picked up from the streets of Dublin. Joshua's sister—the pretty girl they called Barbary—without realizing its application to him, had stated his position. He was a white slave, bought at auction in Philadelphia, and destined to work for his freedom, either for seven years, or until Joshua put him in the way of buying back his bond.

At twelve shillings a month he scarcely saw how he could do that. Yet somehow it seemed important that he should. Barbary's wholly innocent remark had driven deep, and the hurt of it was on his soul. For some reason his mind kept coming back to her, and at last he thought he had puzzled it out. It was because he had nothing, he told himself, that he was so resentful. If he had been independent he would have been able to answer her in a way that would command her respect.

Well, then, he decided, if that was what was needed, then that was what he would win. Nor, he felt, was there any reason why he should not be able to now that he was in America. Once he had earned his bond and pulled himself level with her; once he had made a start of some sort on an honorable fortune and was able to stand on his own feet, he would be able to face her and make a decent, reasonable impression on her.

Why it was important that he should be able to make such an impression was a question he forgot to ask himself before he fell asleep. Yet there was no question but that the feeling was there. It gave him something to hold onto.

8. Drums of Strife

AT THE opposite end of the hall Barbary lost no sleep over Kenny —or, as a matter of fact, over any other young man. She slept soundly, and when the golden fingers of the dawn crept over the great bed she shared with her sister Callie, she leaped out and scrubbed her face with cold water from the icy pitcher standing by the commode, not troubling to wait for the taller jar of warm water that she could have had for the ringing.

Without thinking of it she flung off her night shift upon the bed and caught sight of her own young body, all goose bumps and pale white skin, long straight legs, and well-rounded hips and thighs. The mirror showed her flat stomach and breasts that were bright and firm as young pomegranates. Yet it did not occur to her that there might be any physical attraction in what she saw. She was yet child enough to snatch at the bedcovers and shout: "Up, Callie! Up! They'll all be down before us!"

"Barb'y!" Caroline rolled over and caught at the blankets. "What difference? I declare, I think it's just that you're impatient to see that handsome young Irishman again."

"Hmmmph!" snorted Barbary. "He's not so much!"

"He thinks you are," Callie teased her.

"Stuff!" said Barbary. "He wears a chip on his shoulder—I don't know why!"

"Don't you?" Callie yawned languidly. "Honestly, Barb'y, I can't fathom you. There's Edric Wales just panting to bed with you, and you know 'twould be a good match. But here comes a poor young Irishman, and you encourage him! I admit he's handsome as sin and twice as attractive, but who ever heard of an Irishman that owned anything?"

"Pooh!" cried Barbary. "How did I encourage him? I couldn't open my mouth but he fought with me! Anyway, lazybones, beds are to sleep in. Breakfast's for eating. Get up!"

"Ummm!" Caroline tossed back the covers and sat up on the edge of the bed, thoroughly conscious of her own attraction and contemplating the use of it. "I remember when I'd the same idea. No use to tell you that you're foolish if you don't use everything you have. Men like high-flown words, but they'd rather see a woman in bed any day—or night!"

"Don't judge everyone by your husband!" Barbary flared.

"Or my brother-in-law?" Callie replied dryly.

Barbary was right on one point, at least. The others were all down before them, and the brothers hooted and called them slugabeds. But she noticed that Kenny greeted her politely, if formally, and that he did not smile at the fact that they were the last to appear. As she ate her porridge she studied him covertly, and she was forced to admit that he was handsome, with a sort of tug-at-the-heart appeal that no one else she knew had.

In the fortnight that followed she came to know him, if not well, at least far better; and while she was, in a way, irritated by some of his traits, at the same time she was conscious of an attraction about him that was not altogether of the mind. That Callie should have recognized his masculinity was not surprising. She had always had a preoccupation with breeches. But Barbary had to admit that there seemed a core of solid worth in him such as she had not previously felt.

Of course when she thought about it, which was seldom, she had accepted the general notion that she and Edric Wales would join hands. In a way she thought she rather liked Edric. He thought well of himself, to be sure. But that was a trait, she told herself, she liked in a man. That was one of the troubles with Sam Smith. He was too thoughtful, too self-effacing, always too willing to give way to her opinion, to put the burden of a decision upon her rather than take matters in his own hands and state flatly that this was the way it would be. Either of them, of course, was quite eligible. Edric Wales was well favored, both physically and financially. His father and his brother Ben, Callie's husband, were among the town's leading merchants, and Sam Smith's father was equally prominent. But marriage, she felt, was a long way off; and in the meantime there was no reason why she should not choose her own company. For all they argued constantly, she found a certain likable quality in this young Irishman.

At the same time, however, it was true that they did bicker. Indeed, he seemed to her to be almost hypersensitive. On occasion he would go into a black Irish fit of melancholy, and if it were not for the fact that he was a friend of Joshua's, there were times when she felt impelled to turn him away entirely. He was especially exasperating in his stubborn hostility to both Edric Wales and, in a lesser degree, to Sam Smith. Why he should have resented them, as he appeared to, she could not imagine. Certainly it was not jealousy, for she had felt the sparks that flew between them when they first met, even before she and Kenny had been introduced. But the fact remained that they watched each other as warily as hostile dogs, and it was perhaps because of this belligerence that she herself was more inclined to cordiality toward Sam and Edric than she ordinarily was.

He had no right, she kept telling herself, to be critical of her friends. Yet, curiously enough, she was strangely downcast when at last the *Sydney* sailed for Genoa and the Mediterranean, carrying Joshua and Kenny with her.

They were not much more than gone from the bay, it seemed to her, when events in the Colonies began to explode like a rocket burst against the sky. If Joshua were only there, she told herself over and over, he would be so excited there would be no holding him. The end of April brought word of Lexington and Concord and of the flocking of the colonial troops to the siege of Boston. Maryland at once pledged her support to the war that now seemed inevitable and at once set about raising troops. A company of riflemen was raised in the mountains, and other companies of militia and line troops were formed in Baltimore and the Lower Counties and over on the Eastern Shore. Sam Smith blossomed out in the brilliant scarlet coat and buff waistcoat of Smallwood's Regiment and for the first time seemed to Barbary to be worthy of some notice. In neighboring Virginia, Lord Dunmore added fuel to the fire by carrying on his private war, so to speak, involving the inciting of Indian attacks upon the settlements of the outlying frontier and his proposal to raise and equip "Lord Dunmore's Own Regiment of Indians" and "Lord Dunmore's Ethiopian Regiments" for the purpose of properly chastising any recalcitrant colonials who might offer disobedience to the Crown's will.

Hardly was all this fuel heaped upon the bonfire before galloping couriers fetched word of the Battle of Bunker Hill and the seizure of Fort Ticonderoga, followed by a more leisurely report of General Washington's assumption of command at Cambridge.

All of this might have been little more than an exciting period in her life but for the effect upon Edric and Sam Smith. So far as the latter was concerned, the uniform seemed to do him good. He was more assured, more positive than he had been, though he still tended to leave it to her to decide things.

But no such reticence hampered Edric Wales. If anything, the rebellion roused him to a more outspoken attitude. He was sure of things.

"The fools!" he exclaimed. "What can they hope to accomplish against all the might of England?"

"Do you think, then," she demanded, "that Americans should knuckle under and do just what they're told?"

"Bosh!" he exclaimed. "You talk like Joshua—or that fool of an Irishman he picked up. What's his name? Boyle?"

"What's the matter with Joshua—or Kenny Boyle, for that matter?" she demanded.

"Barbary!" He was mildly placating. "I didn't come to argue. You must see how silly this all is——"

"What do you mean?" she demanded. "I don't see what's silly about it."

The smile he turned on her was bland, but his eyes were puzzled.

"Really, now!" he cried. "You don't mean that, Barbary. It must be plain to you that this handful of rebel rabble will be stamped down. Joshua's misguided, but he'll come around. If it weren't for that Irish lout——"

"Don't you dare speak against my brother!" Barbary cried.

"I don't!" Edric Wales actually laughed. "Truly, Barbary, I like Joshua. But he'll find out where the right cards lie. He's no fool——"

"And don't talk against Kenny, either!" she flared.

"All right! All right!" He grinned. "I won't say anything against either of them—though why the devil you should be interested in an Irish good-for-nothing——"

"What do you mean?" she cried.

"Isn't that what he is?" he demanded.

"How dare you say that?" she retorted, quite without realizing that she was defending Kenny. "Don't you think any man should fight for what he thinks is right?"

"Of course." He was utterly suave. "That's exactly what I say. Barbary, don't you see what foolishness it is to quarrel with such power as England's? Why not accept it and fight alongside it? It will win out in the end, and those who are on the right side of it will stand to benefit by their position."

"What are you driving at?" she demanded.

"I—I hadn't meant to put it bluntly," he told her, "but, Barbary, you must see. I want you to marry me. Let me look out for you and yours. These are troublesome times we are coming into——"

"I don't know," she said hesitantly. "I—I don't know, Edric. There are things——"

"What's the matter?" he demanded roughly. "Don't I offer you enough?"

"It isn't that——" she began.

"Then what?" he interrupted her. "You're not carried away by all this talk of 'liberty' and 'freedom'! After all, a man and a woman——"

He reached for her along the couch, caught her, and drew her to him roughly. He sought for her lips and forced his own against them.

"Edric!" She tried to twist away from him.

"You little witch!" He was breathing heavily. "You knew this was coming. You knew why I was here. I've wanted you for a long time—and you've encouraged me!"

His lips fought for hers again, though now that the first instant of surprise was over she resisted, and his hand fumbled.

"Edric!" she cried once more, and this time it was more than a protest. It was an angry command, and her hand spatted against his cheek. He sat back, startled, rubbing the reddening spot.

"You—you!" she sputtered furiously. "Get out! Get out!"

"You're overwrought, Barb'y!" he laughed. "This is nonsense."

Nevertheless, he rose and moved toward the door.

"I hope I never see you again!" she cried.

"Don't say that," he retorted infuriatingly, "because you will—you will! And you'll be glad of it!"

II

Yankee Men-of-War

1. The "Hornet"

THAT was in midsummer, while Joshua and Kenny were still absent. Barbary's immediate, impulsive wish was that they might both have been there, for surely Edric would never have dared such an approach if they had. In her wrath it did not seem to her significant that she should think of Kenny at such a moment. She was too thoroughly aroused to examine the reasons for her thought. Indeed, she was still fuming when they returned. But by that time, at least, she had cooled enough to be aware of a vague confusion at the sight of him.

The *Sydney* slipped around Whetstone Point quietly late one afternoon soon after the first of October. To the surprise of them all, it was Joshua who commanded her, while Kenny was acting as sailing master. Will Drysdale was dead—gone as suddenly as that; swept overboard in a storm and lost at sea. Supper was on the table when they reached the house, and Joshua told them the grim story as they ate. As a matter of fact, he told it with a sort of relentless relish, for Sam Smith, whose father was owner of the vessel, had picked that evening for a call on Barbary and had to sit and listen with embarrassment, not quite knowing just how he could escape. Joshua was not complimentary, and it was perhaps as well that Alice was not there.

"'Twas a damned, rotten, leaky old bucket your father sent us to sea in, Sam," Joshua taunted.

"I'm sure Father didn't know——" Sam's face was almost as red as his coat.

"He should have!" Joshua snapped. "'Tis an owner's responsibility! We knew before we were fairly down the bay, you may lay to that!"

"What happened, Joshua?" Mary Barney cut in, almost warningly. There was no sense in starting an argument.

"We had bitter weather from the time we'd cleared the capes," Joshua told her. "The old sticks racked and she took water as fast as we could pump her out. We'd the wind in our faces every inch of the way. When we were six weeks out we'd not gone halfway to Gibraltar!"

"Go on," Mary Barney said.

"I was below at the time"—Joshua glanced toward her—"so I never was quite sure what happened. 'Twas night, and she was laboring sorely, for the wind was worse. Will was on deck with the third mate and two men at the helm. I was about to go up to relieve him when I heard the crash. The wind must have come around from the opposite quarter all in a gust, for it laid the ship over on her beam-ends and nigh drove her under. It took the main and mizzen and plucked them out of her as if they were matchwood. When we'd got the mess cut away and a jury rig on her, we could see where the mizzen butt kicked down and across the poop, carrying away the wheel and a good ten feet of the quarter rail. Will and the others must have gone at the same time, for they were all clustered together by the helm, fighting it against the seas."

"You didn't—look for them?" Barbary was appalled.

"How could we?" Joshua smiled at her wryly. "In those seas we'd all we could do to keep afloat and save our own lives! By the time we cleared the hulk and righted her and got a rudder jury rigged, 'twas day and they'd been long gone."

"Then you don't think there was a chance?" his mother asked.

"Never a one!" Kenny interrupted, shaking his head. "He's not t' be blamed, ma'am. They'd never have floated a minute in that heavy gear, let alone fer hours with nothin' t' be clingin' to. In fact, 'twas only be his own quick wit an' th' way he was takin' over and settin' us all t'our tasks that any one o' us come through't alive."

"You should take more credit for your own good skill at navigation, Kenny," Joshua reminded him. "'Twas that fetched us to Gibraltar alive and safe."

"'Twas yerself that kept her afloat so far an' made arrangements for repairs there," Kenny insisted.

"And you that sailed her on to Genoa and then home again!" Joshua grinned. "No, Kenny, I'll take no credit but you share it too."

Barbary was conscious almost of pride at the words, but Mary Barney scarcely seemed to hear them.

"Poor Alice," she whispered. "She must hear it directly. We must go to her and tell her, Joshua—at once. As soon as we've finished supper."

"I mean to," Joshua replied. "There'll be no need for any of the others, I think?"

"Better if 'tis just ourselves," his mother told him. "It's only a short drive over to Bear's Farm. I'll have the carriage made ready as soon as we're done here."

Joshua nodded, then glanced at Sam Smith. Barbary, watching

him, thought she could almost see him force his thoughts into different channels.

"What's the news, Sam? We heard of the war——"

"You heard?" Sam seemed astonished.

"Aye! We were boarded by the sloop *Kingfisher* patrolling off the capes." Joshua chuckled. "They sent a very fire-eater of a midshipman aboard—must have been all of twelve years old, eh, Kenny?"

"Sure he was no bigger than Robin, yonder," Kenny growled.

"I thought I'd burst my buttons!" Joshua grinned. "When the young pup heard Kenny's brogue he came near to pressing him for his crew."

"What did you do?" Barbary looked alarmed.

"I swore he was born and raised in Baltimore"—Joshua smiled—"and that I'd known his mother and father before him, and he couldn't answer that, for I'd written it in the articles myself before ever we sailed!"

The others laughed.

"He let you go then?" Sam Smith asked.

"Would we be here else?" Joshua retorted. "Aye! He found no contraband aboard, and our papers were in order, so he didn't hold us, though I daresay he'd have liked to."

"What did he say?" Sam asked.

"Little enough!" Joshua shrugged. "He told us of Lexington and Concord, and of Bunker Hill after, and how our people were sitting down in front of Boston—all from his own Englishman's point of view, you may be sure. But of anything else that's been done he'd little enough to offer. What about Congress? What are they doing to raise some sort of a defense?"

"Well——" Sam Smith hesitated thoughtfully. "General Washington's taken command of the Army before Boston, and Maryland's taking steps to raise four regiments and two independent companies of riflemen——"

"Oh, forget your Army for a minute!" cried Joshua, laughing. "I mean what have they done that's important? The British have damned long lines of communication. If we can cut those or keep them away from our shores, your Army won't matter two pins in a bucket! What about a navy? What are they doing to send armed ships to sea?"

Sam grinned back at him and shook his head.

"Little enough, I'm afraid," he retorted. "There's been none authorized as yet. Congress keeps bickering about it, but I notice they've not so much as issued letters of marque and reprisal to commission privateers, let alone organize anything more regular. They seem to be leaving the whole thing to the individual states——"

"What are the fools thinking of?" cried Joshua.

"Well, Sam Chase, in Congress the other day, said it would be madness to try to fight the British fleet," Sam retorted.

"Aye? Is it madder then than to attack the British Army in Boston?" Joshua's face was flushed with excitement. "You know Sam Chase is naught but an old sour-guts! Can we hope to win the war with that kind of thought? Be damned to 'em! They can't do this!"

"Hold on, Joshua." Sam Smith shrugged apologetically. " 'Tis not for me to be saying what Congress can or can't do. I'm only telling you what seems to have been done—and what they are doing."

"Well, for God's sake, then!" Joshua cried. "What have they done? What are they doing?"

"The states are organizing their own naval forces—at least Maryland is," Sam told him. "I know that much, for Father has already sold 'em a ship that they've named the *Defense*. I daresay he could arrange for a berth in her if you like."

"Not if she's anything like the *Sydney!*" Joshua retorted.

Sam flushed and evidently chose to ignore the dig.

"Well, then," he offered, "privateers haven't been authorized as yet, but we've every reason to think they will be—and soon. Father's making ready a fleet of them for sea now. If you like I——"

"Pah!" Joshua snorted rudely. "A privateer? I'd as soon sail a damned pirate! No, thank you, Sam. I'll wait, and when the time comes I'll warrant there'll be a naval force. I don't propose to see the privateers draw off all the good seamen——"

Up till this time Kenny had been content to remain more or less quiet, listening, glancing now and again at Barbary, and then looking down thoughtfully at his plate. But at Joshua's explosion he offered protest.

"Where's th' sense in that, now?" he demanded. "I'll be agreein' with ye that a force o' some kind afloat is important. But what's wrong with a privateer? Sure she's manned, furnished, an' equipped all at th' expense o' her owner! She costs th' Congress not so much as a ha'penny, an' certainly she can be doin' as much damage as any naval vessel o' th' same size——"

"That's just the point!" Joshua interrupted him. "She might, but will she? Will a privateer fight with a ship that's heavier-gunned?"

"'Twould depend on her commander," Kenny retorted.

"Stuff!" snorted Joshua. "You know she would not! A privateer's fitted out for profit, and so long as there are fat merchantmen to be taken she'll cut and run from anything more than half her size that shows anything like fight! Would we be able to hold the British fleet in check by such means?"

"I say again it depends on th' captain o' th' ship, if he fights or not, an' I'll dare be sayin' ye'd find it th' same in a navy. There'll always be them will run from a stronger ship—or even one as strong—an' a man-o'-war may take merchantmen too, ye know!"

Barbary glanced at him, interested. It seemed to her that some of the rough edges had been smoothed off in the course of his voyage; and certainly he had gained confidence, for he was not at all abashed in his opposition to her brother. At the same time, she was not sure she cared for that. Whatever Joshua said was gospel so far as she was concerned, and she was not inclined to support any man who argued against him.

"All the more argument in favor of a publicly armed naval force!" Joshua cried. "As you say yourself, they can take merchant ships, the same as privateers. But they'll not dare to run from a fight—not unless they prefer court-martial!"

"If 'twere only for such a reason that they stood an' fought, 'twould be better if they ran!" Kenny shrugged. "Besides, what o' th' motive t' be turnin' an honest penny? Ye'll be admittin' there's a greater share for all hands in a privateer? Will ye not be allowin' th' lads a chance?"

"Ha! Who speaks of profits at a time like this?" Joshua demanded.

"Meself for one!" Kenny retorted. "'Tis all well enough for th' man that'll be havin' no need o't t' be scornin' gold. But for th' lad that's his way t' be makin' 'tis a logical way for him t' serve both himself an' his country at the same time!"

"Hmmph!" Joshua snorted.

"Then I take it, Mr. Boyle"—Sam turned his mild eyes on the Irishman—"you'd be inclined to accept a place in a privateer, if one could be found, rather than in a naval ship?"

Kenny looked at him blandly, stonily.

"As t' that," he retorted, "I'll be makin' up me own mind when th' time comes."

Mary Barney cut the argument short, rising.

"Well! I don't see that it makes much difference!" she said. "Either way 'tis war, and either way men will die. Come, Joshua—we must be on our way."

Sam Smith saw his opportunity to escape and seized it, obviously of no mind to pursue that discussion further, nor yet inclined to serious discussion with Barbary so long as there might be another present. He said his farewells and left, and Joshua and his mother followed soon after, leaving Barbary and Kenny to keep the fires going on the wide hearth. There was an awkward silence for a moment when finally they were gone. Then Kenny rose easily and poked carefully at the fire, though it needed no attention at all.

"D'ye know, Barbary?" he said at length, turning his lean face toward her. It was handsome in the ruddy firelight. "D'ye know, now, I found ye frightenin' when I first came here with Joshua?"

He smiled, but she did not smile back.

"And now you do not?" she asked.

"No!" He shook his head slowly. "Ye see, I'd some reason t' be touchy then. Ye were sharp with me, though 'twas only later I saw that ye did not mean it. Still, ye did hurt t' me heart with yer talk o' white slaves an' black—for, ye see, Barbary, I was one o' them then. An' 'twas yerself said it!"

"What do you mean, Kenny?" she cried, her surprise making her drop a little of her aloofness—a reserve she had built up almost automatically since her experience with Edric. "I didn't mean——"

"I know!" He smiled at her almost encouragingly. "Ye weren't aware o' things. But there's th' truth o't. Joshua held me indentures! He'd bought 'em at Philadelphia at auction, and 'twas why Cap'n Drysdale was able t' ship me before th' mast at half pay. 'Tis not for me t' be thankful for any man's bad luck, but 'tis th' truth an' all that when Joshua came t' th' command an' made me actin' sailin' master, with th' pay that went with it, he also gave me th' means t' be buyin' back me bond. Sure, it's cost me what I made o' th' voyage, but I'm free now, Barbary, an' I'd not ask ye to be thinkin' o' me. But——"

There is no doubt that the shock of her quarrel with Edric Wales had left her with a certain distaste for anything that smacked of romance. It might also have been true that she found herself drawn more sharply toward this handsome young Irishman than even she herself cared to admit, and perhaps her own reluctance to become involved with anyone else, combined with her own vague recognition of his attraction, impelled her to offer harshness where understanding was needed. At least she was ashamed of herself afterward for it.

"But—aren't you reaching higher than your position, Mr. Boyle?" He stared at her, flushing slowly crimson.

"Sure, I've not reached at all—yet," he retorted gravely. "An' I'm thinkin' now that I'll not! I wanted ye t' be knowin', was all! At least I've earned meself th' right t' be talkin' t' ye, an' I was hopin' I might be earnin' somethin' more in time. In th' meantime I'd only th' thought t' be holdin' out me hand in friendship t' ye—as I have t' Joshua."

Embarrassment at her own ill grace was fuel to the fire of her temper.

"I suppose that's why you argued with him in favor of privateering?" she taunted.

"If ye think it wrong for a man t' be betterin' himself——" he began stiffly.

"Of course not!" she retorted. "But no man has a right to better himself at the expense of what he fights for."

"I've not said he should!" he flared. "If a privateersman can be doin' th' task as well——"

"Joshua doesn't think they can," she interrupted him.

"I'm sorry I've not been able t' convince ye!" he cried. "I've spoken me mind honestly, an' I've no wish t' be arguin'. If ye'll excuse me, I think I'll be off upstairs t' bed!"

"If you'd put on a uniform like Sam Smith!" she flung after him. But he was already walking stiffly from the room, and if he heard her he gave no sign of it.

After he was gone she wished she had not been so harsh with him. As he had said, he had done no more than offer his friendship, and she had thrust it away. At least he had offered her no such affront as Edric Wales had done. Indeed, he had not so much as lifted a finger to her.

For his part, Kenny was bewildered. It seemed to him a foolish thing for a man and a woman to be quarreling about, especially when essentially they were both on the same side of things. He was puzzled, for in spite of all he liked her. At the same time he was hurt inside himself that she should so, in a sense, have slapped him; hurt and surprised, too, for after all, it seemed to him, he had offered no harm.

But there it was, and he told himself there was nothing he could do about it. After that he was stiffly formal with her, and though perhaps she would have liked to give him another chance, she could scarcely have made the first move.

She was to remember those days, when he and Joshua were both in Baltimore, at the beginning of things. And so were they. The town was a welter of preparation and excitement, with the companies drilling in the woods and fields all about the little city and the drums banging and rattling in the streets as the recruiting parties marched from one tavern to another. Down by the harbor new ways went up and the clatter and thump of the shipbuilders' hammers and the whine of saws rang out in the early autumn air from dawn to dusk. Whether they were to have a navy or not, someone was certainly preparing to get ships to sea; and all the while it was about, the half-friendly, half-acrimonious argument went on as to whether navy or privateering was the answer, until sometimes Barbary thought it would drive her mad. Kenny and Joshua never seemed to tire of it, and she was constantly aware of Kenny's gray eyes studying her sardonically as he talked.

Curiously enough, it was Sam Smith who settled the point, at least so far as that moment was concerned. He came one midday to the house with a tall, thin, almost cadaverous, smiling young man, already balding a little, yet somehow likably fresh. He was dressed in some sort of odd-looking uniform—a blue coat with red facings, with a red waistcoat and blue trousers, gold buttons, and a golden epaulet upon his left shoulder. But none of them thought much of that. Nearly everyone wore a uniform of some sort in those days. If he were not a member of a company or a battalion with an authorized one, then he made up one for himself—even if it were only a cockade in his hat or a ribbon in his lapel—and some of the fancier ones were a sight to behold!

"This is Lieutenant Isaiah Robinson." Sam presented him politely as soon as they were inside. "He came to Father for advice, and Father thought you might be interested in what he had to say, Joshua —you and Mr. Boyle."

"We're always glad to listen." Joshua nodded, offering his hand. "How can we help you, Lieutenant?"

He was grinning as he said it, but the smile dropped from his face as he heard Robinson's answer.

"Mr. Smith said ye might be interested in a naval berth," Robinson suggested.

Joshua glanced quickly at Kenny.

"I—we are!" he said. "D'you mean——"

"Congress has finally authorized a fleet." Robinson grinned. "'Tis why I'm here. I've been sent to find two ships in Baltimore; to man and victual and furnish 'em——"

"Anything we can do, Lieutenant——" Joshua began. He scarcely troubled to hide his eagerness.

"That's kindly o' ye, Mr. Barney," Robinson replied. "I've found the ships—the sloop *Hornet*, Cap'n Stone, and the schooner *Wasp*, Cap'n Hallock. But we need men an' officers t' get 'em t' sea! Mr. Smith was saying t' me that ye'd a leaning to such service and that ye'd been in command o' one o' his ships—that Mr. Boyle, here, was sailin' master——"

"You've need of such, Lieutenant?" Joshua interrupted.

"Cap'n Hallock's lookin' after th' *Wasp*," the lean officer said slowly, "but I've a berth in th' *Hornet* for a second luff, next under me, an' a sailin' master."

"You've just found your lieutenant—if you'll have me," Joshua told him.

They all looked at Kenny, and it seemed to him that a sort of waiting silence fell upon the room. Both Sam and Barbary were watching him, and Joshua appeared almost worried.

"An' yourself, Mr. Boyle?" Robinson asked.

"Sure I'll be follyin' where Joshua leads," Kenny replied quietly.

Joshua and Lieutenant Robinson smiled abruptly, and even Sam Smith seemed someway pleased. Behind him Kenny almost thought he heard the faint whispering rush of Barbary's pent-up breath.

"There'll be gear for us to get, no doubt," Joshua was saying. "Has a uniform been authorized yet, Lieutenant?"

Robinson glanced down at his own somewhat travel-stained dress in some embarrassment.

"'Tis not much, ye might say," he apologized. "I'd no time t' get th' best tailorin' before I left Philadelphia. But such as 'tis, this is it: blue breeches, red weskit, blue coat with red facin's—— Eh? What's that ye say?"

"I said, 'I'm damned!'" Joshua replied.

2. *The Golden Rock*

THE *Hornet* slipped her cables and stood down the bay late in November in company with the *Wasp,* the first vessels of the young nation's regular new Navy to get to sea. A full month had passed since the day that brought Ike Robinson to the big house on Federal Hill and Joshua and Kenny had raised their hands before him and taken their oaths to support the duly elected Congress of the thirteen federated states and to observe strictly the *Rules for the Regulation of the Navy of the United Colonies,* laid down by it.

But that month had been far from dull. From the moment they were sworn, it seemed to Kenny, Isaiah Robinson had kept them frantically busy—drumming a crew to the recruiting rendezvous, victualing the vessel, seeing her properly armed and braced for the heavier duties of war. He had little time to think of it, for sure, but sometimes at night, before he went to sleep, he pondered it in the dark, and at such times Kenny was not altogether sure he was happy in the new role in which he found himself. Actually, it had been on the impulse of a moment that he had offered to follow where Joshua led. It seemed to him then—and it appeared more so now—that he had set aside his personal ambitions for a cause that could actually offer little to him in the way of reward. To a degree, of course, he recognized he had done it because of Barbary—though whether out of pique at her taunts or from a desire to prove to her that he, too, was capable of sacrifice he himself was scarcely able to say. Whatever the cause, it seemed to him that he was entitled to at least a nod of approval from her for it. But, if anything, she gave him at least the impression that she scorned him the more for having given way to her instead of holding steadfast to his own ideas. He was a little bitter and nonplused by it and more than a little annoyed. It was a case, it seemed to him, of "damned if you do and damned if you don't!"

As a matter of fact, Barbary felt no such scorn. In view of their argument, and in view of the stubborn core she could feel in him, she had been surprised—and she had been oddly pleased too. But she was angry with herself for having been so quick to misjudge him and for being as stubborn in her own way as he was in his, and she could hardly admit that, even to herself. As a result she took out her spite on him and left them both sore and mildly hurt.

But all that was behind now, Kenny told himself, and the thought brought him a curious sense of release and relief. Now that they were away at last, he felt exhilaration. There was a pleasure in feeling again the heave of the deck beneath his feet and the sharp bite of the sea wind in his face. He glanced aloft at the tugging sails and listened with pleasure to the taut whine of the wind in the rigging. The sloop jumped a little to the shock of gunfire as Ike Robinson exercised the green crew at the great guns.

"She draws well!" Kenny remarked to Joshua, who had the deck with him.

"Aye, well enough!" Joshua growled darkly.

"She'll do for my choice to be showin' a smart pair o' heels t' most anythin' she'll have t' run from." Kenny grinned. "An' with Mr. Robinson in charge o' her guns, I'm not fearin' but she'll be standin' up well t' anythin' her size."

"You're forgetting that Ike takes his orders from Captain Stone," Joshua replied darkly.

All of which was quite true, indeed almost prophetic, in the light of events. The *Hornet* was a smart sloop, Bermuda-built, and large enough and stout enough to be able to carry the ten guns with which she had been equipped and to fight them well. She had a reputation about Baltimore as a fast sailer, so that were she pursued by a frigate or a ship of the line whose metal outweighed and outranged her, she would have little difficulty eluding it. At the same time, with a man like Robinson to inspire her fighting men, she should have no fear of anything in her own class. Ashore the lank lieutenant, Ike, had been good-natured, easygoing, and easy indeed to like. Afloat he was seamanly and smart as a whip. He was no sundowner, yet it was clear that he looked for discipline and a taut ship; and that he was a thorough-knowing sailor was evident.

But for all that, Captain Stone was something of an unknown quantity, and in voicing his thoughts Joshua had no more than said what half of them were thinking. Also a Bermudian, William Stone, too, had a reputation about Baltimore as a smart sailor and a daring, crafty one to boot. But they were not long aboard before they began to suspect that *his* reputation, at least, was considerably of his own making. He was a blowhard who never tired of giving himself and his ship a clean bill of health. But Kenny noticed that whenever he came aboard his breath reeked like a Kilmallock still, and Joshua observed that he never seemed to stand by his guns in an argument. He was not alone in wondering if the man would be more inclined to do so when it came to a fight at sea.

But all of that was pure speculation then. They had their orders and they carried them out smartly. The night after they left Baltimore they slipped out through the capes and then doubled up for the Delaware, where they found Commodore Hopkins and the rest of the squadron lying at anchor under the lee of Cape Henlopen.

They were properly impressed with the sight. For all it was yet actually little more than a seagoing rabble, it had a mighty military air of naval order and discipline in their own inexperienced eyes. The fresh sea air that blew from them carried to their innocent noses none of the stench of nepotism, nor warned them that the smallpox had already broken out aboard four of the vessels. They saw only what looked to them to be a powerful array: two ships, the *Alfred*, 24, Captain Saltonstall, carrying Commodore Hopkins's flag, and the *Columbus*, 20, Captain Whipple; two brigs, the *Andrea Doria*, 14, Captain Biddle, and the *Cabot*, 14, Captain John Hopkins—the commodore's son; the sloop *Providence*, 12, Captain Hazard, and the tender *Fly*, 8, Captain Hoystead Hacker. With their own *Hornet*, 10, and their consort, the *Wasp*, 8, they counted eight vessels in all, which seemed a mighty armada to them at the moment, though had they stopped to think about it they must have realized how pitiful a pawn it was with which to try to check the power of Britain's fleet.

Perhaps it was as well that their enthusiasm overrode the thought. As junior officers it was not their privilege to attend the grand council aboard the flagship. They kept the deck and maintained a taut ship until the return of Captain Stone and Lieutenant Robinson brought word of their first undertaking—a projected attack upon the island of New Providence, in the Bahamas, where it was known that a large store of guns and ammunition, of powder and other sorely needed military supplies were kept.

Their excitement knew no bounds at the word, for how were they to know that the commodore was sailing in the direct face of his orders, which were to clear Lord Dunmore's marauders from the mouth and lower reaches of the Chesapeake so that other vessels carrying just such supplies might be able to find their way to port? Alas for their eagerness, however! They were not destined to reach the Bahamas. They got to sea toward the middle of February, and after a bumbling start the fleet turned southward and ran through heavy weather down the coast. Off Hatteras, in the wild darkness of a stormy night, it happened. Running without lights to avoid the enemy prowling in the vicinity, the *Hornet* and the tiny *Fly* rolled close against one another and locked top hamper. There was a rending, protesting shriek of tortured cordage, and then the crash of the *Hornet's* mast as it fell. When morning came they were alone upon a storm-tossed ocean, wallowing, dismasted, and none of the rest of the fleet was anywhere in sight.

It was then that the seamanship of Ike Robinson and Joshua and Kenny came to the fore and the weakness of Captain Stone was revealed, for the captain took to his cabin and chanted psalms in a panic, while the others worked the clock around to get a jury mast rigged and to fight their vessel back. They fished the spar to the broken stump and braced it and got a rag of sail on her. After that they clawed northward, red-eyed and weary, against towering, rushing mountains of green sea water, until they reached the mouth of the Delaware and tried to slip through the Cape May Channel. They might have done it and taken a prize on the way—for the little British tender *Maria*, lighter-gunned and more lightly manned than the *Hornet*, was all that stood in their way. But Captain Stone came rushing on deck at the critical moment, shouting orders to them not to shoot, for he had "no wish to shed blood."

Joshua was furious. He turned and flung his heavy ironshod linstock directly at Stone's head, and the captain only saved himself by ducking back and slamming the door. He did not reappear until they reached port. But the chance was gone. The *Maria* had seen her danger and sheered off, while her mother ship, the British patrol frigate *Roebuck*, was bearing down now to intercept. The *Hornet* had no choice but to fly and battle battering seas for two weeks more, until a lull in the fury of the winter storm let her slip in through the capes like a frightened rabbit, at a time when the *Roebuck* was not looking, and seek safety in Philadelphia.

There was only one good thing about it. Captain Stone slipped ashore and disappeared as if he had been wiped from the face of the earth as soon as they had their lines about the bollards on the quay. But for Joshua and Kenny, the weeks that followed, while they were exciting beyond doubt and profitable to a degree, were hardly satisfying. They hoped for action, but as soon as repairs upon their ship were effected they found themselves assigned to an endless round of convoy duty, like many a naval officer before and since; herding merchant vessels down to the capes and seeing them out to sea, picking up another group and fetching them home again, eluding the British patrols as they went each way.

There seemed nothing but drudgery in it to Joshua and Kenny; and even Ike Robinson, stout seaman though he was, fumed under it. Yet they were learning. Navy ways and navy discipline began to take on some meaning for them. They began to grow aware—even though they were scarcely conscious of it—of the fine line between the good fellow and the commander who had the respect of his men. Paradoxically, the man who recognized that he could be both was a leader. The one who had only one or the other was neither liked nor respected. They took a prize or two—a British supply ship bound up for New York with a cargo of sugar and a privateer that ventured too close. They tasted fire when they had to land a cargo of powder from a grounded brigantine in the shallows of Turtle Gut Inlet under the guns of the entire blockading British force. But the life was dull for them, or so it seemed, and their only compensation was when they met their fellows on convoy duty—Lambert Wickes, John Barry, Richard Dale, and a dozen others—at the taverns in Cape May, during the brief intervals ashore. Strangely enough, it was one of these that drew attention to them.

Lambert Wickes, lean and brown-faced, was twitting round-faced, ruddy, jovial, and altogether Irish John Barry.

"You Irish are traditional haters of the British." He grinned. "A man like yourself, John, should have no trouble raisin' 'em all to our side of it!"

Kenny spoke, almost idly giving tongue to his thoughts.

"So will th' French be," he said. "What about them?"

"What d'ye mean?" Lambert Wickes looked around at him. "There's been peace between 'em for fifteen years."

Having put the cow to pasture, Kenny had to hang a bell on her.

"Aye," he agreed slowly. "But ye'll be admittin', Captain, that if ever there's dirty weather in th' Channel, th' British're screamin' themselves hoarse that there's a Frenchman at th' bottom o't! Wouldn't it be a fine thing now if a dozen or so o' our ships was t' be workin' out o' French ports, sendin' their prizes back into 'em when they were hard pressed? Th' French'd be screamin' blue murder an' swearin' 'twas none o' their doin'. But there'd always be takers for a fine prize, an', mark me words, th' British'd be sure 'twas their work! There'd be war between 'em in no time, with th' French in on our side!"

Luke Matthewman of the *Lexington* laughed at the fantasy of it, but Lambert Wickes's eyes narrowed.

"D'ye know," he grunted, staring at Kenny, "'tis just outlandish enough to have something to it. What was it you said your name was, mister?"

That was in April, and within a week none of them thought anything more of it. May and June went down into the well of the past, and they took a brigantine, the *Three Friends,* laden with rum and sugar for the enemy in New York, and fetched her in to Philadelphia. After that they were transferred to the sloop *Sachem* and were taking a convoy down the river on the fourth of July, when the Colonies proclaimed the Declaration of Independence. But they were back in Philadelphia in a month's time, and their mooring lines were scarcely fast before a green-coated marine came over the side with a letter, bearing the seals of Congress and the Marine Committee, for Isaiah Robinson. He broke the seals almost absently, and Joshua and Kenny could not help reading over his shoulder:

> Will Lieutenants Robinson and Barney, and Mr. Boyle, sailing master, of the sloop-of-war *Sachem,* report immediately to Robert Morris at his office.

That was all it said. But that was enough. Anyone who had aught at all to do with the Navy knew that by this time, at least, the prominent Philadelphia merchant who sat as chairman of it was to all intents and purposes the Marine Committee itself. A request from him was like the finger of God—an order that was laid upon you, and you leaped to obey, whether you anticipated well of it or not.

It seemed to Kenny, when they were ushered one after the other into the big dark oak-paneled room that was his office, that Robert Morris was a man who was quite willing to acknowledge the relationship to the deity—as a younger and perhaps less influential brother. It was not that Morris was conceited or vain. But he was confident, sure of himself, and prepared to concede not one bit of his opinion for any man's. He kept them waiting when they first came in, not even glancing up from the papers he was signing, and they stood stiffly before his desk until he was done. Kenny was almost prepared to dislike him, when he looked up and smiled, and from that moment he held the Irishman—indeed, all of them—in his pocket.

"Gentlemen!" He rose, showing himself not nearly so tall as he had seemed sitting there behind the big rosewood desk, and held out his hand with a smile of welcome. "Forgive me. Those were matters I had to get off. Mr. Robinson—you command the *Sachem*. Mr. Barney —it was you who flung the linstock at Captain Stone? Ah! Don't apologize. A man who'll not fight has no place in this Navy! And you, Mr. Boyle—what I hear of you interests me very much. Sit down, gentlemen. Sit down. Take pipes, find chairs, and light up. This may take a little time."

Kenny found himself a clay in the rack and filled it from the jar, then followed the example of the others and sought a place in one of the comfortable leather armchairs, all the time wondering what the devil there could be about such as himself that might interest this shrewd man with the fine, quick eyes and the straight nose and the thin, tight trap of a mouth. Yet it was at Kenny that Robert Morris looked when they were settled.

"Yes, Mr. Boyle"—he smiled quizzically—"I can't say I've a ship to offer you—yet—though I wish I had. But 'tis the truth, of the three of you—you interest me the most. You see, I've heard of you before."

"I can't be imaginin' where, sir." Kenny was perplexed.

"Do you recall a conversation you had with Captain Wickes at Cape May some time ago?" Morris asked. Then, seeing Kenny still wondering, he prodded. "'Twas something about the French, I believe."

Kenny remembered the incident suddenly and half guiltily.

"Burn me! Th' captain'll be havin' a longer memory than meself! Sure 'twas no more than a flight o' fancy——"

"I know!" The square-faced man behind the desk nodded. "You may have spoken in jest, but the fact that you spoke at all shows the drift of your thoughts. And they were shrewd. It will interest you to know that we are not neglecting the matter."

All three of them sat up a little straighter and exchanged glances. Clearly this was no mere matter of convoy duty. Robert Morris smiled slightly.

"Exactly, gentlemen!" he exclaimed, as if he were reading their minds. "The thing is already being attended to—as Mr. Boyle has suggested. Captain Wickes will sail shortly for European waters— and so may you. But first there are other ways in which you may be more useful, rather similar ways, perhaps. Have you heard—any of you—of Hortalez et Cie.?"

They looked at one another again and then shook their heads slowly.

"I did not really expect that you would." Morris smiled. "After all, it is not well known—we hope! The facts are these. Your plan is in effect, Mr. Boyle, you'll be glad to know. We are working not only through such agents as you suggest, but through other channels toward the same end—through special agents ashore, whose duty is to stir up hostile relations between the two countries; through special missions to those we hope to make our friends. Mr. Deane left not long ago. Arthur Lee is already abroad. And Dr. Franklin will follow soon as the special agent of the Marine Committee."

The three officers nodded; this was a little over their heads, unacquainted as they were with the details of it.

"But naturally," Morris went on, "there are other ways in which we hope to strike. France is traditionally hostile to Britain, and her greatest profit will come from trade in opposition to England's. The King cannot speak openly, but the Crown is not opposed to turning a penny there if it can. So—if M'sieu de Beaumarchais chooses to organize a trading company which he calls Hortalez et Cie., for instance, trading to the West Indies; and if he offers us arms for credit, and supplies and other things we need, can the Royal Arsenal well refuse to sell them to him? Should we complain?"

He gave an exaggerated Gallic shrug and spread his hands. The three officers grinned, and Robert Morris smiled with them.

"Of course not, gentlemen!" he cried. "Tell me! Do any of you know the Golden Rock?"

They looked at one another. Who had not heard of the tiny Dutch island, that infinitesimal dot in the blue wash of the Caribbean? St. Eustatius, scarcely high enough to stop the seasonal rain clouds that passed over it, was not even productive enough for its own support. But with the outbreak of hostilities, its canny Dutch proprietors had been profit-wise enough to declare it a free port, and as a result it had become one of the busiest exchanges of the Western seas. Half the world deposited merchandise in her warehouses and barracoons. The other half came to buy.

But both Joshua and Kenny had to admit they had never seen the place, though they had heard of it.

"I've been there," Robinson put in quietly.

Morris rubbed his hands together and smiled.

"Very good, then, Lieutenant," he said. "You're the very man! The *Andrea Doria* lies at the naval dockyards. You will assume command. Mr. Barney will second you, and Mr. Boyle will take post as sailing master. You will, of course, maintain strict secrecy as to your destination. At 'Statia you will put yourself in contact with the agent of Hortalez et Cie., and he will give you more detailed instructions as to your subsequent movements."

"Aye, aye, sir!" Robinson replied, as much from habit as anything.

"He will tell you what to load and when, and how to return" —Morris smiled—"but I'll add my small bit. Neither going nor coming will you engage ships of the enemy unless it is unavoidable. Nor will you take prizes unless you can do so without risk."

"Very well, sir," replied Robinson.

"Get along, then!" Morris grinned. "Good-by and good luck! I'll see you all again with further orders when you return."

3. The "Andrea Doria"

ST. EUSTATIUS loomed like a green-and-dust-gray cloud out of a sea of the deepest cobalt blue as they approached it in mid-November. In the hollows and folds of its flanks, along the shores and around the white sand-rimmed heads of the little coves and bays, it was lush and tropical; but the shoulders of the ridges and the flanks of its steep slopes wore the pale dustiness of acacia and catch-and-keep, through which the bare, dry yellow ground showed mangily in splotches, while the black rock fangs of the headlands jutted grimly out to where the blue sea curled white around their feet. The *Andrea Doria* poked her bows smartly into the little bay behind which the red and white and blue and pink roofs and walls of Orangetown spattered against the mountainside in pretty disorder. As she passed the little grim gray fort on the headland at the harbor mouth the *Doria's* candy-striped ensign, thirteen alternating red and white bars, with the British jack in the left-hand corner, jerked smartly to the dip, and the guns of the forward battery sent the echoes thundering up the steep slopes—one gun for each of the thirteen states. In reply the colors on the fort dipped, and the saluting battery burst out in booming flour-white puffs, eleven times in response—the first salute ever given by a foreign power to the brand-new United States of America.

Their anchors had scarcely settled in clear view in more than a dozen fathoms before a fat, bustling little Dutchman was scrambling up over their side.

"Mynheer Captain Robinson?" he asked as soon as he came upon the quarter-deck. "We have been expecting you. Mynheer Bingham, your agent in Martinico, has advised us that you will arrive. Jost van Borck my name is, and here am I agent for Hortalez et Cie. I am glad to greet you! Already one cargo we have received from France, and another we are expecting any day now. As soon as it comes we will have you loaded and quickly again on your way. In the meantime, Mynheer Captain, you—and also your officers, too—you are welcome! The hospitality of St. Eustatius is yours!"

He was as good as his word, and there is no doubt that Ike Robinson and Joshua enjoyed their stay on the island to the utmost, for Mynheer van Borck was a jolly and convivial host, and the little Dutch seaport turned itself inside out to entertain these handsome, weather-tanned young representatives of the brave new nation to the north—with whom they hoped to do much business. Kenny, too, would have enjoyed his stay, for Anika van Borck, the Mynheer's daughter, was bright and gay, with straw-blond hair and deep blue eyes and the fresh tint of roses in her cheeks. What was more, she made no secret of her preference for the gray-eyed Irishman. But Kenny's own thoughts and heart were miles away, to the northward. He had been a long time coming to it, but the truth was that the more he thought about it the more he was secretly convinced that he would have neither eyes nor heart again for any other woman but Joshua's dark-eyed, dark-haired sister, Barbary.

And that was curious too. The more he thought about it, the more he was forced to admit it. It was true they bickered and quarreled whenever they met. Indeed, the last time he had seen her she had been outspokenly critical of him and his motives. Yet the fact remained that when he took the deck in the small hours of the night, or when he slept in his hammock below, his thoughts and his dreams kept coming back to her. Her face was always rising before him, laughing, flashing, perhaps a little taunting. And when he was ashore with his fellow officers and these gay Dutch girls who tried so hard to amuse them, it was always of her that he thought.

Perhaps her very criticism, her very doubt of him, was in a way responsible. For he had pride, fierce and determined. He had set a program for himself, and he was bound he would show her. He could be as good as Sam Smith or what-was-his-name?—Wales. He could

make a place for himself in her world; a place he could offer her with
pride and assurance; a place she would not be ashamed to share.
When he stopped to calculate all that he had done so far; how he had
earned his own freedom and made a place for himself in this young
new service; when he added up the sum, yet owing, of his wages as
sailing master and his share of the prizes they had taken, it seemed to
him that he had already made a good stride in that direction. He was
grimly impatient to get back to her and, puppylike, to lay all this at
her feet—as if to say, "There, now! Am I after all such a poor dog as
you thought me?"

But Mynheer van Borck was rather less prompt than his promise.
It was the first week in December before the *Patrie* arrived with the
expected shipment of arms and supplies, and it was the middle of
the month before they were able to sail. As he watched the bar-
rels and cases swing aboard to be stored in the hold below, still with
the fleur de lys of the Royal Arsenal stamped upon them, Kenny
could understand why van Borck had been so insistent that they
wait. Certainly if he were in the Dutchman's shoes he would not care
to have that cargo stacked in his warehouse.

Naturally the British were not without their agents in the Dutch
port. The presence of a Yankee man-of-war in the harbor scarcely
passed unnoticed, nor did it appear to be much of a secret what they
were about. Neither was van Borck without his sources of information. On the eve of their sailing he took them all into conference in
his study.

"Gentlemen," he said. "The English are not fools yet. They know
what we are about. Just over there"—he gestured generally east by
north—"lies St. Kitts and their naval headquarters in the islands.
They will be prepared to intercept you if they can. Already the
Antelope patrols the Culebra Passage, by which you have come
down, and the other eastward passes they also watch! I advise, when
you go from here, that you sail to the north, as if you would go back
by the same way you have come. Then, when falls the darkness, bear
away to the west, under Puerto Rico passing, and at the Mona Passage turn again to the north. So maybe you will come to the Atlantic
where they do not look for you."

"Thanks t' ye, Jost!" Ike Robinson replied. "We'll take care and
keep an eye peeled, eh, lads?"

The Mona Passage opened bright and sparkling under their bows
as they nosed into it on the second day after leaving St. Eustatius. Its

bright blue surface was whipped to a lather of whitecaps by the steady breath of the trades, and the *Doria* heeled far over to larboard as she scuttled through. So far as they could see, as they slipped up into the channel there was nothing in sight but the passage itself and the broad belly of the Atlantic beyond. But as they stood past Mona Island the lookout at the masthead hailed:

"Sail ho!"

"Where away?" Ike Robinson turned anxious eyes aloft, and both Joshua and Kenny stiffened expectantly.

"West nor'west!" The lookout's singsong reply was prompt. "Looks like a small sloop-o'-war, sir! She's makin' this way with a bone in 'er teeth!"

"Very good!" Robinson's reply was punctilious. "Steady as she goes, Mr. Boyle!"

"Aye, aye, sir!" Kenny repeated the order to the helmsman.

"You'll not stand and fight?" Rules did not hamper Joshua.

"We have our orders, Mr. Barney!" Robinson did not even look at him. "If he presses we'll not run away, but our prime purpose is to fetch this cargo through. Come up in the ratlines with your glass. We'll have a look."

Kenny maintained his post as they swarmed up into the mizzen shrouds. It was his duty, at this point, to look to the navigation of the vessel, as it would be his task if they came to battle. One part of the officers and crew, under Joshua, saw to the fighting of the guns. The other, under Kenny's direction, managed and maneuvered her. The responsibility for the over-all results, for the fighting of the ship itself, of course, was Robinson's. But in the way the guns were handled and in the way she tacked and wore according to Kenny's command, the whole outcome would depend. He could not deny that he felt a little prickle of anticipation and excitement at what the next few hours might hold. They had seen action before, of course, all three of them, though never in this vessel. And such fighting as they had done had been more or less desultory, like seagoing guerrillas, during their spell of convoy duty at the mouth of the Delaware.

The sloop was in sight from the deck when Robinson and Joshua swarmed down from the rigging, and Kenny could see her plainly by then; a fast sloop, somewhat smaller than their own brig, and carrying ten guns to their sixteen. From the look of things there was no doubt in her commander's mind as to the course he would follow, for her gun ports were open and triced up and her guns run out, and she was running on a tack to intercept them. Kenny guessed her guns to be of the same weight as their own. Certainly they could be no heavier in so light a vessel. Thus they overmatched her both in size and weight of metal. But with her sleeker lines she probably held the advantage of maneuverability. Thus they were not so unevenly matched as might appear.

"She's one of the patrol," Joshua said excitedly. "There's no doubt she'll fight!"

"She'll have t' come t' us for't if she does!" Robinson replied.

"You don't mean to run from a smaller ship!" Joshua stared at him.

"I've told ye I have me orders, mister!" Robinson retorted, then grinned at the look of almost disgusted disappointment on Joshua's face. "But just th' same, ye'd better get below an' clear for action. Pipe th' men t' quarters! No drums, mind, an' keep th' gun ports closed till I pass ye th' word. No use in lettin' him see what we hold till we're ready to put our cards on th' board! Mr. Boyle, get your men aloft an' prepare t' break out our own colors when I give th' command!"

"Aye, aye, sir!" Both sprang to their appointed tasks, Kenny, at least, with that first vague twinge of nervous excitement that precedes any action. As he turned he could hear the subdued shrill of the bos'n's pipes and the soft pad of bare feet running on the decks as the men swarmed to their stations. As he returned to his post near the helm he saw that already the decks had been cleared of all movable gear such as a whirling ball might smash and toss in deadly dangerous flying splinters. Sand buckets were placed under the bulkheads against the need to cover slippery bloodstains, and below he could hear the groan and squeal of tackles as the guns were loaded and the rumble of the guns on deck as they were made ready to run out. Green-coated marines gathered at the ratlines in readiness to swarm aloft into the fighting tops. In that moment he thought a little grimly of Barbary. Maybe all his impatience had been for naught. Maybe after today it wouldn't matter if she saw him again or not. But he shook away that feeling with an almost impatient shrug. Such thoughts were not fit! And anyway, it was never yourself that the searching ball found out. It was always someone else; someone who never expected it.

Down below, on the gun deck, in the gloom of the battle lanterns, Joshua paced between the grim rows of waiting guns impatiently. His one anxiety at that moment was to get it started and over with

The stranger approached rapidly, altering course just a hair to converge with the *Doria's* steady northward drive. As she drew within range Kenny could see the glow of the gunners' matches in the gloom behind her gun ports. The gap closed, fast now, and then all at once the broad red British ensign burst at the other's masthead, and at the same time an almost arrogant voice hailed:

"What ship is that? Heave to or we'll fire!"

Robinson nodded to Kenny.

"Show him our colors, Mr. Boyle!" And as the striped flag burst upon the breeze he turned back and raised his voice. "This is the United States brig-of-war *Andrea Doria!* If ye want a fight, sir, ye may fire an' be damned!"

He whirled back again sharply to Kenny.

"Smartly now, Mr. Boyle! Fetch her off three points t' larboard! We'll pass astern of him and rake, if he's fool enough t' let us!"

But the Englishman was no such lubberly seaman. The brig's head swung, and as her sails caught the fuller drive of the wind she leaped forward like a horse that feels the touch of the spur. But even as she did so the other vessel spun on her heel. Her spars leaned and her sheets slatted to the new tack, and she bore down almost directly toward them so that the two vessels must pass beam and beam at point-blank range. Kenny grinned without humor. Whatever you might think of the Englishman, he had to admit, it was clear he would not run from a fight.

As the two ships came abreast he felt the deck beneath his feet jump and shudder to the crash of their full broadside. Joshua's timing, as nearly as he could see through the smoke, was perfect. In the same split second he heard the belching, bellowed cough of the enemy's guns. A six-foot splinter, jagged as a smashed two-by-four and as thick through as a man's arm, leaped from the quarter rail and whined eerily above their heads, to splash harmlessly into the sea on the larboard quarter. At the same time they could hear the angry whine of grape in the rigging above, and this time there was a certain grim amusement in Kenny's grin. The Englishman was overanxious. He must have fired at the top of his roll.

"Steady as she goes, Mr. Boyle!" Robinson said dryly.

"Aye, aye, sir!" The response was automatic, but Kenny glanced about and raised inquiring eyebrows at the lean lieutenant.

"Our orders still hold," Robinson explained. "If he still wants a fight, let him follow and force it!"

Kenny nodded. There was logic in that. Quite apart from their instructions, a vessel being followed in such a wind would have a better chance to snatch the weather gauge.

The Englishman wore wide up into the wind and sought to run down upon their weather quarter and use the mask of his own sail shutting off the wind to them, to hang them in irons at his mercy. But Robinson was too smart a sailor to be caught so. He spoke quietly to Kenny once again, and smartly the *Doria* came about, and once again the two vessels came broadside to.

This time, however, the Yankee backed her mainsail, and so they hung upon one another's flanks, blasting shot for shot, hammering blow for blow. All around him Kenny heard the air fill with the whining snarl of flying lead and whirling splinters. Below him he could hear the crash and splinter of wood on the gun deck as some of the enemy's shots took effect, and almost automatically he wondered if Joshua were yet unhurt.

But there was little time for such thoughts. The smoke swirled about them and went drifting off upon the wind. Somewhere a man cried out in bitter agony, and in the waist, before his eyes, a sailor seemed to come apart all at once; to explode abruptly in a spattering mass of blood and bone and entrails that went skittering off across the deck to leave a bloody trail into the scuppers, while only the head, apparently untouched, went rolling crazily, staring, wobbling this way and that, to come to rest finally against the wooden carriage of a gun. At the helm the steersman silently clapped a hand to his side and went down. Kenny took his place quickly, until the man's relief, appointed for such an emergency, came up. Lines parted overhead, and a sail split abruptly in the wind. A yard came crashing down, felling one of the waisters. Repairs claimed Kenny's attention, and he had no notion of how long it took to have them made. Then all at once, abruptly, silence fell with a clap that was almost as sudden as the firing of a gun. The smoke drifted off upon the wind, and a voice cried out:

"She's struck!"

"Cease fire!" Somewhere an answering voice spoke.

Slowly at first, and then more rapidly, the smoke eddied and thinned and then was snatched aside like a curtain that is jerked away to show what lies behind. It was natural that Kenny should look first at his own ship. There was some damage to the *Doria's* rigging, but actually not very much. Her white and carefully scrubbed decks were bloody and grimed, scarred and ripped, and in one place they bulged upward where one of the enemy's shots had found a gun port and passed through and battered underneath.

But when he looked toward the Englishman he felt that sudden mingling of astonishment and pity that always comes when the bitter, hammering damage that has been done to an opponent is suddenly revealed. The once trim sloop lay little more than a broken hulk, wallowing in the trough of the seas. Her mainmast was gone entirely, and her foremast wobbled insecurely as she rolled, held upright only by a single stay. Her decks were a cluttered tangle of torn rigging and bloody, ominously inert heaps of bundled rags and shredded flesh. Her halyards, what there was left of them, still trailed the broken, splintered ends of smashed yards, listlessly, in a hopeless, messy snarl, over the side; and aft, on the quarter-deck, where the helm had once stood, someone was gesturing feebly with a dirty white rag.

4. The Prize Master

THE PRIZE, as it proved, was H.M.S. sloop-of-war *Racehorse*, in the ordinary line of duty tender to H.M.S. *Antelope*, but for the moment detached under command of Lieutenant Jones of the *Boreas*, frigate, to keep watch over the Mona Passage for the *Doria*. Once again, apparently, British contempt for American fighting qualities proved their undoing, for by assigning a lighter vessel of inferior armament to the duty they had permitted the very thing they sought to prevent, and the Americans, in the bargain, had won a stanch ship.

No blame for that, however, could be attached to Lieutenant Jones. He had fought his ship well and courageously and was himself among the severely wounded when the smoke cleared. Indeed, he declared it was only when his foot had been mangled by a four-pound shot and he had been forced below into the hands of the surgeon that some craven coward had struck without authority. But for that, he swore, he would be fighting yet, and even Kenny, scarcely friendly to the British as he was, was grudgingly forced to admire the man's spirit.

The problem of repairs was not so serious as it looked, although it ate away the rest of the day. Joshua had developed rapidly into a smart gunnery officer, not confining himself as did so many of the more hidebound, opposing service to one school of thought or another. Rather he believed in adapting his tactics to conditions, and where the usual run of British officers either aimed first to fetch down the rigging or to silence an enemy's batteries and would not vary that procedure, it was Joshua's theory that where a vessel held the sailing advantage it was best to shoot for her rigging and disable her first, then concentrate on hammering her batteries into submission. Conversely, if an enemy were more heavily gunned but a sluggish sailer, then it was wiser to concentrate upon her batteries and hull from the very start.

Because he had followed this program in this case, and because the *Racehorse* was so much the faster and lighter ship than the *Doria,* the damage she had sustained had been largely superficial. Her masts had been shot to matchwood and her rigging hung in tatters, where it hung at all. But her hull was sound and it was but the work of a feverish afternoon for a specially picked crew from the *Doria* to step their own spare spars in her and to rerig and clothe her in a fresh suit of sails. While this went forward the *Doria's* surgeons worked shoulder to shoulder with those of the captured vessel. The wounded were transferred, and by nightfall Mr. Dunn, the second lieutenant, with a prize crew, was sent aboard and the two ships stood northward once again.

That night proved the captive's abilities as a sailer. Even damaged as she was, she was handier than the *Doria,* and indeed had she been in other hands she would have had no difficulty in showing the brig her heels. As it was, they kept pace with one another, and two days later, somewhat below Hatteras, they came up with the lumbering British snow *Thomas* from Jamaica, bound for London with logwood, fustic, and mahogany. At sight of the Yankee ships she fell clearly into a dithering panic and did not even try to run for it or fire one of the two ancient and rusted four-pounders that she carried. Long before they came up with her she was wallowing, hove to, in the trough of the gray-green seas, with a tablecloth that might once have been white fluttering at her peak in token of submission. Robinson was of a mind to let her go.

" 'Tis a waste of time to carry her in," he growled, "and I can't spare many for a prize crew."

But Joshua was of no mind to let anything slip through their fingers.

"See a penny, pick it up!" he misquoted. "Give me six good men and I'll fetch her home."

Robinson was reluctant, but Joshua begged. He would have taken Kenny with him, too, but on that point at least the elder lieutenant was positive.

"Since ye're bound to it," he growled, "ye can pick six o' th' foremast hands and take command o' her. But I can't spare Boyle. Keep close t' us if ye can. If that's impossible, try first for Philadelphia—after that for any port ye can make!"

"Aye, aye, sir!" Joshua's grin belied the formality of his words, and away he went to the command of his first ship since accepting his commission. Kenny watched him go with a little scowl and a sense of uneasiness. He cared little for this, but as sailing master it was not for him to tell captains and lieutenants what they could or could not do.

Joshua found a crew of a dozen or so aboard the snow—cripples, half-wits, offscourings of the London water front. They were a poor lot; only such as the press gangs of the British Navy had rejected, and they were notoriously not choosy. At least, he consoled himself with a wry grin, they were not apt to give him trouble, and at his call for volunteers to serve at regular pay and a share of the prize money, full half of them stepped forward. Evidently they were not particular whom they served. Joshua went to the rail and hailed.

"There's only a dozen aboard," he called, "and half of them have volunteered! We'll be in Philadelphia before you!"

That was almost the last they saw of him or of the *Thomas* either. Through the night they kept fairly close together, but even before dawn it was apparent that the snow was a sluggish sailer. When day broke it began to make up to weather, and it became more and more difficult to hold the men-of-war to the weary pace. Toward midday Robinson gave it up and waved. Joshua signaled his understanding of the gesture, and two hours later when Kenny glanced back the *Thomas* was hull down astern of them. At dusk, when he found time to look searchingly aft again, the wind was humming ominously in the rigging and the snow was nowhere to be seen.

Left alone upon the ocean, the *Thomas* wallowed northward. Judging from the set of the wind, it was going to blow a gale from the east, but Joshua did not worry especially. Although she was sluggish his prize seemed stout enough. Provided they were not intercepted, he felt no great concern for the future.

He did not calculate, however, that the weather would be as bad as it was. For several days the *Thomas* bumbled sedately along, until he judged they were well north of Hatteras. With each day the gale grew stronger, but yet there seemed no cause for alarm. Once he toyed with the thought of running into Chesapeake Bay and taking his prize to Baltimore. But then, he reflected, both Kenny and Ike Robinson would be sure that he had done it on purpose, in order to snatch a visit with his family! In a day or two the wind would shift and the weather would change, and then he would have no trouble at all in reaching the Delaware.

But the wind did not shift, and the weather did not change. Instead, the blast continued to rise to hurricane proportions, and the great gray-bearded seas thundered down upon them like watery mountains, with the greasy foam and wind-whipped spindrift snatched in steaming rags from their crests, lifting them up, threatening to engulf them, then hurling them down and down and down again, until Joshua began to wonder, each time they dropped, if they would ever be able to claw up once more out of the watery hole.

Just when he began to fight the weather he could never be exactly sure. But he never questioned his sudden shock of despair when, on the very day before Christmas, the lookout's sudden, panic-stricken hail warned of breakers under the lee.

He climbed into the rigging to see for himself, and when he turned and looked where the man pointed he could see the empty beach and the grim, gray dunes behind, and the cleft in the center where the narrow inlet came through. Between lay the welter of torn white water and foaming seas, where the tremendous waves broke across the intervening shoals. The inlet itself, he thought quickly, might be deep enough to float them through to safety in the shelter of the black pine-clad island. But in such seas no ship could ever live to cross those shoals and reach it.

They fought then, against the wind and sea, with redoubled fury, prisoners and prize crew alike, working together for their lives. And for a time it almost seemed as if they were holding their own. Then the wind rose stronger, and inch by inch they slipped backward toward the foaming shoals. When they struck the first time and grated over the bar with a hideous, tooth-shaking wrench and a shrieking groan of racked timbers, Joshua ordered both anchors let go and prayed that they might hold.

Perhaps the prayers did it. For a moment the heavy flukes dragged in the soft sand, and then, with a jerk that snapped their necks and racked the masts in their steps, they dug in, caught, and held. Joshua ordered the men into the rigging and made them lash themselves secure.

All night they hung in the ratlines, soaked to the skin, numb with the cold, and more than half frozen. Often they could not see the decks below for the water that washed over them. When the dawn came it brought Christmas Day but no relief. Once, about midday, a tiny sloop tried to beat out from the inlet to their rescue, and they watched with frost-numbed minds as, with no more than three or four men to handle it, the little vessel battled toward them through the tremendous breakers. At first the thing seemed impossible. And then they appeared to be winning the fight. The men in the snow's rigging offered a feeble cheer. But just as the sloop seemed about to reach them she struck and went all at once to matchwood. For a brief instant they could see the heads of those brave men who had struggled so far in the welter of the seas to help them, dark melon-like balls bouncing in the foam. And then they were gone—dead, drowned, swallowed up. After that they clung again, alone, to the rigging, giving themselves up to a lethargy of despair.

But once the sea had claimed its sacrifice, apparently its appetite was appeased. Joshua was the first to notice that the wind eased a little and shifted to the south. It required a desperate effort to arouse the men, but at last they realized what was happening and saw that the brief respite might not last for long. Under the lash of Joshua's tongue they clambered down through the driving rain to the deck and heaved painfully at the capstans. Under Joshua's goading they got up a rag of sail and picked their way among the shoals, until they came through into the deeper water of the inlet. That night they anchored in the tiny harbor of Chincoteague and slept safe and secure around the clock, Yankee and Englishman alike, never once hearing the wind that shifted again and rose and howled with the wail of shipwrecked souls through the pines of the sheltering island.

For six days they lay at Chincoteague, catching their breath and resting and waiting out the storm. Not until after the New Year and 1777 did the wind die and the weather slack off and the seas become safe again for them to venture forth. On that day Joshua had a difficult decision to make, for then prisoners became prisoners again, and the tiny prize crew became once more the masters.

The Englishmen did not like the thought, and they grumbled openly at being driven again below hatches. Even those who had agreed to help work the ship seemed recalcitrant. But Joshua did not hesitate. Nevertheless, he decided that there was no longer any question of trying to reach the Delaware. In such a situation there was nothing to do but run for the Chesapeake and endure the gibes of his comrades.

The year was not a week old when the snow picked her way out and turned southward toward Cape Charles. When the decision was taken the weather was cold and clear. But even before they were out of the inlet the skies were hazy again and wore a threatening look. Joshua drove the *Thomas* like a frightened heifer down the coast in a frantic effort to reach the bay before another storm could blow up. But it was the luck of the voyage that, just as they came abreast of the capes and brought their clumsy bows about for the run in, the sudden squall burst upon them.

It lashed at them with a sort of mad fury, in a blinding whirl of thick white snow and an obliterating fog that shut out every sight and every star and every landmark. They could not feel their way in through those treacherous waters in that. There was nothing left to do but turn to the eastward once more and claw offshore and ride it out.

When the dawn came up it was still snowing, and the fog was so thick that they could scarcely see twice the length of the ship. Neither Joshua nor anyone else had any inkling that there was another vessel in the heart of the squall. Only when she loomed up out of the fog and slipped past so close that they could all but reach out and touch her black sides and see plainly the yellow strake and count the gun ports were they aware of her. It was equally clear her people were as surprised as themselves. Obviously she was a British man-of-war.

Joshua hoped to take advantage of her surprise, and for once he was thankful for the storm and the covering fog. There was yet time, even if it were but a split instant. He whirled and rapped out his order.

"Up, lads! Look alive! Out courses and come about!"

The Yankees of the prize crew leaped to obey. But the *Thomas's* people stood where they were.

"Shake a leg, damn your eyes!" Joshua barked.

One of the men turned and cursed him sullenly.

"Th' hell with ye, ye stinkin' Yankee hound!"

Joshua's face mottled with fury. He reached inside his coat and jerked out one of the pistols he carried.

"Jump!" he ordered.

The man only spat. Joshua squeezed the trigger. The gun thumped and kicked in his fist, and the fellow spun and fell, end over teakettle, into the scuppers. The others scrambled for the rigging.

But it was too late. Even as they leaped the voice sounded through the fog, almost in their very ears:

"What the devil's that? Come over this way a hair! I say! There she is!"

As if the words were some sort of magic incantation, the bulk of the other ship, swinging back on the opposite tack for a look at them, began to take form. At first no more than a vague turbulence in the mist, her cordage and her masts and yellow spars first began to take shape. Then—Joshua remembered afterward his mild surprise at noticing it—came the billowing cloud of canvas, stark white against the gray rack of the fog. After that she came all in a rush; the same ominous sleek black hull, and the broad bright yellow stripe along her sheer. Through the mist the stripe was broken now with the open, yawning, coal-black caverns of the gun ports, through which frowned the ugly black snouts of a row of twelve-pounders. Ten of them he counted in that one battery alone, against the two rusted, salt-encrusted fours the *Thomas* carried. And behind the guns he could see the grim faces of the gunners as they blew upon their ready matches.

"What ship is that?" came the hail, curt now and sharp with authority. "I see you there, you Yankee dog! Spill your wind and hold your luff while we lay you aboard! Heave to, or we'll blow you out of the water!"

5. *The Navy Regrets*

THE *Doria* and the *Racehorse* also met the full fury of the storm. It was not quite Christmas when they reached the Delaware capes, and in the blow that followed they were forced to claw off and seek safety in deep waters offshore. Not until the beginning of February did they reach Philadelphia, and there they found no word of

Joshua or the *Thomas*. Kenny was worried, and the fact that Ike Robinson was also alarmed was attested by the fact that he delayed reporting in person to Robert Morris for almost two weeks.

In their absence Washington had made his famous dash across Jersey, and for a moment it seemed that Philadelphia must fall. Congress had fled to Baltimore, and the Marine Committee—which was Robert Morris—had gone with it; not so much that Morris agreed with the rabbit-like thinking of the Continental delegates, but obviously no business could be carried on if Congress and the committee were five days apart.

This fact alone gave them the excuse to delay their report, but the summons came at last, calling them to Baltimore, and they had no choice but to comply. They made the five-day journey over the deep-rutted, wintery roads; Robinson in evident apprehension as to what he would say to Robert Morris; Kenny far more concerned with his meeting with Barbary, for he knew the fierce devotion she bore her brother, and it seemed to him no good omen to his cause that he should be the bearer of such tidings. He felt desperately miserable to have to face her with such news.

Ironically, so it seemed to Kenny, Robert Morris had set up offices in the counting rooms of John Smith, on the water front, overlooking the bright bay and somewhat twisting harbor of the Maryland seaport. As they were ushered in he could not help contrasting the smoked oak, the narrow rooms, and the cobwebbed, leaded panes of the windows with the spacious, highly polished walnut and immaculately spotless quarters of Willing and Morris in Philadelphia. Even in his preoccupation it occurred to him that it spoke well for the zeal and concentration of the Philadelphian that he was able to carry on business in that place. Morris himself was pacing up and down, awaiting them, with his hands clasped behind his rather bulbous backside and a frown on his face, his teeth gritted grimly as he glanced now and again out through the dusty windows toward the harbor. He whirled as they entered.

"Well, gentlemen," he cried, "welcome! 'Tis about time I see you home again. I daresay you've news for me?"

"Aye, news, sir," Robinson retorted flatly. "I wrote ye my report from Philadelphia—that we'd fetched home th' cargo that ye sent us t' get, safe an' sound, and picked up th' sloop-o'-war *Racehorse* on th' way. But we've no word yet o' Mr. Barney an' th' *Thomas*. Perhaps ye've had some?"

The blocky gray man whirled on him, his jaw outthrust, his eyes blazing.

"I've had no word!" he snapped. "Though I've combed the coast for it. You know what the weather was at the time. What d'you think?"

"I—I don't know what to think, sir," Robinson replied. "I hope——"

"Aye! You hope—and so do we all!" Morris retorted. "But the fact remains, we can't build a nation on hope alone. We must fear the worst and accept it when it comes. I can't be with the commander of every vessel, to advise him or give him orders that take responsibility for his acts from his own shoulders. You, sir, have been guilty of an error in judgment. You have sacrificed a fine officer and six sorely needed men for the sake of a questionable prize. 'Tis only because of the way you brought the *Doria* through and fought with the *Racehorse* that I incline to leave you your command at all!"

"Sir"—Robinson reddened—"I'd not want to hold place under a cloud. If ye want my commission——"

"Tut, tush!" Morris gestured impatiently. "Put your pride in your pocket, Lieutenant. 'Tis just that I'd plans for the three of you——"

"Aren't ye a bit severe with Mr. Robinson, sir?" Kenny ventured. "'Twas Mr. Barney's own notion an' insistence that he take th' *Thomas*. I——"

"Who asked you?" Morris whirled upon Kenny. "I understand you're acquainted with the Barney family?"

"I'll be that, sir," Kenny retorted stiffly.

"Then you'll be the very man to go with Mr. Robinson and bear the Navy's regrets to them," Morris said grimly. "Perhaps you may soften the blow——"

"Have ye no hope then, sir?" Kenny cried.

"Have you yourself?" Morris retorted. "'Tis two months since he was last seen, and not a word of report since!"

"They could have been retaken!" Kenny thrust out his lower lip stubbornly.

"In that case we'd probably have heard," Morris retorted.

"But if they were carried to England——" Kenny began.

"'Tis not likely!" Morris interrupted him with a shrug and swung back to his desk and picked up a letter bearing the seal of the Marine Committee. "You might as well know, gentlemen, I had intended sending you all three into European waters in the *Lexington* as soon as you returned. In the circumstances, of course, I cannot send Mr.

Robinson on so important a mission. Mr. Barney must be presumed lost. Mr. Johnson will command. You, Mr. Robinson, will retain your post in the *Doria*. Mr. Dale will occupy the post that was to have been Mr. Barney's, and you alone, Mr. Boyle, will take post in the *Lexington* as sailing master, as planned. As soon as you and Mr. Robinson have delivered this letter conveying the Navy's regrets to Mrs. Barney, you will report aboard. Captain Johnson already has his orders and will sail in the morning!"

As they left the office with their unhappy tidings and turned in the direction of Federal Hill, Kenny had to admit that his feet dragged. To return as the simple bearer of the word of his own achievements was one thing. But to be one to bring such news as this was something else again. The tremendous Negress, Cassie, the same whom he had once taken for an Indian, opened the door to them.

"Why, Mist' Boyle!" she cried, beaming at the sight of them. "My, hit good t' see y'all! Hit look lak dat sea done do a pow'ful worl' a good fo' yo'. Come in. Come in, suh."

"Thank ye, Cassie," Kenny replied. "But I'm afraid we won't be as welcome here when we've been passin' on th' word we've come to fetch. Is Mistress Barney at home?"

"Mist'ess Barb'ry?" Cassie beamed.

"Mistress Mary," Kenny told her.

Cassie's face fell into severe lines.

"Oh, Mist' Kenny, don' tell me! Yassuh! They both in th' drawin' room yondeh."

Kenny jerked his head at Robinson and turned abruptly, without a word, and passed into the long familiar room. At sight of them Barbary bounded up, and it seemed to him that there was more than just a set smile of welcome on her lips.

"Kenny!" she cried. "And Lieutenant Robinson! How good to see you! Come in and warm yourselves by the fire."

Mary Barney rose more slowly, but her greeting was no less warm.

"How good to see you boys again!" She smiled. "We've lived so many anxious moments since you left. I suppose Joshua is on duty aboard and can't come up just yet?"

There it was—all at once: the moment he had dreaded. It had come as abruptly as that! It seemed to Kenny that had there been any place to run he would have taken to his heels. As it was, he could only stand where he was and see the hurt done.

"Will ye be forgivin' me, ma'am," he said, "but I've t' be tellin' ye, Joshua's not with th' ship. He took command o' a prize o' war two months back off Hatteras, an' there's been no word o' him since."

He looked at Robinson, hoping that he would pick up the grim report from that point. But the lean lieutenant looked utterly speechless and gray. Neither Barbary nor her mother spoke. Both looked stunned, as if they could not believe what they had heard. Kenny reached over and plucked the official envelope from Ike Robinson's inert fingers and passed it to the elder woman.

"'Tis meself that takes no pleasure in givin' it t' ye, ma'am," he said, "but there'll be th' Navy's report, an' we've our orders t' be passin' it on t' ye. 'Tis Mr. Morris's notion that he must be presumed lost, but if ye'll be allowin' me, 'tis far from me own idea. He could ha' been taken. He could ha' been cast away . . ."

His voice trailed off as Mary Barney, staring at him as if she did not see him, sank back into her chair and slowly broke the seals. There was dead silence while she read, and Kenny himself felt like a thing trodden underfoot. To judge from the look of him, Ike Robinson felt even more stricken. Barbary, thunderstruck at first, reddened and breathed heavily. Perversely, she seemed to be angry at them. Mary Barney said nothing until she had read the letter word for word, taking a world of time at it, as if she must weigh carefully each phrase and sentence. When she was done she let the sheet drop to the floor and covered her eyes with her hands. Then, with a little shake of her head, she stood up wearily.

"F-give me, gentlemen!" she whispered huskily. "I—I must go—go up—upstairs and—and think—please!"

She turned, almost falling as she did so, and Barbary leaped to assist her. The look the girl gave Robinson and Kenny was sharp, almost venomous, but they waited, listening to the hesitant steps on the stairs, and then heard the door of the upstairs bedroom close. Robinson jerked out his handkerchief and swabbed at his brow.

"Christ Jesus!" he gasped. "I didn't figure this'd be part o't!"

"Look!" Kenny turned toward him. "There's no blame t' yerself. He was me own good friend. Why don't ye be leavin' it t' me?"

"I don't like t' do that!" Robinson protested.

"Go along!" cried Kenny. "Is there a reason, now, why I should not be explainin' it as well as yerself?"

He said it with a conviction he did not feel, but Robinson was quick to snatch upon the excuse. On the deck of a fighting ship he might be cool courage itself, but in passing the news to the relatives of casualties his stomach gave way.

"Ye think ye can?"

"Whether or not," Kenny retorted, "there's no need th' both o' us takin' th' heft o't!"

He walked with Robinson to the door and let the lank lieutenant out.

"I'll be off t' Philadelphia," the commander of the *Doria* said. "Let me know how ye come out. I'll get word t' ye if there's any news o' him. A pleasant voyage t' ye on th' *Lexington!* Damme, I wish I were goin' with ye!"

The haste of his departure was enough to indicate how readily he accepted Kenny's suggestion. The latter turned back into the drawing room, to find Barbary come quietly down and waiting there before the fireplace for him.

"Well done, Mr. Boyle!" she said.

Her tone, rather than the words, told of her anger. He stared at her.

"What have I done but break bad news as best I could an' be offerin' me sympathy?" he demanded.

"Sympathy!" she snorted. "Was it from sympathy you broke an old woman's heart and sent her son—my brother, and the man who thought of you as his friend—to his death?"

"I?" he cried. "What had I t' be doin' with that——"

"You could have prevented him from going!" she stormed. "You could have volunteered yourself!"

"How could I stop him? 'Twas his own notion!" Kenny retorted. "As for volunteerin'——"

"That's easy enough to say!" she interrupted, "now that he's gone and you know that nothing will ever bring him back—ever—ever!"

She was close to tears, yet obviously unaccountably furious with him at the same time. His heart went out to her.

"Why would I be lyin' t' ye, Barbary?" he said more softly. "Yerself that's been in th' heart o' me ever since I went away? I tell ye, all th' time we were at 'Statia, an' all th' long way back, it's been in me heart t' be tellin' ye I love ye. Why d'ye disbelieve me? Why——"

"Oh!" His words seemed to make her angrier than ever, almost as if she were disillusioned in him. It was that personal. "Would you?

Would you make love to me at a time like this! Oh, get out, Kenny Boyle! Get out! Get out! Go away and make your greedy, great fortune with never a thought of whom you hurt or what rights you trample on! Don't you think I know why you took up this fight? You'd never have done it if you hadn't been convinced we'd whip the English! Do you think I don't know why you offer me your blarney? 'Tis because you think I'll help you on your way! Well, I'll not! You can go and find someone else to do that for you! Someone else with a brother you can sacrifice——"

She was close to hysterics, but in his own hurt he hardly realized that.

"I told ye——" he began.

"Get out! Get out!" she cried.

He turned away from her abruptly and gathered up his cocked hat and greatcoat.

"There's no sense prolongin' this at all!" he said bitterly. "I was foolish t' be hopin' so lofty. But I'll not be botherin' ye again. I've orders t' th' *Lexington,* an' she's sailin' in th' mornin'. In th' meantime, I'll be leavin' me heart on yer doorstep, ma'am. 'Tis a poor, worthless thing an' not t' be troubled with, for all its devotion t' ye. Ye can be kickin' it off into th' muck when ye're minded to!"

He bowed then once again, stiffly, punctiliously, angrily, and in the next moment the door thumped behind him and he was gone.

III

Prizes and Pitfalls

1. Parole

KENNY had scarcely been gone a week before Joshua came riding back to Baltimore. Barbary herself responded to his knock, and at sight of him her hand flew to her mouth and she cried out:

"You—oh, Joshua! You're alive and safe!"

"What else did you expect?" He grinned, and then sobered, seeing her expression. "Someone's brought you bad news of me?"

"Kenny! 'Twas Kenny," she replied. "He—he thought you lost, and so did Mr. Morris. He brought the Navy's letter, and—and I sent him away angry!"

"You shouldn't have done that," Joshua told her mildly.

"I know!" she admitted. "Oh, Joshua, what are we to do?"

"Tush, tush!" He grinned. "I'll tell him. I didn't know you were so fond of him."

"Nor does he," she retorted. "He tried to tell me he loved me, but I blamed him for your loss and turned him away. I—I—— He's gone in the *Lexington* to France, and I'm afraid you won't be seeing him."

"Damme, now!" he exclaimed. "That does make it more difficult. But come, child! We'll get word to him someway. Mr. Morris will know how 'tis to be done."

"Oh, Joshua, will you ask him?" she cried. "I feel such a little witch to have behaved the way I did. But come now! We must let Mother know you're home. She's been abed ever since she heard you were lost. There's nothing will do her so much good as to see you again."

She was right about that. Mary Barney had languished and aged since she received the Navy's letter. But if Joshua's return could not replace the gray hairs, the sight of him could and did fetch back the color to her cheeks and brighten her dark eyes.

"They kept us almost six weeks aboard the *Perseus*," Joshua told them, "while she patrolled between the capes and Hatteras. George Elphinstone commanded, and I swear to you I looked for him to be one of those stiff British Navy martinets when we were taken aboard at first. But he was a gentleman! He gave me a cabin to myself and the run of the ship, and d'you know what he said to th' dog I'd shot when th' fellow complained?"

"What?" asked Barbary breathlessly.

"I thought he'd clap me in irons at the least," Joshua told her. "But instead he turned on the fellow. 'You damned hound!' he said. 'You agreed with Captain Barney to work your ship for a share of the prize money, and then when you saw us you turned about and went back on it! 'Twas plain mutiny, I tell you! If I'd been in Captain Barney's shoes I'd have shot straighter than he! Get forward to sick bay, and let me hear no more of your sniveling! Captain Barney, sir! You're welcome aboard!' "

"She was taken, then, after that?" Barbary asked.

"God bless you, no!" Joshua grinned. "We cruised offshore until he had a handful of us. Then he sent us ashore under a flag of truce and our parole not to bear arms again against them till we are duly exchanged."

"Oh, Joshua!"

"I must report to Mr. Morris as soon as I can," Joshua said.

"What a shame!" Barbary cried. "Both he and Congress have gone back to Philadelphia. They were here for a while."

"Then I can't stop more than overnight," Joshua told them.

He pushed on the next morning, more than a little concerned, although he did not show it, over the harsh treatment Barbary had shown his friend. He had never said as much, but he had thought of it, and he would have welcomed Kenny as a brother-in-law.

In Philadelphia he found Robert Morris settled once again in the big, highly polished, walnut-paneled offices. At sight of him the blocky financier's eyes bulged. For an instant he looked as if he were seeing a ghost. Then he was up and around his great rosewood desk, with both hands outstretched and a smile of welcome on his lips.

"My boy! My boy!" he cried. "We'd given you up for lost! Indeed, I sent an official letter of condolence to your mother. What pain I must have caused her! I must write at once and offer her my apologies. But tell me, what's happened to you, and why have you been so long? We must set about finding a ship for you!"

"I'm sorry, sir." Joshua smiled. "I'm afraid I'm out of the running—at least until I'm exchanged. You see, I'm on parole."

"The devil!" cried Morris. "And just when we've need for officers with your qualifications! Tell me about it."

Again Joshua went over the story of the voyage and of the snow's recapture; of his own captivity and eventual parole.

"Damn my eyes!" Morris growled. "Who would have believed it? What d'you propose to do now?"

"Well—to begin with"—Joshua looked almost embarrassed—"if it's possible, I'd like to get word to Mr. Boyle."

"Of course!" Morris exclaimed. "There's nothing going direct right now, but there will be a ship for Martinico within the month, and there will be vessels from there. Bring it to me and I'll put it in an official packet for Dr. Franklin in Paris."

"Thank you, sir," Joshua replied. "Then, since I can't serve aboard ship, I daresay you've your hands full here. If I work for the Marine Committee ashore, surely I can't be violating my pledge!"

Robert Morris grinned appreciatively and rubbed his chin.

"That's so!" He chuckled. "My thanks to you for thinking of it. God knows we've work enough here for a dozen. Fetch me that letter, and then we'll see what we can find to keep you out of mischief."

2. Philadelphia

So JOSHUA began his part in the "Battle of the Schuylkill," and indeed Robert Morris had not exaggerated when he had said that there was enough work there for a dozen men. First, of course, Joshua wrote the promised letter to Kenny; a very special letter, in which he revealed not only his own survival but also Barbary's concern. This he delivered to Robert Morris and himself saw the square man, true to his promise, seal it in an official pouch and send it off in the *Sachem* to William Bingham at Martinico, with instructions for its forwarding.

After that he turned to in the outer office with a green-coated, leather-stocked, fish-eyed sergeant of marines for company, and was immediately amazed at the immense amount of paper work and shoreside detail there was to running a navy. There was a daily stream of congressmen and officials through the office, seeking some favor or other. There were orders to be written, ships' inventories to be checked, supplies to be ordered for this vessel or that—provided they could be found or obtained on credit, for the committee's budget was woefully scant. There were members of Congress to placate, who thought one protégé or another entitled to more than he had received, and there were worthy, hard-bitten seamen to see rightly placed—and avoid steping on anyone's toes. Sometimes it was not easy to judge just what category a man fell into. A particular thorn in his side was a Captain John Paul Jones, a short, sandy, sharp-featured little man bursting with energy, who evidently felt himself slighted at his placement on the seniority lists and came all the way from Boston to see justice done. To some extent at least Joshua placated him by giving him command of the *Ranger,* then building at Portsmouth, in New Hampshire, with orders to France when she was done. James Nicholson of Baltimore, with whom Joshua was already none too happily acquainted, was another. In some ways he seemed a sagacious, courageous gentleman. And yet, as Joshua was presently to find out, there were times when he was none of those—just as there were other moments when he could so far surpass them as to be almost superhuman. For all his crankiness and critical attitude; for all his crotchetiness, Joshua took a liking to Paul Jones. On the other hand, for all his suavity and gentlemanly behavior, he held distinct reservations toward Nicholson.

His work, of course, brought him more in contact with Robert Morris than years of serving in the Navy afloat could have done. He came to know the stocky, square-faced merchant as a human being rather than as the financier of the Revolution or as the chairman of the Marine Committee. When Morris issued a draft that called for payment by way of Rotterdam and Vienna and the Dutch East Indies—in those days of sailing ships and tedious communications—Joshua could understand and not be critical. Robert Morris was not above taking a profit for himself if it was there and to be had without cost to the nation. But at the same time, if the federal government needed cash he was prepared to use his own credit to secure it—even if he was not sure that he himself would have the funds to cover the draft when in a year, or two, or three it came back again.

That mutual interest, that will to see the blossoming of the new state first, and any personal considerations second, drew them together as it was bound to do. Naval committeeman and somewhat promising young officer was as much as they were to one another at first, but as the weeks passed and they came to know one another and their common purposes, they came to be better friends; more understanding companions.

"One good victory," Morris said one day, "and we'll have France in with us. 'Tis all they're waiting for!"

"Then let's pray for it," Joshua said grimly.

"Good for us—as a nation, no doubt." Morris smiled grimly. "But I wonder what it will do to our sea service. There's a clique in Congress, you know, that holds that if the French come in we may leave the naval war to them. They've a fleet ready and anxious for a fight."

"Are they fools?" Joshua cried. "You know the British have always held the upper hand there! Granted their ships are fast and smartly armed, but their command is not such as to take the lead. If we were combined, though——"

Morris shrugged.

"I'm only passing on what some say." He grinned. "If Congress hearkens to the argument there'll be little enough you or I can say."

"Oh, damn Congress!" Joshua cried in exasperation.

"You sound like one of George III's ministers." Morris chuckled. "But I know what you mean. At the same time we have to take the sour with the sweet and make the best of it. See here! 'Tis time you began to meet a few people here your own age. I'm going to take you under my wing and see to it. Come out to the house to sup tonight and a bit of a frolic afterwards eh?"

"Why, sir, I take that kindly of you, but I don't want to put you out," Joshua said.

"Nonsense!" Morris snorted. " 'Twill do no such thing. Mrs. Morris is expecting a raft of company, and one more or less will make no difference to her. Tom Willing will be there, and so will his daughter Sally. She's a nice girl, four or five years older than yourself, I daresay, and married to Bill Bingham, our envoy at Martinico. But you'll like her and she'll like you, and that's more to the point! She knows everyone in Philadelphia, and holds the reins for the younger crowd. If she pronounces you fit for company, you'll have more to occupy you than you'll have time for."

"Just as you say, sir," Joshua assented, trying hard to hide his reluctance. He was not at all sure that he would care for such a gorgon as Mr. Morris made this Sally Bingham sound. As for Tom Willing, he already knew him, for the man was Robert Morris's partner in business, and Joshua guessed that they were associated not so much for Willing's business acumen but rather because he was a man Morris could control; a nice enough fellow, but not, as far as Joshua could see, one of great wit.

Perhaps that was one reason why he found the evening so unexpectedly pleasant. Robert Morris's home was gracious, comfortably, even luxuriously appointed, and was run with an ease and elegance that bespoke taste without ostentation. The food and drink were just as one would expect to find in such surroundings—the finest—and the company was gay, scintillating. Mrs. Morris greeted him amiably and with utmost charm, and he did not fail to note that for all she must be approaching middle age she had lost none of her grace and beauty. Tom Willing blossomed, and proved, once away from the office and shut of business worries, to have a rare dry humor and a booming laugh to go with it. As for his daughter, Sally Bingham, she was lively and vivacious, brightly laughing, and though he sensed the force in her that drove her to be the social arbiter that Morris had described, still it was not an obtrusive or unpleasant quality. He liked her at once, and the simple fact that her "Uncle Bob" sponsored him was enough for her. She gave him her hand cordially.

"Welcome, Mr. Barney!" She smiled. "Uncle Bob tells me that you are working temporarily with the Marine Committee until your exchange and release from parole can be arranged."

"I'm afraid it's true, ma'am." Joshua grinned.

"But you'd rather be at sea, eh?" she asked.

"Even though it would mean that I should have to forgo such pleasures as this—I'm afraid I would," he told her.

"There now, Mr. Barney!" She laughed. "Don't apologize. 'Tis a proper way to feel in times like these, and I'm proud to hear you say it."

She turned to Robert Morris.

"Oh, Uncle Bob," she cried, "I was to tell you, the Bedfords can't get over until later. Gunning's been detained——"

"But they are coming?" Morris seemed concerned.

"Oh yes, surely," Sally told him. "Why?"

Morris glanced at Joshua and rubbed his chin.

"I just thought it might be a good idea."

Sally Bingham also flashed the young Baltimorean an almost surprised look.

"Perhaps you're right," she said in a tone that wondered audibly that she had not thought of it herself.

"Would you mind telling me what this is all about?" Joshua laughed.

"You'll find out," Sally Bingham teased him. "And you'll be glad, too, it was left for a surprise!"

In that, however, she was not quite accurate. They dined cheerfully and well, and afterward the gentlemen sat over brandy and cigars until it was time to join the ladies in the drawing room. There the older folk played at loo, while the half dozen young people joined Sally at the piano. Joshua felt a little awkward at this point, for the other young men there—Clement Graham, the lean Luke Matthewman, and Will Brookes—were in uniform; Graham in that of Colonel Lee's Light Horse, Matthewman in the Navy's blue and red, and Brookes in the garb of the Pennsylvania Line. No doubt Joshua, too, was entitled to wear one if he had wished, but being employed with the Marine Committee in a capacity that might, perhaps, admit of some doubt, he felt it best to assume as full a civilian status as possible for the duration of his parole and had laid aside his uniform. Thus he alone of the younger men wore a sober civilian coat of blue serge with pewter buttons and buff smallclothes. In that dress he felt not merely conspicuous but actually somewhat uncomfortable; almost as if he anticipated some misunderstanding.

Nor was his feeling groundless. Mr. Morris had been careful to explain his status to all those present, but obviously he could not do so to those who had not yet arrived. They had not been a quarter of an hour in the drawing room when the front doorbell tinkled and they could hear the steps of the butler crossing the hall outside in response.

"That will be the Bedfords!" Sally Bingham cried.

The outer door opened, and the hall filled with voices. Robert and Mrs. Morris moved to meet their new guests, and before they reached the door the three most recent arrivals appeared.

Mrs. Bedford came first, a stocky, rather stout little gray-haired woman, ruddy-cheeked and bright-eyed, with a quirk of laughter about her mouth. Bringing up the rear came Gunning Bedford, tall, lean, well set up, with a worried look and a serious frown, as if he carried the weight of the world upon his shoulders. His mouth was thin and straight, and his eyes were blue and steady.

But it was the girl between them that caught Joshua's whole attention and caused him to forget the room, the other people in it—

everything, indeed, except her. She was small, not so short as her mother, to be sure, but yet not much more than an inch or two taller. Her hair was tawny, golden yellow, like the leaves of birches in the fall, and her eyes had the same deep blue as the seas off 'Statia. Her cheeks were the color of ripe peaches, and her teeth were the cream to match. Red lips, dark eyebrows, a fine straight nose, and a figure that even under her dress was enough to catch the breath in his throat completed the picture. But these were only the physical attributes. Alone they would have been striking, but hardly arresting as they were. There was a smile in her eyes and a flashing quickness to them that bespoke intelligence. The curve of her lips denoted humor and an ability to laugh at herself as well as with others. And there was life, an almost electric vivacity, about her compact figure that was witness to passion and joy and an honest sharing of all that life held when the right man dropped his heart before her. At the same time it was clear that she did not take herself so seriously as did her parents.

"Hello, everyone!" she cried. "Uncle Bob! Aunt Mary! Sally! Goodness, I never thought I'd get Mamma and Papa started——"

"Hello, Bob," Gunning Bedford said glumly to Robert Morris. "Had an alderman's meeting. Damned fools! God, I thought we'd never get gone."

"Well, you finally got here, anyway!" Morris beamed. "I think you've all met everyone here except young Mr. Barney from Baltimore. Joshua, Mr. and Mrs. Bedford and their daughter, Ann Bedford—may I?"

Joshua jumped guiltily and tore his eyes from the girl.

"Eh—forgive me! Of course!" He bowed punctiliously to Mrs. Bedford and offered his hand to Gunning, who shook it perfunctorily, then bowed again to the girl. " 'Tis a greater pleasure than I can say. I hope you'll forgive me my rudeness for staring. 'Tis not often a man meets such striking beauty."

He meant it for a compliment, of course. But there was no answering spark in her eyes. Instead they were cool, even critical.

"Indeed, Mr. Barney?" she said. "Nor is it often, these days, that one finds an obviously able young man in civilian dress!"

Joshua gulped.

"You're outspoken, ma'am, at least!"

He glanced at Robert Morris, half hoping that the financier would explain matters. But the older man seemed to be enjoying the byplay, and certainly Joshua did not intend to offer a word in his own defense.

After that the evening seemed to him not nearly so warm nor so cheerful. He and Ann Bedford hardly exchanged two words further, though they kept eying one another; and, though it may have been his own imagination, it seemed to him that there was a certain constraint among the others after that. He stayed as long as it was decently polite and took his leave as soon as it was possible, walking home to his quarters, telling himself with every step of the way that it did not matter to him what she thought or if he ever saw her again—although he knew in his heart that he would never have been so vehement with himself if that were true.

Back at Morris's, the naval committeeman strolled over to the piano to stand beside Ann Bedford and rest his elbows on the smooth top of the instrument beside her.

"Don't you think you were a little hard on Mr. Barney?" he asked her slyly.

"Do you think so?" She almost glared at him. "Why isn't he fighting the way Luke, there, or Clem are? Why should he be allowed to fatten as a civilian when these others are giving everything they have? What did you expect me to do—kiss him?"

"As a matter of fact"—Robert Morris grinned; Sally Bingham stopped playing slowly, and everyone turned to listen—"I rather thought you might. He doesn't wear the coat for it—though he's the right to, since he's one of the best young naval officers we have. But right now he's waiting out parole, hoping to be exchanged, since he was captured, and working voluntarily with the Marine Committee!"

There was an instant's silence, while she stared at him. Then she stamped her foot and thumped her fist on the piano top.

"Uncle Bob!" she cried furiously. "Oh, you dog! Oh, how could you? You did that deliberately, and now what will he think? Oh, I hate you! I hate you!"

But Robert Morris only threw back his head and laughed.

3. The "Lexington"

ON THE last day of April 1777, when the Yankee sloop-of-war *Sachem* dropped anchor in the harbor of Martinico, the *Lexington,* with Kenny aboard, had lain almost a month in the harbor of

Bordeaux, while Captain Johnson went up to Paris to deliver his dispatches and to consult with the commissioners. They had made a swift voyage over, taking two prizes in the way, and once Kenny would have been delighted at the captures, seeing nearly a doubling of the small fortune he had gathered. But now he scarcely cared.

So far as his shipmates were concerned he had no complaint. Henry Johnson, their captain, was a gaunt New Englander, twangy with down-East talk, who would have dared the devil himself to fight had the pitchforked gentleman put in his appearance. Rumor had it that, as a prisoner at the Nore, Johnson had boldly and openly walked off the prison hulk and calmly booked his own passage back to Canada, whence he had made his way again to Boston and the command of the *Lexington*. Elijah Bowen, their first lieutenant, was a Connecticut Yankee, sour-dour, as only his kind could be. But Dick Dale, a Norfolk lad and their second, was especially likable, and even despite his own gloom, Kenny felt a quick attachment to him. Jeremiah Holden, master's mate, was a gaunt Philadelphian, while James Connolly, their lieutenant of marines, was as Irish as himself.

The rest of the crew seemed average. Grumblers by the nature of their trade. But that was an occupational complaint. Some were good seamen and some were bad, but on the whole they were neither better nor worse than was to be expected.

For all his gloom, while they lay at Bordeaux, Kenny could not help being curious about the French and their own reception there. A cloud of suspicion seemed to hover over the brig, and forever there were two or three obviously official observers on the *quai*, covertly studying them, all the while pretending diligently to be looking elsewhere. Naturally, neither Kenny nor Dick Dale, nor most of the others, were altogether aware of the difficulties that beset the American commissioners at Paris, or of the suspicion with which the port authorities looked upon themselves. Half of those officials were of a mind to offer them secret aid; while at the same time the other half recoiled in Gallic horror of a possible breach of French neutrality. So long as they lay quietly, offering no offense, either to the French or to the watchful bulldogs across the Narrow Seas, they were left strictly alone, and they only learned of the complications that their presence aroused when Captain Johnson came hotfooting back from Paris with word that they were to join Wickes and the *Reprisal* at Nantes and to make ready for a cruise in English waters. Johnson called the officers together in the tiny cabin.

"Now hark ye, lads!" he told them confidentially. "All this is secret as secret can be, and I warn ye to keep it so! Th' Froggies are as nervous as an old maid in a twenty-room house alone seein' a man under every bed, an' th' British have their agents in every port from Vigo t' th' Texel mouth, as thick as vermin in a Fundyman's galley! Th' French're as excited for their neutrality as a virgin for her virtue, an' th' British're as ready as a cuckold t' yell bloody murder at anythin' at all that looks as if we were bein' encouraged—which is just what we want! Ever' prize we send in an' ever' capture we catch, th' British'll get stiffer an' more big-mouth over! An' th' Frenchmen'll get more mad an' more tempery!

"Now I want ye to know we'll prob'ly not be too welcome in French ports. Maybe they'll seize our prizes an' maybe they'll throw us out of their harbors. Might be they'll even throw us into their jails. But 'tis a good thing we're aimin' for. I want ye to see it plain before we start!"

"Have at it!" growled Kenny. "Let's be done with th' jaw!"

Captain Johnson grinned at him and laid down their plans.

That night under cover of dark Kenny conned the little black-and-yellow brig out of the Gironde, and for a time the British had no notion of where she had gone, until suddenly she reappeared in Nantes and dropped her anchor within hail of the *Reprisal*.

Of the weeks of work and sweat and heartbreak that went into the preparations for that cruise, little more need be said. Neither officers nor men could prevent or foresee everything. Reports from their spies leaped back to Britain that an American squadron was fitting out at a French port. And indeed, if the British spies had not seen to it, certainly American agents would!

The ships of the British Channel Fleet came down and cruised incontinently off the friendly coasts, sailing into French waters with a fine disregard for that same neutrality in whose name they raised such a clamor. The British Ambassador protested, and polite French officials made show of calling upon the Americans to leave their ports and stop embarrassing them, while secretly they offered what help they could. Confusing the issue still further, the wind came on to blow from west northwest and held the ships wind-bound in the Loire.

The activity of preparation—the infinity of detail, the back-breaking labor of it—was good for Kenny. It turned his Irish humor from brooding upon his own hurt. And the cruise that followed offered quite enough to swing him still further from his own troubles.

They got to sea toward the end of May, when the wind shifted suddenly around to the northeast, and the squadron seized opportunity by the whiskers and slipped out of the Loire, past the British blockade.

Action began in the Bay of Biscay, when the *Lexington,* 16 four- and six-pounders, fell in unexpectedly with the line-of-battle ship *Foudroyant,* 80, eighteens, twenty-fours, and forty-twos, and drew a few shots from her. But the odds were too great there for more than a flirt of her lead-colored stern, and the brig showed her heels to the lumbering battleship and escaped without damage.

For a time the wind drove them down toward Finisterre and the coast of Spain; then, clear of the Breton Heads, they swung on a long reach northwestward, round about, to come in again at the north of Ireland and down through the North Channel into the Irish Sea.

They had their heyday there. The enemy's cruisers were all in the south, scouring the Bay of Biscay for them, never dreaming of an attack from that quarter. In a cruise that actually lasted no more than a month, it took the Yankees three weeks to reach their hunting grounds. Then, in the week that remained, within plain sight of the shores of England and Ireland most of the time, they took a total of eighteen prizes, nearly as fast as they could board the ships and provide for their disposal. True, most of them were grimy colliers or insignificant coasters not worth keeping. Still, they boarded all and got rid of them one way or another, for, as Wickes said, the moral effect of their mere presence would be the greater if they demonstrated that British seas were no longer safe even for little men. Eight of the vessels they found worth sending in to French ports in charge of prize crews. Seven they sank. Two smugglers they released, and one vessel they sent in to Whitehaven with the prisoners they had removed from the others. When they had done so much, short of provisions and undermanned by the heavy drains caused by the need for prize crews upon the ships they had sent in, they slipped through the South Channel and cut southeastward once more and dashed for France.

In the early dawn of the twenty-sixth of June they caught sight of a great ship bearing up from the southwestward toward England.

Flushed with the success of their voyage and full of bright dreams of a fat Indiaman to cap the cruise, all three of the little men-of-war swung toward her belligerently.

Whose sharp eyes aboard the *Dolphin*, or whose aboard the *Reprisal*, first recognized her deception is a mystery still. But it is true that the realization came simultaneously to each one of them. Aboard the *Lexington* it was Kenny who sang out:

"Hold hard! Yon's no Indiaman, by God! That's a ship-o'-th'-line!"

The reaction was the same aboard all of them. All three turned on the fantails at the same time and fled eastward toward France like scared rabbits. The great ship suddenly ceased her deceptive waddling and cracked out a billowing mountain of sail, flung open her gun ports, and opened fire with the long eighteens she carried as bow chasers, flinging up mountainous geysers of sea water close aboard.

For an hour they fled before her, and only long after did they learn that she was the *Burford*, 74, Captain Bowyer, who had hoped by trickiness to lure them within range of his main batteries so that he could sink or capture all of the damned Yankee pirates. The *Burford* proved a swift sailer for a ship of her size, and inch by inch over the course of that hour she seemed to gain upon them. By mid-morning her long eighteens were throwing the spray on deck and causing the *Dolphin* to stagger heavily in the wash of the great shells, though her gunners seemed unable to hit them. It was useless for the Americans to attempt to return the fire, for the heaviest gun they carried was a six-pounder, and that would not reach half-way to her, nor would it have done her any damage if it did. Obviously it was only a matter of time before the lumbering battleship's gunners would find the range and lay a shot aboard one or another of them. Lambert Wickes did the only thing he could under the circumstances. Signal flags burst in a bright string at the *Reprisal's* halyards, and Kenny read the message to Johnson:

"*Lexington* bear southeast and make for whatever French port you can. *Dolphin* take northeast reach on like mission. Separate!"

It was not, of course, all spelled out in the flags, but Kenny filled the gaps, and Johnson flung one look at the towering 74 on their heels and spoke dryly:

"No use all o' us fallin' under her guns! Take her off, Mr. Boyle.

Acknowledge an' put her on th' new course: sou'east by south a quarter south."

The *Lexington* came about, and the three vessels scattered like a covey of quail. As Wickes had surmised she would, the *Burford* bore on after his own frigate, the largest of them all. The *Lexington* bucked and twisted, lost sight of them to northward, and finally slipped into Morlaix. Only when they'd had a chance to catch their breath after the flight did they learn that the *Reprisal* had given her pursuer the slip only by throwing over her guns and sawing away her bulwarks, cutting through her timbers to give freeage to her slip through the water. They thought afterward it was that which ate out her heart and destroyed her seaworthiness and sent her to the bottom off Newfoundland on her return voyage with Lambert Wickes and all hands. But for the moment, at least, she found refuge at St. Malo.

While all this was about, Joshua's letter lay at Martinico for weeks, awaiting transshipment. Robert Morris's instructions had been plain, but if there was no ship William Bingham could not invent one. It was almost a month before the ship *La Gloire* dropped anchor in the roads, and it was nearly another six weeks before she sailed again for home. When at last she did depart, carrying Joshua's letter in the thin leathern pouch, she made a bumbling way of it eastward, stopping first at Guadeloupe and then at the Azores, and then for some inexplicable reason running down to the Canaries and finally slipping back up through the Strait of Gibraltar to look in at Alicante before coming to port at Marseilles. There the pouch was sent off with reasonable dispatch by post rider to Paris. Unfortunately, however, Dr. Franklin was away at the moment, engaged upon official business in connection with those very ships, and the letter lay several days upon his desk, awaiting his return, before it came to his attention.

In the meantime all England and three fourths of France were laid by the ears by the incredible daring of the Yankee raiders. The British cried like a child with a broken doll, screamed "Pirates!" hysterically, and shot insurance rates on ships in home waters up to unbelievable new highs. Some of the prizes, thinly disguised, were seized by the French Government and returned to the British. But two or three found buyers and added to the uproar of accusation and recrimination. Demands were made at Paris for the officers and crews of the squadron to be slapped into jail, but the French, ever courteous—and never ones to ignore an opportunity to torment the English—saw to it that Dr. Franklin had plenty of time to appeal to the Ministry of Marine.

But now the English were clamoring for the departure of the American warships from French ports, and nothing that Franklin could do, for all his popularity and his clever sense of politics, could seem to change that.

"In God's name," cried both Wickes and Johnson, in effect, "give us a chance to make repairs and take on stores and ammunition!"

But the French Ministry of Marine was adamant. The Comte de Vergennes, perhaps the least enthusiastic of Dr. Franklin's admirers, was growing impatient with all this shilly-shallying. He complained that here it was September and the ships had lain in port almost since the end of June. It did no good to explain that they were all but impounded, their *quais* guarded day and night, their officers and crews not allowed to set foot ashore, nor supplies or materials to pass out to them. Enough, cried the British. What kind of neutral faith was this? And Vergennes, in the interests of peace, gave them a week in which to leave French waters or face arrest and imprisonment, even possible hanging, for piracy. Dr. Franklin, allowing them as much time as possible to prepare, wrote to both Wickes, at St. Malo, and Johnson, at Morlaix.

> Warrants are being prepared for your arrest, and for the seizure of your vessels, should you fail to leave port within the fortnight. I have been able to arrange for you to take on stores of food and similar necessaries for your subsistence, but any other concession is impossible. You will, therefore, sail immediately you have taken on such supplies, and make for the nearest friendly port, where it is to be hoped that you will be allowed to rearm and refit.

These orders he sealed and sent by his own trusted dispatch rider, and it was only two days later, when, after a fruitless effort to intercede with the King at Fontainebleau, he returned to his study at the Hotel Valentinois at Passy and came across the thin pouch bearing Joshua's letter to Kenny.

He glanced up sharply at young Mr. Williams, his nephew, who was serving as his secretary at the time.

"What date is this?" he demanded.

"Why—the fifteenth," the young man replied.

"Mmmm—there may yet be time," Franklin mused, and summoned another rider and sent the letter on its way.

At Morlaix, Henry Johnson had Dr. Franklin's first dispatch already in his hands, together with another from Lambert Wickes.

"I sail within the hour," was all the latter said.

Captain Johnson flung up his hands.

"Great God!" he cried. "I've only twenty-five rounds of shot in the lockers—not two broadsides altogether!"

"Them's orders—ye can't ignore 'em," said Bowen lugubriously.

"Nope, I can't!" Johnson flung back at him. "But I c'n take in stores an' have one last try."

"Maybe we can get some in Spain," Kenny suggested.

"'Tain't likely!" Johnson retorted.

He went ashore then, showing the special permit that allowed him to do so, but though meat and wine were available, all the stores of powder and shot apparently were closed against him. He gave up after the second day, for time was growing short, and sailed with the tide on the morning of the seventeenth of September.

The *Lexington's* sails were still visible against the blue of the horizon when a messenger on a lathered nag came thundering onto the *quai,* waving a leathern envelope over his head.

"What is it that you have there, *mon vieux?*" the watchman of the docks demanded.

"A message—a letter for the sailing master of the Yankee brig *Lexington,* from the Good Man Richard himself!"

The watchman shrugged and waved his hand seaward.

"She has sailed, *alors?*" cried the messenger.

"*Elle a pris la mer.*" The watchman nodded.

"What then of the letter?" demanded the rider excitedly. "What is it that I shall do with that?"

The watchman shrugged again.

"Take it back to your good Dr. Franklin, I daresay."

Aboard the *Lexington,* Kenny leaned upon the after rail and watched the blue shores of France grow dim. In a way he was disappointed at being thus forced to fly, for he was well aware of the damage they had done; and from the furor the cruise had stirred up, he judged that they had come close to their objective—the involvement of France in the struggle. If they could make only one more such foray, he felt sure, the fat would be in the fire. Still, it was possible to overplay the game and force French sympathies into the

English camp. Perhaps it was as well this way. Matters now might be left to more subtle agents.

But there was another reason, a far more personal one, for his mixed emotions. With French ports closed against them, it was unlikely they would find a welcome in Spain. That could only mean one thing—home—and home meant Barbary. He had a moment to think now, and he knew that nothing—nothing she might say or do— could ever alter his feeling toward her. True, it was she who had turned him away. But she had been mistaken in her belief that he was in any way responsible for Joshua's loss, just as he had been wrong in making no effort to convince her of that mistake. He supposed it was his own grief that had made him give way to her so weakly. But that was past now. He would go back to her and convince her that she had been wrong and that he really did love her; that he had loved Joshua—and he would not take "no" for an answer this time!

So he thought it all out, at any rate. Dick Dale, coming on deck in the dusk and finding him still leaning there moodily against the rail, half guessed his thoughts and taunted him for them.

But that was on the day they sailed. The *Lexington* was two days out from Morlaix when she fell in with the British cutter *Alert*, 10, Lieutenant Bazely commanding, in the early dawn.

"Igod!" Henry Johnson gave his orders to Kenny. "I never thought I'd see the day when I'd run from a pup, but Lord knows we ain't got means t' fight! Let 'er go full afore th' wind, Mr. Boyle. Maybe he won't have th' guts t' follow."

But he was wrong in that. Lieutenant Bazely had the dogged courage of his kind. With a sad eye Henry Johnson watched the swift cutter overhaul the brig.

"Call th' men t' quarters, Mr. Bowen," he grumbled, "an' clear for action. No broadsides now, mind! One gun at a time, an' use that careful. Shoot for his riggin'. If we can fetch down his top hamper, maybe we can slip clear. Steady as she goes, Mr. Boyle! We'll make a runnin' fight o't if we can."

"Aye, aye, sir!" Kenny spoke softly to the helmsman while the drums rattled on the quarter-deck.

He would not soon forget the hours that followed. Even if Lieutenant Bazely had not had his own personal streak of British stubbornness and grit, he must have realized that something was wrong aboard the *Lexington*. When a sixteen-gun brig flies from a ten-gun cutter, either the captain of the larger vessel is a craven coward or he is beset by more practical troubles. He might be short-handed, with crew depleted by the manning of prizes taken or by one or another of the terrible scourges that not infrequently broke out aboard those old wooden sailing ships at sea. He might be short of ammunition. He might have mutiny on his hands. Whatever the cause, it spelled opportunity for a smaller vessel. Bazely drove in pursuit.

Within an hour he was able to open fire with his bow chasers. The Yankee did not return the fire, but held on her course. In two hours the *Alert* struggled abreast of them, and Kenny watched her approach with grim apprehension, remembering his own thoughts by the rail two nights before. It would be grimly ironical if, having reached his decision, he were unable to put it into effect.

By six bells of the morning watch she was in a position to give them a broadside. Nevertheless, grim, glum Elijah Bowen got in the first shot. With that single gun he put a ball into the *Alert's* waist that must have raised havoc in her mid-section and could only have missed the mast by a hair. But even before Kenny could grin, the Englishman answered with his full starboard battery. Huge splinters whined from the *Lexington's* bulwarks, while one of the quarter-deck guns leaped abruptly like a maddened horse gored by a bull and caromed upon its side, mashing two of her crew as if they were no more than flies. The ball that wrecked her carriage whined off at a tangent and laid one of their Frenchmen on the deck with his chest caved in and his side gaping and spilling blood in a bright cascade across the deck planks.

"Steady as she goes, Mr. Boyle," Captain Johnson said quietly, and Kenny realized abruptly that the master's mate, Jeremiah Holden, was down with a jagged ten-foot splinter through the groin.

After that the battle settled down to a grim cannonade. The *Alert's* guns were well handled, though the vessel, fortunately, was light for the seas. Often as not her screaming broadsides flew wide. Nevertheless, time and again her shot found its way aboard, ripping the planking, tearing huge splinters from the rail and spars, smearing the white decks with the blood of the wounded, whose screams of agony rang in their ears. Yet almost as often as the *Alert's* battery thundered, now this gun, now that, aboard the *Lexington* replied. And the American's guns were carefully served. Not a rope or a stitch of canvas aboard the brig parted. But in the cutter the lines twanged with a sound audible to those on the fleeing vessel, while rents appeared in her sails, and about midmorning her jib carried away and her one mast wavered dangerously. Seeing it, Captain Johnson cried out:

"Give her four guns together now, Lije!"

And even as the *Alert's* guns barked once more the four forward guns of the *Lexington's* larboard battery thundered in unison, and the cutter lurched and staggered and fell away.

"We done it! Igod, we done it!" Johnson yelled, thumping Kenny on the back. "We stopped her! Spread every rag, mister! She'll never catch us now."

As he spoke Elijah Bowen staggered through the gun-deck hatch-way with the splintered stump of his left arm sticking through the rags of his bloody shirt.

"That was th' last o't, Cap'n!" he gasped. "There's ever' last bit o' powder an' lead aboard!"

He wavered, and Kenny leaped to support him. Johnson roared: "Jesus Christ, man! Boy! Boy! Fetch th' surgeon!"

That should have been the end of it, and with eight out of ten commanders aboard the cutter, no doubt it would have been. The *Lexington* showed her heels to the *Alert*. But Bazely was not the man to be easily shaken off. Within the hour he had made temporary repairs to his vessel and crowded on all sail, and once again a white wake boiled upon the *Lexington's* heels. Kenny, watching apprehensively over his shoulder, could not help seeing how he crept up on them, and he thought then that it might be a long time before he would have the opportunity to put his plans into action. By midmorning the *Alert* was abreast of them again, and again her guns barked sharply; once again the shot rattled against the *Lexington's* decks, and again the sharp agony of men hurt beyond hiding burst upon their ears.

But this time the *Lexington's* guns did not reply. They could not. For one hour and then another she held to her course; stolidly, silently, save for the faint popping of the muskets of the marines in the tops. Again and again the *Alert* raked her helpless, fleeing foe. One shot, fired high, evidently on the up roll, caught Lieutenant Connolly aloft. Horrified, Kenny watched as the man teetered for a moment and then began a slow, downward, wheeling cartwheel, to crash almost at their feet. Captain Johnson stared an instant at the dead man and then lifted haggard eyes.

"I hate t' do it! Christ knows I hate t' do it, but ye'd best strike, Mr. Boyle, while there's yet some o' us left alive!"

It was past the first day of October. Dr. Franklin, his old eyes bright behind the gray iron rims of his spectacles, sat at his desk in his study in Passy, going methodically through some papers on the tray. Jonathan Williams came in with the latest letters and dispatches and laid them by the old gentleman's elbow. Franklin picked them up and scowled at a thin leathern envelope among them bearing the seal of the Marine Committee.

"What's this?" he demanded.

"Oh—that?" replied Williams negligently. "That'll be that letter for the sailing master of the *Lexington*. The messenger reached Morlaix just after she had sailed."

Franklin shook his head and stared at the letter thoughtfully for an instant. Then quietly he reached out and picked up a copy of a London *News Letter*, several days old.

"We see the English papers here quicker than we do our own dispatches!" he grumbled. "Have you seen this?"

Williams took the paper with an inquiring glance. He read:

LONDON, 25 September. The American brig *Lexington*, 16, Captain Johnson, which lately sailed with the pirate Wickes, departed from Morlaix the 17th Ulto., and fell in on the 19th with H.M. Cutter *Alert*, 10, Captain Bazely, by whom she was taken in the 45th degree of Latitude. All of the officers including the Captain were killed, with the exception of one only, both of whose legs were broke. It is believed that despatches for the rebel congress were Weighted and thrown Overboard during the Engagement!

"You'd think they'd be able to get their own reports right, at least!" Dr. Franklin growled. He looked at the letter in his hands. Then he sighed heavily and tossed it into a high-piled tray at the far side of his desk. "I'll have to do something about that, I daresay!"

4. Of Love and Trumpets

MATTERS were hardly at a standstill in America. On the military side, it was true, events moved for a time in somewhat desultory fashion. Howe, in New York, and Washington, at Morristown, watched each other across the Jersey meadows and the Staten Island Kills expectantly, each waiting some first sign of movement on the part of the other. Late in the spring General Burgoyne prepared to move down upon Albany from Canada by way of Lake Champlain, while another column approached along the Mohawk. When the news was out, even those who were not in the confidence of the English Ministry of War expected that either Howe or Clinton would advance up the Hudson to effect a junction with the other two columns, splitting the Colonies in two.

But to the amazement of all, Howe, instead, embarked his troops upon transports at New York, leaving only enough of a skeleton force to hold that place and a logistic crew to supply his own army, and under the convoy of Admiral Sir Richard and his fleet sailed out and turned south.

Philadelphia seemed the only possible objective, and General Washington and his ragged Continentals skittered across Jersey to take up positions in defense of the capital. The brothers Howe looked into Delaware Bay, to be sure, throwing a dreadful fright, it must be admitted, into the tiny fleet that was all that stood between that mighty armada and the Quaker City. But for some unexplained reasons—like the famous British general who marched his army up the hill, then marched them down again—they merely looked, then turned about and disappeared for some weeks more, to turn up again finally off the Virginia capes.

This time they made no feint, but sailed boldly into Chesapeake Bay and turned north. Baltimore fell into a furor of anticipation—and was almost disappointed when the huge fleet kept right on going past her, looking neither to the right nor to the left, until it came to the height of navigation at the Head of Elk. There the troops were put ashore and the march overland to Philadelphia began. Just why General Howe should have followed such a course is something that no one will probably ever guess. Yet he did so. And indeed, only the fact that General Washington's own force was so small and so ragged and so desperately in need of supplies permitted him to get through at all. When the troops had been landed the fleet, under Sir Richard —"Black Dick," as his men called him—went back down around Cape Charles and up again to the Delaware. And that was where Joshua and the fleet found their hands full; for it was the fleet's duty—officially; and Joshua's, unofficially—to hold them back.

All of that, of course, took most of the summer. Indeed, it carried through into October. During the interim Joshua found his duties with the Marine Committee arduous, if revealing, and at times not a little heartbreaking. They had the word, of course, of Lambert Wickes's great cruise in the Irish Sea in the *Reprisal*, in company with the *Lexington* and the *Dolphin*. And that was encouraging. But it was, of course, too early yet to receive word of the loss of both the *Reprisal* and the *Lexington* on their voyage home.

But it was not all work and heartbreak and scrivening duty during that period for Joshua. He himself had never been called anti-social, nor has Philadelphia been accused of the vice. There was not a thing he could do toward active duty until his exchange came through from Captain Elphinstone of the *Perseus*, so he made up his mind that he might as well make the most of what the city offered. And he did.

He was a frequent visitor at the Morrises' after that first occasion, for despite his discomfiture he still felt a strong friendship for the marine committeeman. By the same token he was also to be found often at the Willings', for he found that Morris's big partner grew upon you as you came to know him better; and, moreover, Sally Bingham took him determinedly in charge and insisted upon sponsoring him. It was largely through her influence that he found himself invited more and more frequently to other homes in the city; found himself taking part more and more in the balls and picnics and garden parties with which the younger group kept themselves entertained despite all the war's alarums and excursions.

It may have been through Sally Bingham that he was invited to the Biddles', the Fitzsimmons', the Gurneys', and the Whartons', or through her that he met General Mifflin and Henry and John Laurens, Philip Freneau, the Livingstons, and the Lippincotts. But there were other forces at work. Ann Bedford appeared to be everywhere he went, although after his first rather sharp encounter with her he went warily there. That did not mean that he did not admire or like her. Indeed, he found the very thought of her a rather disturbing influence to his work. As for her presence, he was delighted when he found her a guest at a party to which he was invited. Just to look at her seemed desirable. But at the same time he was bound he would give her no further opportunity to use what he believed must be an unfortunately sharp tongue upon him. Whenever they met it was with the stiffest, the utmost punctiliousness on his part, and he was at special pains never to reveal to her, by the least shadow of his expression, his real feelings.

If it was not by the same token, perhaps it was for a like reason that she met him upon almost exactly the same terms. This darkly handsome young naval officer pleased and intrigued her. With only a very little encouragement, she knew, she could fall head over heels in love with him. But she herself had wounded and insulted him before a group of strangers, and now he must detest her. His every action proved it, for never by the slightest smile did he show her the tiniest warmth.

She would have apologized to him for her behavior that night at the Morrises'. Surely, being actually in the Navy, he would understand her feelings if only she could explain to him. But during those first months of their friendship, at least, it was almost as if there was a conspiracy among the others of their mutual acquaintance to keep them apart. At dinner they were never partners. At dances they were never paired for longer than a punctilious, formal round, and surely it was not possible to speak out at such a time. At picnics and at the garden parties down by the Schuylkill there were always several others in the group, and neither she nor Joshua—who felt exactly the same about it but dared not say so—noticed that one of the others was invariably Sally Bingham, or that that lady had an almost devilish gleam of amusement in her eyes.

If he did not speak out to Ann, however, Joshua was not so reticent at home. Three times he journeyed to Baltimore to visit with his family, and each time, to Barbary's great amusement, he spoke in glowing terms of the beautiful, the lovely, the delightful Ann Bedford.

"You're very fond of her, aren't you?" Barbary asked him once, mischievously.

Joshua's own very proper horror spoke for itself.

"Fond of her? Good lord, child!" he cried. "Why, I've hardly said a dozen words to her in all the time I've known her! I think she's attractive, that's all."

"You'd better speak to her, then." Barbary laughed. "Lord knows, you'll give none of us any peace until you do!"

Somehow that did not seem at all funny to Joshua.

But Joshua's visits to Baltimore were not altogether taken up with descriptions of Ann. To his irritation and frank distress he discovered that Edric Wales had resumed his visits, and he did not doubt that in time he would also resume his courtship. He was outspokenly grim about that. He called Edric a "damned Tory" to his face and came near to blows with him. They were only separated by the more docile, unctuous Ben—Caroline's husband—who reminded them that gentlemen did not fight in ladies' presences. At that Joshua turned on Edric and retorted that he considered him an empty-headed, shallow-gutted nincompoop who would run with the hare and hunt with the hounds as long as he was able. The result was a definite coolness between them.

When Joshua taxed Barbary with inconstancy, however, she pointed out that Edric invariably took advantage of Callie's and Ben's calls to accompany them, and that she could hardly refuse to admit her own sister and brother-in-law.

"Just let him say something!" she flared.

And Joshua felt that she meant it, for always her first question to him, after her first delighted flurry of greeting, was of Kenny. He told her the news of the *Lexington's* arrival in European waters, and she was delighted with that, although he admitted that so far he had had no reply to his letter. But all, apparently, was well.

That was near the end of June, and Joshua returned to Philadelphia in time to find an invitation awaiting him to attend the evening supper and garden party being given by the Gunning Bedfords in celebration of the young nation's first anniversary on the Fourth of July. Perhaps Barbary's mild gibes made Joshua determined to speak out. Certainly it was more than coincidence that caused Ann Bedford to ask him to come as her particular partner. Now, she thought, let Sally Bingham try to keep me from offering him my apologies!

But it almost seemed to them both that the attempt was doomed to failure. To be sure, Joshua escorted Ann in to supper on his arm, as courtly and polite as anyone could wish. And they sat beside one another and talked of everything but the one thing that really mattered to them both: of the way the war was going, of the most recent decisions of the Congress. And just when Ann thought the moment was approaching when she could speak to him confidentially, Sally Bingham tossed in the perfectly gratuitous and utterly false statement that someone had seen General Washington coming out of a certain house in town, and started a whole new round of general conversation, so that they could not, without making it too conspicuous, talk with one another to the exclusion of the rest.

Their moment came at last, however, during the display of fire-works over the Schuylkill, and Ann never admitted having enlisted aid. Sally Bingham had stuck closer to them than a burr, as if she half suspected Ann's intentions. But Henry Laurens had come, with a smile and a bow for Ann, and dragged the older girl off to see the pinwheels down by the riverbank. Joshua nodded but actually scarcely saw them go. He was staring moodily at the zipping rockets and bursting Roman candles.

"I dislike to say it, Mistress Ann," he remarked, "since your own people have arranged it, but yonder's a most distressing waste of powder."

That was her opportunity—not quite as she had anticipated it, perhaps, but still unmistakable.

"Oh, but 'tis such a little—Lieutenant," she said.

"Yes, but when you think of the need and of how many times that little is multiplied——" he began, and then broke off and stared at her. "You—you knew?"

She smiled at him.

"Of course I knew, Lieutenant Barney," she replied. "I knew after that first night. Uncle Bob told me. How you must dislike me. I am sorry—and I do apologize."

There, she had said it! Now she could do no more.

"Ann! Please!" Joshua cried, and to them both the use of her first name seemed entirely natural. "I don't dislike you. I thought you disliked me. As a matter of fact, I admire you. I—I——"

But just at that moment the return of Sally Bingham and a whole crowd of others interrupted him.

"We've managed to say a lot to each other in just these few min-utes—Joshua," Ann managed to say before they were upon them, and after that things were entirely different for them both.

It was not that they had more opportunity to declare their feeling for one another than they had ever had before. But the feeling was there, and they both knew it and cherished it. After that they were partners often at the summer dances and at supper and garden par-ties. Joshua still did not speak out entirely. No doubt the habit of diffidence had grown upon him, and Ann rather liked him for that. He did not try to sweep her off her feet but sought for something more lasting. But his visits to Baltimore were not nearly so frequent.

At home unfortunately, matters were not altogether so smooth. Edric Wales's visits continued, in company always, and always most punctiliously correct, it must be admitted. Yet Barbary viewed their increasing frequency with growing apprehension and irritation. Sooner or later, she felt, she would have to speak out to him and, being a kind person at heart, she hated the prospect.

Yet it was inevitable. On the day that news arrived in Baltimore of General Howe's embarkation and sailing, Edric Wales had the suave effrontery to call upon her alone, without the usual protection of his brother and her sister.

Barbary did not mince matters.

"I don't know why you come here," she said unflatteringly. "You know how I feel about you!"

But if he was offended he gave her no sign of it. Instead he smiled unctuously at her.

"Now, Barbary," he protested. "You know how much I care for you. I know you've been misled by some foolish folk who think the Americans can stand against England——"

"If you think of Joshua as foolish——" she began hotly.

"Now, now, Barbary," he said. "I didn't say that. I only said that you'd been misguided. You know how much I love you. A little misunderstanding of a moment or so isn't going to make any difference to me. You'll come around to the right point of view, and when you do I'll be here."

"What makes you think I'll come around to your point of view?" she demanded. "Or that it's the right one?"

"Why!" he said, reasoning as if he were talking with a child. "General Howe has sailed for Philadelphia. 'Tis only a matter of weeks—maybe days—before the rebel capital falls, and then the whole rebel movement will collapse like a bubble!"

"You were born in America—and you really think that?" She stared at him, the wonder of it quite overriding his insult to her. "Do you really think, like any European, that when a country's capital falls its cause is lost as well?"

"What else?" He shrugged. "Even if you fight with Philadelphia gone, it can only be a matter of time! After all, who can win against the might of Britain?"

"Oh—you—you!" she cried. "Get out, will you? You might as well go, because I am going upstairs and lock myself in my room until you are gone!"

He did not return again until Howe showed his face inside the Virginia capes and everyone in Baltimore thought that city must be the next object of his attack. The house on Federal Hill was a scene of bustle and activity, with even Callie there rolling up compresses and tearing sheets into bandages, for if the militiamen of the city and the surrounding counties were flocking to the guardian forts at Fell's and Whetstone Points, the women did not mean to be far behind. Edric glanced haughtily about, bowed superciliously to Mary Barney, and then casually drew Barbary aside. She went because she did not wish to create a scene with so many of the other women there.

"My dear!" he exclaimed when he had drawn her away to a corner. "Really! All this is such nonsense, you know. General Howe will have the town before nightfall, and then where will all this be? He will look after the wounded—his own and rebel alike. He has all the facilities, and he's really quite generous——"

"How do you know he'll take the town?" Barbary's lip thrust out belligerently.

"Oh, my sweet!" he cried in a voice loud enough so that the others must have heard. "How can you believe that he will not? Do you think that the city's inefficient militia can stop him? Really, now——"

"I think they can put up a damned good try!" Barbary retorted, forgetting her manners for once. "And even if they fail, I don't want to be associated with you—you—you——"

"Now, now! There, there!" He made a last desperate effort: "Truly, Barbary! I want to say that no matter what happens, when General Howe holds the city, you and your mother can be assured of my care and protection——"

"Will you go?" she screamed, and snatched at the nearest object that was handy. It happened to be a vase of summer flowers, full of water, and she flung it at him, so that he was drenched, both head and shoulders, and the drooping roses hung ludicrously in his hair. The other women laughed. But he marched with the utmost dignity to the door. There he turned with his hand upon the knob.

"I have been patient!" he snarled. "God knows I have been patient with a silly girl! But you and your mother both will suffer for this when General Howe has taken the city. Mark my words!"

He slammed the door behind him, and although they were inclined to laugh with Barbary at his threat, at the same time the other women were forced to look at her sympathetically, for there was little doubt in anyone's mind that, as gallant as the defense might be, it would be only a matter of days before Baltimore would be in English hands.

But to the astonishment of all, the Howes did not bother themselves with anything so insignificant. They sailed on to the Head of Elk, looking neither to the right nor to the left, and Edric Wales, having been so outspoken at the Barney house, fled to the protection of the British Army at Philadelphia, where they were obviously bound.

Barbary, of course, wrote to Joshua about it by a roundabout route as soon as the threat to Baltimore was passed, and Joshua received her note. But he had other matters on his mind just then, for the British were at Brandywine, and the Marine Committee and Congress must be helped to make their escape. Any day now might see Sir Richard in the Delaware itself.

Philadelphia, if the truth be told, was in an even greater panic than Baltimore had been. After all, she had more to lose. Many of her citizens were hand in glove with the rebel government—though some of them sought to hide it; and all of that government centered there. Congress must fly, and the Marine Committee with it; and York, Pennsylvania, beyond the Susquehanna, and off and away from the British line of march seemed the best first refuge. As Barbary had suggested, there was never a thought of surrender. Washington stood at Brandywine, and his ragged troops, underarmed and undisciplined in the face of Howe's overwhelming force, stood well but in the end were forced to withdraw. The way to the city lay open!

Until the last minute Joshua, in shirt sleeves, helped pack necessary records and letters in boxes and loaded them on wagons, burning others. He offered to help make a stand in a rear-guard action, if necessary, but Robert Morris would not hear of that.

"You've done enough, lad!" he said. "If the English ever learn you've done this much there'll be little hope of exchange. You'd best get clear of the town while you can, for if they ever take you, we'll never see you back!"

Joshua shook hands with him and then went directly to Gunning Bedford's home. To his amazement he found all serene there—no effort at any preparation to leave, as there was at most officials'.

"You're not going?" he cried.

Gunning Bedford smiled.

"I'm only an alderman," he replied. "They'll offer no harm to me or mine, and someone must stay behind to keep an eye on things here."

"But—but——" Joshua cried.

Bedford chuckled again.

"This is only a temporary thing," he said. "I'd be willing to wager, if I were a betting man, that they'll not be more than a year in the town. Since I can't fight, I'd sooner be here, where I can watch things and perhaps get word out to you lads now and again. But you'd best be off, for you'll be useful to us, and they'll be on the lookout for such as yourself."

"I daresay you're right," Joshua replied grimly, and showed them Barbary's letter warning him of Edric Wales. He glanced at Ann. "May I have a word with Mistress Ann?"

Gunning Bedford glanced from Joshua to his daughter and smiled, then looked toward his wife.

"Come, Mother," he said. "I've a notion they've things to say that're not for such old ears as ours. Good luck to you, son!"

When they were gone Joshua turned toward the girl.

"Ann! Ann!" he cried. "You know there are things I've not dared say—that I'd not say now but for the fact that I must go. I love you, Ann. I want you to be my wife. If you'll go with me I'll watch over you and protect you—and love you always."

She went to him and took his face in her hands, fondly.

"Joshua! My Joshua!" she told him. "I love you too. You know that. But I can't leave Mother and Father."

He caught her in his arms and drew her close to him.

"Ann!" he cried huskily. "Ann, what should we do?"

She smiled up at him, happy at last to be where she belonged, even though it could be only for a moment.

"You must go, Joshua," she said, "for you are the one in danger now. You go, and don't fear for me. I will be able to take care of myself and keep myself here for you. Don't ever doubt that. When this is over and done and you are able to come back to me, I will be here waiting for you—for I love you too, Joshua. I do love you too!"

He kissed her then as he had never kissed anyone before, and it seemed to him that all the world around them, and time with it, stood still and trembled.

"Now go!" she said at length, breathlessly.

5. *Resume Action*

JOSHUA posted out along the Lancaster road while he could and caught up with Robert Morris and the Marine Committee's wagons before they had passed Paoli. Once they reached the little red brick town beyond the Susquehanna, it was hardly extraordinary that he should be damnably impatient; both to hear word of his own exchange, but even more to hear word of the Bedfords in the captured city and to know how they fared. As to the latter, it was Robert Morris himself who informed him with a grin.

"You'll be pleased to hear, lad," he said, "that the word from within the lines is that the British have burnt no houses nor offered affront to any of the people. Right at this moment the officers are about planning a theatrical entertainment in honor of General Howe——"

"Good God! No wonder they can't win the war!" Joshua cried.

"—and they've appointed Gunning Bedford to see to the provision of their Yankee prisoners of war inside the city," Morris concluded with a grin.

"Then 'tis hardly likely his family will suffer!" Joshua let slip out despite himself.

"Exactly," replied Morris. "'Tis why I told you."

After that Joshua was better able to share the room he had taken with twelve other young naval officers, in which they slept, watch and watch, three at a time to the great bed, eight hours at a time. Nevertheless, he was overjoyed when one morning in October he came down to find a letter awaiting him addressed in an unfamiliar hand.

Idly he tore it open and glanced at it, then looked again and whooped. Breakfast was forgotten. In five minutes he was thundering at the door of Robert Morris's rooms, barging in and waving the letter aloft.

"Exchanged!" he shouted. "I'm to be exchanged! Here's a note from Captain Elphinstone himself to summon me to Hampton for my release!"

Robert Morris took the letter and studied it for a moment, then handed it back to him with a bland smile.

"Then you must be off at once—before someone else can step into your place," he said. "Take your pick of the horses in my stable, and remember me to Governor Henry at Williamsburg when you stop there for his authorization to go aboard the *Perseus*. Good luck to you, Joshua! Report back here to me as soon as you can, and no doubt we'll find something for you. I shall be sorry to lose you, though I know 'tis the thing you want most."

"Thank you, sir," replied Joshua, and was away.

He rode as straight as the roads would take him to Williamsburg, where, within four days of his departure from York, he paused only long enough to call upon the governor, Patrick Henry, and obtain from him the flag of truce that would carry him out to the waiting *Perseus* in the bay. After that he went to the expense of hiring a cutter and dropped down to Hampton Roads and the waiting warship.

Captain Elphinstone, suave and humorously easy, courteously pressed him to stay for a dish of tea and to tell him the news from ashore, but a letter over the captain's signature, stating that he was that day released from his parole in exchange for Lieutenant Moriarty of the *Solebay*, frigate, was as much as he wanted. Once that was in his pocket, he was away again; and by nightfall, refusing all offers of Virginia hospitality, he was riding hell for leather toward the Northern Neck. Three days later he galloped into Baltimore and allowed his nag a day's rest in the big stable behind the brick house on Federal Hill.

He found his family well. They rejoiced with him at his exchange, and he gave Barbary a kiss and reluctantly told her that there was yet no word from Kenny. Blushingly he admitted that he had spoken to Ann and that they had come to an agreement, although she was still in Philadelphia.

After that he had a look around to see what might be in the harbor, although he had a fairly shrewd idea. The Continental frigate *Virginia*, 28, new-built and yet untried, was preparing to get to sea under Captain James Nicholson. That he had little use for Captain Nicholson has already been suggested. The man was a self-seeker and far too fond of his own fleshpots to give them up readily in the interests of his country—as a Baltimorean, Joshua knew that. Still, a ship was a ship, and any skipper was better than none to a sailor cast on the beach. Accordingly he called on Captain Nicholson on board, and though it went against the grain, with a little application of the sweet tongue, which he had learned from Kenny, he managed to persuade the commander to promise him a berth aboard, provided he himself could arrange orders to that effect with the Marine Committee. Of that, at least, Joshua had few doubts, and he consoled himself with the reflection that the *Virginia* was a fine ship. By dawn the red Maryland mud was flying from his horse's galloping hoofs as he posted once more toward York.

He lost no time, once he came to the little frontier village, in seeking out the headquarters of the committee. Robert Morris, who had heard of the victory at Saratoga during his absence, was in an even more than ordinarily affable mood. He greeted Joshua robustly and then listened patiently to his request.

" 'Twill be a step down for you," he suggested. "The only berth open in the *Virginia* is that of third lieutenant. If you'll be content to wait a bit, I'm sure there'll be other ships and better billets."

But Joshua was impatient.

"A man ashore for as long as I've been, sir," he said, "is not like to be choosy!"

"Far be it from me to discourage such a fire-eater!" Morris laughed and wrote out the order. Only when he was on his way back to Baltimore did Joshua realize that he had forgotten to ask if there had been any news of Kenny and the *Lexington*.

But there was no time then, it seemed to him, to turn back and ask. The *Virginia* was expected to get to sea any day, and it was important, for him at least, that he be aboard when she did. He pushed on and, when he came to Baltimore, solaced his own conscience with a small white lie to Barbary, telling her that there was no word, so far as he could find out—which was actually the truth, although he did not know it.

But the *Virginia* did not sail on the day after he reported on board, nor yet the next week nor the next month. The long-nosed, dour Nicholson, it seemed, was having far too fine a time ashore to be much worried about any orders the Marine Committee might issue, and he was adept at finding excuses to postpone the frigate's departure. Indeed, Joshua discovered that the thing had become almost a standing joke among his fellow officers and the men—those who had the patience to remain.

But Joshua had been too long ashore to be patient. He fussed and fretted and grew irritable, the more especially so when he reflected that this very delay of the captain's was prolonging the struggle and keeping him the longer from Ann's side. He buzzed about Nicholson like an obnoxious wasp, and had the captain not suspected something of his standing with the Marine Committee he would probably have been court-martialed out of hand. As it was, Nicholson tried easy, laughing affability, then irritably put him aside. Joshua wrote brief hints to Robert Morris. New orders came down from York to Nicholson—and the latter found new excuses. It seemed the *Virginia's* sheathing had been improperly applied. He had it replaced to his liking. When that was done and it seemed, at last, that all was ready, he reported with his tongue in his cheek that the delay had caused them to use up what provisions they had on board. While they waited for new stores, apparently the crew found opportunity to desert, and they were short-handed.

The day came at last, in December, when Joshua could bear it no longer. Indeed, he was the last of the officers left aboard, except the captain. The rest had found the waiting more than they could bear and had handed in their resignations and gone elsewhere. Under those circumstances Joshua called belligerently upon the captain and warned him of his intention to write directly to Robert Morris unless Captain Nicholson showed a greater inclination to regard the purpose of his ship. Nicholson stared at him. There was no doubt of his fury, but at the same time it was possible this whippersnapper might make it embarrassing for him.

"You know well, Lieutenant," he growled sullenly, "that the *Virginia* is short-handed and lacks supplies!"

"If I can get them for you, will you agree to sail?"

The question caught Nicholson by surprise.

"Certainly!" He blinked. This impetuous young fool, he thought to himself with grim satisfaction, had put himself in a box. Let him ride the roads awhile, and he would lose some of his fiery enthusiasm. In the meantime he, Nicholson, would continue to take his ease in Baltimore.

"Give me leave to appeal to the Marine Committee?" Joshua demanded stoutly.

Nicholson hesitated.

"I can rely on your discretion?"

"Certainly, sir!" Joshua's snort was almost contemptuous.

"Very well." Nicholson grinned. "I will provide you with orders, and you may see what you can do."

Nicholson smiled darkly to himself, but Joshua was not one to act without a plan. By the next night he was in York and laid the matter before Robert Morris.

"When the British took Philadelphia, sir," he said, "the Navy Board for that district fled upriver and took with them most of the men and all of the supplies they could lay their hand on. They went to ground at Bordentown, and most of both are still there, and they've not a bit of use for 'em. Why not send some of them to us?"

"Now there's a thought!" Morris cried. "D'you think you can get 'em through? If so, I'll give you a letter and an order on Bordentown."

"I'd not be here if I did not think so," Joshua retorted.

Morris grinned and drew a sheet of foolscap toward him and started writing.

"While I'm about it"—he chuckled—"I understand that most of the other officers aboard the *Virginia* have given up in disgust and turned in their commissions. If it's all right with you, I'll merely write out your appointment as first lieutenant?"

"As you wish, sir." Joshua was hardly enthusiastic, and Morris's wry smile indicated that he did not miss the implication.

"Have you heard aught from the *Lexington*, sir?" Joshua asked, suddenly remembering.

Morris shook his head.

"Naught since the news of their raid," he replied, "but our dispatches have been damnably slow since the fall of Philadelphia. She's probably on her way home now."

Joshua rode on, round about, through Reading to Bordentown, on the Delaware. There the Navy Board was only too pleased to find employment for its land-bound men and supplies. They loaded five huge wagons and gave him nearly a hundred men and officers; and Joshua, in command of the little column, started the long road back.

It was longer now, however, because the direct route through Philadelphia and Wilmington was occupied by the enemy. He went round through Valley Forge and Rising Sun, and on the way, because he was curious, he stopped overnight at the Army's camp to pay his own respects—and the Navy's—to the Commander in Chief. He was surprised to find the encampment in a state of startling and disorganized confusion, even then undergoing the initial stages of construction. Everywhere cabins and dugouts and plain pole shelters were going up, with no evident attempt at order. When he looked at the men Joshua could see why the British referred contemptuously to them as a "rabble." Such a collection of rags and tatters he had never seen. In the main there were no uniforms—not even strong clothing, as a man would think of such. Sentries walked their posts with sacks wrapped about their feet in place of boots, and any old patch or tatter did for a coat or breeches. To his astonishment the riflemen from the western part of Virginia and from Maryland and Pennsylvania still wore breechclouts and leggings and showed bare bottoms, like Indians! Even among the officers there was only here and there a uniform to be seen, and that was clearly bought out of the wearer's own pocket. Occasionally a staff officer was smartly arrayed, making a conspicuous spot of color. But in the main even those who had regimentals were torn and worn and battle-stained. Usually the officers were simply distinguished by cockades in their hats or varicolored ribbons in their lapels. The men themselves looked battered and hungry, and Joshua felt a certain regret that he had paused with his wagonloads of supplies and his obviously well-fed officers and men.

But for all their grim appearance, there was something strong and forceful about them. They were hard and lean, with the dry, wry humor of men who had faced hard times together and expected to face a good deal more before they were through. They were all kinds, to be sure. But Joshua could see in the glint in their eyes and feel in the very air somehow the intangible power and spirit that drew them and held them together. Their pay and their bellies and the ragged shirts on their backs might loom large in their consciousness. But there was something far greater than that that bound them, and he, for one, was proud as he had never been before to be identified with them.

Having stopped and looked and seen, he would have preferred to go on. The sight of that camp made him impatient to be about his task. Since he had stopped, however, there was no question about it. He must pay his visit of courtesy to the commander. The general greeted him at his headquarters, acknowledged his salute, and shook hands with him pleasantly. He was a tall, very erect man, Joshua noticed, with a rather long nose and a thin slit of a mouth that could close like a trap, and steady, piercing eyes that looked at you and through you, even when he was smiling faintly, almost ironically. Joshua did not miss the slight circles under his eyes or the look of weariness behind them, even though the man seemed serenely confident. Having seen the camp outside, he was hardly surprised.

"Welcome, Lieutenant," the general said. "I hear you've a wagon train in your care. The Navy seems to be better supplied than we are here!"

He chuckled as he said it, removing the sting, and Joshua was embarrassed.

"Believe me, sir," he cried seriously, "I—we had to fight to get these!"

"I know. I can well believe it," the tall man replied. "I've been doing the same thing myself for a long time now. Where are you taking 'em?"

"To Baltimore, sir—to the *Virginia,* so she can sail," Joshua told him.

"Good enough!" the older man exclaimed. "Tell Captain Nicholson I hope he has better luck than we've had so far and that I trust he'll fetch us back far more supplies than he takes away!"

"Aye, aye, sir!" Joshua gulped, not even stopping then to wonder that this tall, serene man should know the name of the *Virginia's* commander without asking.

6. Ann

IN PHILADELPHIA, inside the British lines, Ann, beyond doubt, worried fully as much about Joshua as he did about her. Where he was, what had become of him, what he might be doing, she had no idea, and the uncertainty increased her outspoken hostility to the invaders. Some girls, evidently, could meet and mingle with the young British officers and join in their gaiety, their balls and promenades, their festivities, their Mischianzas and theatricals, without the slightest twinge of conscience. Some even appeared to enjoy themselves, and there was no question but that Philadelphia during that winter was a very gay place indeed.

But Ann, though she might perforce take some part in the easygoing revels of the occupying officers, could not bring herself to enjoy them. Indeed, she was quite outspoken in her criticism of the scarlet-coated dandies who paraded so ostentatiously in the city's streets and salons. She made no effort to hide what she thought, and Joshua, if he had once thought her tongue sharp toward him, would have been delighted if he could hear her now.

But there was a difference here. Now the British were the victors, and the suave and dashing officers did not let Ann's tongue ruffle them—much to her vexation. Rather they were amused by her and among themselves referred to her as "the pretty little rebel." What was worse, so far as she was concerned, was that in their infuriating confidence in their own invincibility they often treated her exactly as if she were not there. Often she heard matters discussed that, in other circumstances, would have been the deepest of secrets—all because of their own serene assurance that she was unable to do anything about them. Sometimes, she was sure, they did it just to taunt her, and the awareness of that only made her all the more determined someday, somehow, to smuggle some of that oh so secret information out to where it would do the most good.

Indeed, it was only that determination that kept her from envying Sally Bingham, who had fled from the city when the British approached. Since her husband was an active and known agent of the rebel colonies, it would scarcely have been safe for her to stay. But the fact of the matter was that she had not gone very far. At that very moment she was safely and snugly hidden away at the Willing farm in that vague no man's land in Bucks County, not very far from the Americans' winter encampment at Valley Forge.

That was a bit of knowledge that Ann never dreamed would be useful to her then. But it was, almost before the winter began. And, curiously enough, it was largely because of Edric Wales that it happened so.

She met Edric at a supper party given by the Howes and Major Loring, to which she and her family had been bidden—for it was early discovered that they did not respond to invitations. She was introduced to him by a mincing young Major André, who was already at work upon the Mischianza and who was later to die so much more heroically than she ever dreamed he could.

"Oh, Mistress Bedford, ma'am!" cried the major, coming up with the handsome, sleek civilian in tow. "May I have the honor? Here's a young man from Baltimore who's been pining away to meet you, and I've sworn he shall not be disappointed. It seems he's heard of you from his brother-in-law, who appears to be something in the Yankee Navy. Mistress Bedford, ma'am—Mr. Wales."

Ann's breath caught in her throat for just an instant, and for just an instant she almost brightened. The first thought that flashed across her mind was that Edric was a messenger from Joshua and that he must have something to tell her. But then, as swiftly on the heels of the idea, some warning signal flashed in her mind.

"Wales? Wales?" She inclined her head perhaps a trifle more politely than she was wont to do. Somehow she felt that she could make use of this young dandy who eyed her so intently as he bowed. "Edric Wales? Oh yes! I do remember now having heard Lieutenant Barney speak of you."

"I'm sure you have, ma'am," cried the irrepressible André. "There's hardly any love lost between 'em, to hear Wales tell it."

"Of course!" Ann by now had definitely made up her mind how she must act. She recalled the letter Barbary had written to Joshua about him, and she was sure this plausible young man had some ulterior motive in singling her out. Whatever it might be, it was not good. Of that much she was sure, and she even guessed that he may have been set to spy upon her and her family by the high command, in which case she meant to see him hanged by his own rope. "Of course, Mr. Wales! Lieutenant Barney did go on in a dreadfully long tirade about you. I do hope you won't prove to be as insufferably boring as he."

For a fleeting instant Edric Wales looked startled. Major André laughed.

"I told you she'd snap your head off!" he told him.

"I thought you were a friend of Barney's," Edric Wales said, almost accusingly.

"Oh lud, no, Mr. Wales!" Ann cried. "Heaven forbid!"

There was a good deal more in the same vein, and each time she spoke harshly of him she sent out a tiny mental prayer to Joshua to beg him to forgive her for making such use of his name. But when the evening was over she was pretty firmly convinced that she had made Edric Wales, at least, believe in her dislike for Joshua, and that, she knew, would make a bond between them. Exactly what she would do with it, or just how she would make use of the young popinjay, she did not yet know, but she felt that somehow, in some way, he would be useful.

After that he came to call on her, not too frequently at first, and then more and more often, until even her father was moved to protest.

"I don't see what you see in the whippersnapper!" he growled. "I've half a mind to forbid him the house!"

"You'll do nothing of the kind, Father," she told him peremptorily. "And you needn't fear that I'll do anything foolish with Mr. Wales. The man sickens me. But I see a potential threat to Joshua in him, and I think, too, he may have been set to keep an eye on us. What better way to forestall him in either case than to throw him off his guard by pretending to be friendly with him?"

"Damme!" Gunning Bedford chuckled. "I should have known better than to worry about you. You've more sense than the lot of us!"

That was in November, not very long after the city had fallen and the British had gone into winter quarters there. It was in December that she found her opportunity, both to make use of the British officers' taunting laxity and to turn Edric Wales to her own needs. It was Major Loring, this time, at another of those hated dinner parties, who was indiscreet in his talk across the table to a Colonel Foote, whose regiment of dragoons had been disembarked from New York only the week before.

"I say, Foote!" Loring cried. "You're all ready for your little sortie, eh? You'd better be! General Howe wants the thing done the eighteenth."

"General Howe need not worry." Colonel Foote, who had not been long enough in Philadelphia to be aware of the customs of the place, looked positively shocked at this open discussion of what should have been a military secret. "I'll be ready."

Ann pricked up her ears. She had given up discouraging these confidences now. Indeed, she openly sought them, hoping by that means to come across something she could use.

"What's that, Major?" she demanded, taunting. "Don't tell me you're going to raid some hay wagons again!"

Her reference was to a fiasco in which a troop of British cavalry had come off second best. Loring was stung, as she knew he would be.

"Not at all," he retorted stiffly. "This time we're shooting for important game."

"Don't tell her!" Foote rapped.

"Oh, tush!" Loring scoffed. "Everyone tells Mistress Bedford everything! We do it to tease her."

"Just the same——" mumbled Foote, red-faced.

"You were saying, Major Loring?" Ann thrust out her tongue at the colonel.

"You see!" Loring laughed. "She even asks for it now. It's become a sort of game, y'know! Haw! Well, mem, since you must know, this time 'tis to be a raid on the headquarters of the Yankee Navy Board at Bordentown. We know they've gone to ground there with all the naval stores and a lot of supplies they took from this place when we came in. Since we can use 'em both, Colonel Foote's to go up the river in whaleboats and make the raid at midnight on the eighteenth."

"Oh no!" Ann pretended a sort of frustrated helplessness. "Oh, Major Loring, don't let him do it! Can't you persuade the general to give it up? They haven't anything at Bordentown, I know. Colonel Foote will just have his jaunt for nothing."

"Then it will be a pleasant little drill for him and his men, eh, Colonel?" Loring gibed.

Ann sank into what she hoped must appear to be miserable silence, while all the time her heart was beating so loudly she was sure that they must be able to hear it. This was the thing she had been waiting for, and now she would be able to kill two birds with one stone, too. She had her plan for that. She calculated quickly. The eighteenth was three days away, and that would give her plenty of time to carry things out. Fortunately Edric Wales was not there and had not heard, so he would never suspect. And, after all, what could be more important to her than a raid on the Navy Board's headquarters at Bordentown? Wasn't Joshua in the Navy? Indeed, he might even be at Bordentown, in which case it was even doubly important to her to get the word of the intended blow to the right people. The only question was, just who were the right people? She thought about that and came to the conclusion that she should take the word to the very top—to General Washington himself, at Valley Forge. He would know what to do.

She made no mention of her scheme to her family. She was not at all sure that they would approve. But she knew well enough that it was the only way the thing could be done. She waited until Edric Wales came to call the next evening, as she well knew he would, and then put on her most pathetic expression.

"Oh, Edric," she cried, "I'm so worried about Sally Bingham."

He looked at her sharply, suddenly attentive.

"Sally Bingham?" he demanded. "You mean William Bingham's wife?"

"Of course!" she said. "We haven't heard from her for days!"

"You——" He gaped at her, and she almost had to laugh in his face, for he thought himself such a fine actor. "You mean you—you hear from her? You know where she is?"

"Certainly!" Ann pretended stupid indignation. "She's just outside of town a little way. She's a very old and very dear friend, you know."

"You said you hadn't heard from her for days?" he said sharply.

"No, we haven't," she replied innocently. "You see, we usually get letters from her in the vegetable wagons that fetch in the supplies, but we can't send any back out by them. We know she's going to have a baby and she always has an awful time when she does—and —and she's all alone there in that great big house! I—I just know something dreadful must have happened. I—I wish there were some way I could go out and see."

She hoped Sally would forgive her for that story when she heard it. After all, Bill Bingham hadn't been home in almost two years! She stared at the young fop wide-eyed and pensively, thinking to herself that just at that moment he looked a little like a beagle on a scent. Then abruptly she looked as if a wonderful idea had just occurred to her, and she clasped her hands together and stared at him pleadingly.

"Edric!" she cried. "I just thought of it, and it's so perfect! You are really the only one who can help me. You can arrange for me to pass through the lines and go to her. You'll do it, won't you? Say you'll do it!"

She held her breath then, for if he were not working secretly for the British, as she suspected, she would have had all her work for nothing. Indeed, she would be in a rather awkward position.

But fortunately the bait that she had dangled before him was all that was necessary, and he snapped at it.

"You can't go alone!" He scowled.

"Of course not," she replied innocently. "I wouldn't dream of it, Edric. You must go with me, to see me safely there and back."

The smirk of satisfaction was so plain upon his face that she could almost have slapped him.

"I'll see what I can do," he promised. "If I can arrange it I'll be here tomorrow evening just after dusk with horses and the passes. You be ready! You said it wasn't far?"

He looked suddenly doubtful.

"Oh no!" she cried convincingly. " 'Tis only ten or a dozen miles, if that. We can do it easily and be back by morning."

He left then, and she lived the next twenty-four hours in a sort of frenzied trance of apprehension. She knew now, of course, that he was all she had believed, for he had been far too quick to agree, far too interested in such a dangerous undertaking for a man who might have difficulty in arranging it. For instance, he had merely assumed the question of the passes as a matter of course, and Ann was sharp enough to know that such things were not simply handed out to everyone. The greatest drawback was that he might appear with a troop in escort—in which case she would simply refuse to go. But she counted upon his own intelligence to realize that possibility and risk it alone. Moreover, she guessed that he was the kind who would prefer to make seizure of the wife of the envoy to Martinico by himself. It would be so much more of a feather in his cap that way.

In a way she felt a little conscience-stricken at what she planned. And yet, she consoled herself with the question, was it any less treacherous than what he himself had in mind? And was he not the enemy of her people—the traitor to his own? Had he not said dreadful things to her about her Joshua—under her encouragement, to be sure, but nevertheless he had said them and meant them.

Nor did she plan to carry with her simply word of the forthcoming raid on Bordentown. So long as she was risking so much, she might as well take everything that might possibly be of use to the Americans. She had spent the afternoon jotting down notes: where all the various officers she could think of had taken up quarters; which of the Americans in town seemed inclined to work with them; where such various regiments as she could remember were stationed, and anything else she had heard regarding their plans. And as a last thought she also grabbed up a bundle of London *News Letters* dating from away back in September. There might be something useful in those.

When he came at last, she was ready, and they mounted and rode out along the Lansdowne Pike. Edric seemed nervous and inclined to be suspicious.

"You said it wasn't far," he reminded her.

"Oh no!" she repeated, lying like a Trojan. " 'Tis just beyond the lines."

That seemed to satisfy him for the moment, at least, for he showed his passes to the sergeant on duty at the outpost, and she was careful to note the password he used—"King George"—as they were waved through. Beyond the lines they rode hard and fast in silence, for she felt sure that sooner or later he would protest at the distance she was leading him. Sure enough, they were not much more than halfway there when he reined in and cried out petulantly:

"See here! You told me it was but a little way, and we've already gone as far as you said it was. I'm going to turn back unless you tell me exactly——"

"You may, but I shan't!" she retorted, and clapped spurs to her mount.

She was away in a spurt and a flurry and was a good fifty yards ahead of him before he could recover himself enough to whip his own nag in pursuit. After that, by dint of constant use of both spur and whip, she managed to maintain her lead, galloping through the countryside like the wind, and holding her breath at every turn lest it bring her face to face with some patrol or raiding party.

But luck was with her. It was a cruel run, and her poor horse was blowing and faltering when she thundered up before the Willing house and flung herself down from the saddle and dashed up the steps. It was with a feeling of intense relief that she heard Sally's voice demanding in answer to her thundering knock:

"Who's that? Who's there?"

"Sally! Sally! Open the door!" Ann shouted loudly, so that anyone who was in the house must hear. She knew Sally Bingham was not there without servants or any help at all, and her own voice must warn them. "'Tis me—Ann Bedford—and I declare I've run all the way from Philadelphia! They're on my heels! Let me in!"

As she said it she heard Edric Wales fling from his horse and run up the steps behind her.

"You little witch!" he panted in her ear as he caught hold of her. "You told me——"

The door in front of them opened, flinging a bright knife blade of yellow light out into the darkness, and Sally Bingham stood staring at them. What was more important, so far as Ann was concerned, behind her stood old Moses, the Willings' family butler, with an enormous blunderbuss clutched tightly in both hands.

"Why, Ann!" cried Sally. "What——"

But Ann turned to Edric Wales.

"I told you you'd meet Sally Bingham," she said. "Sally, this is Edric Wales—a Tory and a spy—or at least he would be if he knew how! He passed me through the lines. May we come in?"

"Please do." Sally looked both amazed and amused. "Are there no more of you?"

"None." Ann shook her head and stood aside. "You first, please, Mr. Wales."

He glanced at her, then at Sally, and finally at old Moses with the gun, and tried to brazen it out.

"Your servant, Mistress Bingham!" he said punctiliously, and then to Ann: "My dear, I'm afraid I don't understand."

"You will!" Ann told him grimly. "Go in."

He shrugged, and they entered, and Sally closed the door behind them, staring from one to the other in as much evident confusion as Edric. She made a motion to Moses.

"That will do, Moses," she said. "We shan't——"

"No! Moses, you stay right here! And don't you let go of that gun, either!" Ann cried, and whirled upon Sally. "Sally, I've got some news I must get to General Washington at once. It's most important, really! I got Edric, here, to pass me through the lines by letting him believe he'd have the chance to seize you and carry you back to Philadelphia. I had to tell him you were having a baby to persuade him that I really had to see you."

"Ann! You didn't!" Sally was shocked, but at the same time she could see the humor of it. She began to laugh. Edric Wales all at once was aware of the use that had been made of him. He reddened and opened his mouth angrily, starting forward. But Moses took a firmer grip on the blunderbuss and pointed the muzzle unwaveringly at him. Edric subsided grimly and waited to see what would happen next.

"Ann," Sally cried, "you're priceless! It's too bad there are none of the American officers here now. There usually are at least a dozen or so of them, but 'tis so late at night now—— If you'll just wait a moment while I run and put on my riding things, I'll be right with you and we'll go directly over to the camp."

"You'll go with me?" cried Ann.

"But of course!" retorted Sally. "I wouldn't miss this for anything. What's more, they know me at the outposts, and we'll have less trouble getting through than you would alone."

Ann glanced at Edric Wales.

"What will we do with——" She nodded in his direction.

"Oh, him!" cried Sally negligently. "Let him stay here. Moses will keep a good watch over him, and when we get to the camp Colonel Hamilton will send a detachment out for him. We can't let him go back, of course. He might do some harm to your people."

"That's so," said Ann slowly. She hadn't thought much about going back before now.

She pondered that problem while Sally went to make herself ready, and when the older girl returned they took once more to the mounts that Ann and Edric had come on, and rode off, leaving Wales slouched sulkily in a great chair by the fireside, brooding on the injustice of his lot and the perfidy of women, under the watchful eye of old Moses.

As they approached the camp Ann was glad that Sally had suggested she come along, for she was recognized by the officer in command at each post, and they were never questioned but were passed along swiftly and without delay. It was near midnight when they came at length to Washington's headquarters, but the place was still alive with activity, and it did not look as if these men ever slept. Colonel Hamilton, the general's aide, looking fresh and dapper and sharp-nosed, met them affably, and when he learned Ann's mission he took them directly in to the general himself.

That was the point at which Ann began to feel quaky at the stomach for fear he would not look upon the word she had brought with as much gravity as she did. But the tall man smiled at her kindly and offered her a chair and encouraged her to tell her story. She began breathlessly with the biggest thing she had to tell—the news of the projected raid—and at mention of Bordentown the general looked suddenly grave and attentive.

"Headquarters of the Navy Board, do you say?" he demanded. "Madam, you've done us a service, indeed, to come and warn us. Not only are there supplies and stores and the Board itself there, but all of the ships of the fleet that were forced to fly from Philadelphia are tied up in the river. They could destroy the whole lot at one swoop!"

"Thank heaven I came!" cried Ann.

"Thank God you did, ma'am!" he corrected her gravely. "Fortunately, since this is a naval matter, there is a naval officer in camp now, passing through on his way southward. Just a moment."

He rose and went to the door and spoke through it to one of his aides. When he was done he came back to his table.

"I've sent for him," he said. "Now then?"

Ann went on. When she came to the part about how she had tricked Edric Wales into passing her through the lines Washington threw back his head and laughed.

"And this Wales is out at Mistress Bingham's house now under guard?" he asked.

"If you call Moses a guard, General," Sally put in.

"We must not ask too much of Moses." Washington smiled. "With your permission, ma'am, I'll send a detail out for him."

"I had hoped you would, General," Sally Bingham replied.

General Washington smiled his approval and summoned Colonel Hamilton and gave him orders to send a platoon to Mistress Bingham's house to pick up the prisoner who was being held there.

"It will be done at once, sir," the colonel assured him. "And, Your Excellency, the lieutenant is waiting."

"Oh yes!" said Washington. "Send him in, will you?"

The colonel went out, and General Washington turned back to Ann. She was resuming her story when the door opened once again, and she uttered a little cry of astonishment and delight at sight of the naval officer who entered.

"Joshua!"

"Ann!" Joshua cried.

In the next instant they met in the middle of the room and were in one another's arms. Neither Sally Bingham nor General Washington himself made any difference to them then. Sally smothered her smile with her hand, and the general covered his decorously with his fingertips. After a proper interval he coughed gently.

"Ahemmm! I see you—know one another?"

Ann and Joshua started apart guiltily, both blushing to the roots of the hair, but Joshua clung to Ann's hand even as he answered.

"We do, indeed, sir! You see—I—that is, we——"

"I see," replied Washington dryly. "I don't suppose Mistress Bedford had any idea that you might be here?"

"Oh, please, sir!" Ann cried. "I did not! I never thought it once. I haven't known where he was since Philadelphia fell. Oh, you must believe——"

"I do!" Washington smiled. "Put yourself at ease, my dear. I understand. But unfortunately this is a matter of rather important official business. I think perhaps, Lieutenant, you'd best hear the thing from Mistress Bedford's own lips."

Once again Ann found herself forced to repeat her story. When she had finished Joshua looked grave.

"Edric Wales fetched you?" he demanded.

Ann nodded.

"You know this Wales?" Washington asked.

"I know him for a traitor and a scoundrel, sir," Joshua told him.

"Excellent!" Washington smiled. "Then we've two counts against him and two witnesses. He sounds to me like prime fodder for the Simsbury Mines! But what about this proposed raid the enemy will make tomorrow night, Lieutenant? Can your people take care of that?"

Joshua frowned thoughtfully.

"As a matter of fact, sir, they're pretty well drawn down to a skeleton force by now. I can turn back, of course, and will, if need be. But I don't know just how much good such a small handful would do! Now if you could spare a small reinforcement——"

"A regiment? Two?"

"Two ought to do it, sir," Joshua replied almost unhappily, no doubt at having to call on the Army for aid. But the circumstances offered no choice. "Unless Foote's dragoons have been increased in strength——"

"They've not." Washington smiled. "Very well then! We'll send the troops along. Perhaps 'twill give the British something more to think about than they bargained for. At least 'twill shake up their livers a little. Suppose we make this a family party, eh? I'll detach Smallwood's Maryland Line and Cresap's riflemen to the duty. That ought to take care of 'em!"

"Thank you, sir," Joshua replied. "I'm sure the Navy Board will be grateful, and I know Mr. Morris will be. How many of my own men should I take along?"

"You've other duties to attend to, you young Mohock!" Washington laughed. "I want you to get those men and supplies down to Baltimore so that the *Virginia* can get to sea and to action. Just let me have a couple of your marines to act as guides, and you can go on your way."

"Thank you, sir," said Joshua again, with something like relief. It was not that he wanted to avoid a fight, but he knew the delays the ship had encountered already and he dreaded any excuse for more.

General Washington leaned back in his chair.

"There, then!" he exclaimed. " 'Tis all settled! Now I daresay you young folks will have things to say to one another——"

"Oh, but I'm not finished!" Ann cried out.

"There's more?" Washington looked at her in surprise.

"Indeed there is, sir!" she replied. "I've made all these notes, and I thought you might find something useful in these copies of the London *News Letter!*"

She reached in the pocket of her riding cape and drew out the papers in question and laid them on his table. Over her shoulder Joshua could not help seeing the sheet that lay on the top of the pile. It was an old *News Letter,* bearing a date line late in September, and prominent in the middle of it was the very notice that Dr. Franklin had pointed out to his nephew. He stared it.

"Th—the *Lexington*—lost!" he muttered.

"What's the matter, Lieutenant?" General Washington demanded. He glanced at the stack of papers. "Is this it? What—did you know someone aboard?"

"I did, sir," Joshua replied dully. "I did indeed."

7. *Tomorrow We Die*

To SAY that Joshua was shocked by the sudden revelation of such tragic news would be to put it far too mildly. It is hardly surprising that he heard little more of that interview, or at least he remembered little of it after, although he naturally rode back to the Willing house with Ann and Sally and gratefully accepted Sally's invitation to spend the night. Only when they were alone at last, however, did he explain fully the terrific impact of the little news item to Ann. As he did so she gazed at him compassionately.

"Oh, Joshua!" she cried. "Oh, my poor love! If I had realized what news I was bringing to you I would never have picked up those papers."

"That does not matter." He gestured almost impatiently. "Better that I should learn it now, since 'tis a fact. But that I should have to learn it at all is what hurts most—that, and that I shall have to tell Barbary. God! How I hate to think what this will do to her!"

Ann stared at him.

"Poor Barbary!" she exclaimed.

"Aye, poor Barbary," he echoed.

She reached over to him then, taking one of his hands in hers, and with her other hand turned his face toward hers earnestly.

"Joshua, my sweet, listen to me," she said. "Let me tell you something we all know—all of us, that is, in Philadelphia. Those reports that are printed in the English *Letters*—they're exaggerated half the time, just for the effect they may have upon us."

"Is that true?" He looked up at her heavily.

She nodded emphatically. She did not know anything of the sort, but she was acting from instinct. She could see what this was doing to him, and she felt that only so could she hold out a tiny crumb of hope. It seemed to her like the right thing to do.

"Of course I know, darling," she told him. "I wouldn't believe that thing for a minute—at least not until I had more official confirmation from our own side. There's no doubt, of course, that the *Lexington* has been captured. They could hardly lie about such a thing as that. But that all of her officers were killed—— Why, 'tis ridiculous on the face of it!"

He seemed half convinced. Yet his shoulders sagged again.

"I'll have to tell Barbary, still."

"If you feel that you must, my dearest," she conceded. "But if you do, be sure and tell her, too, what I have said. I'm sure I'm right, Joshua. 'Tis better than an even chance your friend Kenny still lives!"

So she lifted his spirit more by the force of her love than by logic, and he went on the next morning with a far lighter heart.

Before he left, however, he had the satisfaction of knowing that Ann herself was safe. It was Sally who broached the scheme at the breakfast table.

"Of course you can't go back, Ann!" she cried. "In the first place, we forgot to take the passes from Edric Wales before we left, and there's no doubt that he's destroyed them now, if only to spite you. What's more, 'tis lonely here all by myself. We'll get word to your family that you are safe and sound—there are ways, you know. And then we'll settle down and wait it out together. Aren't I right, Joshua?"

"Of course you are, Sally," he agreed emphatically. "You usually are, and certainly I can think of no one who'd be better company for Ann."

And so it was left. They said a tender farewell, feeling a little better, both of them, for all the poignancy of the moment, for having seen one another. After that Joshua gathered up his command and, after detaching the two marines to guide the Maryland troops back to Bordentown, took up his route again.

But in Baltimore all his old worries and apprehensions came back upon him. There was Barbary still to be faced. He turned over his men and supplies to Captain Nicholson and delivered his orders with none of the enthusiasm he had anticipated when Morris had given them to him. As soon as he was able he went ashore again and climbed up to the house on Federal Hill, where Barbary greeted him with a good cheer that hurt. At least they were alone for the moment, for his mother was down at Callie's.

"Joshua!" cried Barbary with a flash of her old spirit. "It's good to see you back again!"

"I wonder," said Joshua dolefully.

"What do you mean?" She showed her apprehension. "You've heard something!"

"Aye!" He nodded grimly. "Look, child, these things aren't needfully so, but I came back by way of Valley Forge, where I saw Ann and a copy of the London *News Letter*. There was a piece in it about the *Lexington*—she's been lost."

"Lost!" She stared at him, aghast.

"Aye, lost!" he repeated. "Robert Morris had no news of her when I went up. But there was this *News Letter* that—that General Washington had, and I saw. It said the *Lexington* had been captured, and —and all the officers in her killed!"

He was saying it badly and he knew it, but he did not know how else to put it. Her hands came up to her mouth, and for an instant she could not speak. Then she cried out in protest:

"No! Oh, Joshua! No! No! No! It can't be! 'Tis not so! Joshua, you're not saying this——"

"I'm not just saying it!" he replied grimly, hating it but feeling that he must tell her what he had read. "'Tis what the *Letter* said. . . ."

"Oh no! Oh God, no!" she cried again.

"Look, Barbary," he exclaimed, accepting Ann's argument without even being aware whence it came. "Look, child. Half the time these reports in the British *News Letters* are printed just for a stab at us! Half the time they're not true——"

"But—but Kenny, he——" she cried.

"Yes, yes, I know," he replied, almost impatiently. "But 'tis a fact, still, they exaggerate the reports. The *Lexington* has been captured, no doubt. But 'tis not likely that all of her officers are dead. In fact, I'd remind you that we've had no report that Kenny was killed except the enemy's, and if I were you I'd wait for something more before I made up my mind."

She stared at him dumbly.

"Thank you, Joshua," she said finally. "Thank you. I—I'll try. But still——"

"I—I wonder if he ever got my letter," he mused, and added irrelevantly, "The *Virginia'll* be sailing soon!"

But in that, too, he was mistaken. It is true that in January the frigate stood down the bay. But near the mouth of the York she caught sight of the *Emerald,* 36, patrolling the narrow waters and fled all the way back to the sanctuary of Baltimore. There she lay for three full months more, while Captain Nicholson frittered and fussed, and Joshua fumed and swore. At last he could bear it no longer. He sent a long letter to Robert Morris, leaving out no detail of the state of affairs, and the next post rider fetched back such peremptory orders for sea that not even James Nicholson dared refuse.

But the sea-borne career of the *Virginia,* in American service, at least, was both brief and sorry. They shipped a pilot before they ran down the bay; a knowing man, reputedly of some courage. The night they slipped toward the capes was dark and favoring. But evidently their pilot's reputation had been exaggerated, and the lights of the British patrol frigates, the *Emerald* and the *Otter* and the *Solebay,* prowled uncomfortably close. Joshua was forward on the fo'c'sle some time after midnight, ready for the whispered word from aft to shake out the forward courses, and the salt sea air from outside the capes was already beginning to blow fresh. But all at once there was a sudden grinding jolt that knocked him and his men into the scuppers. When they rose it was to find the pilot had put them squarely across the Middle Ground!

With the wind behind them, driving them forward, and the tide running swift astern, they lurched on over the shoals, crashing on bottom at intervals, and even before the frightened whisper came slipping forward Joshua knew from the sound that they had been hurt. Timbers could not rend that way and nothing part. The quartermaster, sent by Captain Nicholson from astern, loomed in the dark at his elbow.

"She's torn away her rudder, sir!"

At the same instant the bos'n showed in the gloom.

"I think she's over, sir! Th' lead shows deeper water under th' forefoot."

"She's still not to be handled without a rudder!" Joshua retorted bitterly. "Let go the anchors, Mr. Breen. We'll have to see what can be done."

There wasn't much. The *Virginia* swung to her anchors under the race of the tide, while Joshua and a crew of men went over the stern. But the damage was severe, and when the gray dawn sent wispy fingers through the shredded mists of the night the frigate still lay helpless and nakedly revealed to all three of the British vessels.

Hopeless as the situation seemed, Joshua was amazed to come round the counter and over the side just in time to see Captain Nicholson's head disappearing hastily on the other. He bounded across the deck and stared down. The captain's gig, fully manned, with the pilot aboard and Captain Nicholson just settling himself in the stern sheets, was just pulling away from the side.

"What the devil?" barked Joshua.

Nicholson's face turned up toward him in a bland heart-shaped smile.

"Sorry, m'boy. Desperate situation! Important papers!" His voice came drifting back across the widening space. "Got t' save 'em! Hard lines, lad! Do what you can for th' ship!"

IV

Stars to Steer By

"If thou," he answered, "follow but
Thy star, thou canst not miss at last
A glorious Haven!"

DANTE

1. Old Mill

As HE let the halyards run swiftly through his fingers and gathered the tattered flag of the *Lexington* in his arms, Kenny Boyle tasted the sour bile of defeat. Often, in times past, it was true, he had known bitterness and despair, misery and desolation and heartache. But never before had he felt that here was an end of all things. Always there had been something ahead.

But this was something else. This combined and overshadowed all the rest. There was the finality of death in the blood on the decks and in the shattered spars and torn rigging. There was bondage before those of them that had survived the engagement with the *Alert;* a bondage from which they could neither buy nor work their freedom. There was no hope of snatching any victory from this defeat. Something more than his own little hopes and plans and schemes lay in ashes about him now, and he was vaguely, distressedly aware of it. This was the end for the *Lexington,* and he could not escape the feeling that it might as well be for him.

That he was premature in his judgment might be perfectly true. Nevertheless, the fact remains that that was the way he felt, and that his feeling was to a greater or lesser extent shared by his shipmates was apparent in their glum faces; in the despair with which they watched the cocky young midshipman from the *Alert* swarm over the side at the head of the prize crew. They gave themselves over to utter gloom, while the cutter, all but prancing with pride at having subdued such a formidable enemy, convoyed them in to Plymouth and brought them to anchor under the Hoe.

The reports circulated by the British press, of course, were grossly exaggerated. The *Lexington's* losses were severe—seven killed and eleven wounded—but they were far from those claimed. And there was no question of the bitter, wounding experience they were still to undergo before they were allowed the grim luxury of a prisoner's anonymity.

There were as yet few facilities in England for the accommodation of prisoners of war. Indeed, the Crown and the King's officers refused to recognize that there was a war. Since the beginning the American commissioners in Paris had been endeavoring to negotiate an agreement for the exchange of captives. But every attempt had been met with arrogance and rebuff. Lord Stormont, the British Ambassador at Versailles, had been goaded by Dr. Franklin into replying to him—but only barely replying—in a curt, unsigned note, that: "The King's Ambassador receives no applications from rebels but when they come to implore His Majesty's mercy!" And this attitude received the blessing of a ministry that presumed to call itself civilized.

The prisoners from the *Lexington* underwent a trial, of course—or the mockery of one. On their arrival in Plymouth they were herded off to the courtroom, where the learned prosecutors hurled legal mumbo-jumbo at them; and their responses, confused though they were, were impatiently interrupted. When the farce was done and they were judged guilty of the crime of "High Treason on His Majesty's Seas," they were sentenced to confinement, at the "Gracious Pleasure of His Majesty," in grim old Mill Prison, and were then marched off under heavy guard to the gloomy, gray-stone walled keep and locked away.

Old Mill, as it was called, lay not far outside of Plymouth. For as long as anyone then living could remember, it had been used primarily for the detention of military prisoners. It consisted of two walls encircling a fairly extensive inner courtyard partially paved with stone cobbles and divided into two sections, each containing an identical set of dreary gray-stone prison buildings. Guards patrolled the outer walls and occasionally made the rounds of the inner enclosures. There was a guard at the outer gate and one at the inner, which Kenny never saw opened, though the market woman and folk from the town with goods to trade were permitted to come that far at stated intervals and offer their wares through the grille. Access to the prison itself, in the main, was by way of a passage between the guard officer's office and the guardroom. But there was only casual contact between the prisoners and the watch.

In the space between the walls were the quarters of the officer in charge and the barracks of the regiment at the moment assigned to guard. "Light duty," it was called, but the men to whom it fell had another name for it. Inside the yard the prisoners were left pretty much to themselves. Twice a day they were fed, and twice a day a lackadaisical roll was called. If a prisoner proved unduly fractious—and fractiousness was left to the definition of the officer in charge—or escaped and was brought back, or otherwise was caught in a breach of the prison rules, he was confined in the solitary cells—the "Black

Hole," it was called—where there was not room to stand erect and where a man was ironed in total blackness on half rations and left to the merciless attacks of the vermin. Regular rations consisted of three quarters of a pound of beef, a pound of bread, a quart of small beer, and some slimy cabbage every other day.

The main complaint was that the food allowed was either rotten or insufficient to maintain life, and the firstcomers, such as Kenny, were fortunate to find grass growing in the yard and a few old bones lying about in the dirt. The former they picked and the latter they pounded, and both they boiled together in a stew that afforded a measure of bulk, if nothing else. Later comers had to be content to pick the snails out of their cold holes in the dank walls and make a nauseous broth of them—a trick they learned from their French allies; although once a stray dog squeezed his way in at the gate and ended his days in a comparatively tasty ragout.

Such were the conditions in which Kenny now found himself and his companions hurled. Bad as they were, there were yet worse aspects to them. The filth and horror and vileness of the physical conditions a man might endure. But, as has been hinted, there was yet no possibility of exchange, for the simple reason that, in European waters, at least, the Crown refused to admit that a state of war existed. The prisoners who might be taken by Americans abroad, as in the case of the *Reprisal's* and the *Lexington's* raid into the Irish Sea, must either be sent all the way home for imprisonment, or released. They could not be lodged in French jails, for the French were not yet at war with England, and any prisoners sent in to their ports to be held would be released anyway.

On the other hand, Yankees who were captured were regarded as treasonable subjects of the Crown; and as Lord Stormont had indicated, no brief was held for them unless they turned coat and crawled for mercy. In America, where actual fighting was in progress and British prisoners could expect like treatment to that given the Americans they took, there was a variety of procedure, depending generally upon the whim of the capturing commander. As in Joshua's case, it might be of the utmost leniency. An officer's word might be accepted and he would be sent home on parole to await his release, with the simple understanding that his pledged word not to bear arms against the Crown until he was relieved of his promise was sufficient as between gentlemen. Or—and this was far more usual—his name would be placed upon a list of those made prisoners and exchanged for a similar list on the other side. Each side then made up a list of those of like rank, and these would then be traded off, so to speak, by formal cartel. But since there were no British prisoners in Europe to be exchanged or to petition the home government for relief from their unbearable conditions, those Americans who were taken there could not look forward to release until the end of hostilities—if, indeed, then. That was something that depended upon who won the war.

Their best chance—and the possibility seemed remote, Kenny had to admit, when he considered it in the light of all evidence—was that France would enter the struggle. In that case, French jails would be opened to receive British prisoners, and in order that their lot—which certainly would be no better than the Americans'—might be relieved, the home government would then be forced, surely, to take measures for a system of exchange.

Under such circumstances it is hardly extraordinary that Kenny and his companions entered the Old Mill with a certain sense of dullness and despair. There were a few exceptions to that rule. Captain Johnson, who had been imprisoned in England before and knew that escape was not impossible, tried to be a tower of strength to his companions—talking to them always of the possibility, laying plans, thinking up new, devious arrangements. Dick Dale took his cue from Captain Johnson. Thankworthy Hand, the gunner's mate, was determined to escape, and Zebulon Varnum, the sergeant of marines, was eager to take part in some plan.

It was Dale who discovered the possibility. The old paving stones in the rear courtyard, some two by three feet square, were loose—loose enough to be lifted by the bare fingers; and underneath them the ground was soft enough to work—with spoons, with tin cups, with odd bits of iron they might pick up here and there.

It was he who gave them the idea and brought them into a plan. After that they went to work, one at a time, digging a tunnel aimed to pass under the two walls at the back, while the rest of them stood watch for any possible round of the guards and to take the dirt as it was dug out and dispose of it.

That was more of a problem than it might seem on the surface. Certainly the guards could not be allowed to see anything suspicious. Some tried eating the stuff. But that did not work well, for they became promptly ill, and the amount they could so dispose of in any case was negligible. Some tried putting it in their laundry bags, but that was discovered, and all work on the project had to stop for weeks while the alarm died down. After that they dropped it by handfuls down the privies, so that it was carried off by the wash of the sewers. Another way that some discovered was to make off with a pocketful of earth and grind it underfoot between some stones far removed from where they were working.

Under such circumstances it was hardly surprising that the thing should take such a long time. They entered the Old Mill in October of 1777, but it was June of '78 before the tunnel idea was conceived, and late autumn of the same year before it was finally thought out in detail and put through.

In the meantime there was many an up and down, many a rumor as to what was happening, although there was no real news that was of encouragement to them. Their guards made gleefully sure that they were told of the fall of Philadelphia; and the Battle of Monmouth, on their lips, became a great British victory. But nothing whatever was said of the defeat of Burgoyne at Saratoga, or of Howe's evacuation of Philadelphia after an occupation of less than a year. Nor were they told anything of the relinquishment of command by the brothers Howe, or of the exploits of the *Ranger* in the Irish Sea. Only by rumor did they learn anything of those events, and then they feared to trust the reports. Indeed, it was only some months after their own incarceration, when the northeast sector of the double inner enclosure was locked off against them and the first French prisoners of war were marched into it, that they learned of the Franco-American alliance.

As sympathetic as they felt toward their fellow prisoners, nevertheless that was a heartening event, for there was no question but that it hastened the day when there would be some chance of exchange. Of course a whole new crop of rumors began at once to circulate like wildfire; an agreement of exchange had been reached, a cartel was already on its way from France to England, lists had been exchanged and names drawn, this one was on it—that one was not!

But it was a long time, really, before there were any concrete results such as they dared hope for or dreamed about. For a few weeks their morale soared, then dropped again to new lows of despond. In the meantime, work on the tunnel went forward, often as little as ten inches or a foot a day. Yet slowly, surely, the shaft drove daily closer to liberty and escape.

Ironically enough, when the day finally did come to break through and make their mass scramble for freedom, Kenny was not among them. He was in the Black Hole.

Naturally, none of them at work on the project could foretell with certainty just when the thing would be done. Nor could they, when at last they did come out upon the moors, just beyond the outer wall, risk discovery by waiting for the release of one of their number from solitary confinement. When Kenny, in a fit of exasperated fury, flung his bowl of an especially viscid and disgusting mess of slops in the face of the sergeant of the guard as he made his rounds, he had known what the consequences must be. A sudden angry impulse alone had moved him, and discretion failed to hold his hand. As a result, when five days after that event the tunnelers broke through onto the starlit brush of the hillside beyond the prison, they felt that it would have been sheer insanity on their part to delay their own escape on his account. And, as a matter of fact, Kenny himself would have been among the first to agree with them.

As it happened, in a sense, his confinement at that time was a blessing in rather wry disguise. Dick Dale and Henry Johnson and nearly sixty others seized the occasion to slip through the hole and escape. But of the lot, not more than half a dozen, all told, succeeded in eluding the pursuit that followed. Henry Johnson, Thankworthy Hand, Zebulon Varnum, Lucius Crowe, Ansell Malone, and Jerusha Payne, it is true, seemed to disappear as if the earth itself had swallowed them up—as, in a way, it had. But all the rest were fetched back and tried and found guilty of "Treason through His Majesty's Earth" and sentenced to sixty days in the Black Hole. Among the last to be brought in, not a whit abashed or repressed by the fact that he had been taken when he had his very foot upon the deck of the vessel that would carry him to Holland and safety, was Dick Dale.

So the attempted escape, at least so far as Kenny and Dale and most of the rest of them were concerned, ended in fiasco. Another opportunity did not present itself for a long time, although Dick Dale swore vehemently that somehow, someway, he would find a way out.

So far as Kenny was concerned, that scarcely mattered, except that to a considerable extent Dale's enthusiasm and determination helped see him through a particularly despondent period. Being Irish, and given to fits of moodiness, he was at first inclined to brood over the fact that the attempt at escape should have come at a time when he could not take part in it. That was his luck, he allowed himself to think in his moments of blackest despair, and, Irish-like, he told himself over and over in the darkness of the dank nights that now he would never see Barbary again; she would never know the strength of his love for her or the sureness of his feeling that he could convince her if only he could get to her side once more.

But that feeling eased a little with time, especially as he watched those who had escaped brought in one by one. The despair remained, it is true. But he could feel that at least he had not set his foot on the very threshold of freedom only to be snatched back. The winter passed amid that gloomy conviction and despond, and he grew thin and hollow-eyed, sunken-cheeked.

Just when he began to feel it, he could not say, but sometime in the spring the conviction began to grow upon him that he would not be much longer there. Curiously enough, it was not a morbid thought, but one that was real and alive with hope. The thought of escape, however, seemed to leave him more than ever cold. He had had one experience with that possibility, and somehow, now, he wanted no more of it. Rather the thing that excited him was the possibility of exchange.

Why that should have been is inexplicable. All through the winter and spring the rumors of an agreement between the American commissioners in Paris and the officers of the Crown had flown thick and fast. But none of them had ever proved grounded. Indeed, if anything, the men came to look upon them as a sort of standing joke, and when at last they were turned out and lined up in the prison yard, none of them gave any serious thought to the possibility that it might at last be actually true. Rather, they thought that some one of their number had committed a breach of prison rules and the authorities were taking this means of finding out who was to blame. Colonel MacCampbell himself was there with a long list of names in his hand, and there was an unusually heavy file of guards stationed about at various points, as if to prevent any outbreak.

When they had been called to heel, Colonel MacCampbell lifted the paper in his hands and began to call off what might have been a roll, except that it hit upon certain names only and gave the rank to go with each.

"Aarons—second lieutenant?"

"Here!"

"Arthur—gunner's mate?"

"Yo!"

"Aspinwall—first lieutenant?"

"Here, sir!"

(There was a subdued sound of booing at that. Colonel Mac-Campbell stopped reading and waited coldly until it was done.)

"Barker—yeoman?"

"Here!"

"Beale—ordinary seaman?"

"Here!"

"Blake—armorer?"

"Here!"

"Boyle—sailing master?"

Kenny's voice caught in his throat, and for an instant he could not speak. Could this be it?

"H-here!" he managed to gasp at length.

Colonel MacCampbell went on reading imperturbably down through the list until more than a hundred names had been called. When he came to the last he closed the roll of paper with a snap. Dale's name was not called.

"You men who have answered to your names," he commanded, "go fetch your dunnage and assemble here in twenty minutes. You have been chosen for exchange."

That was all. Kenny almost fainted as they broke ranks and raced for the last time toward the grim gray-stone barracks. How he fumblingly managed to find his hammock in that yelling, laughing, howling mob of men and make up his meager sack of belongings, he never knew. All that he was conscious of was that her name kept running through his brain in an endless refrain—"Barbary! Barbary! Barbary!" In an hour, perhaps less than that, he would be a free man again, at last. He would be walking aboard the cartel ship that must be waiting in the harbor, and feeling the slight heave and fall of her deck beneath him as she lay at anchor. Best of all he would be going home; this time beyond any question! Home again to lay his heart at her feet. And nothing, he was determined—nothing would stop him now.

That was on July 3, 1779.

2. Of Prison Hulks . . .

As JOSHUA BARNEY leaned upon the quarter rail and waited glumly for the enemy to come and get them, he could not help reflecting bitterly that it was not for nothing that the day should be called "All Fools' Day."

It had been his suggestion that they make one last, desperate try at escape. The wind was set smartly out of the west-northwest. Even rudderless as they were, he pointed out, if they could slip their cables and spread their wings to run full before it, they might, with luck, put the *Virginia* aground on Cape Henry and burn her there, escaping ashore themselves over the bows. But the other officers overrode him. The captain was gone. The rule now should be by the majority, they cried. And the majority pointed out that as the tide set, running strongly out through the rips between the capes, even if they risked piling her on Cape Henry Shoals, the *Virginia* might well miss the bar, and then they would all be carried out, helpless, to sea.

The seamen, seeing Joshua overruled by his fellow officers, took matters into their own hands and sought indulgence in one last fling before they all became prisoners, as they so obviously must. They broke into the rum casks shipped for the voyage, and long before the British boarding boats arrived, more than half of them were dead drunk and rolling in the scuppers. It was a shocking, disheartening thing, the disgrace of which Joshua felt keenly. But the only thing he could do was sadly to gather up all of the *Virginia's* signal books and codes and secret orders—items which, despite his plea of "important papers" as an excuse for so shamefully abandoning his command, James Nicholson had overlooked entirely—and weight them and drop them over the side.

So Joshua became a prisoner again, well before he was able to wet down his new commission with good salt sea water. At that time Kenny had been more than six months in the Old Mill, and it would be better than a year yet before he was to be exchanged. But Joshua knew nothing of that.

The officers and men from the *Virginia* were first distributed among the three British patrol frigates, where they were held for a time, until the big fourth-rate *Saint Albans*, 64, could come bumbling up from the southward for New York. They were all crowded aboard her, then, and carried northward. It was not long after the first of May when the *Saint Albans* finally cast anchor in the Upper Bay and set her prisoners ashore upon the Battery. The day was warm and springlike, and the air was balmy. The birds were twittering in the trees and singing in the shrubbery as the prisoners were marched, more than three hundred of them, under a guard of Hessian soldiers, up through the narrow, crowded, ill-smelling streets to the Old Sugar House Prison. Joshua's heart sank at the sight of those grim, dank walls. But it sank still further when, as senior officer present, he was the first to be herded into the presence of the provost marshal for recording and assignment.

There were several men in the room—a sergeant of the guard and two armed privates by the door. In the center there was a plain, rather grimy deal table, on either side of which stood another pair of guards, and two more lounged at the back of the room.

But it was the man who sat at the table, with an inkwell, a quill pen, and several sheets of foolscap, who caught and held Joshua's eye. He was a big man; a very untidy man with a red face and red-brown hair caught in a slovenly queue at the back of his neck. His mouth was slack and hung half open, as if he found it an effort to breathe, and there were large stains of food and drink, both upon his rusty-brown velvet coat and his red waistcoat.

He was evidently preparing to enter this new lot of prisoners in his records when Joshua was fetched in. He looked up, and his face turned an even brighter, ruddier red at sight of the American. His slack jowls quivered a little—jowls that he had acquired in the years since Joshua had seen him last. His nose twitched as if in anticipation, and the hard blue eyes, like bulbous little marbles, pale and cold, gleamed wickedly. He flung down his quill and washed one huge, grubby paw upon the other in an unctuous, unforgotten gesture.

"Damme eyes!" he cried. "If 'tain't me young friend—leave me see now—Barney, ain't it—Joshua Barney? Yes, be th' hooves o' th' holy sow! That's it, or me own name ain't William Cunnin'ham, an' I ain't provost marshal o' this damned rebel stinkpot! Aye! Sure I remember ye, Mr. Barney. I ought t'! I've been seein' ye long enough in me bad dreams for't! Now damme, 'twill be my turn!"

"Well, get it over with!" growled Joshua. "I've been too long in the same room with you for my own taste!"

The sergeant of the guard swung about and stared with something like awe at the man who would dare to speak so to the provost. As he caught Joshua's eye he tried to give him a look of warning. But Cunningham seemed in a rare good humor.

"Have ye now?" he demanded. "Ah, me little Yankee canary! Ye'll be warblin' a different tune from behind th' bars when ye find th' cage I'll be puttin' ye in! What'd ye say yer rank was?"

"I didn't say," retorted Joshua. "But if you must know, 'tis first lieutenant, late of the *Virginia*."

Cunningham leered.

"Give up without s'much as a spit in yer eye, I hear," he taunted —and wrote: "Josh. Barny, 1st Lieut. *Virginia—Good Hope*."

"All right, Switzer!" Cunningham flung down the quill again and barked at the sergeant. "There's th' first fer th' hulks! Take him away, an' set him aboard th' *Good Hope*."

The sergeant looked aghast.

"But, sir!" he dared to protest. "Him—an officer? In th' *Good Hope?*"

"Be damned t' ye, Switzer!" Cunningham roared, and the sergeant winced. "Ye heard me! Officer?" He spat. "Pah! He's naught but a damned rebel dog. Now be gettin' him th' Jasus out o' here, an' do as I tell ye!"

The *Good Hope*, to which Joshua had been assigned, proved to be a huge old former fourth-rate, one of several honorably retired men-of-war assigned to the duty and anchored at various points about the city, and without question it was one of the largest and oldest and vilest and most overcrowded and most verminous of them all. She lay in the North River, a little above the upper end of the town, resting on the mud flats off the marshy barren of Lispenard's Meadows, and as they were rowed out to her he could see even yet a shadow of the ancient dignity that must have been hers.

She had been stripped down, of course, to the bare skeleton of what she had once been. All that remained of her yards and rigging were the long bowsprit, the jack staff, and a stump of the mainmast, used now for a derrick with which to hoist supplies aboard. The gun ports had been boarded up, and fresh openings, about two feet square and stoutly barred, had replaced them. Permanent gangways had been rigged to receive prisoners and afford access for the guards and more official visitors. But in spite of these indignities the old lines remained. Joshua wondered, as they approached, what ghosts of older days were still aboard.

It was when they drew near, however, and passed around close under her counter in order to approach the proper gangway that Joshua realized no self-respecting ghost could have stayed for more than a moment without shuddering off to limbo, a broken and completely shattered shape. The stench was stomach-racking even before they were aboard, and he could imagine what it must be in those fetid holds. Yet there was something familiar about it. It was only when he started up the gangway, however, that he realized how reminiscent it was of the odor he had noticed about the *Dolphin*.

But if the smell seemed bad from below, it was as sweet as a summer breeze compared with the foul stench that rushed up to greet them as they were herded to the hatchways. There the guards gave them no opportunity to hesitate and retch, but thrust them below without ceremony. As they came down into the gloomy bowels of the ship in the half-light of the 'tween decks, where there was hardly room to stand erect, the men who were already there, skinny, wispy, whiskered wretches in foul rags, greeted each newcomer with jeers and hoots of derision.

"Ah, sweet Christ! Not more!" wailed one.

"Three hundred more, to tell you true," Joshua replied.

"Oh no, merciful Lord!" the man whispered. "There's more'n two hundred o' us now! Where'll we put 'em?"

As soon as the last of them had been crammed inside, the hatch gratings were slammed shut and the heavy bars and locks applied. Joshua thought that would be all, but no! When that was done the ship's boats, in which they had been fetched from shore, were brought on board and stowed over the grilles, so that but for the half dozen tiny barred openings on either side—and how much smaller they looked from the inside than the out!—there was literally no way for those imprisoned within to obtain fresh air.

It was amazing to Joshua that any of them should survive, and yet this was the mere beginning of things for him. Sometimes he wondered if it would have made any difference if the upper decks were laid wide open from stem to stern. Death walked among them constantly, and in the gloom of the lower decks a boy's or an old man's body might often lie for days, until it began to putrefy and bloat, before the fact of death was discovered. To be sure, the guards came around once a day to bellow down the gratings:

"Up, rebels! Turn out yer bloody dead!"

But they never allowed time for a search into the darker corners, nor gave more than a moment or two for such known bodies as there were to be passed up. By such means they hoped to avoid the trouble of too great burial details upon the mud flats ashore.

Nor were their facilities for cleanliness more impressive, unless it be considered that they were impressive for their inadequacy. Only two heads were allowed for all the prisoners, and these were often so foul and choked up that they overflowed. Those who could not fight their way to them perforce must yield obedience to nature where they were. As a result the decks were constantly fouled underfoot, and only once a day were they allowed any opportunity to police the mess. At that time but two moth-eaten mops and half a dozen inadequate buckets were passed down to them, and they were allowed fifteen minutes in which to do the work. Water they must find for themselves, and since they had no way to come at it, there was none save what they were able to provide. To make matters worse, when the task was done as well as it could be, the buckets were hauled aloft and emptied over the side, to lie in the shallow mud flats amid the puddled waters there until another tide could carry it a little away. When mess time came around these very waters over the side were drawn up in huge kettles and used to boil the viscid, crawling slops that the prisoners were served.

For nearly two and a half months Joshua remanied aboard the *Good Hope,* and it speaks well for his wiry constitution that he withstood the ordeal as well as he did. At first his companions were inclined to resent him, for he was the only officer so confined, and perhaps in the first shock of despond he was inclined to ignore their rather pointed sullenness and calculated insults. But as he began to grow more accustomed to his surroundings and instinctively came to realize that his own survival and theirs depended upon making the most of things, the very qualities that had made him an officer in the first place began to assert themselves. Before long he was recognized as the leader among them and certainly as much a friend as any of them had in that crowded, stinking, floating hell.

As a matter of fact, if a man had any qualities of leadership at all, he could not stay long in that foul spot without being moved by his very compassion to do what he could for his fellow sufferers. God knew there was not a great deal that Joshua could do, but certainly he did all he could. He organized details to see that all had an equal opportunity to gasp a few breaths of fresh air at the little grilled windows and that the strong among them did not stay there all day. He set aside a tiny portion of the deck to serve as a sick bay, where those who were feeblest among them might have a little more room to lie and a little more tender care from their mates. He set up other details to receive and dole out fairly the rancid water and thin gruel that was passed down to them daily, by that means preventing the waste of half of it upon the decks through spilling in the scramble for it. He set one squad to search the dark corners of the prison deck every morning before the guards' warning shout for the dead. Others he detailed to take turns with the mops and buckets and do as smart a chore of policing the narrow space as could be. He even set up a sort of rough captain's mast, at which offenders against public peace and private morals were tried and given summary punishment.

In Joshua's eyes it was not much, but he took a certain pride and satisfaction in the achievement. Certainly the *Good Hope* benefited; and although he was unaware of it, Joshua himself was learning much that would presently stand him in good stead. It was toward the end of July when all at once, one late afternoon, the ship seemed to explode abruptly into a great pother and bustle of excitement. Pipes could be heard twittering, guards' feet running. And then astonishingly the gratings were ripped off the hatches and the guards' voices came almost frightenedly down to them.

"All right, rebels! Up now! Look alive! Muster on deck!"

For most it was the first taste of good fresh air and the first visit above since they had been fetched aboard. But as they were herded into some semblance of ranked order it was easy to see the reason for the sudden event. As they watched a barge carrying the burgee of a vice-admiral drew smartly in to the landing stage, and a blocky, ruddy little man, Vice-Admiral Gambier himself, who had but lately come on station to relieve Admiral Howe in the command, stepped out. As he saw him, Joshua thought to himself somewhat wryly that they had probably been called topside because the commander of the prison ship did not dare allow the admiral to see for himself the conditions below.

But the ruddy-faced old sea dog's lowering eye and grim expression, as he came bustling up the accommodation ladder, seemed to indicate that he had a pretty good idea of just what those conditions might be. He ignored the half-pay captain's welcoming salute and scowled upon the man.

"'Twas my understanding, sir, that ye kept prisoners o' war aboard this vessel!" he thundered.

"We—we do, sir!" the captain gulped.

"Then what d'ye mean by keepin' 'em as if they were hogs?" the admiral blared. But the visit turned out to be something more than one of routine inspection. Admiral Gambier spun from the hangdog look of the commanding officer and scowled down grimly at the assembled prisoners in the waist. "I'm told there is an officer among ye! If so, will he step forward and name himself and rank!"

Automatically Joshua moved out a pace.

"Joshua Barney, first lieutenant, late of the United States frigate *Virginia*, sir," he said.

"Hrrmph!" the admiral snorted, glaring down at Joshua for an instant. Then he swung abruptly toward the gangway. "Harummmph! Goddamned outrage, by God, putting an officer aboard this pest ship! Come with me, Mr. Barney!"

Joshua hesitated. He wanted no favors. The pride he felt at what little he had been able to accomplish for his comrades drew him closer to them and deadened his own urgent desires for more comfortable billets ashore.

"Sir, I'm not sure——" he began.

The testy old admiral whirled on him.

"I'm not asking ye, sir! I'm ordering ye!"

He turned and went down the gangway without a backward glance, like a man accustomed to being obeyed. Joshua glanced about him once more, almost defiantly. He was enough of a rebel himself to resent such an approach, and he might have refused, but two of the guards moved forward threateningly, and it was obvious that he had no choice. With a shrug he followed the admiral down the ladder, with the wry thought that it was doubtless the first time they had ever had to drive a prisoner off the *Good Hope*. At the stage the admiral sat in the stern sheets of his barge, and there was a vacant seat beside him.

"Sit here, Mr. Barney," he commanded gruffly. "I want a word with you."

Nevertheless, it was not until they were well away toward the towering *Ardent*, 64, anchored in the Lower Bay, in which the admiral carried his flag, that the old sea dog turned to the ragged lieutenant at his elbow and spoke.

"Now then, Mr. Barney! Now we can breathe easily once more, I want ye to know that I consider it a damnable breach o' the courtesy o' war that ye were ever confined aboard yonder——"

"Sir, I——" Joshua tried again.

"Yes, yes, yes, yes, I know!" the old admiral interrupted him testily. "Ye were about to say that ye sought no favors at my hands and that ye felt ye might do better for your own people aboard the *Good Hope*."

"Exactly, sir," said Joshua stiffly.

"Well, then, ye're wrong, Mr. Barney," the admiral snorted, "for ye can do 'em far more good if ye've quarters aboard my own ship and full charge o' their treatment in all the hulks—not just th' *Good Hope*."

"Sir?" said Joshua, not believing his ears.

"If I must explain it to ye in simple language, Mr. Barney," the admiral snapped, "th' fact is, I've had a look around at one or two o' our hulks here, and 'tis my opinion that th' condition o' th' treatment o' naval prisoners on this station is a stink in th' nostrils o' His Majesty's Navy, an' I propose to do something about it!"

Joshua stared at him unbelievingly.

"Is it permissible for me to say that you are a rare man, Admiral?" he demanded.

"Harrrrummmph!" snorted Admiral Gambier. "Don't mislead yourself, Mr. Barney. I am appointing ye only in part t' make up for th' treatment ye have had at our hands. I have two better reasons—th' first is a slap at my own officers so that they will know—and feel, by God!—my disapproval of their conduct; th' second, because I can think of no one better qualified than yourself, who has been a prisoner aboard one of th' ships and knows th' conditions t' be met at first hand!"

"Thank you, sir—I'll—I'll do my best," Joshua promised.

"Oh, don't fear, Mr. Barney," the admiral growled. "Ye'll be called on t' pay for every privilege ye receive—in work! Ye'll have quarters aboard th' *Ardent*, and th' run o' th' city, as ye like. But I'll ask your parole while you have th' duty, an' I'll expect results! However, ye may expect th' fullest co-operation from me. Anything ye may suggest, short o' issuing each one o' 'em lace panties or turnin' th' lot o' 'em free, will have my consideration an' will probably be granted. But I warn ye! I'll look for definite improvement by my next inspection trip—an' I'll not tell ye when that will be! Now come aboard an' let Captain Turner assign ye to quarters. When ye're washed up an' shipshape, come aft an' sup with me. I'll have a further word with ye on this business."

Joshua may have gone aboard the flagship looking like a scarecrow in rags. And it would be foolish to say that he was not aware of the incongruity of one in his condition stepping aboard the flagship with the admiral himself, to full honors, and never a smile on the wooden faces of the side boys or guards. But he walked on air, and there is the truth, for the berth into which he had just fallen, prisoner still or no, was just such as he had often lulled himself to sleep with at night amid the horrid, noxious stinks of the *Good Hope*. Many a time in the small hours he had dreamed of what he would do if he were in such a post—and here it was, handed to him!

3. And Privateers

As a matter of fact, Joshua was almost disappointed when in the fall the word of his exchange came through and he was released from his parole and given passage through the line.

Actually, of course, he was far from displeased. Yet it is true that he knew a twinge of regret at having to leave a work which he knew was bearing results. Since he had assumed the duty in July he had accomplished a good deal, it seemed to him. He had called upon Admiral Gambier to remove the jurisdiction of naval prisoners from the hands of the provost marshal, who was actually an army appointee, and thus, at one swoop, had eliminated many of the evils of the existing system. For Joshua knew well enough that the rotten provisions, the foul conditions, the bad water, the poverty of the guards, and even the hulks themselves were in a great measure Cunningham's fault. The funds had been provided to allow as reasonably decent accommodations for the prisoners as could be expected, and had only half of it been applied to the purposes for which it was earmarked the men would have had a running chance to survive. But Cunningham strove to pocket all.

Naturally, since the man was under the protection of the Howes and the Lorings, the matter could not be further pursued. But once the thing was done, Joshua had found his way far easier. And he had been able to laugh in Cunningham's face when they met upon the street—which almost gave the burly Irishman a stroke. With Cunningham out of the way Joshua had been able to ease the crowding through the assignment of further hulks. He had been able to have the guards increased so that no single one of them was called upon to do more than he could. He introduced special policing and mess periods and saw to it that every man aboard every hulk had at least one opportunity a day to reach the deck above and take at least some exercise. Gruesome as it might seem, it was at his suggestion that the prisoners themselves were assigned to the burial details. Although there were not so many dead as there were formerly, there were bound to be some. These were now properly interred, deeply enough set so that neither stray dogs nor gnawing crabs nor scavenging gulls nor uncovering tides could violate them. And the prisoners who were assigned the chore, although they grumbled, found beneficial exercise in wielding a pick and shovel.

But the two greatest feathers in Joshua's cap had been the assignment of an especial hulk to serve as a hospital ship for those sick and wounded, and the establishment of a reasonable and fair system of exchange, so that every man had his own good chance and none was slighted. As a result, by the time he left, the number of naval prisoners had been reduced by exchanges from nearly twenty-five hundred to not much more than five hundred.

In short, he knew that he had done as well as could be expected, considering both the time and the means at his disposal. It was plain, too, that Admiral Gambier also recognized it, from the sincerity of his farewell.

"A lucky day for you, me lad!" he growled. "But I'm not so sure 'tis such a lucky one for myself! God bless you and take care o' you, an' have a thought once in a while that we're not all dogs—we Englishmen, eh?"

The thing that gave him most pause at parting was the thought that he was not sure how long all this would continue when he was gone.

Not that such considerations delayed him when it finally came time to take his leave. He shaped his course directly to Philadelphia, which, he had learned only after his rescue by Admiral Gambier, had been evacuated by the British and returned to American hands and was once again the capital. Within two days of his release he was knocking at Gunning Bedford's door. In the next instant the door was opening and Ann herself, lovelier than ever, it seemed to him, was flying into his arms.

"Joshua! Oh, Joshua!" she was crying. "Ever since we heard of the *Virginia's* loss we've been worried about you! Though we knew none of her people were killed, still we've wondered what had happened to you and where you were and—and——"

"Ann! My Ann!" He laughed and held her close. "I've lain awake with the thought of you next to my heart and the warmth of you in my arms and known that, whatever came, I'd have to find my way back to you, one way or another. God knows I couldn't live without you!"

"Why, burn me! If 'tis not Joshua Barney!" cried Gunning Bedford's voice in the hall behind Ann. "Did I intrude? Forgive me. Come in, lad. This house has not seen the sun shine since you were taken, our Ann has worn that long a face. Dear God, you'd think the world had ended!"

"Didn't it?" said Joshua seriously, and Ann laughed while her father chuckled.

"Well, come in anyway! We've missed you."

The evening was a merry one, no question of that. It was only natural that Ann and Joshua should be in a gay mood. Both had stories to tell of all they had been through since they had last seen one another, and Ann's cousin, Gunning Junior, from Delaware, had come north on a visit. His inevitably cheerful humor, as always, never failed to brighten the occasion. But they were glad when the others withdrew discreetly to the upstairs parlor and left them alone. Ann came back into his arms then, and for a time they were content just to sit silently together, feeling comfort in one another's presence. It was Joshua who broke the spell. He sighed heavily.

"D'you know, Ann," he said, "I've been thinking we've made a mistake all along."

She stared at him.

"Joshua, what do you mean?"

"I mean"—he smiled at her—"that we should have been married at once—as soon as we met, right here in Philadelphia. Ah, Ann darling. I was ready for it from our very first meeting out at the Morrises, but I was too stiff-necked to admit it."

"I don't know how you could have loved me after that!" She blushed at the memory.

"Why not?" Joshua demanded. "How were you to know that I was not exactly what you thought me? And in that case you did exactly as I would have wanted you to do."

She looked down at her hands.

"It—it would have been a comfort, at least," she admitted, "to have had that—that sureness of one another, even though we would have been apart so much of the time."

"Aye!" He nodded. "Think of all the trouble and heartache we'd have saved."

She looked at him adoringly.

"But all that's over and done, Joshua," she reminded him. "Let's think of now. I want you to know that I feel it, too, and that I'm ready. We can be married any time—any time you say. Tomorrow, if you like. And after that there won't be any more of this waiting and hoping and yearning——"

She blushed as she said it, but she did so proudly, and with her head up.

"There's just one thing!" In his own turn he flushed crimson at what he had to say. "When we met I had enough for both of us. But in New York, just as anywhere, a prisoner must keep himself in decencies, unless he's to make do with the usual slops that are doled out to him. When he's placed on parole and given privileges, including quarters on the admiral's ship, there are a good many obligations that go with it. 'Tis not cheap, Ann sweet, and the fact is, the long drag of it has cost me every penny I had!"

"Joshua!" She turned to him impulsively. "Don't you know that 'tis yourself I love, not what you have now or may have someday? I don't care if you haven't two cents to rub together! I'd marry you if you were a pauper, if you'd say the word."

He smiled at her and drew her to him, caressing her hair tenderly.

"I know, love," he told her gently. "But we have to be a little bit practical about it. Right now, as much as I want to be married to you, I've neither money nor a job. What would we live on? No, no! Let me see Bob Morris in the morning. He'll have a berth for me, I'm sure. And as soon as he hands me orders—or at the most, as soon as I've made one voyage—there'll be as much as we need to go ahead on."

But Robert Morris, it seemed, did not share that feeling. He greeted his young friend warmly enough, to be sure, and expressed his delight at seeing him free again. But when it came to a ship, he looked grave.

"The devil!" he exclaimed grimly. "I wish I could help."

"You—you mean there's nothing?" Joshua stared at him as if a life preserver at which he had clutched had failed him.

"Things have changed a good deal." Morris shook his head somberly. "For one thing, the French are in it now——"

"What's that got to do with it?"

"A lot!" Morris replied. "Do you mind what I told you some time back about what would happen to the Navy if that came about? Things have turned out much as I predicted."

"The fools!" Joshua cried hotly. "Can't Congress see what it's doing? Still, if you've not been able to convince 'em, I don't suppose there's any use in my talking."

"The truth is"—Morris shook his head—"we've damned little Navy left! Most of the ships we had, built or building, have been lost— the *Alfred*, the *Columbus*, the *Congress*, the *Montgomery*, and the *Virginia*—but I needn't tell you about her! The *Cabot* went aground and was captured off Nova Scotia. The *Reprisal*, lost at sea with all hands! The *Lexington*, captured in European waters——"

"Have you heard aught of her people, by the way?" Joshua looked up quickly.

"Only that the report published by the British was false," Morris replied. "You saw that. Boyle's name was not given to us in the list of either killed or wounded. My guess is that he's a captive, along with the rest, and that we'll be hearing from him before long."

"That's something, anyway!" Joshua said somberly. "What ships have we left in the Navy—or have we any?"

"Well, of course I can't be sure what's been commissioned abroad." Morris smiled grimly. "I understand Jones is to have a ship, under commission from Dr. Franklin. From this side—let's see! The *Ranger, Providence*, and *Boston* were all in European waters at last reports. *Raleigh's* at sea, under Barry. Right now there are the *Warren* and the *Deane* fitting at Boston, and the *Alliance* fitting in the Merrimac—and that's all!"

"What's the matter with one of those?" Joshua demanded.

"Oh God, is there no telling the man?" Morris flung up his hands to the ceiling. "Look, lad! Men, yes! Men we'll take where we can get 'em! Men are hard to come by! We have to lure 'em into the service by any means, fair or foul, for they'd a damn sight rather serve in a privateer, and we've them to compete with. But officers, now! There's a different matter. I have five hundred lieutenants alone, and you're but one. Five hundred men who come crying to me daily for berths—and how many have I to fill, presently commissioned and on this side of the water? Twelve—count 'em! Naturally every one of those is filled. Would you think it fair of me to turn one of those men out of his berth so that you would have work?"

"What d'you suggest I do then?" Joshua demanded.

Morris shook his head glumly.

" 'Tis not an easy problem you face, lad," he said, "and well I know it. You must remember, 'tis partly my own doing." He grinned. "I'll promise you this: One day we will have other ships in commission, and as fast as the berths come up I'll bear you in mind for the best of them, in keeping with your abilities and rank. In the meantime, I'll give you the same advice I've given a hundred others. With the situation as it is, we've no objection to a man finding private employment. An officer like yourself, with a reputation for grit and a fighting heart, should have no trouble finding a berth in a privateer——"

Joshua stared at him.

"There's the last advice I ever expected to hear from you," he said harshly. "Me, a naval officer who's devoted his heart and his soul to the service of his country! Me who's always held against privateers and maintained they did the service a hardship! I'll admit the chances for profit in them are greater, and if it were Kenny Boyle who sat now where I'm sitting, he might take more kindly to it. He always favored the game, and I can understand why. He'd everything to gain and naught to lose——"

"You're overwrought, Joshua," Morris told him shortly, "or you'd not make a remark like that."

"Perhaps so, sir," Joshua replied somberly. "But I tell you, I never thought to hear the suggestion on your lips—not for myself, in any case."

"In any case!" retorted Morris dryly. His patience was growing a little short. "A man must eat! Don't close the door entirely. Think it over! See what Ann has to say about it. And let me know what you decide."

"I will, sir," Joshua promised, but there was little conviction in his tone.

Joshua returned to Ann's house, a different man from the cocky lad who went away that morning. He told her the story of his interview dispiritedly.

"There's the situation," he said glumly. "I never thought he'd advise me so."

"You didn't tell him right out that you'd take whatever you could?" She stared at him.

"Look, Ann!" he cried. "I don't even think I'd mind shipping before the mast—if they'd let me. But a privateer——"

She grew a little angry herself.

"Joshua Barney!" she cried. "I don't believe you care enough for me to care whether we are married or not——"

"Ann!" He was aghast and sorely hurt. "How can you say that? Are you, too——"

"Joshua, my own love!" She softened toward him a little. "Perhaps I shouldn't have said that. I know you want to marry me. And God knows I want to be married to you! I—I ache all over sometimes with the want of it! But that isn't why I would advise you to take what you can—in a privateer or anything. I know you, Joshua. Sometimes I think I know you better than you know yourself, and I know how miserable you'd be fretting away your time ashore. There's nothing you can do here to serve the cause we all put first. There's nothing to be had in the Navy. Then accept a berth in a privateer until there is! That way, you'll at least be doing what you can. You'll be striking at them where you can strike—and you'll be winning back some of that proud sense of self-respect that I love so much about you. I'll wait for you, Joshua, my sweet. Never worry about that. If it takes forever, I'll be right here—and waiting till you come back."

He looked at her with a new light in his eye, almost as if he really saw her now for the first time since he had come back.

"Ann!" he cried. "Ann darling! I—you've seemed to straighten things out for me. I—I think I see things more clearly now. 'Tis a disappointment, aye! I'll not deny it. But what you've said is true."

"Oh, Joshua!" she cried, looking suddenly happy again for him. "I knew you'd see it so when you got over your first bitterness. I'm sure you'll not find it so hard an experience once you've resigned yourself to it. You'll tell Uncle Bob?"

He laughed and caught her to him, kissing her roughly.

"I declare, ma'am," he cried, "I almost think you want to get rid of me. Yes, I'll stop at his office and tell him first thing in the morning. But I must go to Baltimore before I can take anything, for 'tis only right I should let them know I'm back in the land of the living."

He was as good as his word. As soon as he took his leave of her the next morning he called again upon the naval committeeman. Morris grinned at him.

"I'd a notion Ann would put a little sense into that stubborn head!" He chuckled. "So you've decided to come round to it?"

"'Tis better than rotting ashore." Joshua nodded. "And perhaps we'll be able to do something."

"I daresay," Morris agreed dryly. "I tell you what—there are a couple of privateers and letters of marque that I know of that might fill your bill. Suppose I drop a line to their commanders. If they've anything open, I'll ask 'em to get in touch with you, eh? No promises now, mind you, and I'll name no names. But I'll guarantee you'll be satisfied if anything comes of it. What do you say?"

"I'd say thanks to you, sir, a thousand times over!" Joshua grinned back at him. "Anything that you may put in my way I'll be sure is to be relied on, and I'll be grateful to you for it."

The journey to Baltimore was as rough as usual, but the greeting he found at home made up for it. Mary Barney, aged with the passage of time, folded him in her arms and cried over him, called him her "baby," and made much of him. Barbary was equally demonstrative and seemed quite gay and cheerful now that he was home again. He wondered at that but had to wait until they had a moment alone to ask her about it.

"You seem almighty happy, young lady," he exclaimed. "Have *you* had some word from Kenny that the rest of us have not?"

She shook her head.

"I was just going to ask you if you had heard anything."

"I don't understand." He was puzzled. "Why this cheer, then? Last time I saw you, you were pretty glum—remember?"

She nodded.

"I—I heard from your Ann, Joshua. She wrote to me, such a good—good heartening letter. It helped me over a bad time, and now, I guess, I've caught her spirit, for I feel that he's alive. I know it, Joshua, I just know it!"

He smiled at her. It was like Ann not to tell him that she had written to his sister; to leave it for him to find out.

"Well, miss!" he teased her. "Just to give that feeling of yours a little something to feed itself on, there's been no actual direct news of him, or where he is. But the lists are in, and we do know that he was not among the killed or wounded. Robert Morris believes that he is probably a prisoner somewhere and that we should be hearing from him soon."

He did not add his own grim thought; that the life of a prisoner of war was oftentimes precarious at best. That he knew from his own experience.

"Oh, Joshua!" she cried, her eyes shining.

But at that moment they were interrupted by the knocker and found Sam Smith come to call.

The war had done Sam good in many ways, Joshua thought as they shook hands. He was leaner, straighter, more purposeful, for all he still retained a good deal of his old diffidence. He had commanded at Fort Mifflin in the Delaware and had taken a ball in the leg there, a shattering one that had put him out of the running so far as any further soldiering was concerned. Consequently he had returned home to don sober civilian clothes and take charge of his father's business and become one of the town's most eligible bachelors; although, as always in the past, he seemed to have neither eyes nor heart for anyone but Barbary.

Joshua was not sure he cared for that. But Sam did not stay long when he found Barbary occupied. He made much of Joshua's return from captivity and then took his leave. When he was gone Joshua taxed his sister with it.

"Pooh!" cried Barbary. "You needn't worry. You know where my heart has gone. And after all, I can't tell Sam never to come around here again. He is persistent, you know."

Joshua nodded and decided that it was probably all right.

"Just don't let his persistence carry you away," he growled.

"No fear—now!" She laughed.

It was a day or two after that when they were interrupted again, just at suppertime, by the sudden appearance of Joshua's old commander, Isaiah Robinson. Joshua whooped.

"Ike!" he cried. "Come in! Here, let me take your things and have another place set out for supper. You'll take pot luck with us and stay the night?"

"I don't know as I dare." Robinson grinned, bowing to Mary Barney and Barbary. "I wan't exactly warmly welcomed last time I looked in here."

Barbary flushed.

"That's all forgotten now, Captain Robinson," she said, "and forgiven—and I hope you'll find it in your heart to forgive us."

"Could any man not?" demanded Robinson gallantly. "Ah, Joshua, 'tis a pity Kevin Boyle is not here now to make things complete."

"Aye, it is!" Joshua glanced quickly at Barbary, and Robinson did not miss his look.

"Damme!" he cried. "Have I put my foot in it again?"

"Not exactly." Joshua grinned at him. "You heard he was missing?"

"Aye, taken in th' *Lexington*, I'm told." Robinson nodded.

"Well, you see," Joshua explained, despite Barbary's furious shake of the head, "he and Barbary, here——"

"No!" exclaimed Ike Robinson in surprise. "Why, then, damme double! We must find him, and that's sure!"

Joshua looked at him sharply. He did not miss Robinson's "we," and he knew Ike well enough to know that he was not a man to hint idly at things. However, there was no time to ask what he meant just then, for Cassie called them all to supper. As they settled themselves at the table Joshua glanced across quizzically at the lean lieutenant on the other side.

"And what brings you to Baltimore, Ike?" he demanded.

"Yourself!" retorted Robinson laconically.

"Me?" cried Joshua in genuine surprise now.

"Aye," Robinson told him gravely. "Mr. Morris writes me from Philadelphia that you're on the beach——"

"And you've a ship?" Joshua cried, his eyes gleaming.

"Such as she is." Robinson shrugged. "Right now she ain't such a hell—excuse me, ma'am!—such a much of a vessel, but she's sound and has good possibilities. Her rigging's a bit on the worn side, and she's got one of the damnedest—ma'am, I must ask your pardon again!—one of the—the—the doggonedest collections of guns aboard you ever did see! I'll bet there ain't two of them the same caliber. But as I say, she's a sound bottom, and we sail direct for Bordeaux with tobacco, to refit and rearm. If ye'll sail with me, I've a place for a first luff, and I'll be glad to see that you share and share alike with myself in any prizes we might take."

"I'll not take that, Ike!" cried Joshua. "But I'll take the berth! All I ask is the usual share, and I'd not think of cutting into your own."

"Done!" cried Robinson.

"Done!" retorted Joshua, and lifted his glass.

They drank, letting the good red wine seal the bargain.

"By the way," said Joshua as they put their glasses down, "what's her name?"

"She's the *General Mercer,* loading now at Alexandria," Robinson told him.

"Then here's to the *General Mercer!*" Joshua cried, refilling their glasses and lifting his again.

4. *The Commodore*

KENNY BOYLE'S RELEASE from Mill Prison and exchange came early in July, 1779. But it was only when he could feel the solid planks of the cartel ship that had come for them from France, and the slight heave and tug of her as she lay to her cables, that he could be sure that all of this was not just a dream. When that moment came at last he all but fell down upon his knees and kissed the timbers. He was free at last! He was exchanged and going home to America; to America and Barbary.

But that there were some who had other plans was evident. There was a short man on the quarter-deck alongside the lean French captain—beside whom he seemed roly-poly. His stomach was round, and his face was red as an apple, but with a New England severity around the mouth. He wore an enormous old-fashioned curly peruke, and on top of that his great three-cornered hat looked a little ridiculous.

This man stayed by the captain until they were well clear of Plymouth Sound. Then he came down among the released, none too savory-smelling prisoners and passed, smiling bleakly, from group to group, offering a few words here and there, nodding, and passing on. Kenny was alone by the rail when he came up and paused.

"What's your name?" he asked.

"Boyle!" Kenny told him shortly. "What's yours?"

If the little man was put out he did not let on.

"John Adams," he said. "I'm one of the commissioners."

"Yer servant, sir!" Kenny bowed his apology stiffly.

Adams acknowledged the gesture with a curt nod.

"You were sailing master aboard the *Lexington?*"

"I was that!"

"Hmmm!" mused Adams. "The frigate *Alliance,* Captain Landais, is in France and has need for a man of your qualifications."

"Will she be sailin' for America?" Kenny eyed him.

"I believe she'll be operating in these waters for some time."

"Thanks t' yerself, sir!" Kenny laughed. "I've been a long time away from home. There'll be those that think me dead. I must be gettin' back to 'em at all speed."

"I'll be glad to send word to anyone you name of your survival— or pass on any other message," Adams suggested.

"Me thanks again, sir," Kenny replied. "This is a thing I can be doin' only meself."

"Ah?" Adams raised precise eyebrows. "Well! Think about it, young man, and let me remind you, this is no time to be worrying about ourselves."

He moved on to the next group. Kenny stared after him. Cursed old goat! he thought to himself, but it seemed to him that a little of the sharp, brisk brightness had gone from the day.

The cartel landed them at Nantes. As he waited his turn to go down the gangway Kenny caught Adams's eye, and in response to the little round man's one lifted eyebrow shook his head. Damn the fellow, he thought. He was making it accursedly hard. He felt a twinge of conscience. But he put that behind him. It was two years, he reminded himself, since he had seen Barbary. In that time he had made one good cruise and spent months in prison. He had earned the right to go home, and he was going! From that he would not allow himself to be diverted.

But Adams, it seemed, was but the first of a gantlet he had to run. He had scarcely left his sea bag at the sign of La Corunne and descended to the taproom, where he proposed to indulge in the luxury of a good toddy, when he was accosted by a short man; a wiry man in a blue coat with red facings and a captain's epaulets. The man's face was sharp and thin and weathered, and his eyes were wide-spaced and quick. Kenny could not recall having seen him before. His hair was sandy and his nose pointed but lifted in a definite tilt, while his mouth was level and thin-lipped, with little lines at the corners that hinted at a certain wry humor.

"Mr. Boyle?"

"Yer servant, Captain!"

"Captain Jones of the *Bonhomme Richard*," the man introduced himself. "May I have a word with you?"

"As many——" Kenny began. But at that instant a stout, oily Frenchman came bustling up and thrust himself between them.

"M'sieu Boyle!" he cried. "*Le concierge* have point you out to me.

You wish a ship? I have the very one—a fine privateer, which lies now at Bordeaux! Ah! I tell to you, of the most magnificent she is——"

Captain Jones rounded upon him.

"Damn you, Giroux!" he cried. "How dare you interrupt when you see I am talking to this gentleman?"

He swung around again to Kenny.

"Mr. Boyle! I'm most damnably hard up for men myself——"

"Gentlemen! Gentlemen!" Kenny threw up his hand. "'Tis obvious ye know who I am——"

"But certain!" the Frenchman cried. "You are the great Kevin Boyle who was sailing master in the *Lexington*. You have but just land from the cartel ship."

Kenny gave him a sour look.

"Y'are but part right!" he exclaimed. "I'm not after bein' 'great' an' I'm but just turned out o' prison! I've an appetite that's as great as both yer ships combined. I can't be thinkin' till I've supped. If ye'll be excusin' me, gentlemen——"

Captain Jones laughed and seized one arm. Giroux, not to be lost so easily, took the other.

"To be sure!" cried Jones. "We can talk while we eat—and then the choice be yours!"

Between them they led him down the street to a fine little tavern, where Kenny, with his mouth watering, called for one of the enormous lobsters for which that coast is famous and washed it down with a fine muscadet.

"M'sieu!" cried Giroux, not to be second in the talking. "This ship of which I say—such a vessel you have never seen! Two hundred and sixty tons burden an' all found, new-rigged an' new-armed. In Bordeaux she has taken on the new gun—twenty six- an' twelve-pounder, with powder an' shot for burn!"

"Aye!" growled Jones. "'Tis ready enough for privateers with cash! But let a public man-o'-war seek credit, and there's none to be had!"

Kenny, chewing, glanced at him, remembering abruptly his own experience in the *Lexington*. He looked back at the Frenchman.

"Who commands?" he demanded.

"Ah, this I cannot tell! I do not know his name, this *capitaine*." Giroux shrugged. "But a very fire-eat, so I am assure. Already in the voyage out he has taken two prize an' have fight the running battle with an English privateer. In the reward for these you will share! An' she loads now at Bordeaux for Philadelphia in America. Myself, I am agent for her owners at this place."

"What's her name?" Kenny demanded.

"The *General Mercer* she is called," the Frenchman told him.

The name meant nothing to Kenny. He glanced at Jones.

"And yourself, Captain?" he asked. "We've heard little of your side of the story."

John Paul Jones smiled bleakly.

"I've little enough to offer against that, God knows," he replied. "But as I have said to you, Mr. Boyle, I'm damnably hard up for men. I've combed every port between Antwerp and the Gironde, and little enough to show for my efforts I've found, I'll tell you! I've an old East Indiaman, 42, commissioned by Dr. Franklin and named for him the *Bonhomme Richard*. There'll be six or seven of us in the squadron, the American *Alliance*, commanded by Captain Landais, a French frigate or two, and as many privateers as we can gather to our midst. I can't offer you anything like M'sieu Giroux here. The pay will be as usual, and the prize money will be—well, as you know, prize money, this side of the water, is always uncertain. We'll be taking a dangerous mission—cruising in British waters, with all the home fleet against us. And there you are! 'Tis as honest as I can be. I can't do more than appeal to your own sense of patriotism."

Kenny tossed his napkin on the table thoughtfully. The ship that Giroux had offered was exactly the sort of thing he had in mind. At heart he had always been a privateersman. There was the way to get rich—quick prizes and a fat share. And, what was more, he would be sailing home to Barbary if he signed in her. What Jones suggested was exactly what he had told himself over and over again he did not want—danger, more service abroad, and at the least the prospect of a much longer time before ever he could come home again; if not, indeed, the probability of being caught and sent back to an English prison.

There should be no doubt whatever in his mind as to which he would choose, and yet there was. He could not bring himself to say either "yes" to the Frenchman or "no" to Captain Jones.

"I must have time to think, gentlemen."

"As much as you like!" cried Giroux.

"An hour?" said Jones.

Kenny glanced at him. That remark told him as much as anything the captain had said of his desperate need.

He left them then and walked down by the river, staring out with unseeing eyes at Port Fluvial. The moon rode high, with a fleecy lace of clouds scudding across its face, casting a sheen upon the waters of the Loire. From downstream came a faint breeze, and with it the tang of the sea. Kenny, as he sniffed it, pondered. The decision should not be difficult. On the one hand the *General Mercer* waited in Bordeaux. If he went in her he would be home in a few months, and they might have the luck to pick up a few prizes on the way, in addition to those in which he would share if he signed aboard her now. On the other hand there was Captain Jones and the *Bonhomme Richard*. If he listened to him and signed for the cruise, even if they won through, it would certainly be months before he could sail for home.

Yet he lifted his face to the night and the light wind, and pondered. As he glanced up at the moon riding through the sky like a silver race horse amid the clouds, he recalled the day—July the Fourth! Three years ago—three long, weary years of war—the Declaration of American Independence had been proclaimed. For three years they had fought and bled and many had died. Surely he had earned the right to return. He had tasted the bitter slime of defeat and known almost two years of prison. He had paid his way, and surely none could criticize him if he went home now.

And yet the independence for which they fought had not been won. Barbary lay there to the west, where the wind came from, and he yearned to see her. But America lay to the west, too, and she put her faith in the strength and courage and fighting heart of the men who struggled for her. She looked to them to win the independence she had so proudly proclaimed. What kind of man, he wondered, would he be in his own eyes to abandon that faith for his own small dreams? When independence was won and the war ended at last, America would be his—his and Barbary's; the birthright of every man, woman, and child who had helped fight her battle. That would be time enough. Then they would have won the right to reach out to one another—but then, and only then.

He turned on his heel and went back through the darkened streets, along the ringing cobbles, to the inn at the sign of La Corunne. As he pushed open the door and stepped into the smoky, dim-lit taproom, the Frenchman, Hyacinthe Giroux, bounced up from a table, full of vigor and confidence. Behind him Captain Jones rose also, more slowly, as if he had already decided and had not much hope.

"Well, M'sieu Boyle?" cried Giroux. "You have make up the mind?"

Kenny nodded to him curtly.

"I have, mounseer!" he said shortly, and turned abruptly to the captain in the background.

"If ye'll have me, sir," he said, "I'll be one man fer ye!"

5. *The Great Cruise*

KENNY was aware of an immediate sense of relief as soon as he had made his announcement. Of course he regretted bitterly the need to lay his dreams aside. But in his own conscience he felt that his first duty lay here. Now that he was free again he planned to write to Barbary at the very first opportunity. But in the meantime there was work to be done, and he flung himself into it with vigor. He signed Captain Jones's articles the next morning and then immediately proceeded to L'Orient in charge of the recruits the captain had been able to scrape together—some sixty of them—while Jones went on in search of more.

He found the little fleet lying in Groix Roads. Under the new American ensign—thirteen alternating red and white stripes with a blue field containing a circlet of thirteen white stars in the upper left-hand corner, adopted by Congress on June 14, 1777, some months before his capture in the *Lexington*—there were five men-of-war. The *Bonhomme Richard,* of course, was the flagship, in command of Captain Jones, which made him, by courtesy, at least, the commodore of the squadron. She was an ancient East Indiaman, the former *Duc de Duras,* pierced now for forty-two guns. At the moment she was undergoing repairs to her bowsprit and rigging, occasioned by a collision at sea with the *Alliance,* and it was plain to see that her timbers were old and half rotten. For anything but an emergency she was hardly to be considered as a ship of war, and, indeed, even since her conversion a number of errors had been committed by the carpenters and naval architects set to work on her, not the least grave of which was the placing of the main battery of six eighteen-pounders in the after part of the gun room, where their ports were cut so close to the water line that it was impossible to use them in any but the gentlest of seas.

The *Alliance* had none of these faults. Built at Salisbury Point in the Merrimac, she was an American frigate carrying thirty-two guns. She was, curiously enough, commanded by Captain Pierre Landais, a bombastic little Frenchman, and even though she was at the moment careened upon the sands with her crew scraping her bottom in preparation for her cruise, her rake and her lines unquestionably showed her American origin.

In addition to these two were the French ships referred to by Captain Jones; ships loaned by the French Crown, though sailing for the moment under Yankee colors. They were the frigate *Pallas,* 32, Captain Cottineau; the brigantine *Vengeance,* 12, Captain Ricot; and the cutter *Cerf,* 18, Captain Varage. Recent reinforcements, in the shape of two privateers who had indicated a desire to join the expedition, were the *Monsieur,* 40, Captain de Roberdeau, and the *Granville,* 14.

Despite their impatience, they lay six full weeks at L'Orient while they struggled to fit their ships for sea. During that time, although he fretted at the delay, Kenny had an opportunity to study his ship-mates and the commanders of the other vessels. Captains Cottineau, Varage, Ricot, and de Roberdeau seemed average enough, though with full share of their countrymen's temperament. De Roberdeau, perhaps, was a little more volatile and impetuous than the rest, yet he was honest, honorable, and no doubt courageous.

Pierre Landais, on the other hand, was a thorn in everyone's side, even those of his compatriots. He was a pompous, puffed-up, strutting little Gascon of a man; full of wind and fury, but very little else. He had a long, prominent beak of a nose, eyebrows as carefully tended as a belle's, and a pinched, petulant mouth. His dress was impeccable; his manners far from nice. He quarreled with everyone, sneered at Captain Jones, fought with Captain de Roberdeau, who could not bear the sight of his rotund little form. One would have thought that at least such a fire-eater would prove a valuable ally in a fight. Alas for that! He seemed to have neither the common sense to command his beautiful new vessel nor the ordinary stomach for battle when it came.

Fortunately Kenny had almost no contact with him. His concern, naturally, was far more with his own shipmates. In the wardroom, among the officers, he found little to excite astonishment, hetero-geneous though they were. Henry and Cutting Lunt, second lieu-tenant and master, respectively, were brothers; gaunt New Englanders and recent exchanges from Forton Prison. The third and fourth lieutenants and master's first mate were Irishmen like Kenny himself, volunteers from Walsh's Irish Regiment in the service of France: Edward Stack, Eugene McCarty, and James Gerald, the O'Kelley himself. John White, a quiet little man from Norfolk, was master's second mate, while Kenny himself was third, at the bottom of the list. Laurens Brooke had come all the way from Virginia to volunteer as surgeon; while the purser was Matthew Mease, a visiting Philadelphia merchant, who had offered himself for the post. Colonel Wiebert and Lieutenant Colonel Chamillard commanded the detachment of 137 French marines loaned for the service by the French Government. Not one of them had ever been to sea! In the steerage, the bosun, Jack Robinson, was an escapee from Portsea Gaol, as were midshipmen Nat Fanning, John Mayrant, and Tom Potter. These four had broken prison and stolen a barge, which they had *rowed* across the Channel, arriving at Nantes just in time to join.

But it was the crew itself which made Kenny gasp. Such a mixture of races and nationalities was seldom seen all at once. Scotsmen, Swedes, Norwegians, Danes, Hollanders, a handful of Irishmen, and a leavening of Americans rubbed elbows with a great many French peasants. (Captain Jones was strictly forbidden by the French Government to enlist any French seamen, although he was permitted to take on board some 186 Portuguese, Malay, and Maltese sailors who were in its service.) There was even, to top the list, one American Indian, Anthony Jeremiah by name.

Into this bubbling babel of tongues, early in August, Kenny was delighted to see John Paul Jones himself come swarming dourly over the side. And at his heels, to take post as first lieutenant, who should follow but the bright-faced, happy-go-lucky Dick Dale, who had at last made his escape from the Old Mill.

They got to sea toward the middle of August, and it was only when they did that Kenny realized, too late, that in the hurly-burly of preparation he had forgotten to write his letter to Barbary. It was not that he had forgotten her. She had been often in his thoughts and always in his heart, but never had he seemed able to find a moment in which to sit down and write a line to her. Now that they were away he consoled himself with the thought that it probably did not matter anyway. The French *Poste* was notoriously unreliable, and as for any ship sailing for home, he knew of none except the *General Mercer*. So far as she was concerned, he could scarcely ask M. Giroux to see to putting a letter aboard her for him, in view of what had happened. As a matter of fact, he was not at all sure that the *Mercer* had not already sailed. Indeed, he rather suspected that she had, for as her agent had spoken it had certainly sounded as if she were all but ready to leave on the next tide. Nevertheless, on the chance that they might fall in with some ship homeward bound in the course of their cruise, he went below and took the time to set down the words that were closest to his heart. When it was done he sealed the letter and put it away in his sea bag against the day when he might be able to send it on its way.

In these circumstances his surprise may be imagined when, at the flush of dawn one morning, not more than three days out, while Kenny himself had the deck watch, they all but ran down and brought to a strange sail. She was a fast ship, obviously, new-rigged and well armed; a privateer, from the look of her, though of what nationality it was impossible to guess. In fact, if they had not come upon her in the half-dark, just before the break of day, before she had caught sight of them, Kenny judged they would probably not have come up with her at all. Had she seen them first there was little doubt she would have taken to her heels and might easily have outsailed them all. As it was, she broached to and bristled for a fight. They could hear the twitter of the pipes aboard her and the clatter of her gun ports as they flapped open. At the same time, of course, the *Richard's* own drums rumbled to quarters, and everything was smartly cleared for action even before Captain Jones appeared on deck. As watch officer, it was for Kenny to hail--and delay action, if necessary.

"Ahoy, there!" he thundered. "What ship is that?"

There was a brief instant's hesitation across the water, and then the reply:

"What ship is *that?*"

Kenny grinned faintly in the half-light. They were sparring for time, obviously. But the squadron held the advantage by more than eight to one, in weight of metal at least. It would be better from their point of view if she did not have time to ready herself to run or fight. None of the vessels as yet, of course, showed their colors. But now the *Richard* should declare herself. Give her an honest answer and force their hand!

"This is the United States ship-of-war *Bonhomme Richard*, 42, Captain Jones!" Kenny replied, and made sign to the signalman to break out their own flag. At the same time he repeated his own question once more: "What ship is that? Answer or we fire!"

The response was prompt, almost gusty in relief, and at the same instant the bright American colors broke upon her mizzen halyards and floated on the wind.

"This is the letter of marque *General Mercer*, 20, Captain Robinson, Bordeaux for Philadelphia! Cap'n's compliments to th' commodore!"

The name meant nothing to Kenny. There were a good many Robinsons afloat. At his elbow a grimly approving voice sounded: "Smartly done, Mr. Boyle! Return him my own compliments and ask him if he'll do us the courtesy to lie to until we can put letters and dispatches for home aboard. After that, pipe the men down and ready a boat."

"Aye, aye, sir!" replied Kenny. "If ye please, sir——"

Jones was swinging away when Kenny's voice arrested him. He swung back, scowling, for he was not long on unseamanly behavior, and there were times when it did his popularity no good. He came close to being a sundowner.

"Yes, Mr. Boyle?"

"If ye please, sir," said Kenny again correctly, "with th' captain's permission, I'd like t' be puttin' a letter aboard her me own self——"

"Will you have time to write one?" Jones's brow darkened.

"Sir, 'tis ready written," Kenny told him. "I'd no time t' be sendin' it while we were in port, an' if ye'll be allowin' me now, sir, I'd like t' have it go. 'Tis important t' me that they sh'ld be knowin' that I'm alive an' free again an' where it is that I've been these two years an' more since I came away."

Jones's frown softened a little at the reminder that Kenny had voluntarily undertaken this duty when he might so easily have been homeward bound upon this very vessel they had halted.

"I'll be relieved o' th' watch by th' time th' dispatches are ready, sir." Kenny threw that in by way of extra persuasion. "There'll be time for me to go an' get it."

"Very well, Mr. Boyle." This time Jones actually smiled. "Fetch your letter and stand ready. I'll ask you to put the packet aboard her."

As the *Richard's* whaleboat swooped and lifted across the long Biscay rollers between the two ships, Kenny was conscious only of a certain satisfaction, sprung from the knowledge that at last he would be able to let Barbary know what had become of him. Whether or not she cared was a thing he would have to discover when he finally did get back. But at least she would know that he was alive and that he loved her. The *Mercer's* ladder was out when they came alongside, and he reached for it and climbed aboard. The privateer's men were smartly drawn up, prepared to receive him, the Navy's official representative. But as his head cleared the gangway and his eye fell upon the lieutenant commanding the detail, his jaw dropped and he all but fell backward into the ocean.

"Joshua!" he yelped. "Joshua Barney!"

The effect on Joshua was hardly less startling.

"What——" he began. Then: "Holy God! Kenny! Kenny Boyle! Oh Jesus! Ike! Ike Robinson, come here!"

They met in the middle of the deck then, and there was none of the usual flummery of salutes and compliments. Joshua's sword was forgotten, and for the moment Kenny's dispatches lay in limbo. They seized one another by the shoulders and shook them, then thumped each other on the back; and then, for all they were closer to the English than the French tradition, they fell into one another's arms and again thumped and pounded and bawled at each other.

"Joshua! Joshua! Ye're not dead, after all! Ye're live an' real?"

"Kenny! Ah, Kenny! Where the devil have you been all these years? Don't you know that you've had the Barneys looking half the world over for you? Ike! Ike Robinson! God damn you! To hell with your lousy quarter-deck! Come down here and see what we've got!"

Ike Robinson was not a man to stand on ceremony in such a case, fortunately. The seamen and marines of the *Mercer's* carefully drawn-up guard of honor, smart as any aboard the *Richard*, were grinning from ear to ear. Robinson came down from the quarter-deck and pumped Kenny's hand and thumped him on the back with almost as much enthusiasm as had Joshua.

"By th' Lord, 'tis good t' see ye!" he cried. "We'd all but thought ye lost! Where've ye been all this time?"

"Mill Prison, most of it!" Kenny told them.

"Mill Prison!" Robinson grinned at Joshua. "By God, we'll have news t' carry home now, eh?"

The remark was a reminder to Joshua.

"Did you get my letter?" he demanded.

"Letter?" Kenny stared at him. "What letter? I had none!"

"None? None at all?" cried Joshua. "I wrote to you! I wrote as soon as I was back, not three weeks after you'd gone. I told you about Barbary——"

"Barbary?" Kenny interrupted him eagerly.

"Aye, Barbary!" Joshua grinned. "The child has worried herself sick about you. She thinks maybe she sent you off to die, hating her—and, I'll tell you, Kenny, she thinks more of you than ever she's let on."

The deck under Kenny's feet reeled and wobbled.

"Joshua!" he cried. "Joshua—in th' name o' God, ye don't mean it?"

One of the *Mercer's* quartermasters broke in upon them apologetically:

"Excuse me, sir. Th' flagship's signalin'."

Kenny glanced toward the string of flags that had broken out upon the *Richard's* halyards and could guess instantly Captain Jones's impatience.

"I—I must be going!" he exclaimed. "But, Joshua—— Would God there was a way I could be comin' with ye. Almost, I did! I'll be tellin' ye o' that one day. But now I must be gettin' back or th' commodore'll have me before th' mast! Look, Joshua, there's a letter there—in yonder packet. 'Tis for Barbary. Will ye be seein' that she gets it? An' tell her I've not changed a bit—an' t' be waitin' for me, eh? I'll be back!"

"I'll tell her," Joshua promised, chuckling. "Be sure I will! I wish there were some way we could change places, but——"

Another set of flags broke out impatiently on the *Richard's* string. Kenny saw them and gulped.

"Now yonder's a most unreasonable impatient man!" he cried. "I must be goin'! Luck t' ye! An', Joshua, me love t' Barbary!"

The *Bonhomme Richard* and her consorts stood north-northwest after that, in the general direction of the southwest coast of Ireland, following the same route that Kenny had taken two years ago in the *Lexington*. Within an hour they had dropped the *Mercer* over the southwestern horizon. But, at least so far as Kenny was concerned, it mattered little which way they went or what they did. If John Paul Jones had chosen that moment to sail his little fleet straight into London Dock and challenge the might of England there, he would have gone along cheerfully and never questioned the prudence of it. He had seen Joshua—*her* brother! He was not dead! They had talked, and Joshua had promised to deliver his message to her. She would know now, and so long as he could not go straight to her himself he was happy enough to have it so.

But Kenny was not given long to walk among the clouds. There was the business of war to be attended, and promotion was to come to him with breath-taking suddenness. To begin the events of the cruise, on the day after they left the *Mercer* they overhauled and took a Dutchman, the *Verwagting*. Properly she was the prize of the squadron and should be duly sent in to the charge of M. le Ray de Chaumont, the representative of the French Ministry of War at Le Havre, and incidentally Dr. Franklin's landlord. Indeed, Captain Jones had already placed a prize crew aboard her under command of Mr. O'Kelley, when Captain de Roberdeau decided suddenly, and with Gallic impetuosity, that she rightly belonged to the *Monsieur*. Further, he declared that if Captain Jones would not keep hands off her he would fight for her. Rather than risk a battle among themselves, Jones let him have the prize, and when last seen both the *Monsieur* and the *Verwagting*, James Gerald O'Kelley and prize crew and all, were standing off to the eastward, in the direction of France.

A few days later they took a brigantine, the *Mayflower*, and Captain Jones immediately sent Mr. White aboard with a prize crew and sent her away at once, lest some similar fate overtake her. Then, near the Skallocks, and almost in sight of Kenny's birthplace, they set out in chase of an East Indiaman.

But the wind was light and the tide was contrary. Captain Jones sent the *Richard's* barge ahead to tow the ship out of danger. Unfortunately, the choice of oarsmen was left to the bosun's mate in charge, a disgruntled man; and, whether on purpose or not, he picked nearly all Englishmen—prisoners released from the French jails in return for their promise to serve against their own countrymen. Scarcely had this unsavory lot cleared the ship's side than they cut the hawser and pulled for the shore.

Captain Jones did not observe the event as it happened, but the sailing master, Cutting Lunt, on duty at the time, did so. He did not wait either for permission or orders, but himself ordered away a boat in pursuit, and before he could return to the ship was lost in the dense fog that came rolling in.

As a result of these three depletions in almost as many days, Kenny found himself abruptly catapulted into the post of sailing master. But this was no more than the beginning. Hardly had they lost their barge and the pursuing boat than Captain Landais made off on his own in the *Alliance*. He quarreled blatantly with Captain Jones and even dared state that only he was qualified to command such an undertaking. When Captain Jones ventured to differ with him he took matters into his own hands and departed. Next the *Cerf* took advantage of Jones's orders to search for the missing boats and vanished in the fog. A few days later the *Granville* disappeared in pursuit of a prize—and did not return.

The three ships that remained, the *Richard*, the *Pallas*, and the *Vengeance*, continued on their course and were both surprised and delighted when, in the North Channel, the *Alliance* rejoined them, though Captain Landais showed no greater inclination to subordination than ever. That was on the thirty-first of August, and for several days they held together. Then, rounding the Shetlands, the wind blew—a stout gale, but certainly not a storm—and Landais flew dispersal signals, when everyone knew there was no need for them.

Whether or not, away he went with all the prizes they had taken— some eighteen of them—to a port in Norway, as it turned out, in complete disregard of orders, and there all of the captured vessels were returned to their British owners. Indeed, the *Alliance* herself narrowly missed internment. Naturally Landais was not impatient to rejoin Jones after that.

The remnants of the little squadron, again only the *Richard*, the *Pallas*, and the *Vengeance*, kept on south, along the eastern coast of Scotland, sinking colliers, catching coasters, and hoping—but never very stoutly convinced of it—that fatter game lay just ahead.

Indeed, it is hardly extraordinary, in view of all the quarrelings and bickerings and hard luck that had been theirs, that those who remained should feel a certain disgruntlement at the results. Even Kenny was conscious of a sense of disappointment and a desire to have the thing over with as quickly as might be. It seemed to him that the whole aim, to contrive something of lasting worth to the struggle, was lost. They had taken prizes, to be sure—many of them— and they had evidently thrown British coastal shipping into something of a panic. But they had taken nothing really worth while. The gains had been small in comparison with the sacrifice. But for his surrender to a patriotic whim, he could not help feeling a little bitterly, he might even now be in Baltimore, with Barbary in his arms.

For an instant, however, it almost seemed as if all of their heart-break and trouble might be worth while. In an effort to rescue the whole expedition from complete failure Captain Jones proposed a raid upon the Scottish city of Leith; the bold seizure of the town, and the levying upon it of an enormous ransom, under penalty of being laid in ashes in retaliation for similar destruction of Falmouth and Norfolk. They sailed into the Firth of Forth, disguised as English naval vessels, and so successful was their disguise, so far as the landsmen were concerned at least, that the sleepy British home guards revealed to them the utter helplessness of Edinburgh Castle, which was supposed to guard the approaches from the sea, by sending out to them and begging a few kegs of powder with which to defend themselves against the "Yankee pirate," Jones, who was known to be in the vicinity. Indeed, the Americans had even cleared their ships for action and were in the process of heating the balls with which to fire the town in the event of its refusal to redeem itself, when their luck—almost as usual, it seemed—turned against them. The wind swung about contrary and blew a storm out of the northwest, which drove them from the very gates of the town and out of the narrow firth and off to sea. What was worse, in the course of the gale, which did the poor old *Richard's* ancient timbers no good, they were seen and recognized for what they were by British naval units, with the result that any hope of carrying out their design when the storm had blown itself out was spoiled.

So they ran, and after the gale had passed off to sea they bumbled southward, quite unaware of the furor their passing was creating ashore, nor realizing that every landowner from Scotland to the British Midlands was burying his plate and gathering up his family and fleeing to the interior.

Flamborough Head juts from the ragged coast of Yorkshire like the bend of a thumb from the palm of a hand, grim and rugged and bleak, looming above the green-tossed waters of the North Sea. A little to the northward lies the little seaport town of Scarborough, while southward, in the shelter of the hollow, lies Bridlington and its shallow bay. Not far below this again is the jut of the Spurn, with Grimsby and the Humber Mouth under it. It was off Flamborough Head that Paul Jones had long ago set the general rendezvous, in the event the squadron became separated at sea. Here the ships were to gather before swinging over toward the Holland coast and ending their voyage in the shelter of the Texel. Here, too, it was just possible, though no one considered it very probable, that the missing *Cerf* and *Alliance* might put in their appearance.

The *Richard* and her companions met there a day or two beforehand and were lucky enough, as they cruised on and off, to seize a pair of fat colliers and a merchant brigantine belonging to Sunderland, out of Holland, laden with butter and cheese and flax, and to drive yet another collier aground in the shallows below Bridlington. They hoped to catch either the Leith convoy, northbound from London, or the Baltic convoy as it came south. But their greatest prize was a pilot schooner which they were able to lure out of the Humber Mouth by resorting to their English disguises. She had aboard all her codes and secret signals, but it seemed hardly likely that they would find any use for them this late in the day.

On the night before they were to assemble they sighted and chased a strange sail ghosting through the darkness, which they overhauled and brought to. Although they showed the recognition signals agreed upon beforehand, the stranger returned but half of them, and consequently they lay gun to gun, with ports open and gunners blowing on their matches throughout the hours of dark, until the faint lightening of the dawn revealed to them the *Alliance*. Captain Landais had come down to the rendezvous in order to be able to run in with them to the Texel, and to be able to answer with his innocence and his presence any charges they might make of desertion.

6. Night of Battle

THAT was on the twenty-third of September, 1779.

At the beginning of the day even Captain Jones seemed convinced that the end was near; that the cruise was over, save for the brief journey to Holland, and that to remain longer in these waters would only be to court disaster, for surely by now their presence must be known. But until the last minute he postponed the order summoning the other captains on board for the final conference. Apparently it was in his mind to do just so and have it done with when the lookout cried that a lone brigantine was standing along inshore. From his post near the wheel Kenny could almost see the captain's thoughts pivot. One last prize, perhaps, before it was done!

The chase was a long one. The other vessel tried at first to get in under the Spurn. When she saw that was impossible she turned about and sought to double Flamborough Head. They were all hampered by lack of wind, for the day was bright, and mild, and warm—almost still. At midday, seeing that it would be impossible to escape around the point, the brigantine turned once more and made a desperate effort to find safety in the shallows of Bridlington Bay.

As she did so, a large merchantman appeared in the north, coming down around the cape. Here was a far more worthy catch, and accordingly Captain Jones put Lieutenant Lunt and a picked crew in the pilot schooner and sent her after the brigantine, while the *Richard* and her companions stood up toward this new prey. The stranger came on toward them, apparently with all the confidence of innocence, and the white sails of the schooner became a distant speck against the darker loom of the land. They were still well under the Head when Kenny saw the others, and his yell of startled surprise fetched a frown of disapproval from Jones.

"Great God, sir! Will ye look there now?"

"That will do, Mr. Boyle!"

"Look, sir!" yelled Kenny, gesturing violently north-northeast. "Yer pardon, Captain! But, Holy Mary, was ever such a sight?"

In spite of himself Jones turned and looked, and one by one other heads came up and about too. The *Richard's* people stared with a mingling of surprise and anticipation, and a little apprehension as well. Far off in the distance, almost hull down and well at sea, northeast of Flamborough Head, and on a course almost at right angles to their own, so thick that their massed sails formed a long, low-lying white cloud between the edge of the sea and the sky, was an enormous fleet. At that distance it was impossible to count them, but it was obvious that here was such a convoy as they had never dreamed of meeting. Paul Jones jerked up his glass and studied them. When he lowered it even his carefully wooden features were split in a smile.

"Gentlemen!" he barked. "There'll be work for us now!"

"Any fleet as big as that, sir"—Dale's remark was a reminder—"will be well guarded."

"Of course!" Jones shot him a glance. "Mr. Boyle! Signal the schooner to rejoin at once, and call the other vessels to general chase. When you've done that, alter course three points to starboard to intercept, and crowd on every rag! Mr. Dale, prepare for general quarters!"

When they returned to their posts Jones greeted them with a grim chuckle.

"Our luck's in at last, gentlemen, if we act smartly," he said. "There are forty-one sail in that fleet. I counted 'em!"

The sea was blue, clear, almost unruffled save for a tiny cat's-paw here and there. Actually there was barely enough wind to keep way on the cumbersome ships, and such as there was lay west-southwest. The *Richard* and her companions, at dawn, had been well offshore. But the pursuit of the two merchantmen had drawn them in close to the jutting promontory, and now they were standing northward, up the coast, when the huge concourse of sails came in sight north-northeast of them, following a course east-southeast, so that the Yankees must pass astern of them if they held their way. It was to compensate for this, and to fetch his ships on a tack to intercept, that Captain Jones had brought them about northeast by north; and it was this alteration of their direction that prevented the little schooner from returning to them. Kenny cast several apprehensive glances back toward her.

"I doubt th' schooner can catch us, sir," he reported.

"Can't wait!" Jones retorted impatiently. "Make signal to 'em, Mr. Boyle—do the best they can!"

As the two forces converged across the shimmering seas the great fleet took on form and substance. From the *Richard* they were able to pick out first the individual sails and then the hulls of the ships themselves. Their prime interest, of course, was in the convoying vessels, for if they did their duty they would interpose for the protection of their charges, and, as Dale had said, so vast a fleet was bound to be well convoyed.

It was difficult at first to make out the convoying ships, for with guns run under and ports tightly closed, they could be any of a dozen. But as they drew closer Captain Jones hazarded a guess and pointed out one large vessel, well astern of the van, that might be a two-decker, and another, smaller ship, of perhaps twenty guns, at the far forward edge of the fleet, that might be a man-of-war.

It seemed too good to be true—two warships only, and one of those of minor force. Yet, as it proved, it was a fact. For a time the fleet held majestically on its way, scarcely seeming to move in the light air. Then a gun to weatherward in the large ship spouted twice in a signal of warning to the convoy of a possible enemy in the neighborhood. At the same time a string of signal flags ran up on her halyards and burst in bright alarm. Royals and skysails blossomed on the man-of-war's yards.

At the ominous signal the convoy fell into a confusion of panic, letting fly top gallant sheets and firing off warning guns at one another, while some drove one way and some another. It was only after a long interval, while the American squadron plodded steadily toward them, that the farther, smaller vessel came round the head of the fleet, like a frantic shepherd beating in his flock, and got the last of them headed back toward the shelter of Scarborough Castle. After that the two warships stood down between their charges and the oncoming squadron, to investigate these strangers and to fight if need be, but in any case to give their frightened merchantmen a chance to reach safety. As they converged Jones studied the other two through his glass until Dale, on the deck beside him, became fidgety.

"I can't make the big one out," Jones said finally. "She's new to my book—a fourth-rate, likely. The other looks like the *Countess of Scarborough*. Plague on them! And plague on this wind! Between them they'll delay us long enough, likely, to let the entire fleet slip through our fingers!"

Kenny grinned to himself. What matter? he dared wonder—and doubtless every man aboard felt the same. If they could come to grips with a British fourth-rate and whip her in her own home waters—in very sight of the English coast—would the British ever again dare sneer at the naval strength of America? Such an event would be worth all the heartbreak and failures of the cruise.

"Mr. Boyle!" Captain Jones interrupted his musing. "Is this the best speed you can get out of this hooker?"

"I could spread me coat, sir!" Kenny grinned.

"Ummp!" grunted Jones, unamused. "Then there's no more to be asked of her. Signal the other vessels to form line of battle astern of us! Mr. Dale, beat to quarters while there's yet light. Send the midshipmen and marines to the tops, and see to it that the holds are well battened down. I'd not care to have the prisoners break free below decks. See every man to his battle station, guns loaded and 'tompkins' out, but leave the ports closed and guns run in until I give the word. We'll work as close to 'em as we can before we come to action!"

Kenny bent on the signal to the other ships, and as he did so he noticed that crawling figures were beginning to swarm on Flamborough Head, seeking points of vantage to watch what was evidently to be a spectacular fight. As was almost to be expected, the

Alliance blandly ignored the *Richard's* signal and ran down ahead of the *Pallas*.

"What in God's name is the fool doing now?" Jones raged. "Mr. Boyle! Get up the *Alliance's* signal and command her to take her place at once!"

It was past midafternoon when that signal was given, but in consequence of Captain Landais's tactics, a full hour was lost before Jones could bring the *Richard* into her proper position, with the rest of the ships behind him. In the meantime the convoy had recovered some semblance of order, and all except the two men-of-war were falling back to the shelter of Scarborough. Seeing their charges safely out of danger, the warships themselves hauled about and tacked inshore, as if they, too, were of a mind to take shelter under the guns of the castle.

Observing the movement, Captain Jones hauled the *Richard* around quickly, northwest by north, to head them off, and the timorous Landais, marking the swift maneuver and afraid, so he said later, that the English prisoners below the decks had broken out and seized the ship, drew the *Alliance* out of line and wore away to a safe distance, where he hove to and lay by to watch developments in safety.

"Burn his cowardly soul in hell!" Jones raged. "Signal him to rejoin at once, Mr. Boyle!"

"Shall we wait for him, sir?"

"Be damned to that! Hold her as she goes. Let him make use of his speed if he's of a mind to come in with us. If not, to hell with him! We'll tackle her alone!"

Already the signals had been sent to the other ships. *Alliance* and *Richard* were to attack the larger enemy vessel. *Pallas* and *Vengeance* were to tackle the *Countess of Scarborough*. Kenny bent on the fresh signal to the *Alliance*, though without any more expectation that it would be obeyed than their commander. Even as he sent it aloft the dusk began to thicken and the wind dropped off to a whisper. The two Englishmen were yet some distance ahead. Kenny, finding a brief moment to think of other things, had a sudden quick flash of Barbary; of the dark, smooth hair and the flashing eyes. "Lord, let me fight a good fight for her," he found himself whispering, "and if I come through, let it be for her sake." Captain Jones, at his elbow, glanced at him sharply. Kenny said nothing but reddened slowly, and after that concentrated on his task.

The ships drew together slowly as the night closed in, and though they were less than half a mile apart when night fell, it was so dark they could not make out the enemy from the decks of the *Richard* with the naked eye. Overhead the stars glittered, but there was yet no moon to shed its track upon the water. Neither force showed a light, and as the night spread her cloak of invisibility about them the word was passed in whispers from the quarter-deck:

"Up gun ports! Easy now! Keep your matches muffled!"

Kenny was conscious of the faint creaking of the port covers and of the low rumble of the heavy guns as their snouts thrust out. He was conscious, too, of the little prickle of anticipation that began in his stomach, always before any action, and spread down into his legs and up into his chest and seemed to bind his lungs and make his breath come fast. Silence settled on the vessel, the hush of wait-ing, and he had time to wonder many things, though he kept them to himself. What were Barbary and Joshua doing now? Did every man aboard have the same sensations he did? Did they have that same tiny trickle of sweat running down the middle of their backs? Overhead the rigging creaked a little with the lift of the ship to the swell, and he jumped nervously. Then all at once the other ship was there beside them, not half a cable's length away, a slightly darker patch of black against the blackness of the night. A voice rang out, challenging:

"What ship is that?"

Kenny thought that in the dark they must have overshot their mark a little. But Captain Jones seemed satisfied.

"Well done, Mr. Boyle. We're not in the direct line of her broad-side, but if he's any kind of a sailor he'll try to wear and bring us under his guns. Try to keep her on our quarter." He swung away, and his answering hail to the Englishman was low. "I can't hear you!"

Kenny whispered to the helmsman to bring the *Richard's* stern a little toward the wind. Behind him he could hear Jones's whisper to the Indian quartermaster.

"Pass the word to Mr. Dale. He may open fire with his starboard battery as soon as he judges her in position."

"I say, what ship is that?" bawled the Englishman again.

"*Princess Royal!*" Jones replied.

There was a long moment of hesitation, while the two vessels drifted nearer until they lay within pistol shot. Evidently the enemy was confused; not sure yet whether to act or not. Those precious seconds were being put to good use aboard the *Richard*.

"What port?" demanded the Englishman.

Jones made no reply. Possibly he could not trust his voice. Aboard the *Richard* every man was tense and waiting.

"Answer!" the Englishman bawled through the dark. "Answer or, by God, I'll fire into you!"

From somewhere on the gun deck below, answering in a Yankee twang, breaking the tension, came a voice:

"Fire away, then, an' be God damned t' ye!"

It came then. Which ship was first Kenny never afterward could tell. There could not have been a split second between them. The night was slashed with a blistering belch of flame and smoke. In the thunderous, acrid clap of pitchy blackness that followed, wispy little sparklets of half-burnt powder dropped hissing into the sea. Under his feet Kenny felt the deck bulge suddenly upward and heard the screams of wounded men. Wood splintered and whined in the dark, and the *Richard* reeled and staggered under the shock. He heard the crack of timbers, then saw the glare of fire as it rose and spread upon the narrow blackened seas between. In the *Richard's* tops the muskets and swivels and coehorns crackled, and a hail of leaden death swept cross the Englishman's deck. On their own gun deck the second battery belched again, and immediately after came the fire of the fo'c'sle and quarter-deck guns. By their light and by the glow of fire that was leaping up from somewhere, they could see the Englishman now, close alongside—so close that the two ships' yards were almost touching; a great ship with a lower tier of gun ports, open and shedding the dim blue light of the battle lanterns, so that they could see the cavernous muzzles of half a score of eighteen-pounders that seemed to gulp their breaths in readiness.

In the confusion, ordered as it was, Kenny only half heard the shouts around him; only half saw the action that took place. No man's eyes and ears could follow everything.

"The eighteens in the lower battery burst!" he heard someone shout, and Jones's crisp order followed, cutting sharply through the wrenching bedlam:

"Secure that lower battery! Make fast the gun ports! Send those men to serve the upper guns! Put those that aren't needed at the other batteries to the tops! Fill, Mr. Boyle, and wear across in front of her!"

"Aye, aye, sir!"

The enemy's eighteen-pounders crashed, and the *Richard* staggered under the blow. Underfoot more cries of wounded men rose to mingle with the crunch of timbers and the answering thunder of their own guns. With both came the panicked shriek and puny pounding at the bulkheads of the two hundred trapped prisoners below, frantic lest they should be drowned like rats in their prison holds at the hands of their own countrymen. But the *Richard* wore ahead, still answering to her helm and sails, and crossed in front of the Englishman, to bring her larboard batteries to bear.

Below decks the fire that had broken out when the two eighteen-pounders of the lower battery had burst—ancient guns, they had been, pocked and pitted and long ago discarded by the French, accepted only by the Americans because nothing better was offered —had been brought under control. But the light that it shed was scarcely missed now in the almost continuous glare of the bellowing guns. Like brawny fighters, they stood toe to toe and hammered at one another, and in the *Bonhomme Richard,* at least, the thunder of the cannon, of the twelve-pounders on the gun deck, and the nine-pounders on fo'c'sle and quarter-deck was a steady roar. Above the lower-noted rumble of the fight Kenny could hear the pop and crackle of the muskets aloft, and the rip of parting canvas, the dull snap of breaking rope, and always the shrill, keening scream of sorely wounded men.

They were to leeward now, and the smoke of battle drifted across their decks, red with the glare of battle. He could see, too, the darker red of blood that trickled this way and that across the white planks. Somehow he was not afraid now. Action seemed entirely automatic. An eighteen-pound shot caught one of their nine-pounders by the muzzle, lifted it, and sent it slamming across, through the opposite bulwarks, into the sea, sheering away a stanchion as it went, smashing two of its gunners into a bloody, pulpy smear across the deck, and mangling the legs of a third so that they were no longer recognizable. Yet even when the man screamed and screamed and screamed away his life with the pumping blood, Kenny scarcely seemed to hear him in the welter of noise. His ear was tuned only for the things he ought to hear in the midst of that bedlam; and for the wounded man there was not even time for a throb of the heart. He was the loblolly boys' duty, and presently they came and carried him away.

Aloft, sails and rigging were parting, stays giving way. It was Kenny's duty to see them replaced or repaired as quickly as might be by the skeleton sailing crew. It was to him the carpenter came, white-faced and tugging at his forelock.

"She's had half a dozen eighteen-pounders under th' water line, sir! She's makin' water fast amidships!" he reported.

"Get down what men ye must have from aloft," Kenny told him, far more calmly than he felt. "Set 'em t' th' pumps, an' be makin' th' best repairs ye can. If ye wear 'em out, send 'em aloft again an' fetch down a fresh lot. We've got t' keep 'er afloat!"

"Aye, aye, sir!" As the man left Kenny was aware of Captain Jones at his elbow, smiling grimly in approval, nodding.

"That's well, Boyle! Close if you can! She'll cut us to ribbons with her heavier guns if we don't!"

A quartermaster loomed and plucked at the captain's sleeve.

"There's but four twelve-pounders left in th' larboard battery, sir," he reported. "An' there's fire forrad in th' gun deck. Mr. Dale has it under control, but he says if——"

He never finished. A shot took him under the arm as he spoke. Before their eyes the upper quarter of him disappeared in a spatter of blood, and the rest of the headless, shoulderless body skittered into the starboard scuppers and lay there flopping for an instant as a hen will when her head is cut off. For the one time in the fight Kenny felt his stomach turn over and the nauseous taste of bile rise in his throat. When he turned back Jones had swung away and was bawling commands down into the waist.

The *Richard* carried a battle glass slung by the wheel. It was one of Kenny's duties to turn it, so long as it remained intact; accordingly he knew the fight to have lasted no more than a half-hour at that point. It was only a moment later—though in the crash and whine of the fight it seemed like an age—when one of the gunners came up to report the larboard battery below completely silenced. At the same instant Mr. Mease, the purser, who had charge of the quarter-deck nines, took a musket ball over the right eye and dropped to the deck —a ball, incidentally, which in the course of two hours' surgery during the battle Mr. Brooke, in the smoky cockpit, removed from its resting place against the brain, trepanning a piece of living skull in place of the shattered bone, and sending the purser back to fight and live again!

Captain Jones turned at the report and swept the upper deck. The ancient eighteens on the gun deck had proven their uselessness and been discarded. Now all fourteen twelves in the larboard battery were silenced, and abovedecks only two of the four remaining nines on that side continued in action. One nine was still upright to starboard on the quarter-deck, and as Jones himself leaped to replace the fallen purser he barked over his shoulder.

"Fetch up some of the gunners, Mr. Boyle! Work that ninepounder over here and serve her!"

How it was done Kenny himself was never sure. The gunner who fetched the report himself vanished in the smoke to call the men, while Kenny, in the midst of the hail of lead, bent to the tackles and freed the gun. By the time it was done a dozen Frenchmen and Yankees and two of the Malays and a Maltese, men who had been working the guns below, were at his elbow with bights of rope and crowbars. Between them they hauled the gun from its position and worked the piece around into place in the opposite battery at last. When they finally opened fire with it there were but three small guns aboard the *Bonhomme Richard,* besides the coehorns and the muskets in the tops, to bark in answer to almost the full battery of the enemy frigate. A man folded silently on the slippery deck. Another grunted, as if it mattered:

"There's th' moon comin' up now!"

It was true. In the ghostly, silvery light the two ships, battered and stark against the blackness of the sea, stood muzzle to muzzle, and the streaks of gunfire were paler in the moon's wash. Kenny leaped back quickly to the glass and found that the fight had been going on only little more than an hour. He turned it and returned to his gun.

The *Richard's* high poop gave her a slight advantage. To dismount the few guns the Americans could bring to bear the English had to elevate their own, and this could be done only by taking advantage of their own vessel's up roll. At the same time the *Richard's* height enabled her people to sweep the Englishman's deck. Jones, quick to see the advantage, seized it and loaded the guns with grape and canister, and between them and the blistering fire that poured from the American's tops the enemy's upper decks for a moment were swept clean and her shrouds and rigging cut to shreds. After that the guns were double-shotted and aimed for the masts.

The Englishman sensed his danger. Somehow he got men aloft and sail on. He forged ahead, to swing across the *Richard's* bows and rake with his middle batteries. But in the light airs he miscalculated and yawed and threw his helm alee, which fetched the ships in line ahead. In this position the *Bonhomme Richard*, having the greater way on, overran him and thrust her bowsprit over his stern. So for a trembling moment the two vessels hung locked. There came a momentary lull in the fire.

Kenny remembered long afterward the chill curl in the pit of his stomach as it occurred to him that the British boarders would be swarming in a moment over their bows. Possibly, although it did not come to him then, the English themselves felt a like fear of the Yankee sea wolves. Somewhere far below he could hear the ominous crackle of flames and the dull, steady clank of the pumps. The howling of the prisoners had died away to a sort of muffled, heartless moan.

The interval lasted but an instant, and then the Englishman's hail came drifting back to them:

"Ahoy there! Have you surrendered?"

Captain Jones himself leaped onto the *Richard's* bulwarks.

"Surrender be damned, sir!" he bawled. "We've just begun to fight!"

In response, the Englishman, having evidently brought the fires that could be seen through his lower ports under control, backed his topsails, and the ships broke free.

Still with the intention of raking the *Richard*, he shivered his after sails and put his helm hard down, lay all aback forward, and wore short around on his heel. But once again he misjudged the length of his turning circle. It was shorter than he realized, and despite his intention to pass astern of the American, his long jib boom bore down upon the all but helpless *Richard* and passed directly through the mizzen shrouds, to foul with the rigging and the mizzenmast, while his high bows ground with a crunching rack of timbers into the *Richard's* side.

They heeled far over under the impact and dipped their larboard under, then righted slowly as the Englishman himself literally held them afloat. Kenny clung for support to the hot butt of the gun he had been serving, never even feeling the blisters the hot metal raised upon his arms and hands and against his side, aghast at what seemed to him a new disaster.

But there was no disaster in John Paul Jones's book. He saw the opportunity and leaped into the rigging to lash the enemy's yard to their own mast.

"Make her fast, lads," he cried, "before she can fill away! We've a chance at her yet at close quarters!"

His voice was like a clearing tonic to Kenny. In an instant he was swarming up to help.

So again they lay, bow and flank this time, with the English ship unable to back away without dragging the American after him, while the *Richard* was now able to bring the few remaining guns of her starboard batteries into play. In desperation the British captain tried to pull away, backing his wind and throwing his helm hard over, closing his starboard ports, lest the maneuver bring them flank to flank and the Yankees swarm aboard through the openings.

But the effort availed him nothing, and only the wind at last accomplished for him some of what he, with all his seamanship, had been unable to do. Stronger, with the rising of the moon, it wore the *Richard* around against the Englishman's flank, and by the leverage tore away the American's tattered mizzen shrouds and snapped the enemy's stout bowsprit with a rending crack. The twang of it made the American's aftermast whip like a catapult and threw two men off their small platform in the mizzentop, to send them hurtling down, narrowly missing Kenny as he leaped to bear a hand. But he was scarcely aware of that, for he had Jones's own example before him, passing a cable around the shattered stump of the Englishman's jib boom.

It was a bit of luck that as the two ships swung the Englishman's spare anchor, which had been overhanging the *Richard's* rail, fouled her bulwarks and caught. The timbers held, and in the next instant the stout hawser from the *Richard* passed around the shattered bowsprit, while amidships and astern of the American the grappling irons flew out and caught and held.

In the hope that the wind might shake them free the Englishman let go his anchors. But Jones could play at that game too. Fore and aft the *Richard's* anchors splashed into the murky waters and caught, and thenceforward the two ships thundered at each other, flank to flank and bow to stern, so close that the gun crews, ramming home their charges, had to reach across into the other vessel to thrust their long poles down the muzzles of their guns!

As has been told, the Englishman had closed down his lower ports lest the Americans swarm aboard through them, so that now he was faced either with abandoning his eighteen-pounders or firing through the very flanks of his own ship, for they were at such close quarters that the ports could not be raised again. He chose to fire, and the splinters of the British ship crashed clear across the *Richard's* deck, while the wads of each, used to ram the powder home, fell in smoldering chunks inboard of both vessels and started fires in each.

The acrid smell of wood smoke rose through the pungent vapor of burning powder. Jones was quick to realize what was happening. He thrust his mouth close to Kenny's ear.

"Get your seamen below, Boyle! Fight fires! Send Mr. Dale on deck with all the men he can spare from the guns to repel boarders! If we can clear his decks once and hold off his first attempt we'll have 'em!"

It took Kenny a moment to order his crew below and send up Dick Dale, bloody and powder-grimed but still grinning, at the head of a swarm of fighting men. Then as the guns crashed, muzzle to muzzle, Kenny and his sailors battled the stubborn fires in that hellish welter of swirling smoke and smashing shot and crackling flame. The decks below were a shambles, grimmer than ever he had dreamed. Blood dripped from the bulkheads and from the overhead, and the deck itself was slippery with the mingled slime of gore and human entrails mixed with the spillings of burnt powder and sloshing sea water. At the same time the aged *Richard's* half-rotted sides were all but smashed away, so that as he looked at the gaping holes Kenny wondered that the decks above had not collapsed upon the lower ones. Dead men lay in bloodstained heaps beside their guns, or crushed beneath the overturned cannon, and the thumping and the yammering of the prisoners in the holds was louder here than above. As they fought the flames desperately, Kenny felt a cold prickle at the base of his scalp, a sense of apprehension, far from unfounded, for already the bulkheads were splintering under the prisoners' onslaught.

Frantically he and his men worked with soaked mops and bucket lines. So close were the two ships that half a dozen of the *Richard's* gun ports had been battered into a single gaping hole, and not once, but frequently, the enemy's round shot whined clear through the 'tween decks and splashed into the sea upon the far side without touching a stick in passing.

In that swarming, smoking hell, with the stench of burning human flesh in their nostrils, Kenny and his men struggled. Sweat ran in rivulets down their powder-grimed bodies, leaving little tracks, interlaced, behind them. Despite the danger from the enemy's shots, the yawning rents in the old ship's sides served a useful purpose, for they let a little wind blow through to clear away some of the stinging smoke and allowed some air to reach them. At the same time, the men could lean out to fill and pass the buckets of sea water with which they fought the stubborn flames. They let in the sea, too, as the ships rolled together in the trough of the waves. Each time the old ship dipped, a slopping of water poured in at her wounds. But though some of it would trickle down into her bilges, Kenny was yet thankful for it, for it helped them to gain slow control.

He went below with thirty men, and he saw them drop beside him as they worked—one by one. Yet slowly, agonizedly, it seemed to him, for the moment at least, they beat back the flames. When they had finished it appeared that the enemy's fire had slackened somewhat, and he led the seven men who were left to him back to the upper deck.

There he saw why. Lying side by side, bound together as they were, the *Richard's* yards projected over the Englishman's decks. The withering fire from the American tops had cleared the Englishman's rigging of every vestige of life and swept her decks bare. Even the English commander had taken refuge below, and as Kenny came on deck one of the Yankee seamen aloft clambered out to the end of the main yard with a bucket of grenades and smoldering tow, and dropped it squarely through the Englishman's open scuttle below.

Apparently the bucket, scattering its contents across the gun deck, found a vital spot, for instantly there came a terrific explosion aboard the English ship. The decks lifted and her seams gaped with the fire within. The blast from the inferno shot skyward. For an instant there was an almost deafening silence. Then the voices of the remaining American officers rose in the night.

"Boarders! Away boarders!"

But that was the very moment at which the *Alliance* chose to sweep across the *Richard's* stern, and Kenny found time to think of Joshua Barney and wish that he had been in command of the other ship instead of Pierre Landais.

Perhaps there was some excuse for Landais's first fire, poured directly into the *Richard's* stern. Despite the full moonlight that must have revealed their outlines with some clarity, hooked together as they were, perhaps he could not make out the three recognition lanterns that Captain Jones had ordered hung out over the bows. His

full broadside crashed into the *Richard's* counter, smashing the helm
and the rudder, and carrying away half of what the Englishman's fire
had not already wrecked in that quarter.

For an instant there was dead silence. Then the cries of newly
wounded men, hurt by the fire of their own allies, rose in the night.
After them, and mingling with them, came the shouts of horror-
stricken survivors.

"Wear round! Wear round, man! The other is the Englishman!"

"*Ventre St. Gris, monsieur!*" came the protesting shouts of the
Frenchmen aboard the *Alliance* itself. "*Pour l'amour de Dieu! Ce
n'est pas par la! Tirez à l'autre côté! Ça, c'est le Bonhomme Richard!*"

Perhaps that first fire was an error, but there was no excuse for the
second broadside that poured into the *Richard's* larboard bows. That
crashing burst smashed two of the recognition lanterns hanging
where they could not help being seen, and tore great holes below as
well, so that the seas gushed into the already flooded bilges. Worse,
the crashing round shot carried away the pumps and the men who
were working them.

Kenny was not ashamed to own later that after that first volley he
huddled for shelter under the mainmast. Cries and curses and an
understandable panic followed the second broadside, as Captain
Landais, having done his damage, sailed proudly off into the night
with the oaths and maledictions of his own countrymen rising after
him. Nor did he offer any further "assistance."

In the *Richard* the confusion was indescribable. The carpenter,
well aware of the floods the ship was already taking, not even ex-
amining the fresh damage below the water line, seeing the pumps
wrecked, and believing no means left to keep the ship afloat beneath
them, cried out that they were lost and ran aft, shrieking, "Quarter!
Quarter!"

A blow from a nearby sailor's fist, a man of more stomach than
himself, stretched him on the deck, and for a moment Kenny himself
held the quarter-deck, for Captain Jones and Dick Dale had streaked
below to examine the damage to the pumps. He was there, holding
the few ship's people around him by the fury of his own fists, when
the captain came again on deck and started toward the jack staff.

Undoubtedly it was Jones's own intention to surrender. But on the
quarter-deck he could see by the bright moonlight that already the
jack staff had been carried away. And his second glance showed him
Kenny, by the useless helm, still fighting for the ship.

Perhaps the sight persuaded him. Perhaps that one reminder that there were others who would stand behind him appealed to his own fighting heart. In any case, when the Englishman called again to know if they had surrendered and wished quarter, Jones lifted his own voice in reply:

"Be damned to you! All hands on deck to repel boarders!"

There was a brief struggle at the rail, then foot by foot the British were beaten back to their own decks. The American tops blossomed again with streamers of fire, and the enemy scuttled for cover.

As a result the Americans found a breath of hope. They were able to turn from their efforts to save their own ship, to right their guns and serve them again. Aboard the Englishman the fire slackened, while, contrary to their expectations, the American fire increased and steadied. New fires broke out in several places aboard the English frigate. One by one his guns were knocked over and silenced, while the Yankee fire appeared to grow stronger.

It lacked an hour of midnight when Kenny dragged himself on deck from overseeing the rigging of the jury pumps on the deck below. The British prisoners had come in handy, after all, for Kenny's Irish wit had found great delight in telling them that the Englishman was sinking, and the only way to save their own lives was to turn to the pumps with all their might. Aboard the enemy only one gun remained in service in the starboard battery, and even as Kenny stumbled to the quarter-deck the British captain himself stepped to his own halyards and struck.

In the smoke of the fire and battle, however, it was not immediately seen. Only when the enemy's mainmast toppled to leeward, dragging the mizzentop with it, did Captain Jones become aware that the other ship was his.

"Away boarders, Mr. Dale!" he shouted.

With the first wave Kenny snatched a cutlass from the rack and clambered across the Englishman's bulwarks. On the enemy's fo'c'sle an English gunner, himself not yet aware that his ship had already surrendered, sighted his swivel at the inpouring Yankees and fired.

As Kenny's feet touched the rail and he crouched to leap down upon the other deck, one arm upraised as he held to a stay for support, something seemed to snatch at his side and he felt himself turned helplessly askew in the air. The bloody decks rushed up to meet him as he fell, and the black skies above plunged down to blanket him. Then all at once everything about him was dark, and he was falling—falling—was it into Barbary's arms?

For a long time he lay and bled quietly in the shelter of the bulwarks, unconscious, a huddled, shapeless mass, while wave after wave of Yankee and French and Malay and Portuguese and Maltese seamen leaped unseeingly over him.

V

Should Auld Acquaintance . . .

1. *"Charming Molly"*

Joshua barney and Ike Robinson, in the *General Mercer,* slipped back into Philadelphia toward mid-October with three stout merchantmen and a British privateer taken en route. The merchant vessels were laden with rum, sugar, and molasses for the enemy's forces at New York and offered no resistance. The privateer was a stout vessel, however, mounting twenty twelves and long nines, and she had given them a running fight that lasted nearly twenty-four hours. The *Mercer's* own cargo consisted of 81 pipes of brandy, 116 hogsheads and 110 cases of claret. Joshua's share of the total was a reasonably tidy little sum—enough, certainly, to stifle any other qualms he might have had about getting married.

Indeed, he lost no time in going straight to the Bedford house with his news, where Gunning and Mrs. Bedford wrung his hand and Ann greeted him with such heart-warming delight that every moment he had been gone seemed to become suddenly worth all the dreariness and worry and waiting that it had cost.

"Joshua!" she cried, gazing up at him out of the circle of his arms. "If you only knew how I'd looked forward to this moment—to have you back again, here! Holding me——"

He smiled and kissed her hungrily.

"Aye!" he cried. "Holding you, Ann. And not meaning ever to let you go."

That was a slight exaggeration, of course, but there was no doubt that it came from his heart. If they could have had their way they would have been off to the justice of the peace the very next morning and had it over and done.

But, if only out of deference to Mrs. Bedford, to whom such haste was unseemly, to say the least, they had to be a little more decorous about it. And, as a matter of fact, but for the wear and tear upon their own young patience, they were better off for a brief wait. For one thing, it permitted the prizes fetched in by the *Mercer* to be condemned and sold and the prize money distributed, so that they were not forced to start out with no more than Joshua's wages for the voyage in his pocket. Also, it allowed time for him to make a flying visit to Baltimore and fetch back his mother and sister to meet their soon-to-be Philadelphia relatives and to attend the ceremony itself.

After a good deal of bickering and dickering with Ann's folks, the date was finally set for Thanksgiving Day, nearly six weeks away; and though Joshua declared he did not know how he would be able to live so long apart from her and Ann declared that she would go into a languishing decline if they were not married before then, Mrs. Bedford was determined, and that was the best they could do. They had to be satisfied.

Not until that had been settled did Joshua stop to think that he should at least pay his respects to Robert Morris, and belatedly called at the committeeman's paneled offices.

"I heard you were back and wondered when I'd see you," Robert Morris greeted him dryly as he came around his great desk to seize Joshua's hand with a warmth that belied his gibe. "You'd a successful voyage, I'm told?"

Joshua flushed, recalling his own stubbornness.

"I can't deny 'twas more profitable than any I could have made in a man-o'-war," he replied.

"Wasn't that what was needed?" Morris grinned. "Would you have preferred another service?"

"Perhaps, in the circumstances," Joshua admitted a little sheepishly. "I don't suppose there's been any change so far as naval matters are concerned?"

"What? What?" Morris chided him, smiling. "Here you're not yet even married, and you're already looking for a berth? I'd not have expected that so soon!"

"You knew?" Joshua blushed furiously this time. "I didn't mean—— I was just asking——"

"I know!" Morris laughed outright. "Gunning's been dropping a hint or two around while you were away. So far as the other's concerned—no, there's been no change. But I don't suppose that will really matter to you, eh?"

Joshua chuckled, admitting the accusation.

"I must say I shan't object to a turn ashore right now," he agreed. "But it seemed wise to ask."

"Well, set your conscience at rest." Morris nodded approvingly. "If anything, so far as the Navy's concerned, the situation is worse. In fact, even privateering's beginning to be slow. So you've no need to fret, lad. You may marry and find a home for your bride without any thought of neglecting your duty. I'll let you know when there's a change, you may be sure of that. By the way—when's it to be?"

"Next month, sir. You'll come?"

"You couldn't keep me away!" Morris laughed. "She's a rare fine prize, Joshua. My congratulations to you."

"Thank you, sir." Joshua accepted his hand on that and rose to leave; then abruptly remembered. "Incidentally, sir, I almost forgot to tell you I saw Boyle."

"Did you?" Robert Morris looked up abruptly. "Now that *is* something! Where? When?"

"He's aboard the *Bonhomme Richard,* sir, with Captain Jones." Joshua told him how they had met at sea. "He said he had been in Mill Prison since the *Lexington* was taken and had only been exchanged a few weeks before."

"And he chose to sail with Jones rather than come straight home?" Morris stared at him.

"I gathered, sir," Joshua replied, "that he was on his way when he fell in with Captain Jones and decided that the *Richard's* need for men was a thing that could not be ignored. As a matter of fact, he hinted that he had almost sailed in the *Mercer* with us—although he obviously did not know we were aboard."

"Think of it, now!" Morris continued to gaze at him with a mingling of wonder and disbelief. "All that time he was in prison, and then, as soon as he is free, he turns around and offers himself immediately where he feels he is most needed. Take note of that, Joshua! I tell you, there's such devotion to the thing we fight for as is not often seen. I feel proud and humble in the face of it. I hope you'll see that the word of it reaches the right place?"

"I leave for Baltimore tomorrow, sir," Joshua assured him.

He could not remember any other home-coming that was as pleasurably exciting as that one. To be sure, it was not so very long since he himself had come back almost literally from the dead. But as a sailor that seemed to him commonplace. This time, he felt, he brought news—real news. He brought word that Kenny lived and was safe—and that he thought of Barbary. And he brought word of his own forthcoming wedding.

It was not because he thought his own affairs more important that he spoke of them first. That was just the way it happened. Both his mother and Barbary greeted him with all their usual delight, such as they showed whenever he returned from a cruise. When the first flurry of welcome was over Mary Barney held him out at arm's length and studied him.

"Great heavens! Look at you, Joshua!" she cried. "You've grown so straight and tall and thin! Who'd ever think you were once my little boy? I suppose one of these days you'll be fetching home a wife of your own."

"Well—as a matter of fact, Mother"—Joshua turned red to the ears —"that's something I wanted to tell you about."

"You're not going to say——" Mary Barney cried. "My land, Joshua! Where is she? Why didn't you——"

"Now, now! Don't get so excited." Joshua grinned. " 'Tis not done yet. I came back through Philadelphia, and Ann and I have set the date——"

"When?" his mother interrupted him.

"Next month—Thanksgiving." He laughed. "And you've got to be there—both of you!"

"Oh dear——" began Mrs. Barney.

"Why take on so?" Joshua chuckled. "It's not as though I hadn't given you plenty of warning——"

"I know, I know," his mother sighed. " 'Tis just that it's hard to believe, is all. It needs a little getting used to, I guess. Of course we'll be there, Son. We'll go right up next week so we can have a good long visit."

All this time Barbary had said nothing but had stood studying Joshua with an almost puzzled expression. For his part, he was holding himself in, biting his lip to keep in the news he had for her. Somehow she sensed that he had something more to say.

"I—I know I ought to act more surprised, Joshua," she burst out abruptly. "I—I ought to be more excited. I ought to tell you how thrilling it is. And don't think I don't feel all that. I—I am glad, Joshua. And thrilled and excited and delighted. But you *have* hinted at it, you know—and—and somehow I feel that this is only a part of what you were going to say. There's something else, isn't there, Joshua?"

"Whatever makes you think that, miss?" He turned toward her teasingly, his smile widening now to a broad grin that he could no longer hold back.

Her hand crept out and found the back of a nearby chair and clutched at it.

"Joshua!" her voice was sharp with the tension in her. "Joshua— what is it? What else——"

He sobered abruptly, seeing her trembling intensity, and slipped an arm about her shoulders fondly.

"I shan't torment you longer, Barbary," he told her. "There is something else I must be saying, something very extra special for you. He's alive, Barbary. Kenny's alive! I've seen him and talked to him, and he loves you. He gave me this to bring you, and he asked me to tell you he'll be back."

He reached in his pocket and drew out the letter Kenny had given him and laid it in her hands. She stared at it, almost as if it were not real.

"Kenny!" she whispered. Then, "Joshua—— Oh—oh, Joshua! I— I——"

Her voice broke suddenly, and all the pent-up emotions of those years in which she had held herself in and controlled herself by the very force of her love and hope and longing burst through in a sudden rush of helpless tears. She turned to him and buried her face in his coat.

"Joshua! Oh, Joshua! I—I—I ought to be happy! And I am—I am! But—I—I just can't help it."

He took her in his arms and sought to quiet her.

"There, now. There, Barbary," he said a little bewilderedly. "There, child. All these years while he was gone and you didn't know whether he was dead or alive, you held it in and never let a peep out of you. Now you know he's safe—now you know he's alive—and you let it all out in a rush."

Mary Barney came forward and also sought to offer some comfort. It seemed to her that if Barbary had a moment to herself in her room she might gain control the sooner. She took her gently by the shoulders.

"Come now, Barbary. Come, child," she said.

But Barbary shook her off.

"No!" she cried. "No, Mother, please don't ask me. Don't you see? I can't go anywhere now—not until Joshua has told me—everything. I—I'm sorry, Joshua. It—it's just that it's been so long! And n-now all at once—— You do understand, don't you? I want to know! I want to hear—everything. How is he? How does he look? Where—where did you see him? Why——"

"All right, Barbary." Joshua chuckled. "The gale's blown itself out. Now let's sit down and I'll tell it to you—everything I know."

They drew their little circle of easy chairs up before the bright warm fire, all three of them, and the blaze, which had been freshly stirred when he came in, sank to red coals and was forgotten as he told them of his meeting at sea with Kenny; of what Kenny had found time to tell him of the loss of the *Lexington* and the long grim years in prison, and of how he had come to sign aboard the *Bonhomme Richard* at the last moment.

What Mary Barney thought of it, she did not say. But it was curious that Barbary should lift her dark eyes to Joshua's and repeat, in different words, almost exactly what Robert Morris had said.

"Should I feel hurt, do you think, that he did not come to me straight when he had the chance?" she asked. "No, Joshua. I'm glad—— No, perhaps I should not say that. I'm not glad. But I'm proud that he should do as he has. Ah, Joshua, I know how you've sometimes wondered—and so have I, too. The way he used to argue in favor of privateering as against the Navy! I wasn't sure. Was he an opportunist? Did he only want to pull himself up? I—I've loved him! I'd never deny it! But I've always had that fear—that maybe he just used this—us—to sweep his own ambition along. But now—now, Joshua, thank God, I know! He's honest and strong and decent, and he's worth everything that I have to offer—and far more! 'Tis not easy to say I'd rather he did what he did. And I know 'twas not easy for him to decide it. But, Joshua, I'm happy—yes, happy and—and flattered beyond telling—that he should have such faith in me that he should know I'd rather he did that than—than—that he should come home to me when he knew that there was a real need for him there!"

She stood up abruptly and smiled down at them both, such a gay, lighthearted smile as they had not seen on her lips or in her eyes for years.

"Now," she cried, "now I can read his letter—and answer it—as I should! If I write to him, Joshua, you'll ask Mr. Morris to send it, won't you?"

"He never got my other letter," Joshua replied, never thinking if the answer matched her mood.

"No matter!" she retorted. "He will this one! You'll see to it, won't you?"

"Of course!" He grinned. "Good night, Barbary. And sweet dreams."

She flashed him a smile and went straight to her room, where she curled up on the bed with Kenny's long letter. It was past midnight when she finished, yet she sat down at once and began her reply: "I love you," was the gist of it, "and I'm proud of you for what you've done. Come to me when you can, Kenny. Come to me any way at all. I will be here, waiting."

Joshua's wedding to Ann Bedford was modest, quiet, as Joshua and Ann both wanted it; though it was properly dignified and elegant, as was in keeping with Mrs. Bedford's wishes. Ann had Sally Bingham as matron of honor, and two attendants, and Ike Robinson stood as best man for Joshua. The guests afterward were gay and numerous, and of course Barbary and Joshua's mother came up to Philadelphia for the event. In fact, Mrs. Bedford and Mrs. Barney took an immediate liking to one another, while Ann and Barbary were at once so close that Ann insisted that Joshua's sister be one of her attendants.

Indeed, the whole day seemed to them, in Philadelphia at least, full of good omens. In the morning there were the usual church bells, summoning all to the giving of due thanks for the blessings of the year past. But in the afternoon the bells burst out again in a wilder peal of joy, and Joshua stuck his head out of the window just before the wedding march, in time to hear the crier pass, shouting:

"OYEZ! OYEZ! OYEZ! Hear ye now! This day is come news that the United States ship *Bonhomme Richard*, 42, Captain John Paul Jones, has met and taken, within sight of Flamborough Head, on the east coast of England, the British frigate *Serapis*, 50, Captain Pearson, after a desperate fight lasting more than six hours! OYEZ—Oyez—OYEZ——"

Joshua pulled in his head and had just time to pass that word to Ann and Barbary.

"That was Kenny's ship!"

Then came the march and the ceremony, and Joshua stood up bursting with a double excitement, for surely the announcement of an American victory at this hour could only mean that their own beginning together was bound to be successful.

After they had both pledged their word and embraced and then swung into the reception that Mrs. Bedford had insisted was only proper, Joshua watched his moment to draw Ann and Barbary and Robert Morris a little to one side.

"This concerns us all," he said. "Bob—Mr. Morris, have you met my sister Barbary? She has especial reason for interest in this. Tell me, what's the news of this battle? Have you anything more than the crier has told us?"

Robert Morris did not smile.

"Little!" he admitted. "As much as has come to us has been the word that a battle has been fought and—that we came off victorious. About what you heard is all that we know. But"—he smiled broadly now—"I'll tell you, I'd put such a victory next to Saratoga itself, so far as its influence abroad is concerned!"

"Then let's hope 'tis so!" cried Barbary.

"Oh, there's no doubt of it," replied Morris.

Joshua would have asked more, but he caught a warning glance from Morris and held his tongue. He was puzzled, but he said nothing, and the rest of the afternoon and evening, until it was time for them to leave, passed in gay laughter. Only a little before their own escape did he manage to draw Morris aside again and tax him with his almost extraordinary glumness.

"Have you heard more than you're telling?" he demanded.

Morris smiled at him.

"Look you, Joshua," he said. "I know what the situation is as between yourself and Boyle. I'd tell you if I'd heard more, even at the risk of spoiling such an occasion as this. But I've heard nothing. No more has come to me than you've heard the crier announce on the streets. If that's true, 'tis a great thing. But omelets are not made without breaking eggs. Battles are not fought without casualties. 'Tis that that has me worried. As soon as I have word I'll pass it along to you. There's my promise. May I say you have a lovely sister—to say nothing of a charming bride?"

Joshua waved his hand impatiently.

"Look!" he cried. "Barbary could not bear it if she thought anything had been withheld from her. You're sure you've had no other news?"

"Not a word, Joshua." Morris smiled and shook his head. "Please believe it. Captain Jones makes very complete reports, but his has not yet been received. As soon as it is I'll let you know—there's a promise. Now go out, and for God's sake, enjoy life while you may!"

Joshua had every intention of doing exactly that. After all, this was his wedding day, and he proposed to let others do the worrying. Since Morris assured him that no other word had been received, he put the matter out of his mind and turned his thoughts and his heart toward this business of making a life for himself and for Ann.

There was a period in Philadelphia during the early winter in which they visited and were visited. And after that they went to Baltimore for a month or six weeks, in which time they saw and were made much of by all Joshua's old companions—to say nothing of his family. When that—no one in those days called it a honeymoon, though that is exactly what it was—was over, they returned to Philadelphia and thence went to Dover, in Delaware, where young Gunning Bedford lived and where, so he assured them, they could find the most comfortable living and the most agreeable life.

He was certainly not far wrong in that. Cheerful bachelor though he was, he helped them find a small brick house in Loockerman Lane, not far off what had been King Street but now was called State. He introduced the young Barneys to Dover social circles—to the Rodneys and the McKeans, to the Ridgelys and the Richardsons and Haslets and Comegys and Pennewells and Bassetts—so that they did not long remain strangers in the town. But unfortunately, perhaps, that state of things was not destined to continue long. Joshua was a naval officer, and there was a war to be fought.

That was not his fault. That he loved Ann dearly is certainly never to be doubted. But he was a sailor, fundamentally, and that was equally true. He might be happy for a brief spell ashore; he might look forward to holding Ann in his arms again. But the sea was in him, and the sea called. As hard as he might try, he could never deny it.

Indeed, that winter things to some extent worked against him. At the outset, of course, his life with Ann was of such a shattering sweetness that he could never have wished any other. But he was not honed to the social life nor cut out to be a drawing-room dandy. He might enjoy that for a moment, and then more serious considerations would begin to gnaw at him. For one thing, though they waited, no news came from Robert Morris with regard to the details of the *Bonhomme Richard-Serapis* fight. Barbary, in her letters, prodded him on that score. Nor was there any word from Kenny, though they waited, watching for it day by day.

These things undoubtedly made him restless to be off and doing—anything he could—rather than just lazing away his time there, as pleasant as it might be. He was already beginning to taste the bitterness of frustration, when Ann admitted to him that she was convinced she was going to bear their child. He looked into his pocket then and next day went off to Philadelphia to see Robert Morris.

"No, Joshua," said the naval committeeman disappointingly. "I'm sorry, but things have not changed much yet. There are a couple of ships getting ready, and as soon as they are I'll let you know. In the meantime there's naught to be done afloat or ashore. You know that privateering's almost stopped in the last few months since the British clamped on their blockade?"

Joshua nodded.

"You've heard nothing yet of Kenny Boyle, I suppose?"

"Nothing yet." Morris shook his head. "We've not had the reports from Jones himself, in fact. But you know how slow communications are these days. Look in again next time you're up. In the meantime, if I hear anything I'll surely let you know."

Since there was nothing more than that to be had at the moment, Joshua had to be satisfied with it. He went back to Dover, where he grew crotchety as an old she-bear with cubs, watching the posts, and waiting, and hoping that some word would be forthcoming from Philadelphia. Instead, one day in July—a year, lacking a month, Joshua could not help remembering, from the day he had met Kenny at sea—Barbary stepped down from the Baltimore stage and came to visit with them.

"I can't help it, Joshua," she told him that night at dinner. "I can't help but feel that there's something wrong. It's been all this time since the battle between the *Richard* and the *Serapis*, and yet we've not heard. There's been no official report, and I've had no answer to my letter. There must be something! I came to see if you'd go with me to Philadelphia to see Mr. Morris and see if there isn't some way we can come at the truth——"

She put into words vague fears that he himself had felt increasingly during the last few months, although he had mentioned them to no one—not even Ann. He gave his wife a slight warning glance.

"I'll go up with you, Barbary," he promised gravely.

Robert Morris's greeting to them, when they looked into his office two days later, was as agreeable as ever, though yet with a restraint that Joshua had not known in the man before. In a way he looked as if, at sight of them, he would gladly bolt out the back door, but he was trapped.

"Joshua Barney!" he exclaimed. "And Mistress Barbary! I declare,

I was just about to write to you, though I must say I'd not quite decided what——"

"You've had news then, sir?" Joshua cried.

Morris looked gravely at Barbary and turned toward his desk.

"The reports from Captain Jones have arrived," he said. "They were delayed at Paris by the Ministry of Marine, which felt that certain matters regarding Captain Landais, in the *Alliance*, should be investigated. Here! Perhaps you'd best look them over yourselves. They express far better than anything I might say the exact state of things."

He held out the thick sheaf of papers to Joshua, who took them soberly and began to read.

"What——" Barbary half cried out, and then stopped her mouth with her fist.

Robert Morris turned away abruptly and went to the window, where he stood staring moodily out into the sunny street. Joshua read swiftly, flipping the pages—and there were many of them, closely filled with neat, careful handwriting. Barbary held her breath as long as she could, then managed an agonized whisper.

"Joshua—what does it say, Joshua?"

He waved his finger at her, concentrating, and shook his head. Then, toward the end of the report, he read aloud to her:

"Especially to be recommended for their conspicuous gallantry in action are Richard Dale, first lieutenant, Kevin Boyle, sailing master, Nathaniel Fanning, John Mayrant, Reuben Chase, Benjamin Stubbs, midshipmen——"

"Yes! Yes!" she cried impatiently. "But what——"

He flipped the page quickly and came to the close-scrawled casualty lists. The length of that giving the names of those killed in the action made even him, accustomed as he was to such things, blanch. Yet though he went through it carefully, twice he could not find Kenny's name.

"He's not listed as killed!" he announced.

Barbary's breath caught in a little choking gasp in her throat. Robert Morris turned about sharply from the window and looked at them glumly. Joshua scarcely noticed. His finger was racing rapidly down the list of wounded.

"He's not here either!" he cried.

"Joshua——" Barbary choked.

"Turn the page!" Morris's voice rasped.

Joshua obeyed and read aloud:

"The following were so severely wounded in the action that they are not expected to survive:
Kevin Boyle, sailing master——"

It was Ann Barney's own good common sense—call it intuition, if you will—that prompted her to come up from Dover with them, and it was she now who took Barbary into her heart and arms and comforted her. Although she did not go to the offices of Willing and Morris with them, she could and did insist that Barbary stay with them at the Bedford house. Indeed, after that brief heartbreaking visit, she took the girl home with her to Dover and insisted that she stay with her and keep her company through the rest of the summer.

That was good for Barbary—and it was good for Ann, for Robert Morris had had other things to say beside showing them the report.

"I shouldn't give up entirely, ma'am," he said to Barbary, trying to soften the blow a little, perhaps. "After all, that report's nearly a year old, and we've had no other to indicate that—that anything of the sort has happened. Let me send forward a special inquiry to Dr. Franklin and see what he has to say before we accept it as final—eh?"

She thanked him gratefully, of course, though without much hope, and he smiled his understanding and sympathy and turned to her brother.

"There's a new ship fitting, Joshua," he said, perhaps offering him the post in atonement for having so abruptly given them this harsh news. "The *Saratoga*, 18, Captain Young, is making ready for sea. She needs a first luff. If you like, the berth is yours."

Joshua hesitated only an instant, glancing at his sister.

"Thank you, sir. I'll report aboard as soon as you send me my orders."

So Joshua went to sea again in mid-August. That first cruise was little more than a shakedown voyage, though they did convoy the brigantine *Mercury* to sea, carrying Henry Laurens on a mission to the Dutch. After that they fought an action with the British dispatch brig *Keppel* and found the *Saratoga* too lightly ballasted to be able to hold her own in any but the lightest airs. On the return, however, they managed to save face somewhat by taking the rich snow *Sarah*, bound from Nevis for New York with rum, which netted them enough, at least, to see Ann through the winter.

After that Joshua went out again in the *Saratoga,* and this time, it seemed, luck was with them, for one after another they took four quick prizes. The sloop *Elizabeth,* with Indian corn, spars, and Negro slaves, they sent in to Philadelphia. The *Charming Molly,* 22, from Jamaica for New York, with rum and sugar, showed fight and was severely damaged in the taking. But her rich cargo remained intact, and Joshua and a prize crew were set aboard her with orders to maintain contact with the *Saratoga.* Next day they took another ship, *Elizabeth,* 14, and a brig, *Nancy,* 4, both also laden with rum and sugar and bound from Jamaica for New York. With rum selling at three dollars a gallon, and nearly two thousand hogsheads of it aboard their prizes, it is hardly extraordinary that Joshua had bright dreams of a fine birthing present for Ann when they returned to port.

But fortune proved fickle with her favors. That very night fresh gales blew up, and Joshua, in the wallowing *Molly,* had to give up the effort to remain with the swift-sailing *Saratoga* and run for safety in Chesapeake Bay. When the dawn came up it was to find themselves squarely caught between H.M. line-of-battle ship *Intrepid,* 64, Captain James Pye Malloy, and the frigate *Raleigh,* 32, which the British had not long before captured from the Americans and put into their own service. In the circumstances, with a leaky, bumbling, badly battered ship under him, and only eight men in his prize crew, Joshua had little choice. Within the hour he stood again upon a British deck, once more a prisoner of war.

2. *Amsterdam*

THAT Kenny did not fulfill the gloomy predictions of John Paul Jones in his report was no evidence of undue pessimism on the captain's part. Even today a man carried from the battlefield with side laid open from armpit to knee by a gunshot blast; whose thigh and hip are shattered and ribs caved; whose face, though lacerated, has only been saved by his upraised arm; and whose right hand has been blown off at the wrist, would hardly be given more than an even chance to live. In those days it was an almost foregone conclusion that he would not.

It was a tribute to the surgical skill and medical knowledge—far in advance of his time—of the surgeon of the *Bonhomme Richard* that Kenny did live. Indeed, if the English gunner had aimed his swivel five—or even four—inches to the left, there would have been nothing that even Laurens Brooke could do. As it was, when they found him crumpled and bleeding in the scuppers, there remained yet a spark of life in Kenny's huddled form; and that spark was a challenge to the Norfolk surgeon. He nursed it and blew upon it, working over the unconscious Irishman for hours at a time, removing bits of bone and chunks of lead, fetching the broken ends of the bones together and binding them in place, suturing the wounds as delicately as he could. He tied off the ends of the veins and arteries of the wrist and smoothed the shattered bone, dressed down the remaining skin in a neat flap, and cauterized the whole with boiling pitch, grateful at least for the fact that Kenny was unconscious then and could not feel that greater pain. How he avoided gangrene, the bête noire of the military surgeon of the time, or how he managed to keep that tiny spark of life aglow in the limp form in the absence of transfusions or any knowledge of them, is a mystery. At least it speaks well for Kenny's own wiry strength.

As it was, more than a week went by before Kenny opened his eyes to anything like coherent consciousness. When he did, it was to find himself ashore, already in the care of the Poor Clares, where he had been lodged temporarily with several other wounded. A cherry-cheeked, white-coifed Dutch nun watched him open his eyes.

"Rest you so there!" she whispered, and flew to call Dr. Brooke, who had been waiting for that moment. But though she was not more than five minutes in summoning him, by the time she returned with Brooke in tow Kenny had lapsed again unconscious, and after that it was a long, bitter drag before he could again shake off the delirium and come back once more into the land of the living. When he did finally struggle slowly up again, eight more full weeks had passed; eight weeks in which the nuns had had to feed him by force, and much had happened and much was happening for his shipmates to be telling.

No doubt it was a merciful thing for Kenny that he did lie so long in a state of insensibility, for it gave him time to regain at least a little of his physical strength before he was brought to the shocking discovery of what had happened to him. The full extent of it, of course, he did not realize at first. He was fortunate enough this time to open his eyes and look directly up into the round, smiling face and lively blue eyes of Dick Dale, who had stopped in but a few moments before, as he made it a practice to do at frequent intervals, to see if there was any sign of returning consciousness on his friend's part. It was Dale who lifted a finger to the nun nearby and sent her scurrying for the doctor. He himself grinned cheerfully down at the bandaged figure lying so thin and still in the plain wooden bed.

"So ye've made up your mind to come around again, after all, and stay with us awhile, have ye?" Dale chuckled.

Kenny blinked up at him, somehow feeling unutterably weary and aching in every bone. Where his bones did not ache his flesh seemed on fire, and where he was not burning up, it seemed to him he itched abominably—especially the side of his face. It also seemed to him there was something not altogether right with his vision, for Dale's face was only half clear. The rest of it looked a shapeless gibbering blob. He tried to lift his hand and rub it across his eyes. But, perhaps fortunately, the excruciating pain of the movement sent the blades of hot knives probing all up and down his side and made him cry out in agony and go reeling—so it seemed to him—off into a bloody, flaming haze of near unconsciousness. After that he did not try to move, but once again struggled back to where he had been, this time coming out of it to find Laurens Brooke standing beside Dale and watching him anxiously.

As he looked up Brooke smiled a little with a mingling of anxiety and relief, to say nothing of pride and sharp professional observation.

"How d'ye feel?" The question was purely automatic, a courtesy as commonplace as "Good morning." Both Dale and Brooke knew well enough that he felt bad, though not even the doctor could know how bad.

Kenny swallowed and rolled his eyes gingerly about, taking care not to move his head, which seemed to hurt him. He could not see much, but from what he could observe of the long plain whitewashed room, he was no longer aboard the *Richard* or any other ship. Nor did this in any way resemble the barracks or the infirmary at Mill Prison.

"Where—what——" he managed to gasp.

"Ye're all right now, lad!" It was Dale who answered. "Thanks t' Dr. Brooke here. Ye were hit at the very last minute, it looked like, and we brought ye ashore here in Amsterdam. Ye're at th' monastery o' th' Poor Clares—an' I'll warrant ye, in th' best o' hands!"

"I—don't——" Kenny was bewildered. It all seemed so sudden. Not ten minutes before, it seemed to him, the battle had been just reaching its peak. And now: "What of him—th' Englishman?"

"Him!" Dale laughed. "Bless ye! 'Tis so long since, I'd almost forgot ye did not know. She was a fine new ship, a frigate, but just fitted out, the *Serapis*, Captain Pearson—forty-four they rated her, though she'd fifty guns aboard when we took her——"

"Took her?" In his startled surprise Kenny half raised himself and then went whirling down again into the fiery red haze of pain. He gasped and cried out involuntarily and then came back again. "I—I'm sorry. I didn't mean to yell like that. Sure, I must ha' been hit worse than I'd any notion—at least it hurts! But what is it ye're after tellin' me? We took her, did ye say?"

The expression that flitted across Laurens Brooke's face as he spoke was beyond Kenny's powers of the moment to identify, and it seemed to him that even the laughing Dale looked grim for just an instant.

"Took her, aye!" he said quickly, and his grin returned. "The *Serapis* and the *Scarborough* both——"

"The—the *Richard?*" Kenny asked feebly.

"Matchwood!" replied Dale. "There was naught left o' her but a platform for th' guns, floatin' on a raft o' matchwood. We were lucky to have taken th' Englishman, for she was sinking under our feet when we did!"

Dr. Brooke plucked at his sleeve.

"There's enough for now," he said. "Let him get back a little more strength before you try to talk to him too much."

He took a cup from the nun who appeared silently at his elbow and dropped some powders into it from a folded paper he took out of his waistcoat, then held the cup to Kenny's lips.

"Here, now, my lad," he urged. "Drink this. 'Twill help you sleep a bit. Then when you've gained a bit more, Dick here can tell you the rest."

Kenny turned his head slightly so that his lips left the rim of the cup, and stared at Dale.

"Ye were sayin' 'twas so long since," he reminded him. "What did ye mean by that?"

Dale grinned at him.

"Naught but a matter o' two months or so——" he began.

"Two months!" Kenny almost knocked the cup from Dr. Brooke's hand, and so violent was his start that once again he felt overwhelmed by that sudden, swirling blanket of bloody pain.

When he opened his eyes again he was not quite in time to hear what it was that the doctor said to Dale, but whatever it was must have been sharp and angry, for the lieutenant looked chagrined and abashed. Brooke turned quickly back to him and again pressed the cup against his lips, nor this time did he refuse it or attempt to say anything further. They watched him for a moment and then seemed to draw farther and farther away, until all at once, quite without realizing it, he slept.

After that it seemed to him that whenever he opened his eyes there would be one or another of his shipmates, waiting, watching— quick to jump in response to his needs, to talk, to fetch and carry for him and wait on him, and even, when a little time had gone by, to laugh and joke with him. Dick Dale was the one perhaps most frequently there, then Dr. Brooke, and their two Irish lieutenants, Edward Stack and Eugene McCarty. Even Captain Jones himself seemed to find time to sit with him in addition to all the rest he was doing; and of course there were dozens of others, all of whom seemed to be far more interested in him now than they had been aboard ship: Nat Fanning and John Mayrant, and Chase and Stubbs—all midshipmen—Jack Robinson, the bosun, and even Anthony Jeremiah, their Indian quartermaster, and Colonel Wiebert and Lieutenant Colonel Chamillard of the French Marines.

From these, for all he was scarcely strong enough to lift a cup of water to his own lips—even if they had allowed him to try— he learned much of what had happened; how they had lain almost a week in the Channel after the fight and then run in to the Texel; how the English had protested to the Dutch, and how the Dutch themselves had been split into two completely opposing camps, so that it was hoped that they might also be drawn into the struggle. How Pierre Landais had stormed and fumed and at last taken himself off to Paris to present his case, while Captain Jones summarily relieved him of his command. Little by little Kenny picked up the threads and put the picture together—all except his own state. So far as that was concerned, he knew that he was far too weak and crippled yet to be of any use in a sea fight. But he had hopes—he had fond hopes—and his friends saw to it assiduously that he did not learn actually how things stood with him, not at least until he had regained sufficient strength to be able to withstand the shock.

But they could not keep it from him indefinitely. For all Brooke's care and for all the efforts of his friends, he must learn it sometime. It came to him in the middle of the night, finally, when there was none of them around—and that, perhaps, was just as well.

It was not often he felt the need of a drink of water when he woke, but when he had, thus far, there had always been someone close at hand to reach for it quickly. This time there was no one around— only the dim glow of a night lamp on the bedside table, placed for some odd reason at the left-hand side of his bed. As he turned his head he could see the small pitcher and the glass—perhaps left there thoughtlessly—and his thirst rose in his throat.

With an effort he eased himself gently onto his left side and reached out for the pitcher. Oddly, nothing came in contact with his feeling fingers. His arm swung, in the semigloom, straight past the handle, when it should have stopped, and for a moment the pain of it dazed him and prevented him from seeing why. He rested for a bit, panting, and then again opened his eyes and reached for the pitcher.

But this time he saw it. He could feel it. When he reached the hand, the fingers—all of it was there. Yet as he looked—it was not. Only the stub of his wrist reached out—and the stub of his wrist had no feeling ends, such as he was all but positive were there. He tried—and tried again. And then slowly, nauseatingly, he brought back his arm and looked closely in the semidark. It wasn't—it couldn't be! He could flex the fingers and all but touch the thumb. But yet —it wasn't there. He had no hand!

That was near midnight. It was unusual for Captain Jones to come to his bedside before midday, yet it seemed to him, in the daze of hours that dragged by after that, that it was scarcely daylight before the commodore appeared.

"I'm sorry to be so early, Boyle——" Jones began, then glanced sharply at Kenny's face. "Forgive me! If I'd realized I'd have been here sooner. I see you've learned."

Kenny nodded but could not bring himself to speak. Jones looked uncomfortable.

"I—I don't know what to say, Boyle—as between man and man," he grated at last. "I know a little, I think, how you must feel—and I—I wish there were something I could do. But there's not! Let me tell you, at least, there's not one of us that's not proud of the way you fought and full of feeling for you for what's happened! But I know that doesn't replace what you've lost."

Kenny stared at him dully.

"Thanks—thanks t' ye, Captain," he got out at last. "I'll manage."

Something flickered deep in Jones's eyes, something very close to admiration.

"I'm sure you will, Boyle!" he exclaimed. "I came early today to tell you that Dale and I—and the rest of us—are ordered out in the *Alliance*. We—we wish you were going with us, but since that can't be we want you to know you've the good wishes and the friendship of us all. We don't like to leave you unattended, but Mr. Adams will be here shortly from Paris, and you can count on him for anything you need. In the meantime—at least you are alive! Isn't there someone you'd want me to write to—someone you'd like me to tell how stoutly you've served and how deeply we all feel for you? Isn't there someone to whom I can say, 'He will be back with you soon'?"

With an effort Kenny lifted the stump of his wrist and looked at it.

"Like this, sir?" he demanded. "No, thank ye!"

3. Yet, Freedom!

JOSHUA and his men were carried to New York aboard the *Intrepid*, and it is a fact that Captain Malloy proved a man of far different stamp from those to whom he had previously surrendered. There were no good quarters during that voyage. As a matter of fact, Joshua and the rest of the prisoners were herded in summer uniforms, just as they were taken, into the pen amidships, ordinarily reserved for the hogs, and there held to wait disposition until they reached the gangling city on the island, sometimes called Manhattan. On the way they passed through three snowstorms, and four of their number, who had the misfortune to be frozen to death, were incontinently pitched over the sides by their guards.

Joshua, seething within, came to New York in the full expectation of some degree of justice. But it was his misfortune that he had not kept abreast of the changes in the British command since his own departure. They had been swift and many, and at the moment when he and his fellows were brought in, the quarrel was between Admiral Collier, who cared little what became of prisoners of war, and Admiral Rodney, who seemed even less concerned and indeed appeared only interested in what share of the prize money might be his.

Under such circumstances it was not surprising that William Cunningham should be again in charge of them. Joshua glared at him.

"Are you still here?" he cried. "And back again in charge of naval prisoners? Has Admiral Gambier——"

"Gambier? Hah!" Cunningham lay back his head and laughed, though there was no laughter in his hard blue eyes. "That old Nellie! Be damned, Mr. Barney! Gambier's gone long since, an' things here have been returned to the 'statues quop'—I think ye'd be callin' it! An' I must say 'tis a pleasure t' be havin' ye with us again—a fine pleasure, ye c'n imagine!"

"If——" began Joshua with some heat.

"If—and be damned t' ye!" snarled Cunningham, and he snatched up the heavy riding crop that lay at his elbow and slashed Joshua across the cheek and back, leaving a three-inch gash. "That for yer damned Admiral Gambier! We got rid o' him easy enough. An' now we've reasonable men t' be workin' with. Men that think no more o' ye stinkin' rebels than I do meself."

Joshua lunged at him, but the guards caught and held him. Cunningham slashed at him again and again, until his arm seemed to grow tired, and Joshua's face, turn it this way and that way though he might, was a bloody pulp. Then the provost sat down again and scrabbled through his papers. It was significant that he sent Joshua aboard a ship that would carry him out of his jurisdiction—almost as if he feared that somehow the Yankee might yet again slip around him and destroy his purpose.

"Put him aboard th' *Yarmouth!*" he growled. "We'll see what th' son of a bitch has t' say when Lutwidge gets 'em where they're goin'!"

The *Yarmouth*, surprisingly enough to Joshua, was a fourth-rate; a sixty-four, decently armed, well manned, and as such should have been well commanded, at least. Although Skeffington Lutwidge, her captain, appeared almost fanatically bitter at the American rebellion, he was presumed to be a man of intelligence and breeding. He had commanded an expedition toward the northern pole with such midshipmen in his charge as Horatio Nelson. But evidently more than that was needed. His prisoners were set down in the hold, five decks under, on top of the ship's water casks, where the air was already foul with the stink of the vessel's bilges, and there the hatches were clapped tight upon them, seventy-one of them—

damned rebels all, who deserved, according to Skeffington Lutwidge, all that was coming to them.

They were forty days there, according to Joshua's count, not one of them able to stand erect, and all crowded into a space less than twenty feet square. When they left New York was easy enough to tell from the racket of the incoming cable in the chain locker overhead. But where they were when they arrived was something else again. The guards snatched off the hatch covers and shouted down: "Out, rebels! Up with ye!"

But not a one of them was strong enough to walk, and indeed, eleven of them were dead and foul. The rest, including Joshua, were lifted out in slings and sent for a week to a prison ship nearby, where the stink and the food were foul enough, God knew, for all they were comparatively luxurious beside those they had known. As soon as they had recovered sufficient strength so that their passage through the streets would not be a disgrace to "British Humanity," they were passed ashore under guard, to find themselves in England —in Plymouth—not long after Christmas Day. From the landing they were marched—under heavy guard, for many of the folk who watched them pass were almost openly sympathetic—to Mill Prison. There, without the formality of a trial, they were driven through into the inner enclosure and locked away on charges of treason.

Joshua, it must be admitted, entered the grim old prison yard with more curiosity than most, for he had heard many a tale of the Old Mill and had known many a shipmate who had lain there. It is likely, too, that he came to it with even more than the usual impatience, for far away at home Ann would be approaching her time, and he felt a certain desperation at the knowledge that he would not be there beside her when she needed him most. Since he could not possibly be there now in time to assist at the birthing of his son—somehow the sex of the child was never in doubt so far as he was concerned—then, by all means, he must get there as swiftly as he could.

The gate had not much more than clanged behind him and his scrawny, emaciated fellows before he was contemplating the notion. Exchange, of course, was a slow and tedious process, and he had grave doubts as to whether it was possible from this place. American engagements in European waters since the battle between the *Bonhomme Richard* and the *Serapis* had been too infrequent to insure a flow of English prisoners who could be offered in place of

Yankee captives there. No, if he waited for exchange, the chances were he would rot where he was till the end of the war—and that he had no intention of doing.

Escape, then, offered the quickest possibility of a return to his own, and in this he was not actually sighting his bow at the moon as much as it might seem. He knew of the flight of Johnson and Dale and a dozen others from that very place. And he knew, too, that similar breaks from Forton and Portsea, and even the Nore, were so commonplace that if they were not regarded as the rule they were at least not looked upon as astonishing.

But the means—that was the problem. For one thing, because of just such repeated breaks and attempts as he remembered, the guards themselves had grown more wise and wary, and the thing was more difficult. To begin with, he tried the most obvious route. He secured a handful of fellow prisoners and swore them to secrecy. After that they lifted one of the stones in the back court and started to tunnel their way to freedom. But that was too old and worn a trick, had they but known it, and they had not driven half a dozen feet in the direction of the walls, digging painfully and assiduously, before it was discovered by the guard and filled in and sealed up. Fortunately the discovery was made at a time when none of them was at work on the undertaking, and though the entire prison was lined up and made to stand for hours while the commandant stormed and threatened in an effort to find the culprits, no one spoke. Consequently that attempt, at least, went unpunished.

Their next effort was not so happy. With several of his mates Joshua let himself down through the holes in the privies, into the sewers, whence they crawled along, following the general flow of the slime, only to find, when at last daylight showed through to them and they were actually within sight of the very bay, that their way was barred by a stout iron grille set in stones and concrete.

Of course they were forced to return the way they had come. But once they reached the outlets at the privies they discovered that going down was one thing. Getting back up again was quite another matter. In the end the guards had to be called, and to their ribald jokes and even the snickers of their friends they were dug out and hauled off to confinement in the Black Hole, where they lay for forty days on half rations so that they might have time to consider the enormity of their crime.

It was mid-April before Joshua was released again to the comparative freedom of the prison yard, and for once he was content to sit in the sunlight against the barrack wall while he contemplated his next effort. As was to be expected, he had lost a good deal of strength and vigor in the Black Hole, and he came out thin and emaciated, hollow-eyed and sunken-cheeked. But he had also had time to consider that subtlety was likely to get him farther than more blundering, direct methods. Twice now he had attempted escape. The third effort must be successful—if ever he was to be successful—for if he was caught again he would likely be chained in the Hole as a chronic offender. This time he must succeed, even if it was necessary to buy his freedom.

And that idea was not one that was impossible either, though it would be necessary for him to proceed warily, until he was sure he had found the right guard to bribe. Fortunately the question of money raised little problem. As an officer he was accorded some privileges. One of these was that of cashing small drafts, up to the amount of five pounds, to defray the cost of such small luxuries as he might wish to buy on market days at the gate. Ever since his arrival he had been assiduous in this, passing his weekly drafts through the guard office and drawing them against Lady Grant, a Tory relative of Ann's who lived in London and who he knew could scarcely refuse to honor them for fear of future retaliation on some of her own closer kin in America. By this means he had managed to amass a tidy little sum, which he had secreted in a canvas money belt he had made himself and tied about his middle against his need of it when once he was free. The question of strength was important, too, for naturally he was weakened by his sojourn in the Black Hole. But this, also, was in a fair way to taking care of itself, for he was resilient, and once out in the open air he recovered swiftly. He was, however, wise enough by now not to let the fact become suspected.

It happened that one day he was sitting on the paving stones with his back against the side of the barracks, not far from the back corner, when one of the patrolling redcoats came striding around in a very devil of a hurry to get his tour of duty done and over with and take himself down to the taverns in the town. Joshua sprawled with his legs thrust out before him, and the man did not see him at first. Indeed, he stumbled and almost fell across Joshua's knees. He turned, glowering bleakly—not an old man, but perhaps ten or fifteen years older than Joshua, with wide-set eyes and a fringe of reddish hair and the map of Ireland plain to be seen in his square face.

"Why th' divil don't yez be sittin' where ivirywan that's passin' by'll not be fallin' all over yez?" he demanded.

"Why th' divil don't ye be lookin' where ye're goin' yerself, man, an' not be flingin' around a corner as if ye'd th' whole run o' th' place?" Joshua's retort in the soft, broad brogue of the south of Ireland that he had picked up from Kenny was purely automatic. It was so he had used to tease his friend, and now something in the guard's slight slur brought it back to him. He said it without thinking. But the guard's eyes widened.

"Be Jasus, an' Irishman, an' from County Kerry at that, or begod I'll be eatin' me own muskit, primin' an' all!"

"'Twill be most unpalatable, I'm afraid!" Joshua grinned at him. "For as much as I hate to disappoint you, I was born in Baltimore, in Maryland. But one or two of my very best friends were from the south part of Ireland you mention. I take it you're a Kerryman yourself?"

"Indeed I am that!" cried the soldier, putting the butt of his musket on the ground and leaning on the muzzle, staring the while at Joshua with interest. "An' who wad they be after bein', these friends o' yours ye mention?"

Joshua smiled a little wryly.

"I'm not so sure they're yet alive, for I've heard from neither for a long time," he replied. "But the very best friend a man ever had was a lad from Tralee, of the name of Boyle. The other was a lass from Limerick."

The man looked even more interested, as only an Irishman can.

"Tralee, is it?" he cried. "I'll be knowin' th' place well meself! 'Twas there eight-ten years ago th' bloody damned recruitin' sergeant crossed me palm with th' King's shillin' an' says t' me, 'John Michael O'Gorman, ye're a poor, bad bargain of a recruit, ye are! But such as ye be, begod, ye're a bloody damned lobsterback from now on,' he says—an' so, begod, I've been! But Boyle, now—Boyle! 'Twould seem t' me I know th' name. Wad he be after bein' anny relative o' Big Sean O'Boyle, th' free trader, that th' bloody damned Sassenach previtive min were after takin' an' hangin' at his own door——"

He broke off abruptly, realizing where and what he was. Joshua almost grinned. He nodded.

"That would have been Kenny's father," he said. "He told me about it. 'Twas one of the reasons why he fought so hard for us. But you're a strange one to be wearing the coat you are."

"Ah, am I not just after tellin' yez I couldn't be helpin' meself?" the man cried. "An' don't be gettin' th' notion I'll be th' only wan, either! Sure, 'tis manny a year th' bloody red boogers've been drummin' th' lanes an' highways o' Ireland for th' likes o' us, an' manny's th' trick they'll be usin' t' catch us, too! But, hist! We must not be seen talkin'. I'll be on djuty be th' inner gate tomorry at market time. Do yez be comin' down thin, if ye're so minded, an' if there's anny little thing ye may be wantin' from town, maybe 'tis John Michael O'Gorman himself can be puttin' his hands on it for yez!"

He winked and was about to turn away when Joshua cried out: "Wait!"

He slipped a hand into his pocket and drew out a guinea, which he flipped and the guard caught expertly and slipped into his own coat after a quick look around.

"Drink a pot or two for me to the memory of Kenny Boyle," Joshua told him.

"I will that, yer honor," the soldier promised, and was gone.

Joshua was at the gate the next day, pretending to be looking over the bundles of greens and knit socks that the women from town had brought to offer, and there, sure enough, as large as life and looking perhaps a little the worse for wear but nonetheless happy for it, was John Michael O'Gorman. Joshua eased around toward him, and the guard whispered out of the corner of his mouth:

"Ah, an' a grand good day it is t' ye, sir, though I can't be sure I'll be seein' it right! D'ye know? I've been thinkin'. Ye spoke o' a lass from Limerick that ye knew. Wad it be her name was Moira O'Connell, now?"

"You know her?" Joshua gaped at him.

"Hist!" whispered O'Gorman warningly, and grinned. "Indade! Is there an' Irishman in th' bloody damned British Army that's served in America that does not?"

"I'll be damned!" whispered Joshua in genuine astonishment.

O'Gorman chuckled.

"Oh, 'tis not such a curious coincinence as ye seem t' be thinkin' yerself, sir!" he went on. "For sure she was in Boston whin th' fightin' began, an' she went from there t' Halyfax with us. And after that she was follyin' us down t' New Yark an' thin t' Philadelphy an' back again. What with th' trade she did—an' a fine gey bugarock wench she was!—'twould be more curiouser be a long shot if I shouldn't be knowin' her! What's more, it was after I left but yesterday I got t' thinkin'. She was forever an' a day talkin' about a couple o' lads that had been after doin' her a good turn onct. Wan o' 'em was Boyle, that was for sure! An' t'other was Joshua Barney—an' that's after bein' yerself, for I went straight t' th' rolls an' had a look an' it come t' me thin whin I seen it!"

"The devil!" Joshua exclaimed, still amazed. "What do you suppose ever became of her?"

"Moira?" O'Gorman grinned. "Sure I can be tellin' yez that! She's in London. She took up with a sergeant—Mike Moriarty—that was wounded at Monmouth, an' she come back with him whin he come. Thin what'll ye be thinkin' th' bloody boogers do but up an' send him off t' Inja as soon's he's after bein' recovered. So now she's there alone an' all, gone back t' th' trade she had before, workin' Vauxhall Gardens, they do be sayin', an' livin' not far away in Blackfriars Alley!"

He sighed.

"Ah, man, I'm after tellin' yez! There's times I wisht I was in London me own self!" He grinned. "But, sure! If wishes was to be harses I'd be ownin' me own stage line! An' since ye're a frind o' Moira O'Connell, what is it I can be gettin' fer ye down below in th' town?"

"You wouldn't happen to know of a quiet little tailor shop where you could pick up the uniform of a lieutenant in the British Navy—about my size—now would you?" Joshua grinned, as if he were joking when he said it. But his heart was in his throat for all that.

O'Gorman's eyes slanted toward him and held for a moment. Then one eyelid fluttered.

"It just happened t' come t' me," he said. "Maybe I do at that!"

That was the beginning of it, and the rest is simply told, although it was by no means as simple of execution. John Michael O'Gorman, once he had taken his hand in the game, became almost the moving force behind it; certainly far more than mere go-between. Nor would he accept more than a few guineas with which to drink a health to them all now and again. He seemed to regard it as something of a lark, a means to enliven his own dull existence as prison guard, and perhaps, in a sort of secret way, a chance to get in his own knock at his British masters, for whom he had no love.

It was he who procured the uniform and smuggled it in to Joshua in a bundle of greens. It was his notion that Joshua should pretend to sprain his ankle while playing at leapfrog in the courtyard. After that he fetched in the long shabby overcoat, which covered the American from chin to the tops of his shoes, and a pair of crutches, and advised Joshua to hobble about for several days, so that the other guards would see him and become accustomed both to the coat and to his helplessness. The choice of a confederate within the walls, to bear a hand at the right moment, he left to Joshua. But it was he who made the contacts within the town and arranged the means by which Joshua was to find shelter. When the day itself came, in May, he was again on guard at the inner gate, and when Joshua, feeling far more excited than he looked, hobbled past, O'Gorman whispered out of the corner of his mouth:

"Noon!"

Joshua barely nodded. That would be the time when the officers were at dinner and there would be only the few guards scattered about at infrequent intervals to observe. At midday Joshua and Silas Talbot, whom he had picked to help, wandered over near the wall, not far from the gate, through which they could see the guard, O'Gorman. O'Gorman looked about, wooden-faced. Joshua fidgeted. The guard at the top of the outer wall appeared to be the stumbling block. He was moving slowly. But at last he turned the corner of the wall and was lost to view behind the barracks. For an instant the only redcoat in sight was O'Gorman himself.

The latter nodded abruptly, almost as if he were only shaking a fly from his nose. Joshua dropped coat and crutches, while Talbot leaned against the wall and made a cup of his hands.

"Good luck, Silas!" Joshua whispered.

"Same t' ye!" retorted Talbot. "Over ye go!"

Joshua put his toe in the other's cupped hands and went up the side and over the inner wall. In the next instant he had dropped catlike into the enclose between the inner and outer walls. It took but a second to dust himself lightly and snatch out his cocked hat from inside his coat. He walked toward the outer gate. A sergeant of the guard came out of the guardroom under the arch and glanced at him.

"Good day, Leftenant!" he said smartly, and saluted.

The guard at the door snapped his musket to the present. Joshua returned the salute grimly and without a word strode straight through and down the hill.

4. The Eagle's Flight

THE BACK of his neck prickled, and as he walked Joshua had the feeling of all the eyes on the hill following him. Yet though he was sorely tempted to do both he neither looked back nor broke into a run. Once he was within the town itself, he felt better. There he followed O'Gorman's directions until he came to a corner with a greengrocer's shop on one side, as the Irishman had described. Sure enough, there was a young man lounging there; not a prepossessing young man, but nonetheless one to fit the description. That should be Edward Beckwith, whose father was the Anglican rector of All Saints, on the hill, and who made it his interest to look after Americans. Joshua approached him confidently.

"I say!" he said, adopting the haughty superiority of the British naval officer. "Would you be so good as to direct me to the Crown and Garter?"

The youth straightened.

"Certainly, sir!" he replied. "Since I'm going that way myself, I'll be glad to show you."

That was all there was to it. The password had been given and the reply received. In silence they wound this way and that through the rambling old town and eventually came to the rectory of All Saints, where the Reverend Lindsey Beckwith and his wife Elizabeth greeted Joshua as hospitably as if he were Baltimore kissing kin out for a visit, while Edward Beckwith stood by grinning a little with pride at the smooth way it had all gone, yet looking a little disappointed that it had not been more exciting.

To Joshua's genuine pleasure and surprise there were two other Americans and their Negro servant staying at the Beckwiths'. Dr. Hyndman and Colonel Richardson, both of Salisbury, Maryland, had been captured when the sloop in which they had taken northward passage from Guadeloupe had been overhauled near St. Kitts by the British frigate *Boreas*. As passengers, of course, they were not subject to confinement in the Old Mill, as they would have been had they been taken in the act of bearing arms against the Crown. Nevertheless, they were prisoners, in a sort of loose way, since there was little chance that they would be able to find a ship from Plymouth so long as the war lasted; and though they were both nearly desperate, with that peculiar sort of helpless anxiety that comes to some middle-aged men, to get home to their friends and families, neither one of them seemed to have enough imagination to know quite how to go about it. Joshua took them in tow.

Beyond the Beckwiths, John O'Gorman's plans had not gone. Let Joshua come thus far, he had reasoned, and there would be a number of alternatives. In Hyndman and Richardson, Joshua felt sure he saw a ready-made answer to all their prayers. He himself did not have enough money to accomplish it alone, but if all three of them clubbed together they could buy a fishing smack in which, with Joshua to sail them and their servant to help, they could all go directly to France. After that it would merely be a matter of finding homeward passage.

He broached the matter at teatime that evening, and his enthusiasm was infectious. Both of the Marylanders were easily persuaded, and Edward Beckwith brightened a little at the prospect of further activity for him. Indeed, only Dr. Hyndman's man, Willoughby, seemed at all timid about it. Yet he could scarcely refuse to take part, and in the end it was he who solved one of their most serious problems for them.

That was the selection of a boat. Edward Beckwith knew nothing of such matters, although he was the logical one to make the purchase once the craft was selected. John Michael O'Gorman, who looked in to be sure that everything was going well, was equally ignorant. As for Hyndman and Richardson, they hardly knew the difference between a Chesapeake schooner and an Arabian dhow. Naturally Joshua dared not show his face outside the house. But the man Willoughby, for all his pessimism, had been brought up in Chestertown, and if he did not have much experience with ocean-going vessels, he at least knew a good seaworthy fishing boat when he saw one. It was he, acting on orders from Dr. Hyndman, who settled on the bluff-bowed lugger; Edward Beckwith, who bought it.

The boat stank of fish—enough to turn your stomach almost as she rode at anchor in the still waters of the harbor, Joshua thought as he clambered aboard her in the dark of the second night. But he said nothing of that. At least she was seaworthy and sound, if she would roll like a chip in a tub with any kind of sea. She had but the one mast and sail for him to handle, and he was beginning to suspect that if they were to make it he would have to be captain, navigator, and crew all in one.

They went aboard toward midnight after saying farewell to their friends, and Joshua pressed an extra guinea or two on O'Gorman with which to help drink them over the Channel waves. Richardson and Hyndman seemed to develop a certain nervousness at the stomach as soon as they were on board and retired to the stuffy little cabin below as soon as they had set foot on deck. Willoughby, like Joshua, seemed to prefer the night air on deck, at least until they were well away, when he, too, disappeared below. However, he remained on deck long enough to help Joshua get up the anchor and set the sail at the outward turn of the tide, and that was as much as Joshua cared. After that, he felt, he could manage well enough by himself.

They got under way a little before dawn, and the sky was just lightening with the first pale hint of gray as they swung out of the Catwater into Plymouth Sound and found the whole of Admiral Digby's British home fleet at anchor before them. Joshua gulped at the sight and was glad he had taken the precaution to throw on a tarry old seaman's watchcoat over his uniform and replace his naval cocked hat with a three-cornered tarpaulin. Nevertheless, he held his breath as they threaded their way amid the towering frigates and two-deckers lying at anchor, scarcely daring to glance left or right for fear he might be challenged by one of the prowling sentries or alert watch officers aboard. But he was in luck, apparently. None of them had eyes for a stinking little fishing smack creeping out to sea in the dawn. By the time it was broad day they had cleared the Shagstone and found a brisk sea running down through the Channel. Joshua made fast the tiller and went forward to call the others with the suggestion that they broach the jug of rum they had brought for the occasion, only to find them all rolling in misery in the bunks below—master and man alike—and not caring whether they lived or died.

It was heartless of him, no doubt, but he could not help it. He laughed at them and wet his own whistle. After that he offered them each a bit of salt pork, which he swore was good for all ills, and after they had indignantly refused he returned on deck and set his sails and his course for the jut of the Breton coast.

But his luck had been almost too good to last, as he began to suspect when, actually within sight of the French coast, a Jersey privateer took a look at him and then came about and bore down to speak.

He tried to bluff it out when the boarding officer came over the side. He threw open his seaman's coat to display his British officer's uniform and declared that he was on a most secret mission to France and that the Admiralty and the Crown itself would be more than a little vexed if he was in any way detained. The boarding officer, a lean Guernseyman, was impressed. That was clear. But he could shift the responsibility to his captain, and when that rotund gentleman was called and Joshua refused to reveal his "important mission" to him, he, too, showed that he could be stubborn. In that case, he said, he would have no choice but to take Joshua and the lugger back to Plymouth, where surely Joshua would not object to revealing the nature of his so secret journey to Admiral Digby. If the admiral was satisfied, then, said the Jerseyman, so would he be. But at least he would have the satisfaction of knowing that he had done his plain duty—and that was that!

Joshua fumed and swore and acted as arrogant and haughty as any English naval officer who deigned to talk to a lubberly privateersman. The delay would jeopardize the thing he had been sent to do, he declared. The Jerseyman was sorry. If Joshua would not reveal his mission to him, then he would have to tell the admiral. If it was jeopardized by his own stubbornness, then that would be on Joshua's own head. Was he to reveal the Crown secrets to every stinking, fishmongering merchantman-turned-pirate who chose to stop him? Joshua demanded. The Jerseyman shrugged. It was clear he was not too fond of the high-and-mighty junior officers of the Royal Navy, in any case. The best Joshua could do was threaten. Once they were aboard the admiral's ship, by the Lord, he would see to it that a press gang went at once aboard the privateer and fetched off the best of the Jerseyman's men for service in the fleet. But though that might ordinarily have given the privateer pause, for the fleet was hard up for men and a trained crew such as his would be at a premium, his own anger was aroused, and nothing would do but that the lugger must come about, under the care of a prize crew, and wallow through the night, back again to Plymouth where the captain and mate themselves went aboard the admiral's flagship to present their story, leaving Joshua and his mates aboard the privateer to cool their heels until their return with the admiral's orders.

A man's fate, however, will hang often by the slenderest of threads. Joshua's threat, uttered in a fit of purest bluster, was evidently the one thing that saved him, for, approaching Plymouth, the Jerseyman thought best to anchor at as great a distance from the fleet as possible, at Cawsand, whence he rowed across several miles of open water to the waiting flagship. Hardly was he gone before the crew of the privateer, almost to a man, fled ashore to escape the irate lieutenant's threat of impressment and went to ground in the various taverns and taprooms of the village.

Joshua saw his chance. There was a dinghy lying at the tow astern, and it would be but the work of an instant to haul this alongside and slip over into it and row ashore. He took Hyndman and Richardson aside and told them his plans, pointing out that he had no alternative but that. Since he had been taken in a British naval uniform his very life depended on escape now. They, however, had neither broken prison nor pretended to be other than they were. Indeed, they had said nothing. No harm was likely to befall them. He offered to take them with him but actually was as well pleased when they elected to stay aboard and await the privateersman's return.

They did, however, agree to divert the steward and such other crew members as still remained aboard, and this they did with the jug of rum that had been put aboard the lugger. Under such cover Joshua had no difficulty slipping away and sliding down the rope into the dinghy and hastening ashore. But one man on the beach had seen him come, and he walked over half idly as Joshua leaped out onto the sand. To forestall any interference Joshua once more showed his uniform.

"Bear a hand here, my man!" he commanded arrogantly. "Fetch this boat up out of reach of the tide! Where will I find our people? Can you tell me?"

"Aye, aye, sir!" The man was obviously an old hand, for automatically he touched his forelock and then laid hold of the dinghy's gunwales. "I think they be all up yawnder be th' inn, nigh t' Plymout' Road!"

Joshua thanked him and strode off. Needless to say, he did not stop at the inn "nigh t' Plymout' Road" but kept straight on past the place. Nor did he pause again until, just at nightfall, he came back once more by back ways and alleys to the rectory at All Saints and the temporary shelter of the Beckwiths' hearth.

To say that the Beckwiths were merely distressed and astounded at his sudden reappearance would be a distinct understatement.

They were alarmed and apprehensive, both for him and for themselves, for they saw plainly the threat to him, and now that a hue and cry may have been raised they were afraid it might lead straight to their door. Swift action was necessary, but fortunately Joshua was equal to the problem. Edward Beckwith was about of a size with him. He must have a spare suit of clothing. Joshua would buy it and pay well. That done, Edward was sent out to engage a post chaise in which he might drive to Exeter. Within an hour of the time he appeared at their door Joshua had once again said farewell to his clerical friends and was driving at near top speed for the town at the mouth of the Exe.

At Exeter he surrendered his chaise at the Royal Clarence just in time to catch the Bristol coach that left with the dawn. At Bristol he went to ground for a week with the Americans' secret agent at that place—a collector of His Majesty's Customs!—until he could obtain several more complete changes of clothing. After that, as jaunty as any British gentleman, he rode the top seat of the stage all the way to London and there dropped off at the Temple and disappeared into the blessed anonymity of the city.

Joshua was far from so foolish, however, as to believe himself safe simply because he had won this far. Nor had he come to that place without a plan. It was early evening when he dropped from the Bristol stage, and it was just growing dusk when twenty minutes later he turned in at the Vauxhall Gardens. There he began his search quietly, unobtrusively, strolling along the garden paths unconcernedly, unhurriedly, as if he did not jump inside at the sight of every uniform that crossed his way. There were far too many of those hereabout for his taste. He had the feeling that at any moment he might find himself face to face with Captain Elphinstone or Captain Conway or one of Admiral Gambier's bright young men —any one of a dozen who might recognize him. But that was a risk he must run, he told himself. He had crossed the Gardens twice, past the playhouse where *The Beaux Stratagem* was showing, past the pavilion where a string ensemble was playing something very British and not at all conducive to the romance the place was supposed to engender. He was beginning to look in some doubt at these larger buildings, wondering if he should not search in there, when he saw her turning laughingly away from a stiff-backed officer of dragoons, who had just shaken his head haughtily at her, much as to say he needed none of her favors.

"Moira!" he cried.

She turned in the dusk and came toward him, peering as if to see who could have called.

"Did someone——" she began. Then all at once she recognized him. "Joshua! Oh, Holy Mother av all th' saints! Joshua! What——"

She hardly gave him a chance to answer but flung herself upon him and wrapped her arms about his neck, as gay and excited as a child. He caught her almost in self-defense and held her to him.

"Moira!" he cried, and added in a lower tone: "Hist! This is no safe place for me. Is there somewhere we can go and talk—some place we'll not be observed—some quiet spot?"

"Av course, ye ninny!" She laughed. "Me own rooms—where else? They're but just around th' corner!"

He held her off and looked at her. Whatever she might have been doing these six years past, it hardly seemed to have touched her. Indeed, if anything, she seemed even more handsome than ever in a maturer way.

"D'you think we should?" he asked soberly. "I mean is it right?"

She laughed again, almost teasingly, at that.

"Why not?" she demanded. "What d'ye think I'd be doin' but entertainin' me own friends there? Sure 'twill be a novelty fer me t' be fetchin' home a friend fer a cup av tea that I met so long, long, long ago!"

He did not miss the little barb of bitterness that went with that last remark as he took her by the arm and turned her about on the path.

"Don't, Moira!" he said in a low tone. "I'm not here to torment you. I helped you once. I've come to you now because you may be able to help me."

She stopped and stared at him in surprise.

"Me help ye?" she demanded incredulously. "How?"

"I'll tell you when we've—got out of here," he replied.

They walked for a moment in silence after that, each with his own thoughts racing.

"What about—him?" she asked abruptly.

"Kenny?" He shot a glance at her in the dusk and shook his head. "I wish I could tell you for sure. He was aboard the *Bonhomme Richard* and was badly wounded—so badly, indeed, that Captain Jones reported he did not believe he would live. We've heard naught of him since."

Her fingers tightened on his arm.

"Oh no!" she half cried, half whispered. Then she turned to him insistently. "Tell me what ye will be knowin'! Tell me everythin'! There's a good lad, Joshua."

As they walked out through the Gardens and turned into Black-friars Lane he told her much of what had happened to both himself and Kenny. She nodded approval when she heard how he had bid in the other's indentures and taken him home, and she looked proud when she heard that Kenny had gone into the naval service with him. She even seemed pleased when she learned of Kenny's and Barbary's love. Then all at once she remembered and turned sober.

"Poor lambs!" she whispered. "Poor, poor lambs!"

She turned him off at that point, out of Blackfriars Lane and into the narrow alley that bears the same name, where the pointed half-timbered houses leaned out toward one another as if reaching for an embrace. Halfway along the cul-de-sac she stopped and thrust open a door that led into a dim hallway.

"Here we are now!" she cried. "Ah, Joshua, me duck! Never a thought did I have in me head that one av these nights 'twould be yerself I'd be bringing t' this door!"

They entered, and Joshua sniffed the moldering, half-dead air of the hall. But halfway along Moira stopped at yet another door, and with a key yet warm from her own handsome bosom unlocked it and thrust it open before him.

The room they entered, warm and cozy and neat and tidy, with a fire of sea coals upon the grate and the kettle singing merrily upon them, was as different from the hall outside as a snug cottage from a barnyard litter. Moira shut the door behind them while Joshua stared about him.

"Why, Moira," he cried, " 'tis cozy and fine, and snug as anything, and it has the marks of your own sweet hand on everything."

She beamed, obviously pleased as a child with this compliment. Laughing, she tossed off her hat and cape and slipped into a rear room, evidently the bedroom, to reappear in an instant with a canister of tea and a squat black bottle. With deft hands she plucked down the teapot and measured out the tea, pouring the boiling water over it and lacing the steaming cups with rum.

"A drink we'll be havin' t' seein' one another again!" She smiled.

"An' then ye'll be tellin' me about yerself an' how it is that I can be helpin' ye."

They sipped at their warming mugs, and Joshua felt the glow of the liquor spread through him. All at once he felt vastly relieved and relaxed, as if now, at last, he were close to safe ground and could breathe a little easier again. At her prompting he told her all that had happened to him in the recent months, and when he spoke of the soldier O'Gorman, Moira gave a gay little laugh and clapped her hands.

"Why, then, if 'tis Johnny O'Gorman ye've been talkin' with there'll be no need av me tellin' ye a thing about meself, for sure he knows everythin' that's happened t' me, an' no secret would he be makin' av it either!"

"He told me a good deal of you, that's a fact!" Joshua nodded. "In fact, 'tis because he told me where I might find you that I'm here at all. Moira, I must get out of England, and I can think only of yourself that may be able to help me do it."

She looked at him softly, soberly.

"Whatever it is I can be doin', Joshua," she told him, "ye've but t' be askin' it. Ye know that."

"I was sure of it!" He smiled. "And really 'tis not much. As you know, I can't be seen around. I'll give you the money and get you to buy me a place on the Ostend packet. Then if I can find a place to stay——"

She looked utterly offended.

"Whist now!" she cried. "Where else'd ye be stayin' but right here?"

"But——" he started to protest. And he glanced involuntarily at the open door of the single bedroom, then turned pink to the ears.

"Tosh!" She laughed. " 'Tis big enough fer th' two av us, an' purposely so, indeed!" And then she sobered. "An' sure, Joshua, I'd not be botherin' ye, if 'tis that ye're thinkin' about."

" 'Tis not yourself bothering me, Moira," he cried, "but just the other way round! D'you realize how long it is since I've laid eyes on a woman—let alone lain beside one?"

She tossed her head with a grin.

"D'ye think that'd trouble me?" she demanded.

" 'Twould trouble me!" he said soberly. "I've my own conscience to live with—and a wife, and a child I've never seen waiting at home for me!"

"Ah, an' why must th' best men av ye be always bringin' that up?" she cried almost harshly. "Who asks t' be sharin' yer love? All that th' likes av meself could be askin' 'd be t' give ye a little t' comfort yer needs, an' perhaps be takin' some av th' warmth av yer body and stren'th av yer arms in return! How could a wife be missin' so little?"

Joshua shook his head somberly.

" 'Tis just that 'tis so much a part of the bargain, I guess," he said. "I only know that I'd not feel right!"

"Aaarr!" She made a hurt little sound in her throat and rose abruptly. "Well, annyways, there's supper t' be gettin'! If ye prefer it that way we'll be takin' turns with it! Ye sleep in it while I'm out, an' I'll be havin' me crack at it later."

He shook his head but did not answer, and they discussed it no more while she deftly set about fixing a meal for them. All at once he realized that he was both desperately hungry and bitterly tired. The excitement that had carried him here from Plymouth, on the crest of a wave in a way, had sapped his strength and at the same time curtailed his appetite. Now that he was here he felt both of them strike with telling force. When the supper of beef and kidney pie and hot biscuits and tea was ready he realized, too, that Moira was a superb cook. With her to urge him on subtly he did not stint himself in the eating. But when it was done he found himself nodding while she washed up the dishes. Indeed, he was all but asleep by the grate when she turned and saw him.

"Ah, ye poor lamb!" she cried suddenly, sympathetically. " 'Tis fair dead on yer feet ye are yerself! Go on with yez! Into th' bed yonder an' get some sleep! We'll talk more av this in th' mornin'!"

He was too drugged with fatigue to argue with her. She pushed him into the bedroom and closed the door behind him. When she was gone, more than half automatically he pulled off his clothes and fell into the great, faintly perfumed bed. But he never noticed that, for his head had scarcely touched the pillow before he was asleep, soundly, completely, dead to the world.

What time it was when he awoke he did not know. But it was dark. Moira was lying on the bed beside him; not in it, in her night shift, as she had every right to be in her own bed surely, but on top of the covers, fully dressed but for a loosening of her stays, and wrapped loosely against the chill of the night in an old quilt. She lay far over on the side of the bed so as not to disturb him.

Sleepily, half instinctively, he put out his hand toward her and without the least intent dropped it squarely upon her breast. For an instant, it seemed to him, she stiffened and trembled. Then gently, lightly, her hand reached down to his and carried it up to her cheek, where she pillowed it. As sleepy as he was, the move touched him.

"Ummm-um!" He half yawned. "Moira, you're a good girl!"

There was a long moment of silence. Then abruptly he felt a warm wetness against the palm of his hand under her cheek.

"Moira!" He sat up, all at once quite wide awake. "Moira, child! You're crying! What the——"

"I—I—I'm sorry, Joshua," she gulped, striving to hold back the tears now and not quite succeeding. "'Twas no thought I had t' be distressin' ye. But—but—'tis a long time since annywan was sayin' that t' me!"

5. Reunion in the Lowlands

KENNY lay for a long, long time at the monastery of the Poor Clares after the departure of Paul Jones and the rest of his shipmates in the *Alliance*. He was weak, abominably weak, and sorely hurt. Such wounds as he had taken were not to be healed overnight, and this would account for much of his slow recovery, though it could not truly be blamed for all. His own bitterness had something to do with it; a bitterness that sprang not so much from a blame of any-one or anything for what had happened, or from regret for a decision taken, but rather because he felt himself to be a broken, useless thing; a hulk, to be tended and fed and constantly cared for, never able to do for himself many of even the most ordinary things. Far better, was his constant self-reminder, for all concerned, if he had died!

But once it has reached a certain stage, physical progress cannot be halted. Bones knit and flesh heals—slowly, perhaps, but none-theless surely. The wounds on Kenny's face were the first to heal, being the most superficial; though, like the rest, they left behind them livid nicks and streaks and stripes, ugly, unsightly scars that he knew he would carry through the rest of his life. Next came his side and the wounds under his arm. After them his thigh healed. Then, almost the slowest and most painful, was his hip. His wrist ached for years.

A good part of his slow recovery, to be sure, was due to the fact that all of his wounds were on the same side. Once his side and armpit had healed sufficiently to allow him to hobble around upon a crutch, he found even that impossible, for he had no hand with which to grasp the crutch's staff. Thus he had to lie abed until the bones and flesh of hip and thigh had knit enough to allow him to stand upon them. Perhaps this accounted for the fact that his right leg healed shorter than his left by almost three inches; or that, when at last he could stand and hobble about, it was necessary to teach himself to walk all over again, and that he accomplished only with a pronounced twisting, limping gait, almost a hitching movement, that was yet another bitter, rancid pill to swallow.

John Adams came from Paris in March—nearly seven months after the battle. At the request of John Paul Jones he looked in upon Kenny and was deeply shocked at what he found. Kenny was lying still abed, thin, unshaven, hollow-eyed. He did not turn his face to look at the older man. Instead he continued to stare moodily at the wall.

"Mr. Boyle?" said Adams.

John Adams had not become prominent through lack of memory or slowness of wit or imperception. He recognized Kenny, of course. He remembered their interview as if it had happened only the day before.

"What d'ye want?" said Kenny.

"There's no use telling you 'tis the misfortunes of war," Adams replied as he hitched a chair over to Kenny's bedside and dropped his rotund form into it. "I'm sorry to see you so badly hurt. I hope you'll believe that."

"All right!" growled Kenny. "I believe it."

"When I saw you aboard the cartel——" Adams had a knack for ignoring what he did not wish to hear. Kenny turned his face toward him, and the surprise in his eyes was the first expression he had shown.

"Will ye be recallin' that, then?"

"Of course!" Adams retorted almost indignantly. "I was about to say—when I saw you there you spoke of getting home with all possible speed to let someone know that you were alive and free again. I want you to know I admire your courage and your sacrifice, the one of which Captain Jones has told me, and the other I can see for myself. But have you written home to let them know what's happened? That you still live?"

Kenny's lips twisted in a bitter grin. He lifted the stump of his wrist.

"How would I be writin'?" he demanded. "Sure I was never worth a damn with me left."

Adams shook his head sympathetically.

"I'd be glad to——" he began.

"No!" said Kenny sharply, and then apologized. "Beggin' yer pardon, sir! I'm a touch distressed. I daresay ye'll be understandin'. I'd rather not."

"Think it over."

He went away then, but that did not mean that he dropped the matter nor that he had lost interest. On the contrary, having seen Kenny, he was more than ever concerned. The lad needed help, that was certain, even though he might be too proud to ask for it. And in view of what he had done, the cherry-cheeked New Englander felt, it was the nation's duty, through him, to see that he had it.

He sought out the mother superior and had a long earnest conversation with her. From there he went to the small, snug home of Hans and Katje van Kloop, a jolly, buxom, bright-faced middle-aged Dutch couple who lived not too far from the heart of Amsterdam and both of whom spoke English of a sort. Hans was a cabinetmaker, expert with knife and chisel, a wood carver, an artist, and craftsman. Katje cooked and sewed and cleaned. Her house was spotless, her table of the best. They had no children. They listened to Adams's story with ever-lengthening faces. When he finished and offered his suggestion they both clucked sympathetically and cried out:

"Ach! Poor boy! Ya! Ya! By every means! Bring him to stay with us!"

John Adams returned to Kenny at the Poor Clares.

"I'm afraid we'll have to move you, my lad," he said.

"Why?" Kenny looked at him suspiciously.

"Why? 'Tis obvious you can't stay here with the nuns forever!" Adams shrugged. "You can get around a little now. I've found a place in the city where they'll look out for you until you're on your feet again and able to do for yourself——"

"When will that be?" demanded Kenny. "Will it be ever, are ye thinkin'?"

"Of course!" Adams retorted. "And sooner than you think. In the meantime, you'll be comfortable with these folk. There are just the two of them—the old gentleman and his wife. They'll not be troubling you, and you'll be no trouble to them."

So Kenny moved from the Poor Clares to the house of Hans van Kloop, while John Adams returned to Paris. At the outset Kenny was almost perversely determined he would not like it, but in spite of himself he found himself drawn to these cheerful folk. They fed him well. They helped him when he needed it. But they laughed and joked and never referred, even obliquely, to his own difficulties. Almost without being aware of it he began to be a little lifted out of himself, though sometimes, in the lonely hours of the night, when he lay awake and brooding, when he thought of Barbary, he would be plunged again into the blackness of despair.

In the evenings, after supper, when the table was cleared and Katje hummed cheerfully over the dishes and her household chores, which never seemed to be done, Hans van Kloop would fetch out the jar of tobacco and a pair of long clay pipes and a bottle of schnapps and the chessboard with the elaborate men he had carved himself. He would set them up, and then they would play, Kenny using his left hand more and more deftly to move his pieces, and never even noticing that the pipe was always filled when Hans handed it to him. Over the weeks he learned to speak a little Dutch, while they learned more English, and more and more he became expert with his left hand, though he could never learn to write with it, and either Hans or Katje had to cut his meat for him—two circumstances which irked him bitterly. Nevertheless, even so slight a human contact did him good without his being aware of it. In much the same way, under the necessary exercise of going up and down stairs, his bones knit more rapidly and grew stronger. He still had his limp, definite and pronounced, to be sure. Yet almost without his knowing it he was walking more smoothly, more naturally.

John Adams came back again from Paris in June and one evening looked in on the van Kloops and their guest. The change both astonished and pleased him, though he was careful not to let on. Kenny was shaven and his eye was bright. If there were still traces of the broody mood that sometimes descended upon him, at least they were nowhere near so bitter as they had been.

"Well, Boyle, my lad!" cried Adams, as if he were surprised to find him still there. " 'Tis good to see you! And how are you now?"

"Much better, thanks t' ye, sir!" Kenny grinned. " 'Tis beginnin'

t' get around a bit now, I am. An' Hans here has been introducin'
me t' schnapps an' chess. Give me a week or two more, an' I declare
t' ye I'll be beatin' him!"

Adams chuckled.

"Aye! And by the time we've a new ship fitted out you'll be ready
for a berth in her."

Kenny's smile was a little wry at that, and Adams did not pursue
the subject.

"I saw Captain Jones in Paris," he said. "He asked for you, and
he gave me this for you. Dr. Franklin, when he heard your name
mentioned, also remembered this—it came some time back, just after
the *Lexington* had left Morlaix."

He held out the two packets: one the letter from Barbary, written
just after she had heard from Joshua that Kenny was aboard the
Richard, the other the letter written by Joshua himself so long ago.

Kenny stared at them, and his expression went bleak. Nevertheless, he accepted them and put them in his pocket.

"Thank ye, sir," he said grimly.

"Are you not going to read them?" Adams cried.

"Later—perhaps," Kenny replied shortly.

Adams shook his head and took his leave, pausing at the door for
a brief word with Hans van Kloop, who went with him that far.

"The lad's better—much better," he said. "But there's a long way to
go yet. Keep up your good work, Mynheer. We'll make it worth
your while."

"Ya! Ya!" Hans van Kloop flushed at the mention of money. "As
you say, so much there is yet to be done! But of the pay do not be
thinking. Like a son to us he is."

It lacked an hour till suppertime when he left. While Hans went
with Adams to the door, Kenny turned abruptly and without a word
to Katje slowly, laboriously climbed the stairs to his own room.
Inside he drew the two packets from his pocket and stared at them
but made no move to open them. Presently he propped them on his
bureau and then went to sit on his bed. He was still sitting there in
the dusk, staring at the untouched letters, when Katje came to call
him down to the meal she had prepared.

He came down a few moments later, looking glum and morose,
to find them already seated at the table and awaiting him with a
great air of suppressed glee and expectation, as if they might suddenly burst out into a song about happy birthdays and fetch a cake

and candles and all out of the oven. He found the reason at his place as he was about to sit down, and he stopped and stared down at it, while Hans and Katje held their breath, wondering what he would do.

Slowly he reached out with his left hand and picked it up—a curious contraption; a perfectly carved, entirely natural wooden hand, carefully painted, so lifelike that it almost seemed he could see the grain of the skin upon it. At the upper end, at the wrist, there was a socket and a tongue of wood, hollowed out to go around his wrist, with a set of straps and another tongue on the underside to hold it steady. Obviously Hans had made it, secretly carving away at it in his spare time until he had it just so. Kenny looked at it as he sat down slowly, then blinked and blinked again and gulped.

"I——" he choked. "Hans! Katje, see? Why, th' blessin' o' God be on th' pair o' ye! 'Tis perfect—per-fect! God love ye! If I was t' be puttin' a glove on it now an' pulled me sleeve down, there's none'd ever be tellin' it from th' real thing!"

Katje got up quickly and went to fuss over the stove, and even Hans cleared his throat roughly.

"Ho!" He laughed his deep, Dutch, booming chuckle. "*Nein!* That is not the same, but at least it is better than nothing, no? Look! Even I have made it so that with the other hand it is easy to put on —see?"

He took Kenny's wrist and fitted the hand in place, showing how by a simple snapping of the catches it would fit and hold.

"By gorry, now!" cried Kenny. "Sure 'tis as good as real!"

To demonstrate he seized a glass of wine and with his left hand fitted it between thumb and finger and made as if to drink. But the glass was not well wedged, and when it came off balance it slipped and spilled, spreading a broad blood-red stain across the clean white tablecloth. There was an instant's silence.

"Ach! There!" cried Katje quickly. "It does not matter! A little practice it will take. Then you will see."

That saved the moment, at least. Kenny took her at her word, and they made a jolly evening of it after that—jolly, that is, through the supper and well into the evening after, when Katje was cleaning up the dishes and Hans had fetched out the board and they began to play. They laughed and drank their wine and schnapps, and Kenny hardly even noticed when Katje cut up his cutlet for him.

But all was not right. Perhaps it was the letters that sat still upstairs on his bureau, unopened, to which his mind kept turning. Perhaps it was the hand which was new and a little clumsy and not quite snug. It wobbled, and twice after he spilled the wine Kenny knocked things over. The last straw came when he was about to make a move on the chessboard. Half automatically he reached out with the new hand to lift the piece. But there was no feeling in it and it wobbled slightly, touching two of the nearby men. They fell and rolled, and Kenny nervously grabbed for them—or attempted to—and the whole array went toppling. The reminder was more than he could bear.

"Bah!" he cried, and with his left hand knocked the board across the room. Angrily he snatched at the wooden hand and jerked it off and flung it in a corner. "Th' hell with it! Th' hell with th' whole damned thing! I'm goin' up t' bed!"

He turned and, stumping angrily, stormed up the stairs and slammed his door behind him.

Below, Katje and Hans exchanged glances. Katje shook her head. After a bit Hans rose and retrieved the hand and studied it, turning it over and over.

"Look, Katje," he said suddenly. "Look, here—and here! If I make this longer, and here a piece add, and pack the socket so tight it fits, and then a crook in this finger, and a little bend in that—— Ya! I think we make it right yet, you see!"

Kenny came down the next morning feeling shamed and apologetic.

"I lost me temper," he said, "not at yerselves, me good friends, though I was hurtin' yer feelin's, be it, I'm afraid. 'Twas angry at meself I was. I hope ye'll be forgivin' me!"

"Ach, nein!" they cried. "Let us no more be thinking of that, and no more be saying!"

So it was forgiven and, by Kenny, at least for the moment, forgotten. Hans went off to his shop, and after a while Katje noticed that Kenny went upstairs and fetched down the letters that John Adams had brought. He sat down by the fire and, awkwardly holding them down with the stub of his wrist, tore them open with his left hand. Then one by one, with great difficulty in turning the pages, he read them. When he was done she noticed that he sat for a long time staring moodily into the grate. Then he rose, clutching the letters in his good hand, and went to the little table in the nook, where he sat down and buried his face in his arms.

For a long time she did not disturb him. Then at last she went to him and touched his shoulder gently.

"Kenny!" she said. "Kenny, would you like an answer to those letters I write for you? Not so good I do maybe—but I could try."

He looked up at her, and the agony in his eyes wrung her heart. But he said nothing. He only shook his head slowly, then dropped it again onto his arms. After a while she went away and left him alone.

Several nights later Hans came home late. Katje was already setting the supper table. Hans had a package under his arm, and this time he did not wait for any surprises but instead beckoned to Kenny and unwrapped the package, taking out the rebuilt hand, improved according to the way he had figured it. The two tongues above and below had been lengthened so as to come nearly up to the elbow, and two side strips had been added. Several more clamps had been put on to bind the piece to his arm, and the inside of the socket itself had been padded with soft lamb's wool to prevent chafing. More important than those improvements, however, was the fact that instead of being comparatively straight, all four fingers had been removed and replaced by a new set, each curved so that they still looked natural, yet each formed a little step above the next, while the thumb had been set on a stiff pivot so that with the left hand it could be swung against anything the fingers might support and would so hold it in place.

"See!" cried Hans, demonstrating. He fastened the hand in place and then turned and snatched up a glass of wine and deftly slipped it into grip so that the little pedestal of the tiny goblet rested on the platform of the third finger, while the stem was braced against the crook of the first and second. Then he swung the thumb over so that it rested against the bottom of the glass. "Now drink! Spill it will not!"

Kenny stared at the glass first, then at Hans. Then silently he tried it. The glass rode evenly, steadily to his lips, and he drank the contents without spilling a drop.

"Hans!" he cried excitedly. "It really works now!"

Then abruptly he sobered.

"I—I'm sorry to have been as I was that night," he said. "Sure ye must be thinkin' me a poor sort——"

"Pooh!" snorted Hans. "Often many things we must try three, four times before we have them right, no? Why not with this too? Now it works! If any way we can make it better, so we will do, eh?"

It would be difficult to tell all that that one small thing did for Kenny. The hours of thought and care that Hans had spent on the hand were far from wasted. Indeed, they were a godsend, for that one thing alone seemed to take Kenny out of his hell of despair. He wore the hand after that from morning to night, only laying it aside when he went to bed, and once when Hans took it back to the shop to make a model of it and add a few special clamps to the fingers, where they would not show, for the easier holding of difficult objects. With their help Kenny was even able to teach himself to write a little—a rough scrawl, but still legible, that improved with practice. He found that with it he could dress and undress himself with ease. He could cut his own meat and hold his own glass. He could even pour out of a bottle and load his own pipe—as for chess, he did beat Hans within a week, and he no longer fumbled for the men. Katje was particularly pleased one evening to notice that he was rereading his letters—with a far different expression—and holding them quite naturally and entirely unconsciously in his artificial hand.

But the hand had even greater value than that. From the model he had taken Hans made several more identical ones so that he would have a change in case of need, while Katje made a number of special gloves to be worn over it. As soon as she gave them to him he whooped with glee and that very afternoon went out for a stroll— something he had not done since the loblolly boys had picked him up from under the bulwarks of the *Serapis,* where he had fallen.

But there was even yet another way in which it helped, for somehow it turned his own mind from contemplation of a future in which he dragged himself from one small charity to another, to one of life to be lived, of a service to be done, of a contribution that he himself could make. And that, above all else, won back his self-esteem and enabled him to lift his head and look his fellows in the eye. Even the move from the monastery had not done that for him.

All this, of course, did not happen overnight. The summer passed. The winter came and went. Kenny became more and more active; more and more like his old self. The limp which had improved astonishingly after his removal to the van Kloops' changed still further in that time. It was a limp still, and it would always be a limp. But it was no longer a hitching, almost creeping sort of thing. His right leg reached a little farther to compensate for its shortness, that was all, and as a result his gait became almost more cocky and nautical than ever.

But his improvement was not all physical. He was mentally more alive and alert, and a good deal of his time was given to his effort to work out his own personal problem. He did well with it, as a matter of fact. Only Barbary remained his stumbling block. So far as she was concerned, he felt matters were finished. There was nothing personal in that, he told himself. He would feel the same about any woman he loved or who loved him. There were many things he could do or could learn to do. But the fact would still remain that to such a one he would be only a part of a man; a battered, broken bit of flesh with life, to be pitied and looked after—and perhaps, in the end, hated.

But there were still things that he could be doing. He could not stay indefinitely in Holland, living with the van Kloops. Neither could he go to England or Ireland, even if he wanted to. He contemplated going to Paris, but then he realized that Paul Jones was gone, and now there were no American vessels fitting in French ports. It might be difficult for him to find anything to do there except as an object of charity, and that he did not want.

On the other hand, the fight was not over. Britain and America were still at war, and until that had been won, he asked himself, had he any right to quit? What was almost as much to the point was that at home—in America—there were Navy men who knew him for a sound seaman. They would know that his ability as a sailor had not been much impaired. Perhaps they would be able to find a place for him where he would be able to carry on the struggle until it was won. After that would be time enough to see what could be done.

The spring passed while he was thinking that out, and it so happened that the word had also come that Henry Laurens, who had been accredited to the Dutch with instructions to draw them into the war against the British if possible, had been captured and hustled away to the Tower of London. His task was hastily assigned to John Adams, who already was in Europe, and for several months the roly-poly New Englander shuttled back and forth between Paris and The Hague, until at last, in the early summer, his efforts were crowned with success and he was made minister plenipotentiary and envoy extraordinary to our new allies. Accordingly, it was directly to him that Kenny went in July.

John Adams was busy, but when he heard his visitor's name he dropped everything and called him in.

"Why, Kenny!" he cried, for it was no longer "Boyle" and "sir" now. "Stab me! But I'd hardly know you!"

"I take that kindly o' ye, Mr. Adams," Kenny replied.

"What's on your mind?" Adams demanded, and Kenny sat down and told him seriously. When he was done Adams smiled broadly.

"So you've come round to it at last, have you?" he cried. "Thank the Lord for that! Now maybe I can help you. You know Commodore Gillon is getting the *South Carolina* ready for sea——"

"That one!" Kenny interrupted almost contemptuously. "Aye, I know him! 'The Red Ribbon Commodore,' Captain Jones used t' be callin' him. And th' *South Carolina*'ll be th' old *Indien* that Jones was t' have! Two years now he's been gettin' ready——"

"Ah!" said Adams wisely. "All that is true, but now Holland is in the fight, and Commodore Gillon's creditors grow impatient. Unless I miss my guess he will be sailing soon—and Charleston will be seeing him before Europe does again, or I am very much mistaken."

"Sure I don't move in his circles!" Kenny said.

Adams laughed outright—a most unusual thing for him.

"We'll fix that!" he retorted. "I'll give you a letter to him, and I'll guarantee 'twill be good for a passage."

They were interrupted by the secretary's knock, and Adams glanced up as the young man thrust his head in the door.

"Excuse me, sir," the secretary said. "There's a gentleman here who's just come from London by way of Ostend—a naval officer, he says, just escaped from Mill Prison. He wants to know if you can arrange for him to meet Commodore Gillon."

"Gillon, eh?" Adams glanced at Kenny. "Well, well! Might as well kill two birds with one stone, eh? Send him in."

The secretary withdrew, and Adams looked across his desk at the younger man.

"Perhaps you'll have company," he said.

"Perhaps so," replied Kenny darkly. "At least I'll be able t' tell ye if th' man's a fraud or no. Remember, 'twas two years I lay in Old Mill me own self!"

The door behind Kenny opened once more and the secretary stepped in. Both Kenny and Adams were rising, and Kenny was swinging round toward the door as the man began his announcement.

"Lieutenant Joshua Barney to see you, Mr. Adams!"

VI

A Better Spring

So shall a better spring
  Less bitter fruits bring forth
    Childe Harold—iv, xcviii

1. Prodigals' Return

Joshua did not even see John Adams.

"Kenny!" he shouted.

"Saints o' th' mornin'!" gasped Kenny. "'Tis Joshua himself!"

They met in the middle of the room and embraced and thumped each other on the back, and Joshua was too excited to notice either Kenny's scars or his limp. As for his hand, so good was Hans's woodwork that he never so much as suspected it until, when all the rest was done and they offered one another their hands it was the left that Kenny gave him.

"What?" said Joshua, puzzled. "Did you hurt the other?"

"Hurt it?" Kenny laughed a little grimly. "No, begod, for sure there's no feelin' in it at all!"

With that he calmly rolled up his sleeve and undid the clamps, removed the artificial hand, and held up the stump of his wrist for Joshua to see.

"Oh, great God! Kenny, I'm sorry!" cried Joshua.

"'Tis naught!" Kenny shrugged with exaggerated negligence. "Sure I'm used to't be now."

"We'd heard you were bad hit," Joshua told him. "In fact, 'twas reported you were not expected to live." He held Kenny off and examined him more closely. "Aye! I can see it now. 'Tis good to find you still alive and well—believe me!"

John Adams cleared his throat.

"I see you two have met before." He chuckled. "I take it you can vouch for this gentleman, Kenny?"

"Begod, an' that I can!" Kenny assured him. "'Twas himself fetched me out of Ireland an' brought me into all this."

"Then he deserves commendation, if only for that," Adams replied. "Lieutenant Barney, your servant, sir!"

"And your own, Mr. Adams!" Joshua bowed.

They stayed a bit in idle talk, and it was then that Kenny learned that Joshua had seen Moira in London, though Joshua did not think it wise to reveal that he had stayed almost a fortnight hidden in her rooms, while she found passage for him in the Ostend packet and they awaited the sailing. Even Kenny, he felt, would be hard pressed to believe that their relationship throughout that time had been wholly platonic, particularly in view of Moira's profession. Indeed, Joshua himself did not like to think of it. In the circumstances it had not been easy.

Perhaps in a somewhat like manner Joshua learned only a part of the struggle Kenny had been through. The physical aspects of it, the fight for recovery, and the gradual return to something like a normal viewpoint were sketched in for him briefly. But it was only as they made their way to Commodore Gillon's quarters in the Kalverstraat that Kenny, swinging along beside him with his half-limp half-roll, turned suddenly sober.

"Joshua," he said abruptly, "before I can be goin' back with ye, there's a favor I must be askin' o' ye. Indeed, I must be demandin' it! Not a word o' this mind t' Barbary! She must not know that I'm alive."

Joshua stopped in his tracks.

"What?" he cried. "But why, Kenny? What the devil——"

"Think o't a minute for yerself, Joshua." Kenny shrugged. "Ye'll see th' why o't! Aye, aye! I know she loves me. An' God knows I love her! But what have I t' be offerin' any woman now? 'Twould be naught for her but misery an' heartbreak, an' sure she deserves better than that!"

"That's nonsense!" exclaimed Joshua almost angrily.

" 'Tis not nonsense!" Kenny retorted, and the jut of his jaw showed that there was no "almost" in the way he felt. " 'Tis th' hard truth that I must be facin'. 'Tis better for her t' be stayin' ignorant that I live— t' be thinkin' me dead an' gone, than t' be faced with th' same terrible thought! I tell ye, Joshua, 'tis easier so for her, an' I must be insistin' on yer promise, or begod I'll not be goin' so far as Gillon's with ye, let alone all th' way t' Philadelphia!"

Joshua studied him for a long moment and saw that he was determined.

" 'Tis a hard thing you ask me to do!" he said at length. "You know how fond I am of Barbary."

"I know." Kenny nodded. "But this is a personal thing between herself an' me. I ask only that ye hold yer tongue!"

"Very well!" said Joshua shortly. "God knows I've no intention of losing sight of you again. But——"

"But what?" Kenny demanded.

"Oh, nothing!" Joshua retorted roughly. "Come on!"

When they presented their letters, which John Adams had given them, to Commodore Gillon of the South Carolina State Navy, they found that although that gentleman may well have been every bit as much a fraud and a scoundrel as he had been painted at least he had all the polish of his Charleston home. He greeted them affably and with extreme courtesy, and nothing seemed too much for him to do for them.

So Joshua and Kenny went aboard the fine new frigate after Kenny had presented his friend to the van Kloops, of course, and taken an earnest and all but tearful farewell of them. But, though the commodore was glib enough about their sailing, he dawdled, and when at last he did leave Holland he took such a roundabout route that they despaired of ever reaching home with him. Accordingly they transferred at La Coruña, in Spain, to a privateer, the *Cicero*, 20, out of Beverly, Massachusetts. But even she frittered away her time in Bilbao, so that it was past midwinter—indeed, it was the end of March—before they approached Philadelphia, and then they came from the north. It was in Joshua's mind that because of his long absence Ann would probably have closed up the house in Dover and gone to wait for him at her parents'. And there, at least, he was right.

As they neared the end of their journey, however, Kenny found himself growing more and more apprehensive. Philadelphia was no great distance, he reminded himself, from Baltimore. Was he not risking a great deal—not for himself, but for her? For curiously enough, though by now he lacked no confidence in his own ability to stand upon a deck and guide a vessel through all the hazards of a voyage, still nothing would convince him that marriage to him would not bring her anything but bleak misery and disaster. Upon that one point he yet retained all his old fears and doubts and uncertainties, and it was that feeling that prompted him to remind Joshua of his promise.

"I gave you my word!" snapped Joshua bleakly. "There's an end to it!"

"I meant only t' be sure ye recalled it!" Kenny retorted stiffly.

Joshua softened a little. After all, he was a fighting man and he loved his Ann, but he felt he could understand a little.

"You'll stay with us until you can find a berth?" he invited.

"As long as ye'll have me." Kenny nodded, and that, too, showed his fundamental sense of insecurity.

It was Ann herself who opened the door to them, and the delight with which she went into Joshua's arms, the little cry of surprise and gladness that she gave, and the way in which they clung to one another gave Kenny a sort of nostalgic pleasure and tore at the very core of his heart. It could not help suggesting to him something of what he himself must have lost. He stood carefully aside, pretending absence, while they embraced. For a moment Joshua forgot everything else in his own joy and happiness. They kissed and even began their stories of all that had happened, both at once, before he remembered abruptly. Then he did not release her but swung round with his arm about her waist.

"But here, Ann!" he cried. "I was forgetting. I'm not alone! This is Kenny Boyle! I found him in Amsterdam!"

Ann stared at him for an instant.

"Kenny! Kenny Boyle!" she whispered. Then she tore herself from Joshua's encircling arm and before Kenny could back away had thrown her arms about his neck and kissed him.

"There!" she cried gaily. "There! That's for the long-lost friend—and—and, really, Kenny, is it you? I—I've heard so much about you from both Joshua and Barbary that I feel as if you were one of the family already."

There was a moment's brief, awkward silence as Kenny turned beet red and his left hand crept up to his cheek, where her lips had touched. The look in his eyes was almost one of panic, but Joshua covered for him.

"My dear, you embarrass the lad. Did I never tell you that he's very shy?"

"That's not what Barbary says!" Ann cried.

But by that time Kenny had recovered. He made a proper leg.

"Sure if 'tis so ye'd greet a brother, ma'am!" he said. "Joshua, ye're a very lucky man!"

Ann tossed her head at Joshua, much as to say, "See?" and then turned, laughing.

"But come in, both of you! And, Joshua, you've not asked once about your son! Don't you want to see him?"

"I certainly do!" Joshua retorted. "But what chance have you given me to ask for him? Let me see him at once, madam!"

She led them into the downstairs drawing room, where the rest of the Bedford family were awaiting the call to supper. A bright log fire crackled on the hearth, and William Bedford Barney watched the activities of the little group with a sort of commanding triumph from his place in the big wooden cradle beside it. Both Gunning and Mother Bedford greeted Joshua with tears of delight and were most cordial to Kenny. But it was the baby, most naturally, who proved the greatest attraction. He cooed and he laughed and he gurgled when Ann took them across and presented them both as properly as if he were an adult and quite old enough to appreciate it. There was no questioning her pride. Joshua thrust a forefinger at the child, being a little awed by such a very little bit of humanity and more than a little afraid he might break it if he attempted to pick it up.

The child gurgled and caught at his finger. Joshua snatched it back almost as if he were frightened. At the other side of the cradle Kenny, grinning, thrust forward his still gloved hand. The baby snatched at it and clamped his jaws, just beginning to show the white edge of teeth, upon it.

"Aha!" cried Kenny. "I have th' advantage o' ye, Joshua. Go on, Billy! Bite down hard on 't! Sure an' ye can be cuttin' yer teeth on yer old uncle Kenny's fingers, an' never a bit o' a bite will he be feelin'!"

Ann looked at Joshua almost in alarm, but he shook his head almost imperceptibly and behind Kenny's back his lips formed the word "Later!"

When the servant called them all in to supper there was a new place set for Kenny at one side of the table, between Gunning Bedford at one end and Mrs. Bedford at the other. A like place had been put at the opposite side, next to Ann, for Joshua; and Kenny, from where he sat across from them, wished a little bitterly that he, too, might have been able to bring with him such happiness. As he watched he stripped the glove from his artificial hand quite automatically, so accustomed to it had he become, and so naturally that it was not until he began to eat with it that any of the others noticed it. They saw it then only because Kenny had to adjust the thumb for eating or drinking and because he was perhaps a little awkward—though not very much so—at certain operations. Joshua, who realized Kenny's sensitiveness, was the most uncomfortable and certainly seemed far more concerned than Kenny himself.

But there was no necessity for him to cover anything. The rest might notice, but they were far too courteous to mention it until Kenny himself did, and in the end it was he who called attention to it.

Ann in her bubbling enthusiasm was plunging ahead, now that she had her Joshua home again, full of grand hopes and great ideas. "There's so much to plan and so much to do!" she cried. "I wish Kenny could stay with us for a bit—but I know you're anxious to get on to Barbary, Kenny. Otherwise I'd urge you!"

The awkwardness of the silence that followed this time was definitely pronounced. Ann looked a flash bewildered. Joshua spoke quickly.

"I've already asked him, Ann, and he's accepted."

But that only seemed to make the silence deeper. It was Kenny at length who spoke.

"I'm not goin', Ann," he said. "I'll not be seein' Barbary."

Ann stared at him, startled at first, and then almost angrily.

"You—— Why not?" she demanded.

With a bitter expression Kenny held up his hand.

"This," he said, "an' what 'tis fastened on!"

He turned it in the light so that all could see. Then he lifted the stiff immobile hand to the scar on his cheek and neck.

"These!" he said. He thumped his game hip and thigh.

"And these—and all those other things ye can't be seein'!"

Ann's eyes filled with tears as he made each move, more at the bitterness with which he did it than at sight of the thing he displayed. When he was done she turned and hid her face for an instant on Joshua's shoulder. For a long silent moment no one spoke. Then abruptly Ann turned back.

"No! No, Kenny!" she cried. "You mustn't! You mustn't feel so!"

"Is that aught t' be offerin' to anyone in th' place o' a whole man, d'ye think?" Kenny demanded harshly. "I've no mind t' be distressin' ye, but——"

"But she loves you, Kenny!" she protested. "She'd not feel that way—I'm sure."

"I'm sure she'd not say so if she did!" Kenny retorted. "No, Ann, 'tis best for her sake——"

"I don't believe it! I won't——" Ann began.

Joshua cut in quickly:

"'Tis Kenny's problem, my dear."

She turned on him.

"You mean you don't intend to do anything?" she cried. "You don't intend to tell Barbary?"

"I gave Kenny my word," he replied. "I'll keep it!"

"But I——" she began.

"I said it is Kenny's problem, my dear!" he said sharply. "'Twill be best if we don't discuss it any more."

Something in the tone of his voice brought her up short. She looked from him to Kenny and then made a supreme effort to recover the gaiety of the evening.

"Of course! Kenny may stay with us as long as he likes!" she cried. "Isn't that how this all started? He can come with us and help us look for a house of our own."

Joshua chuckled but shook his head.

"I'm afraid I must disappoint you even there," he said. "Kenny and I will have to report to Mr. Morris and go looking for a fresh billet for each. This business of being a prisoner isn't cheap, you know. I'm afraid I shall have to earn some more money before I can think of buying a house."

"But the war's over!" Mrs. Bedford protested.

"Not quite, Mother," Joshua replied. "Ashore—yes, the fighting's done. Neither General Washington nor Sir Guy Carleton have seen any sense in shedding more blood since Yorktown, when the thing's so obviously done. But at sea 'tis another story. The Royal Navy has been stung and 'twill not admit an end to things till peace is actually proclaimed. They still take our ships; they still blockade our coasts; they still fling our seamen into their prisons! And until the ink is dry on the treaty there'll be work afloat for the Navy and slim chance of any peacetime pursuits for either of us—eh, Kenny?"

"I'm afraid ye're right, Joshua," Kenny replied. "Though for th' sake o' these others here, I wish 'twere not so."

The talk then turned upon the war and their own journeyings, and it was not until some time later, when Kenny had been shown his room and Ann and Joshua had withdrawn to theirs, that she was able to turn almost angrily upon her husband.

"Joshua Barney, I—honestly! I'm ashamed of you!"

"Whoa! Hold on now! Not so loud and not so fast, my sweet." He grinned at her. "I told you that I'd made Kenny a promise——"

"But whatever possessed you?" she stormed.

"Gently! Gently!" he soothed. "He had me in a corner—that's what possessed me! I had to make him such a promise in order to get him home. I tell you, he's eaten his heart out over the thing and he would not have come at all if I had not given my word."

"Ah, poor dear!" she cried. "'Tis easy enough to see that. But what——"

"What prompted me to cut you off so sharply?" He chuckled. "Why, if I had not, I daresay he'd have backed you into just some such a corner yourself, and then you'd have had to promise too. I tell you, Ann, the lad's sharp."

She stared at him with slowly dawning comprehension.

"And then I'd have been bound too!" she mused. "But, as it is—— Why, Joshua Barney! You old rogue!"

And all at once it seemed to her that all the joy and gladness and cheer that had gone so suddenly out of things downstairs came flooding back, and everything was right once more.

Joshua and Kenny left the house early the next morning. As they went out the door Joshua paused to kiss his wife good-by.

"Now, sweet Ann"—he grinned at her—"I'll leave you to see to all we talked of last night. Kenny and I'll be back as soon as we've seen Bob Morris and heard what he has to say."

She gave him a lingering embrace and then sent them away, closing the door behind them. Hardly had the latch clicked than she was off, scampering away upstairs to her writing desk.

"Where are you going, dear?" her mother called anxiously after her. "What are you doing?"

"Just tending things, Mother!" she called back.

When they were ushered into his office Robert Morris bounced out of his chair as if he had been shot from a gun.

"Joshua Barney!" he cried. "And Kevin Boyle! Both at once! I declare, this is almost too good to be true! Here, sit down and tell me all about what's happened to you both!"

They told him their stories, a piece at a time, so that he had the thing in full chronological order. When Kenny came to the point at which he was wounded in the battle between the *Richard* and the *Serapis*, purposely making little of it, Morris nodded and interrupted.

"Yes, yes! I know all about how lightly you were wounded!" He grinned. "Don't belittle yourself, Mr. Boyle. There's more happens in the world than you're aware of."

"Ye knew?" Kenny gaped at him.

"Of course!" Morris was half teasing. "First there was Captain Jones's report. Then I'd—er—interest enough to inquire about you from Dr. Franklin. I've been in touch with Mr. Adams, and of course Captain Jones has been back here himself since he left you. So you see, I know a great deal more about you than you'd think."

"Ye don't——" Kenny's throat was almost dry. He felt panic-stricken. "I mean ye won't——"

"I suppose you'll be wanting to go straight to Baltimore?" Morris almost seemed to switch the subject deliberately.

"No, sir!" replied Kenny. "Th' fact is, both Joshua an' meself, sir, we were hopin' ye might know of a berth or two?"

"Not going to Baltimore?" Morris demanded. "Why not?"

"If ye please, sir!" Kenny signed wearily. " 'Tis me own personal affair, an' it seems t' me everyone in th' world is interested—I've explained me feelin's t' that many. Would ye mind, sir, if we said no more o't?"

Morris glanced almost quizzically at Joshua.

"Hmmm!" he grunted. "Well, no doubt you're right. Let's say no more of it. Now as to berths for the pair of you! Of course there's nothing going right now in the service. Lord knows we're as bad off as ever. But Pennsylvania is fitting out a ship for her own state navy—the *Hyder Ally*."

"What's she to do?" Joshua demanded.

"Not much, I'm afraid, from both your points of view." Morris grinned at him. "The British have been blockading the bay, and the Tory 'refugee boats'—freebooters and river pirates, to be exact—have been active. Pennsylvania proposes to protect her own. The *Hyder Ally* will convoy vessels from here to sea and not more than two miles beyond the capes. After that she'll turn around and fetch back up whatever ships are gathered there. 'Twill not be exciting, and she's not much, I grant, but 'twill be a command. Will you take her, Joshua?"

"Command? I?" Joshua blinked at him.

"I'm sure—indeed, I know it can be arranged," Morris replied.

"Why—why—if I can have Kenny Boyle, here, for first luff!" Joshua said stoutly.

"I would have suggested it myself if you had not," Robert Morris told him. He rose, and they rose with him. "Then 'tis done, eh? I'll ask Frank Gurney to send around your commissions to you this very afternoon—— Oh, and by the way, Boyle, in view of your services against the *Serapis* and the injuries you received in that battle, you have been recommended for promotion to lieutenant in the regular service. Shall I send that commission around with the other? I take it you're staying with Joshua at Gunning's place?"

"Y-yes, *sir!*" Kenny gulped.

If the deep-piled carpet that led out of Morris's office and across the antechamber and into the hall had been made of clouds it could scarcely have felt any different under their feet as they left.

The door had hardly closed behind them before Morris was back again at his desk. He snatched a sheet of foolscap toward him and began to write. His quill scratched steadily for several moments. Then he read what he had written, sanded it, folded it, and sealed it with hot wax and wrote the direction upon the outside. When that was done he rang the bell at his elbow violently, and, like the genie of the lamp, a green-coated marine sergeant appeared from beyond the door.

"I want a dispatch rider!" Morris ordered. "I want this to go off to Baltimore—to the address shown—without delay!"

"Aye, aye, sir!" replied the marine.

"And, Sergeant," Morris added.

"Aye, sir?"

"When you've got that off," Morris said, "you may ask Mr. Gurney if he'll be so kind as to step this way."

2. *The "Hyder Ally"*

THAT lacked but a day or two of the end of March. It was on the second of April that Barbary Barney, in Baltimore, received two letters from the North. The first was addressed in Ann's neat, crisp hand. The other bore the official seal of the Marine Committee. Barbary, looking at them both and wondering which to open first, womanlike settled for Ann's because the other seemed so cold and official, and it somehow gave her a turn to look at it. She broke the seals and then abruptly cried out.

"Mother! He's back! Kenny's back!"

It was some moments before she could read further, but at length she was able to smooth the paper again and read aloud, so that Mary Barney might share its excitement:

"Dearest Barbary,

"They're back! Both Kenny and Joshua came in last night from Boston! Joshua has been in Mill Prison, in England, from which he made his escape, to find Kenny still in Amsterdam. Joshua looks thin and hollow-eyed, but we will put some meat on his bones, Papa says. As you know, Kenny was horribly wounded on the *Bonhomme Richard*—wounded, Barbary, both physically and in spirit. He has some silly notion that you will not want to see him now or that you will pretend to love him merely from a sense of duty. So he has made up his mind he will not come on to you or ever let you know that he is here and *alive!*

"Barbary darling, I haven't time to tell you everything now. The boys have just gone out to Mr. Morris's and may be back at any minute, and I must get this off to you before they do. Kenny made Joshua promise not to tell you about him. But *I* made no such promise!

"Anyway—you are the only one who can persuade him how wrong he is. And you must see him yourself to understand. I hope you can come up. I hope you can come at once, for I am so afraid they may find a ship, and now that he is here we must not lose him again!

"Ever your loving sister-in-law,
Ann"

Only when she had finished reading and had lowered the letter did Barbary glance at her mother. Mary Barney's eyes were filled with tears of joy.

"They're back!" she said. "Joshua's back—and Kenny too! Thank the good Lord for that!"

"I'm sorry, Mother." Barbary flushed. "I should have spoken about Joshua too. But I—I——"

"I know, child!" Mary Barney replied. "What does the other one say?"

Barbary remembered the more official packet. Hastily she tore open the seals and again read aloud:

"My dear Mistress Barbary,

"While it is not one of the duties of the Marine Committee to play Cupid to its officers, I feel it only right to let you know that *Lieutenant* Boyle has returned from Amsterdam with your brother, Lieutenant Barney, and that he is at present in Philadelphia. He clings persistently to certain ideas resulting from his injuries in the *Bonhomme Richard* and has asked me to find him a vessel. Perhaps by a bit of chicanery, for which I trust God will forgive me, I have secured from the Penn[a] Comm'rs the command of the ship *Hyder Ally*, of the Penn[a] State Navy, for your brother, and placed Lieutenant Boyle in her as second-in-command. The duties of this ship will be simply to convoy merchant vessels down the river to the capes and return. Thus, I believe, I have secured them against any possibility of dangerous action. However, I feel very strongly that you should see and talk with Lieutenant Boyle as soon as may be. For that reason I urge you to come to Philadelphia with all possible speed!

"My sincerest regards to your most charming mother, if you please; and will you convey to her my congratulations upon the return of Lieutenant Barney.

"Assuredly, my dear, y[r] Most humble
and Obd[t] Serv[t]
ROBERT MORRIS"

Barbary crumpled both letters excitedly in her bosom and turned toward the door.

"*Lieutenant* Boyle! Did you hear that, Mother?" she cried over her shoulder as she ran.

"Barbary, where are you going?" Mary Barney called after her.

"Upstairs—to pack!" Barbary replied without halting.

"There's no need to be in such a rush," her mother cried. "There's no stage until Monday. We'll go right up then."

"Monday nothing!" Barbary's voice came floating back from the stairs. "I'm going today! This very afternoon! Cassie's husband, Cassius, can drive me in our carriage. It'll be much quicker, and if I hurry I may be able to get to Reisterstown tonight!"

In Philadelphia, Robert Morris was as good as his word to Joshua and Kenny. Their commissions arrived that very afternoon. To Ann's relief, however, there was much to be done to the *Hyder Ally*. She had to be rerigged and new-braced throughout. Her decks and sides and timbers needed strengthening to withstand her heavier batteries and the more exacting duties she might be called upon to perform as a warship. Gun ports had to be cut and their covers fitted and placed. Sixteen six-pounders had to be set and tackles rigged, the magazines filled, ammunition stowed away in her lockers, and cutlass racks and stands of muskets made ready in the armory. A crew had to be recruited and mustered.

In the shipyard the hammers clattered. On the streets the recruiting drums rolled, and Philip Freneau contributed a poem for the recruiting posters that went:

> Come all ye lads that know no fear,
> To wealth and honor we will steer
> In the *Hyder Ally* privateer,
>   Commanded by Bold Barney!
>
> She's new and true and tight and sound
> Well rigged aloft and all well found—
> Come and be with laurel crowned—
>   Away and leave your lasses!

It was most effective.

As may be imagined, it was a feverish week. And for that matter, so did Ann Barney seem feverish! Fifteen and twenty times a day she would go to the window and peep out, until Joshua had to chide her.

"For heaven's sake, Ann, be careful or he will grow suspicious. You can't hurry things. She'll get here when she gets here—not before."

"Oh dear, Joshua!" Ann wrung her hands. "I hope she gets here before you sail. She must!"

But she did not. That was on the fourth. On the fifth the crew was complete, the repairs done. By the seventh Joshua knew he could wait no longer. He signaled the other vessels of the convoy, and one by one they cast off and stood away. Their white sails could still be seen far downstream from the lower part of the city when Barbary drove up to the Bedford house uptown and flew from the carriage into Ann's arms.

"Oh, Barbary! Barbary!" Ann was actually crying with disappointment. "You've just missed them! They've just sailed!"

Seeing Ann's distress, Barbary tried to hide her own under a cloak of good cheer.

"No matter!" She laughed. "Mr. Morris wrote me that they were confined to river duty in the *Hyder Ally*, so they won't be very long. A week or ten days, at the most, will see them home again. In the meantime you can tell me everything I should know."

Ann shook her head, still under the spell of her own vexation.

"I know—they should be back soon!" she said. "I'm just afraid of what Joshua might do. You know it would be just like him to take the *Ally* outside for a cruise and tell the commissioners that the wind drove him off when he comes back."

But even so neither Ann nor Barbary realized how swiftly things could happen with Joshua in command.

The *Hyder Ally* had a favoring wind and a helping tide, and with them behind her she made Cape May by sundown. There the wind came about contrary, and they were forced to come to anchor under the shore, in the shallow Cape May channel. When the dawn came up it was Kenny who had the watch and took the lookout's hail:

"Sail ho!"

"Where away?"

"Sou'east by east, sir. A sloop-o'-war an' a big frigate layin' off about three leagues t' seaward, at th' mouth o' th' channel, looks like!"

Kenny had no trouble finding them in his glass and swore. Obviously they had seen the *Ally* and her convoy and had moved in to choke off their exit to the sea. The frigate, he felt sure, would be the *Quebec*, currently on patrol on that station. The sloop he did not recognize. He turned to the marine on duty, one of a hand-picked group of Pennsylvania Riflemen, independent, fractious, undisciplined, but expert.

"Ask Captain Barney to step up here at once, please," he ordered. "Tell him 'tis urgent!"

"Y'betcha, Lieutenant!" The man grinned and was gone.

Joshua came on deck promptly, so promptly, indeed, that there was lather still behind his ears and a towel tucked under his chin. Kenny pointed out the enemy, and Joshua studied them carefully through the glass.

"The frigate'll be too big to venture into these waters," he growled. "The other looks like the *General Monk*."

"Ye know her?" Kenny glanced at him.

"She used to be the *General Washington*, privateer," Joshua replied, still studying them, "till the British took her. Since then she's raised hob with shipping off our coast. If that's her, she's fast and rangy, a handy ship in any waters, and not too big for these—and she mounts twenty guns, all nines! If you were the Englishman, what'd you do?"

"Sure, now, that's simple!" retorted Kenny. "I'd send th' sloop in after us an' take th' frigate meself, as fast I could, around th' Overfalls t' cut off th' convoy."

"So would I," agreed Joshua, and there was no doubt of the gleam in his eye. Clearly he had no notion of evading action. "In fact, 'tis so obvious, we must assume he'll do the same. Best take steps to send the convoy promptly to safety. Ask the sailing master to signal 'Enemy in Sight,' and bend on the order to weigh and return upriver at once!"

Kenny started, abruptly realizing that he was no longer sailing master but instead was first lieutenant and as such was the one who would command the gun deck. He ventured to offer his opinion.

"If they act quick aboard th' frigate, just th' same, she should be havin' no trouble overtakin' 'em," he said.

"We must try!" retorted Joshua. "Muster the men amidships, Mr. Boyle, if you please. I'd like a word with 'em before any possible action."

Kenny passed the order and the pipes shrilled. The signal flags jerked aloft, balled fists on a string, to break in bright warning at a tug at the lanyard as they reached the peak. Kenny was aware of sudden confusion amid the huddled merchantmen. Anchors clanked in, dripping river mud. Sails bellied gray in the breaking dawn, and ships moved this way and that across one another's course, according to their commanders' whims. Despite the seeming disorder, however, most of the merchantmen fetched around and stood back upstream. Two—the *Charming Sally* of Philadelphia, which went fast on the Overfalls and stayed there, and the *General Greene*, 12—failed to complete the *Ally's* order. The *Greene* stood up under the *Hyder Ally's* lee.

"Ahoy, *Ally!*" came her skipper's voice. "Damn 'em! If 'tis a fight they want, we'll back ye up!"

"Thank you, *Greene!*" Joshua replied. "Cover the convoy, please, and see 'em safe. We'll tend things here!"

"Be damned t' that!" They were very belligerent aboard the *Greene*. "They'll be all right. I'd ruther support ye!"

"Come about then," bawled Joshua, "and lay to! We'll have our hands full in a bit!"

The *Greene* hove round cockily under the *Hyder Ally's* counter and lay there, breathing fire and brimstone from the look of her. There were signs of activity aboard the Englishmen by now, and Joshua stepped to the quarter rail and was about to speak to his own men when the lookout cried again:

"Sail ho!"

"Where away?" Joshua glanced up.

"East nor'east! Three ships, sir! Enemy privateers, they look like. Leastways, th' sloop's made signal to 'em!"

Joshua did not bother to look seaward. Instead he looked down at the men in the waist.

"You heard, lads!" he barked. "'Twas likely to be a fight before. We're bound to get it now, and with the odds against us! Can I count on you?"

"Aye!" It came in a growling shout that made Kenny grin without humor.

"Good!" Joshua's dark eyes flashed, and he gave them a wolfish smile. "Mark this, then! Today's orders go by rule of contrary. If I command 'Starboard,' lay her to larboard. If I say 'Bank and Fill,' shoot ahead! Pipe the men to quarters, Mr. Boyle. Double-shot all guns, but keep 'em run in; free all gun ports, but don't open 'em until we're ready to fire!"

The bosun's pipes shrilled, and bare feet pounded on the deck. Marines with rifles swarmed into the fighting tops, and all at once the decks appeared miraculously swept clean of anything that might splinter. Powder monkeys ran to be served out shot and ammunition from the lockers, and filled sand buckets appeared suddenly in a score of places.

Joshua and Kenny turned their attention to the newcomers. Only one—she turned out to be the privateer ship *Fair American*, 14—responded to the signals of the *General Monk*. The others were coy, laying off, doubtless hoping to pick up the odds and ends of the convoy as they fled, without risk to themselves. The *Quebec* dawdled, evidently waiting for them. Joshua grinned.

"The longer she delays, the better chance for the convoy to escape!"

Not until midmorning did the *Quebec* weigh and stand about the Overfalls, where there was water enough for her draft. Nor till she moved could the *General Monk* and *Fair American* stand in toward the waiting Yankees in the Cape May stream.

"Fair enough!" Joshua showed his satisfaction. "Let 'em come! The convoy's safe away by now! Best get to your post on the gun deck, Mr. Boyle!"

"Aye, aye, sir!" Kenny was turning when Joshua caught his arm. "You're not worried, are you?"

"Me?" Kenny stared at him. "What's for me t' be worryin' about? 'Tis not me first action, an' I daresay 'twould be better if——"

"Belay that!" Joshua told him sharply. "Now get below, and re-member we're counting on you! You're in command there. Your judg-ment and the way you serve the guns'll count as much as anything I do here."

The post in the gun deck was a new thing to Kenny, and he was not sure that he liked it. To be above, where he could watch what was happening and understand the navigation of the ship, was the thing to which he was accustomed. Now it was committed to an-other, to a stranger's hand and judgment, and it was for him to fight the guns. Through a port opened just a little he watched the two enemy ships come on. But he could not see the *General Greene* ab-ruptly decide that it might be healthier elsewhere and take to her heels, only to go aground on Cape May Sands.

He could hear the grumble of the *Hyder Ally's* cable coming in. He could feel the shiver and swing of the vessel as she got under way. She was fluttering like a wounded duck, of course, trying to draw the enemy as far as possible from the stranded vessel. But naturally he knew nothing of that. He was sure he could have sailed her better.

Through the narrow opening the view was limited. For a few mo-ments he lost sight of the enemy. Then all at once he could see the *Fair American* loom up within a cable's length. At the same instant there was a marine at his elbow.

"Hold it, Lieutenant!" the man cried. "Hold yer fire, sir! There's better game comin'! No contrary 'bout this'n! Wait now! Wait'll ye get th' word!"

As he spoke the privateer loosed her broadside. But her guns were aimed at the *Ally's* tops. Not one of them found their mark. Her second broadside, which she was able to get away quickly before she passed on in pursuit of the distant convoy, drummed against the *Hyder Ally's* sides, filling her with a bilious rumble but leaving no harmful effects, and plumped into the seas alongside.

Kenny gritted his teeth but held his fire, mindful of Joshua's orders. The gunners looked toward him hopefully. He shook his head. Neither he nor they had the satisfaction of seeing the *Fair American* run hard on Egg Island flats, so that she was out of any action. But the *General Monk* was close behind. Kenny felt the *Hyder Ally* swerve, broaching sharply at right angles, and all at once the same marine was at his side.

"Now, Lieutenant!" he yelped. "Now! Rake 'er! Eeeyow!"

That was enough for Kenny.

"Let 'em go!" he bawled.

The gun ports flew open. The guns rumbled out. Even Kenny was startled to see the Englishman bearing down directly upon them, scarcely a pistol shot away.

Two feeble bow chasers the *Monk* fired. But the *Hyder Ally's* entire broadside, double-shotted to rake the enemy's decks, loosed in a withering hail the full length of the Englishman. Despite the carnage, the enemy wore and ran parallel with the *Ally*, so close that in either one a man could have tossed a cannon ball across by hand. Aboard the *Ally*, Kenny's gunners were reloading and returning their pieces to position. In the *Monk* the guns were being run out.

The Englishman managed to fire one broadside, and Kenny felt the *Hyder Ally* reel beneath the impact even as her own guns flared for the second time. The recoil of her fire made the Yankee decks jump vividly. Smoke and the thunder of the guns and the cries of the wounded filled the narrow gun deck. Splinters flew and whined and cracked against the bulkheads. If Kenny had thought about it, it would have reminded him of the hellish, slamming din of battle aboard the *Richard*, and he might have tasted fear. But there was no time for thought now. Only the guns that must be served.

"At will, lads!" he yelled above the crashing roar. "Fire at will!"

On the deck above, Joshua found himself come at last to that position toward which he had so carefully planned his whole course of action. The Englishman was slightly astern of them on their larboard quarter, but fast coming up. This was the time for the maneuver. But it must be done swiftly, and those below must see their opportunity through the open ports. A good first luff counted much at this stage.

"Starboard your helm!" bawled Joshua with a nod and a wink to the sailing master. "Starboard! Damme! D'you want him to run us aboard?"

He did not try to hold his voice down, but instead raised it to the utmost, so that the sound of it would carry down to Kenny below and across the water to the Englishman, who was trying to outmaneuver him. Naturally the British captain laid his own helm to starboard, with the intention of keeping the two vessels more or less parallel, where his heavier guns must tell.

But this command was by Joshua's "Rule of Contrary." Instead of laying down his helm, Joshua's quartermaster flung it hard up. Like a careering horse at a tug of the rein, the *Ally* reared and swung across the *Monk's* bows. And slowly, just as inexorably, the *General Monk's* jib boom came around and poked through the *Hyder Ally's* main shrouds. Thunderously the two ships came together in a grinding crash. Joshua leaped from the quarter-deck, with a handful of men at his heels, to make them fast. At the same time, Kenny, on the gun deck, saw his opportunity and poured blast after blast of grape along the enemy's crowded decks.

Her men went down as if mowed by a scythe. There was a moment's confusion, panic; the roar and crash of the guns and the scream and whine of the grape as it swept along the *Monk's* decks; the sharp smell of gun smoke and the agonized cries of the wounded. And then, all at once, aboard the English vessel someone waved a hat and ran toward the halyards.

"No more! No more! Don't shoot! Quarter! Quarter!"

"Away, boarders!" yelled Joshua. "Don't fight 'em, lads! They've struck!"

The action took twenty minutes. In less than three quarters of an hour the two ships were standing upstream after the convoy. Beyond the Overfalls, the *Quebec,* evidently under the impression that the outcome of the fight was exactly the opposite of what it was, dropped anchor and flew a string of unintelligible signals, doubtless ordering the *Monk* and her presumed prize to go on after the merchantmen. She did not attempt to follow, at least, as the two vessels stood up the river, and the next day the *Hyder Ally* and her prize dropped anchor off Philadelphia.

Their reception there was to both Kenny and Joshua the most astonishing result of the battle. After all, they had both been in far more desperate engagements; harder-won fights that seemed to them to have attracted less notice. To be sure, they had been outgunned and outmanned, and the *Monk* was a notoriously handy sailer. Still, they suspected that it was the fact that they had whipped the heavier ship and taken her on their very doorstep that set the Philadelphians off into such a whooping, shouting transport of celebration. Joshua and Kenny had scarcely stepped from their boat onto the quay before they were recognized and scooped up onto the shoulders of the dancing, singing, cavorting mob and carried in triumph through the streets to the very door of the Bedford house.

There, perhaps out of deference to Captain Barney's family, the mob withdrew a little to a respectful distance and stood watching. Joshua and Kenny made a dash for the door. But there was no need to knock. Joshua's hand was on the brass when the door opened and Ann, laughing and shining in thrilled delight, stood before them.

In the crowd that watched someone whooped, and a great cheer rose as they went into one another's arms. But Kenny scarcely heard, for there, behind Ann, in the shadow of the hallway, stood Barbary—and she was smiling at him.

3. *Barbary*

EVEN as he caught sight of her the great door thumped shut behind him, and Kenny's first impulse, a panic-stricken urge to flight, was blocked. His smile froze on his lips, and he looked sharply at Joshua with accusation hot in his eyes.

"Don't look at me!" Joshua grinned. "I never said a word!"

Ann moved a little forward, almost protectively, lifting her chin defiantly at Kenny.

"I did it!" she declared. "I wrote to Barbary and told her that you were here. You never made me promise anything, Kenny Boyle, and I——"

"And Mr. Morris wrote too, Kenny," Barbary interrupted. She was still smiling, as if she frankly enjoyed his surprise where once, he felt, she would have been offended—inclined to flare out at him.

"Robert Morris?" he cried incredulously.

"I know no other," Barbary replied. "Aren't you even going to say 'Hello,' Kenny?"

Abruptly he remembered his manners and bowed stiffly.

"Mistress Barbary!" he exclaimed with an almost visible effort at control. "Will ye forgive me? 'Tis so surprised I am——"

"Oh!" Ann all but stamped her foot in her vexation at such stubbornness, and Barbary herself looked as if her own patience were close to its end. Joshua grinned again.

"Well, lord! We don't have to stand here in the hall!" he said. "Let's at least go into the drawing room, where we can be comfortable."

So easily that it seemed quite natural, he took Kenny's arm and turned him toward the door, while Ann and Barbary went before them. Barbary entered the comfortable room, with its fire burning cheerfully on the hearth, at once. But Ann hung back, her head turned to one side a little, as if she were listening. Kenny and Joshua stopped, waiting for her to go first, but she looked at Joshua.

"I thought I heard the baby," she said. "Joshua, will you——"

Joshua went bounding up the stairs two steps at a time. The child's slightest whimper was enough to set him fretting with concern. As he went Ann turned to Kenny.

"And now, Mr. Boyle!" she exclaimed. "You go straight in there and talk to Barbary, and let's have no more of this oafish nonsense! I declare, I've never seen anyone so stubbornly selfish in all my life!"

"Me?" Kenny gaped at her. "Selfish?"

She snatched him by the shoulders and with all the strength of her wiry little body turned him and pushed him into the room.

"Yes, you!" she cried, and snatched at the brass lever of the door handle. "There, Barbary! There he is! I wish you joy of him!"

She banged the door behind her with a slam that shook the house, and left them alone together.

Slowly Kenny turned toward Barbary.

"I!" he said in an amazed tone. "She called me selfish——"

Barbary nodded, and the smile was yet in her eyes.

"That's the way it looks to some, Kenny."

He missed the full implication of that.

"But, Barbary, I——" he cried. "But 'tis not for myself that—— Oh, th' devil! How am I t' be sayin' it?"

In his agitation he swung from her and limped toward the fireplace. She watched him go with tender concern. She wanted to take him in her arms and touch his scars and tell him that they did not matter to her but that she was sorry for him; for all he had been through. But his very attitude warned her that this was exactly a part of what he did not want. His pride would allow him to accept no one's pity. Instead she said simply:

"Yes, I know!"

This time he did not miss it. Beside the fireplace, his right arm stretched along the mantel, he turned toward her again.

"What d'ye know, Barbary?" he demanded.

"Kenny!" She forced herself to hold her patience and came forward to stand in front of him at the other side of the fireplace. "Let's not quarrel. Always before, when we've seen each other, we've bickered and fought because we were too stubborn to admit what we felt. That last time I saw you I was overwrought. I flew out at you. I blamed you for something that could not have been your fault, even if it had been true. I told you I hated you, though even when I said it I knew in my heart that I loved you. I sent you away from me and told you that I never wanted to see you again. That was five years ago! Five long, horrible years——"

"And two months!" he interrupted her.

"—and two months!" she went on, smiling just a little, for as bitter as it was, his remark told her a great deal. He counted the days too! "Five years and two months in which we've not seen each other, though we've thought of each other constantly. Five years and two months in which I've wondered and worried and feared—yes, feared! Feared that I'd killed the one I loved—or, even more dreadful, that I'd sent him out to be hurt horribly, with the last thing I had said to him—'I hate you'! Do you know what it's like, Kenny, to feel like that? To know that the one you love most in all the world is gone—and that you did it?"

"Barbary—I——" he tried to interrupt.

"Let me go on, Kenny," she said. "Let me say to you what I must. You hadn't been gone a week before Joshua was back——"

"He told me," he said soberly.

"I know," she said. "And he wrote to you. But we didn't hear from you, and all the while I was sure I had sent you away——"

"But you didn't!" he protested. "I had me orders then!"

"Yes, but I'd said I hated you, and you'd gone out so proud and hurt!" she cried. "You tried to tell me—and I'd turned you away——"

He lifted his left hand toward her, almost as if to take her in his arms; and then, abruptly, seemed to remember and snatched it away again to thrust it behind his back.

"Go on!" he said harshly.

She drew a deep, tremulous breath.

"And then," she said, "and then we heard that the *Lexington* was lost and that all the officers in her had been killed."

"'Twas false!" he growled.

"Obviously." She smiled. "Still, we didn't know that. We didn't know anything, Kenny, about you—whether you were alive or dead—until Joshua came back with your letter and told me that he had seen you on board the *Bonhomme Richard!* Oh, Kenny, you don't know how grateful I was for that! How grateful, and how happy, and how relieved, and how—how—how full of—of joy. For I loved you, Kenny, do you see? And now I knew that I hadn't driven you away! I knew that you loved me and that you were alive and well and that you were coming back to me as soon as you could!"

"Maybe 'twould have been better——" he began.

"No, no!" she cried. "I understood. You tried to tell me in your letter why you went aboard the *Richard* instead of coming straight home to me. You didn't put it very well, Kenny, but I could read between the lines and see what was in your heart and in your mind, and I was proud of you—and happier for that. It told me a lot about you, Kenny, that I'd been in doubt about before—and I loved you the more because you were big enough to put your own love and mine in back of you for the time being and give yourself to America's needs!"

She paused, but he only shook his head, thinking back to that night on the *quai* at Nantes.

"Then," she went on quickly, "we heard about the battle between the *Bonhomme Richard* and the *Serapis,* though we'd no report of the casualties yet. I was proud of you, Kenny—proud to know that you had been there and taken a part in such a victory. But then we had Captain Jones's report—a long time after the first news of the battle. He said that you were hurt—so badly hurt that you weren't expected to live!"

He looked at her, studying her sympathetically. This was the first he had heard of that, for he had given Joshua no chance to tell him about it before he had extracted his promise. After that Joshua had held his tongue.

"Can you think what that must have been like then, Kenny?" she demanded. "Can you imagine what hell it was? Oh, my dear, I know it was hell for you too—far, far worse than any I knew. But—but I want you to understand what it was like here—just a little bit."

"I think I do." He nodded gravely.

"I'm sure you do," she replied. "You wouldn't be—Kenny, if you didn't. It was Mr. Morris who really helped me then, who kept me from sinking in complete despair."

"Morris?"

"Robert Morris." She nodded, smiling. "He wrote to Dr. Franklin and asked about you, and that was how we found that you were in Amsterdam and that you were recovering—slowly, but still recovering. That's how we found, too, how badly you'd been hurt——"

"You knew?" he gaped at her.

"Of course!" She nodded. "And we knew more than that, Kenny. Why do you think I'm here? Mr. Morris heard from John Adams after he wrote to him, and it was Mr. Adams who told us first of your own deep inner hurt and your bitterness at what had happened to you; of how you would not let him—or anyone—write to me—to tell me! And then Captain Jones himself came home to Philadelphia, and Mr. Morris summoned me from Baltimore to talk to him—and he told us the same thing, of how you felt inside—and it was easy to understand!"

"You knew all this—all the time?" Kenny stared at her. "You knew, and you——"

"Of course I knew, and I understand, Kenny!" she replied soberly. "I won't pretend to say that I know all of what it must be like. But I love you, Kenny, and I think I know enough about you and what makes you the way you are to see why it should make you feel so. Oh, Kenny, if you hadn't come here to Philadelphia I would surely have come to Amsterdam in search of you as soon as they would let me! It was only the war that prevented me, as it was!"

He turned from her abruptly and put his forehead down upon his hand that rested against the mantel—the wooden hand. There was no feeling in it. It was as if he had laid his face against a statue, and the feel of it reminded him of the things he himself had thought.

Almost roughly he turned back to her.

"That's all very well!" he cried harshly. "But it only opens old wounds! What about this?"

He lifted his hand and brought it crashing down against the bricks of the fireplace.

"What about all the rest—the shattered leg and the torn body that's hard and gnarled with scars like these, only far worse?" He lifted his good hand to touch the livid streaks on his face and neck. "Is that something, d'ye think, Barbary, for me t' be offerin' ye and askin' ye t' be happy with? I love ye! God knows I love ye still—and will forever! But how can I——"

"Kenny!" she interrupted him. "Do you really think that matters? What kind of a woman do you think me? Do you think I love you for your handsome looks and your perfect body? Ah, Kenny! Men and women have married before under circumstances just like this—and been happy! Perhaps happier than they might be otherwise! Those are honest scars, Kenny. You've a right to be proud of them and flaunt them if you like! Those are the wounds of valor, and they're not to be ashamed of! And if you'd ever a doubt of your ability to stand among other men and do as well as they, you've only to look back to yesterday and remember the part you played in taking the *General Monk!*"

"But I'm not whole, Barbary!" His resistance was crumbling.

"Whole!" She laughed almost wildly. "Whole? Look at me! Do you see me a whole woman? No! For I can never be whole without a man to make me so. A man is whole when he is born, Kenny. But a woman is not whole until she has children! That's the way God made things so that they would go on. I am not whole, Kenny, nor will I ever be if I can't have you, for I'll bear none but yours—I swear it!"

"Barbary!" Kenny cried. "Barbary—ye don't mean that!"

"I do mean it, Kenny!" she retorted. "Would I say it if I did not? A woman has pride, too, Kenny, and I've come to you on my knees, putting pride behind me, because I love you! Because I want you beside me——"

He reached for her then and caught her almost roughly, drawing her to him hungrily.

"Then get up off them!" he cried. "For I'll not have ye grovelin' t' me! If that's the way it is ye feel, an' sure ye are o't, then let it be so! An' praise be t' God for it! 'Tis a thing I've wanted an' thought I'd lost. I'd given it up, an' I would have lost it but for your own stout courage. God bless ye, Barbary! Can ye forgive me? I can see now a little why it was that Ann called me selfish!"

She laughed up at him from his arms, happy now, at last.

"Forgive?" she cried. "Pooh! Nonsense! What's to forgive? I'm proud of you, Kenny, and I'll cherish that thought that you had for me always—and always!"

"Will ye, Barbary?" he cried, as if that were something wonderful. "Then what's delayin' us? God knows I've no mind t' be runnin' th' risk o' losin' ye again!"

"So! Now you are impatient!" she teased him.

"I am that!" he retorted. "Set th' day, Barbary."

"Next week? Tomorrow? This very afternoon?" She laughed.

But the knock at the door interrupted his answer. Indeed, they did not even have time to break apart before Joshua looked in.

"Oho!" cried Joshua. "Forgive me for breaking in, but, Kenny, Robert Morris has sent a messenger to summon us. We're to report to his office immediately. Can you tear yourself away?"

"Th' devil!" Kenny swore. "I hate to, but I suppose it must be."

He turned to Barbary and kissed her, unabashed either by Joshua in the doorway or by Ann, who had come to join him.

"Ye'll have heard him, me sweet Barbary," he said. " 'Twill be like forever, after this, each minute that I'm gone from yer side. But I'll be back as fast as ever I can. I promise ye!"

He went out with Joshua, and the door had no more than thudded behind them than Ann turned.

"Oh, Barbary!" she cried. "Oh, Barbary, it's really true?"

There was a familiar redolence of good tobacco and polished wood in the office of Robert Morris as they were ushered in by the marine guard. Morris himself was already on his feet to greet them, and he came forward with both hands outstretched and a smile of welcome on his face.

"Captain Barney and Lieutenant Boyle!" he cried. "My congratulations upon your magnificent victory! I want to be the first to extend 'em officially!"

He shook hands with each of them solemnly, yet smiling his pleasure.

"And yourself, Lieutenant Boyle," he said when that was done, "have you seen—— Ah, yes! I see by your eye that you have. Well, then, may I hope that still further congratulations are to be expected?"

"Ye may that, sir!" Kenny grinned and blushed.

"Good! Good!" cried Morris gleefully. "At least there's one work I can do when the war's ended. If all else fails me, I can open a marriage bureau! You'll recommend me?"

He laughed with them at that, and then sobered abruptly.

"I don't like to be the skeleton at the feast, gentlemen," he said, "but the fact is, 'twas not altogether on account of congratulations I brought you here. As I just hinted, the war is not ended—yet. We still have our work cut out for us. Take chairs, gentlemen, and let me draw you the picture!"

It was early in the afternoon when Kenny and Joshua left the house, and though the girls fretted and fussed and waited for them by the fire, it was well on toward a late suppertime before the door opened at last and they were back. Then, even before they came into the drawing room, something in the dragging sound of their steps warned Barbary that the news they bore was not of the best.

"Well!" cried Ann as they appeared in the doorway. "It's about time—— Joshua! What is it?"

Joshua walked heavily to the fireplace.

"Damme if I ever thought I'd feel so about being offered a command—and such a command!" he said. "But——" He nodded toward his companion. "Let Kenny tell it. 'Tis even harder for him."

Barbary rose abruptly and crossed to where Kenny sat, staring moodily into the fire, and dropped to her knees beside him.

"Kenny!" she said. "Kenny, what happened?"

"I—I'm afraid we'll have t' wait, Barbary," he said huskily.

"Oh, Kenny—not——" she protested.

"Not long, I hope," he replied, "but long enough at least for one voyage."

"One voyage—to where?"

"To France."

"Oh—no!" she cried.

"'Tis so I feel meself, sweet!" He smiled at her. "But wait till ye hear. Then if ye still say 'No'—I'll turn in me sword!"

Ann glanced abruptly at Joshua and then without saying anything went to stand beside him and took his hand in hers. If either Kenny or Barbary noticed they gave no sign.

"D'ye mind, Barbary," he said, "how I came t' sail in th' *Richard?* When I came ashore at Nantes from th' cartel ship 'twas to meet Captain Jones an' a Frenchman, name o' Giroux, that represented th' *General Mercer*—th' very ship that Joshua was on, though I didn't know that then."

He drew a deep breath.

"Th' long an' th' short o't was that they both offered me berths. Th' one that Giroux offered was th' very thing I'd been hopin' t' find—a privateer, bound home, bringin' me t' ye, Barbary. I could be servin' in her an' doin' some good—but I'd be servin' meself th' more. An' after I'd heard what Jones had t' say 'twas not th' same. 'Twas a hard decision t' make, ye've said it yerself. But it had t' be. When I took th' time for it an' walked down by th' river an' looked t' th' west, 'twas almost as if I could see ye then, Barbary, lyin' here, asleep an' safe!"

Her hand tightened against his upon her shoulder.

"But, d'ye see, I could see, too, where it was ye were lyin' so safe asleep," he went on. "'Twas here in America that I'd made me own an' pledged me word to defend. She lay here too, though not safe nor asleep. An' she put her faith in me an' in a few thousands o' others like me! I knew then that I'd not th' right t' lay down th' arms I was carryin' until th' fight was won an' done an' she was safe—safe for ye,

Barbary, an' for ye, Joshua, an' ye, Ann, an' for th' little tyke upstairs —an' never mind about me!"

There was deep silence as he paused. Then he went on:

"So I sailed in the *Richard*, an' what happened was th' risk I took when I signed. I knew that! But I knew why I took th' risk too! 'Twas hard it should happen so, it was indeed! It left a bitter taste in me mouth for a bit after. But I came round again to th' same thing in Amsterdam before ever I ran into ye, Joshua. Already then I'd asked meself had I th' right t' quit before the battle was done. An' I'd found me own answer in me heart. I could not!"

"We know that, Kenny"—Barbary smiled up at his troubled eyes encouragingly—"or at least we guessed it. But what has that to do——"

"Just this!" he interrupted her. "The *General Monk* is a swift sailer an' a handy ship. She is t' be refitted and returned to her old name, the *General Washington*, an' taken into th' service o' Congress—an' sent t' France t' fetch back th' treaty o' peace itself!"

"Oh, Kenny!" Barbary cried. "But why, then——"

Kenny nodded toward Joshua and then looked down at her.

"Th' war's not done yet, Barbary," he told her. "Nor it won't be done till the treaty is fetched back here t' Philadelphia an' delivered. Joshua's been asked t' command th' *Washington*, an' 'tis meself that's been named first luff. Have I th' right, d'ye think, t' be refusin' it, Barbary? 'Tis America that asks! Can I be sayin' 'No' an' still think o' meself as American?"

Barbary stood up and held out her hands to him, and Kenny also rose then and went to her.

"Kenny!" she said earnestly as she held tight to his lapels. "And you too, Joshua! We'd be pretty poor folk ourselves, Ann and I, if we were to stand in your way at such a time as this. No, my dears! No indeed, we will not! Go! Go as fast as you can and bring back the treaty. And when you do the fight will be won. The battle will be fought and finished, and America will be ours—yours and mine, Kenny, and yours and Ann's and little Billy's, Joshua—for we will be real Americans then, once and for all!"

"Barbary!" cried Kenny. "Ah, Barbary! So it was I knew ye'd be feelin'! Praise God for it!"

She smiled up at him and imitated his brogue in the old way that she and Joshua used to do.

"An' so will ye be seein' that there's how 'tis t' be!" she said. "But sure, Mr. Boyle, it does seem t' me that ye've been altogether too gloomy about some bits o' this!"

"What d'ye mean?" He blinked at her, half suspecting some joke she was about to play on him.

"Well," she demanded, "an' how long will it be takin' them t' be refittin' th' *General Washington* for sea?"

"Weeks! Maybe even a month or two with all the damage she took in the fight with the *Ally!*" he assured her seriously. Then all at once what she was driving at burst upon him.

"Barbary!" he shouted.

"An' what was it, Mr. Boyle"—she smiled at him—"that ye were sayin' when Joshua interrupted us?"

3/5
CLASS
149